About the Author

James Carrac's new thriller novel, *Shanghai Calling*, takes the reader on a riveting journey with the main character. Carrac, an ex-lecturer, who lives in Warwickshire, UK, with his wife and family. James enjoys many sports, in particular golf, and most genres of music, playing guitar and drums. He now works part-time as a TV and film extra. Check out *Red Light*, his previous novel.

Shanghai Calling

James Carrac

Shanghai Calling

James Carrac

Vanguard Press

VANGUARD PAPERBACK

© Copyright 2023
James Carrac

A CIP catalogue record for this title is
available from the British Library.

ISBN 978 1 80016 687 5

*Vanguard Press is an imprint of
Pegasus Elliot Mackenzie Publishers Ltd.*
www.pegasuspublishers.com

First Published in 2023

**Vanguard Press
Sheraton House Castle Park
Cambridge England**

Printed & Bound in Great Britain

Special thanks to Lorraine Cooke and Josie Brown.

CHAPTER ONE

Anne Peters was muttering to herself, as she paced up and down the beige lounge carpet of her two-bedroomed bungalow. "He said he would ring at three o'clock in the afternoon, exactly three, it's now five past." Jeff, Anne's husband for twenty-five 'happy' years, ignored his wife's comment and carried on reading the Sunday paper, paying particular attention to the football results from the day before, and where his favourite team, Chelsham, were in the league. Jeff and Anne had lived in the detached bungalow for eight years, moving from a mid-terraced house that they bought when they first got married. Anne almost jumped out of her skin as the phone started to ring.

She purposely waited for it to ring four times, so as to pretend she wasn't overly keen. Anne picked up the receiver. "Hello." A typical bland answer when receiving a call.

"Hi Mum, how are you and Dad?" Anne felt herself flush with excitement. She missed her son, David, so much, and wished he was back home. At least he would have decent meals, she would see to that.

Anne calmed herself, purposely pausing. "We are fine, your father is more interested in the football results." She sat on the arm at the end of the black leather settee. She forgave David for ringing late. "What's going on at your end?"

"Great news, I've got the job, I'll be starting tomorrow, Monday morning, beginning with a two-day induction. They have timetabled me three classes every day, from years ten to twelve. Isn't it fantastic?"

"That's wonderful," Anne lied. She was hoping David wouldn't get the teaching job he applied for and would settle down a 'stone's throw' from where her and Jeff lived. "So, you'll be teaching four and a half hours every day, from Monday to Friday. Have you much spare time?" She now moved from the settee end onto the settee seat, not bothering to look at Jeff, who sat on one of the two chairs opposite.

"I've just got two classes on Friday, both in the morning. I can't wait to start, everybody has been so kind and friendly, you never know, I might emigrate." David laughed, he was in a buoyant mood. "And guess what." Anne started to feel unwell. "I've met the most beautiful girl in the world, she is wonderful!"

Anne moved the phone to the other ear, switching hands as she did, and now wished she hadn't answered the phone when it rang. She glanced at Jeff for crumbs of comfort, he was still reading the sports page, typical, in her hour of need, he was miles away. "I'm so pleased everything is going so swimmingly for you," she lied again. "Come on, what's the lucky girl's name?"

"Chynna, Chynna Ling, she's twenty-one. I'll send a photo of her to your mobile phone. We're going to get a flat together, also, I've already met her parents, very nice people, and I think they like me."

Anne almost dropped the phone, living together, getting a flat, meeting the parents, David would be married next. She put on a brave front and chuckled down the phone. "Well, I am pleased," she lied once more. "Don't get too carried away, David, one step at a time." She felt guilty saying one step at a time, because it might dampen his spirits, but she had to try and rescue the situation. Anne decided to change the subject, that at least might take David's mind of Chynna. "What do you think of Shanghai?" She looked at Jeff and tutted.

"It's an amazing city, so much hustle and bustle. There are twenty-seven million people here, twenty-seven million, can you imagine that, Mum?" He raised his voice to emphasise the huge population. "I think it's the third most populated city in the world, after Tokyo and Delhi. Wherever you go, there are crowds of people, it's like an ants' nest. Chynna took me to see the Old City and Yu Garden, yesterday, that was a nice experience."

Typical, Anne thought, *Chynna 'in on the act'*.

"We are staying about ten minutes' walk from the Bund, on Nanjing Road, not far from the Huangpu River."

Anne 'ummed', she pretended to sound interested. "Where exactly in China is Shanghai?"

"It's halfway between Hong Kong to the south and Beijing which is northwards. Beijing, the capital of China, is parallel to North Korea."

David had to think geographically. "On the east coast, it's where the Yellow Sea and East China Sea meet, at the estuary of the 'mighty' Yangtze River, the third longest river in the world!" He raised his voice slightly as he said 'mighty'. He also felt Chynna's hands on his chest.

In many ways Anne was pleased for her son, and only child, but she worried about him whenever he was out of her sight, which was often these days. Ever since he had left school to go to university, to study for a teaching degree. Firstly, she looked to the ceiling, and noticed a small mark that required touching up. *Jeff will have to do it first opportunity,* she thought. Anne then glanced at the wallpaper, the flower pattern on a cream background was quite comforting. "You sound like you are really enjoying yourself," she said begrudgingly. "Take one step at a time and be careful. Do you want a quick word with your father?"

"Yes, of course I do."

Anne handed the phone over to Jeff, who put his paper down, then held the phone to his left ear, whilst still sitting in his chair. Anne then starting pacing again, much to his irritation. "Hello son, it sounds great, what time is it in China?"

He had been listening after all, Anne mused.

"Hi Dad, it's twenty minutes past ten in the evening, we are seven hours ahead of you. The surrounding area is all lit up, it looks brilliant, we can see the Oriental Pearl Tower in Pudong, which is on the other side of the river Huangpu. I'm in the hotel, as we speak, on the sixteenth of twenty floors. It's a superb view. How are you?"

Jeff looked at Anne, she envied the close bond David had with Jeff, she knew he would tell his father secrets that she would then have to squeeze out of Jeff, usually in bed after a drink or two.

"I'm fine, same old, same old, you know, work's okay, nothing's changed. Chelsham won yesterday, they're now fourth in the league. I'm playing doubles this afternoon. I hope I serve better today than the last time I played."

Anne couldn't believe the rubbish Jeff talked to David about, football, tennis, work, he should have found out more about that, bloody girl, what's her name, Chanye?

"Send me a photo of that girl of yours, Chynna, you always pick pretty ones."

Jeff could hear David laughing, he could just make out another person giggling in the background. "Yes, I'll attach it to a text as soon as possible, anyway I'd better sign off as I've got an early start tomorrow morning. I'll take a quick shower and go to bed. Bye Dad, take care."

Jeff knew that David, although he'd go to bed, wouldn't be sleeping for a couple of hours, he'd be frolicking in bed with Chynna — lucky so and so. "Bye, son, watch what you're doing." He quickly handed the phone back to Anne, who almost snatched it out of his hand. He was tempted to drop it, just for a laugh, but that thought quickly vanished.

"Bye, David, be careful, and don't forget to wash behind your neck." It was now Jeff's turn to tut.

"Bye, Mum."

Anne replaced the phone back in its base, which was located on a small table in the middle of the large lounge, against the external wall, by the fireplace. Jeff got out of his chair. He was going to get ready to go to the tennis club, for the usual mixed doubles Sunday afternoon matches. "Well, that's excellent news, Anne, isn't it. He's got a job, a girlfriend, Shanghai sounds interesting." He started to hum a song, which immediately irritated Anne.

"I'm not so sure, Shanghai is a very big city, there are all sorts of undesirables creeping about, besides, David's a bit naïve and too good natured, people could take advantage of him." Jeff ignored Anne's protestations and went into the bedroom to change and get his tennis kit out of a drawer. Anne could hear him humming that stupid song. *What was it.* She racked her brains. *Ah, I know,* she thought. *'China in your hand', by T'Pau, a big hit in 1987. Typical of Jeff, always looking on the bright side.*

Jeff changed into his tennis kit and put his tracksuit over the top, then looked in the full-length bedroom mirror. *Not bad for a forty-six-year-old,* he thought. Jeff was five foot nine inches tall, medium built, with a reasonable head of blond hair, and was just above average looking, with blue eyes. He worked as an engineer in a factory, which was a thirty-minute car drive away from his home, depending on traffic and the time of day. He put a change of clothes, towel and fresh underwear in his sports bag, gathered two rackets, a tube of balls then headed for the front door, still humming; he was pleased for his son. "I'm off then Anne, I might see you later." And then he sang, "Don't push too far your dreams are China in your hand," as he opened the main door to the bungalow.

"Play well, see you later." Anne waved her husband off, envying his optimism and close relationship that father and son had, and knew that Jeff worshiped the ground David walked on. Anne had a nagging feeling that it all sounded too good. She was inwardly worried, Shanghai could be a dangerous place. She had every right to be anxious — David was being stalked!

CHAPTER TWO

Jeff arrived at the local tennis club ten minutes after leaving his bungalow. He parked his mid-range blue saloon in the club car park, took his sports bag out of the back seat of his car, and walked to the entrance of the club, singing, "Chynna in David's hands". He'd been a member of Hiltin tennis and squash club for many years and knew almost everybody there. There were plenty of 'hellos' and 'hiyas' as he made his way to the gents' changing room; which was in the middle of the single storey building, behind the reception and bar and in front of the six squash courts.

Hiltin T & S Club had been founded in the 1950s, and was named after the local area in Chelsham, situated in the suburbs of the west side of the town. The architecture was typical of that period, quite bland, with no interesting features, such as bow or bay windows, or arches over the door or window openings. Hiltin, a top squash and tennis club, was one of the best in the country, with many up-and-coming future world champions playing there. The reception area was positioned at the front main entrance of the club, which was small, the size of a typical house living room. It was in many ways furnished in typical office layout: two desks in the middle of the room, supported with comfortable office chairs. The desks were topped with computers and large diaries. The reception faced out to the front and south side of the building, which overlooked the eight tennis courts. Both external walls had large windows, which allowed for substantial daylight and views of arriving visitors. The walls were finished with magnolia matt paint, and decorated with signed photographs of famous tennis and squash players. These included: Jahangir Khan, Jonah Barrington and Heather McKay, all past world squash champions, plus John McEnroe, Pete Sampras and Steffi Graf from the tennis fraternity. The reception floor was covered with wall-to-wall light brown carpet.

Jeff placed his sports bag on a spare clothes hook, towards the left-hand end of the changing room. He preferred that end as it was closest to the six showers, making it more convenient and quicker to get showered and dressed after the matches. The changing room was typical in layout, rows of benches around the wall perimeter, and in the middle section, with clothes hooks spaced body width apart and fixed at eye level. The walls were painted in the same colour and texture as the reception, with a thin blue carpet on the floor. The room was half full of people, some due to be playing squash, others in the tennis round robin matches that started at four o'clock, Sunday afternoon. Jeff spoke to several people as he picked up his car keys, phone, wallet, rackets and balls. The usual banter. "Hi, play well, have a good one, see you later." He made his way out of the changing room, through a side door leading to the tennis courts. It was a pleasant mid-April afternoon, sunny, not much breeze, a hint of cloud. *Perfect for tennis* Jeff thought. The usual 'suspects' were there, including his regular playing partner, Rosemary Shaft, who greeted Jeff with a peck on the left cheek. The format consisted of pairs playing against each other, and swapping around after one set, the winners being determined by which pair had the most total number of wins. The group chatted casually for a few minutes, then the mixed doubles organiser called order.

Rosemary was in her late thirties, small, petite, above average in looks, and had her hair dyed 'off blonde' wearing it shoulder length, bob-style. She was happily married to her husband Geoff and was mother of two teenage girls. Rosemary worked as a cashier at a large bank in the town centre. The pair had been tennis partners for three years and got on exceptionally well, some say too well. She enjoyed a good laugh and played to a reasonable standard, having a particularly good backhand.

Sixteen members turned up, which made it easy for the mixed doubles captain, Max James, to organise. The pairs split into four groups taking the first four tennis courts, leaving four courts available for non-participants. Jeff and Rosemary walked to court two, their first opponents were John Miller and Hayley Skye. Pleasantries were exchanged, a quick warm-up ensued, Jeff spun his racket to determine which team served first. Jeff would be receiving John's serve.

Jeff was a good player, very steady and played mainly from the baseline. John won his service game; Jeff now served to him. Rosemary crouched by the net ready to intercept a weak passing shot. She bent down, Jeff glanced at what she was wearing, a skimpy white thong — instead of her usual white shorts. That was the signal for 'after match practice'.

It started when Jeff offered Rosemary a lift to the Christmas meal, two years previously. They'd both had a drink, Jeff was on the driving limit, plus Rosemary had drunk too much wine. When they left the club for the drive home, she got into the passenger seat of Jeff's car, then 'accidentally' slipped, her right hand landing in Jeff's groin, who didn't see it coming and jumped, not sure what to do. She manipulated his trousers down to his knees and proceeded to use her hands and mouth, insisting that he just enjoyed it and it would be his turn another time. They developed a ruling that there would be no kissing, one gave, the other received and no full sex. A code was used, serve meant hands, volley meant mouth, slam meant the receiver grabbed the giver by the back of the head, slamming it into their groin area. This 'bit of fun' usually happened once a month, the signal being if Rosemary wore either a thong or no underwear, instead of her usual attire. They would often use their code whilst playing to build up the anticipation, their opposition being oblivious to Rosemary laughing when Jeff said, "I must work on my slam a bit more." It was Rosemary's turn to receive this particular Sunday evening.

They lost the first match, but won the other seven, finishing second to John and Hayley. Each set lasted roughly thirty minutes, so they'd been playing for four hours. It was now eight o'clock in the evening, time for a shower, spruce up and drink in the bar. Jeff shaved after his shower, he knew Rosemary didn't like stubble. He wore cream chinos, a black polo shirt and light blue deck shoes.

The mixed group sat around a set of tables and chairs, on the right-hand side of the bar. The bar room was the size of an average pub lounge, with the bar situated at the far end. It was decorated the same as the reception, and also included many photos of top squash and tennis players, many of them visiting the club whilst touring, and obligingly signing a photo taken in the club grounds. A small kitchen located to the left-hand end of the bar, prepared basic pub grub. Max ordered sandwiches and drinks and everybody generally lounged about, talking mainly about how they played and any other topical subject. All the players in the tennis group chipped in for the cost of the sandwiches, except the winning pair, although they usually did as well. Jeff and Rosemary purposely sat apart. The bar was crowded that evening, with a lot of squash players enjoying the hospitality. Most of the group had one drink, a quick sandwich and then left. Jeff waited until it was dark before taking his leave.

He went back to the changing room, picked up his sports bag, walked to his car and manoeuvred it so it was close to Rosemary's, facing in the opposite direction. Jeff waited twenty minutes before he heard her car fob click the locks. He quickly looked around. *Good no one about*, he thought, then slipped out of his door and into Rosemary's passenger seat in less than two seconds, moving the blanket, which was used for emergency cover, onto the centre consul of her Mercedes, keeping low in case somebody was looking. Rosemary opened her door, pulled the driver chair back, and slipped in, pulling her skirt up as she did, then took out her phone and placed it against her right ear, feigning an important phone call — all part of the charade.

"Okay Jeff, I'll have a 'serve'." Jeff worked his fingers, she kept a lookout, neither of them spoke, she just moaned a bit. Seven minutes later, "I'd like a 'volley'." Jeff willingly did as instructed, she really enjoyed the 'volley'. After nine minutes of 'volley', she demanded, "'Serve and volley', Jeff." Then she quickly looked around, put the phone down and grabbed the back of Jeff's head. "Slam me!"

"Rosemary, are you okay?"

Shit it was Elaine Rogers, she was walking towards Rosemary's 'Merc'. Quickly she threw the blanket over Jeff, pulled her skirt down and got out of her car.

"Yes, of course I am, I was just calling Geoff to tell him I'm coming, coming home and not to make me any supper, as I've had two sandwiches. Why, what's the matter?"

Elaine tried to see inside Rosemary's car, it was dark. *The interior light didn't come on as she got out of her car, strange,* she thought. "I wondered if you could give me a lift as my car won't start, it's on your way, that's if it's not inconvenient?"

Yes, it bloody well is, Rosemary thought, trying to think of what to do. "Yes, of course I will, it will be nice to have company."

Jeff was suffocating under the blanket; they'd only needed it once before. He wondered what the hell Rosemary was playing at. *What's she doing?*

"I need to quickly nip to the loo, as I've drank too much lemon and lime, you can tell me what's wrong with your car, on the walk back to the clubhouse."

Jeff almost burst out laughing. *Clever Rosemary*, he thought. Once the pair were back at the club, Jeff slid out of Rosemary's Mercedes, gently closed the passenger door and walked off, out of the car park.

"I thought you were having a fit or something, you looked like you were shaking," Elaine quipped, as they walked into the ladies' toilets, which was situated next to the reception, just outside the bar.

Busybody, I was just about to have 'the mother' of all orgasms, until I heard your big gob, she felt like saying. Rosemary ignored her quip and nipped into the first cubicle, using the tissue to wipe herself down, had a quick pee and flushed the toilet. "I felt a bit faint as I was talking to Geoff, I don't know what came over me," she finally replied, as she washed her hands in one of two basins. Elaine had also used the loo. On the walk back to the 'Merc', Rosemary told Elaine how much she disliked Jeff and was looking for another playing partner, a complete lie of course, but it might stop any gossip. When they got to the Mercedes, Jeff came walking up the driveway to the club. "Jeff where on earth have you been?" Rosemary asked.

"I went for a walk to clear my head, I think I had one more drink than I should have, I feel better now." He had been hiding behind bushes at the driveway entrance waiting for them to come back to her car. "See you both next week." Jeff jumped in his car and quickly drove off, giving a cursory wave.

On the drive home he thought about their practice arrangement. To him it was just a bit of titillation, no harm really. Although Jeff liked Rosemary, he loved Anne, it was like foreplay, he would make love to Anne at the first opportunity, and knew Geoff would be burning energy that evening. He had a clear conscience, he could look his wife in the eye. "No, Anne, I have never had sexual intercourse with another woman." On the drive home, he came near the turn for Burlington Road, where he lived, and his mind drifted back to more important matters, the news from David. Jeff was over the moon, a job, girlfriend, everything sounded good for David. He started humming that song as he approached number twenty-five Burlington Road, parking on the wide, two-car drive. It was nearly eleven o'clock in the evening, he wondered what time it was in Shanghai.

CHAPTER THREE

David dragged himself off Chynna, it was five thirty a.m., Monday morning, Shanghai time. David's first day teaching at the school. Jeff was right, David and Chynna had been making love most of the night. They had been inseparable since they first met, at David's first interview for the teaching job.

David had replied to an advert in a national newspaper.

English teacher required, temporary post, with possible permanent position, immediate start, Shanghai, People's Republic of China.

He completed the application, more on a whim, and then emailed it to the headmaster's secretary, Miss Chynna Ling. David was surprised and pleased that the school had shortlisted him for an interview two weeks later, inviting him to attend the first part of the selection process, and also contributing half towards the travel expenses. He arrived in Shanghai two days before the interview, booking into a hotel located relatively close to the school. On the morning of the interview, he checked into the school reception and was shown to the headmaster's office, where he first met Chynna. It was love at first sight, for both of them.

In some ways they were completely the opposite. David was tall, just under six feet, blond hair, and had blue eyes, whereas Chynna was small, five foot three inches, black hair, and dark brown eyes. However, what they had in common was that they were both good looking and had a good figure/physique. On the way out of the school, after David's first interview, he made an excuse to see the headmaster's secretary, apparently, he'd left a document in his application form envelope. As Chynna looked for his birth certificate (which wasn't there), he asked her out. She accepted, they then saw each other every evening after that.

The first interview, which consisted of meeting the six candidates, showing them around the school, and generally checking their educational and suitability credentials, was conducted in an informal atmosphere; the second was formal.

David was shortlisted for the second interview, which was narrowed down to him, an American and an Australian. After the preliminary questions, the interview commenced. He assumed (with Chynna's help, of course), that the interview panel, which consisted of the headmaster, the principal of languages and the director of academic affairs, would ask him what he knew of the Chinese education system. He was right. "David, can you give us an overview of the education system in Shanghai," the principal asked.

"Education is split into three categories: basic, higher, and adult education. By law, each child must have nine years of compulsory education, consisting of six years of primary and three years of junior." David paused, looked at the principal, then continued. "Basic education includes preschool education lasting three years, primary usually starting at the age of six and then secondary educational, a further six years." David looked at the headmaster, waited for him to nod, and then continued.

"Secondary education has two routes, academic and specialised. The academic route consists of three years of junior and three at senior middle schools." David purposely looked at the director. "Junior middle school pupils wishing to continue their education take a local entrance exam. They will have the option of continuing in an academic senior middle school or entering a vocational middle school to receive two to four years of training." The headmaster briefly whispered to the director of academic affairs and nodded at David. "Senior middle school students wishing to go to universities must take the difficult National Higher Education Entrance Exam called the GaoKao. Due to fierce competitiveness to get into good universities, the pressure to do well for GaoKao is intense." He hoped he pronounced GaoKao correctly and then continued, trying not to sound too robotic. "Many schools hold extra morning classes in science and maths for three to four hours on Saturdays. If schools don't have Saturday morning classes, most parents would send their children to expensive 'hothouse' school weekends, or organise one-to-one private tuition for their children over the weekend, working through past practice papers." David paused, and looked at the three interviewers. Chynna had 'drilled' this information into David, emphasising the importance of this knowledge.

"What do you know about higher education in China?" the director asked.

David hadn't studied the higher education (H.E.) aspect as throughly, so he just repeated what Chynna had told him the previous night, whilst she was performing a striptease. She asked him a question, if he got the answer correct, she removed an item of clothing, if wrong, she put something back on. Consequently, he'd never concentrated so hard in all his life. Unfortunately for them, they'd left the hotel room curtains undrawn, somebody was watching them from the pavement, through binoculars, and didn't like what he saw. "H.E. is divided into two categories, universities that offer four or five-year undergraduate degrees, awarding academic degree qualifications, or colleges that offer three-year diploma or certificate courses, on both academic and vocational subjects."

"What about postgraduate and doctoral programmes," she then asked.

"Oh, they are only offered at universities." David left it at that.

The headmaster cleared his throat with a cough. "What about the daily routine of school life?"

This was an important but basic question. "Most schools start from early morning, usually seven thirty a.m. finishing about six p.m., with a two-hour lunch break. Many schools, as this one does, have evening self-study classes running from seven to nine p.m., so students can finish their homework and prepare for tests." He knew that from Chynna. "If schools do not run self-study evening classes, pupils still have to do their homework at home, usually up to ten p.m. On average, a primary school pupil spends about seven to eight hours at school whilst, a secondary school student spends about twelve to fourteen hours at school, if including lunchtime and evening classes."

The principal then chipped in. "Are you familiar with the structure of the academic year?"

"It is divided into two terms for all the educational institutions, February to mid-July with a six-week summer vacation, and then September to mid/late-January with a four-week winter vacation, there are no half terms." David knew this before he left home.

The headmaster looked at his interview notes, then threw David a 'curve ball'. "What about adult education, David, can you tell us about that?"

David dug deep into his memory, he'd watched a video clip of Asian education whilst at university. *Here we go*, he said to himself. "Adult education ranges from primary education to higher education. For example, adult primary education includes workers' primary schools and peasants' primary schools in an effort to raise literacy level in remote areas." He then paused, quickly looking at the three panellists. "Adult secondary education includes specialised secondary schools and adult higher education includes traditional radio/TV universities delivered online, most of which offer certificates or diplomas but a few offer regular undergraduate degrees." *He wasn't sure if he'd got it right but it was a good answer. He might end up teaching adults English,* he thought.

The interview was going well. "David, this is an opportunity for you to make any comments or ask any questions," the headmaster said, and then leant back in his chair.

David had anticipated this chance to stamp his personality on the interview panel. "If possible, I would like to introduce various English speaking accents, not only from the UK but from other English speaking countries." David decided to go for broke. "I think it's very important that 'our' pupils can speak to, and understand where people are from. It's essential that 'our' students' English is perfect, but that they can also pick up nuances and react accordingly." David purposely used 'our' to reinforce his position. He originally applied for the job as an adventure, but, since meeting Chynna, now desperately wanted it. "Even being aware of colloquial expressions is essential, for example, 'cockney rhyme'."

The headmaster almost fell off his chair. "What an earth is that, poetry?"

David smiled at the panel, he felt like laughing. "It's rhyming slang, first used in the early nineteenth century in the East End of London, for example, 'apples and pears' means stairs. Knowledge or awareness of accents and colloquialisms could be very useful, when 'our' ex-pupils are negotiating with business people from all around the world."

The interview finished, David thanked the panel. They would let him know the result via the headmaster's secretary, who would phone him in two days' time. He walked out of the school, undid his red tie and took off his cream jacket. It was sunny, therefore, he slipped his shades on, and ambled to a local coffee shop, which was a ten-minute walk from the school entrance. It was now two thirty in the afternoon, the interview had lasted an hour. Three Shanghai, undesirables, were following him. David purposely didn't look for Chynna at the school because he didn't want any tongues wagging, and, as he would see her later.

David ordered a large latte and sat outside and spoke a 'smattering' of Chinese, which was pre-requisite for the post, when ordering his drink. There were six tables outside the coffee bar, four chairs to each, three of which were free. He mused over the interview as he took his first sip. *How did it go, should he have mentioned the faults of other English speaking nationalities, such as, the Americans pronouncing words spelt with a double 't' as ds, for example, 'letter', would be pronounced 'ledda' and continuous words beginning and ending with the same letter are joined, for example, 'partying gift', pronounced as 'partingift'.* He weighed it up, and thought that it might come across critical and negative, hence why he decided not to go, down that path.

He was preoccupied and didn't notice three men sitting at the table next to his, drinking coffee and watching him. The expression on their faces wasn't pleasant. One in particular, a large, hard faced individual, with short, cropped hair, stared intensely at David; his eyes full of hate.

No, all in all, he thought, *I've done a very good job.* With Chynna's help of course, he'd have to give her a special treat tonight as a means of gratitude. He looked at his watch, it was now three o'clock. I'll give Mum and Dad a quick call just to let them know how it went, it's eight a.m. back home, he decided. He finished his coffee, picked his jacket up off the spare chair at his table, and started to walk towards the Wusong (Suzhou) river. As he passed the adjacent table, the biggest of the group of three stuck his leg out tripping David, who stumbled slightly. He assumed it was his fault, and apologised (in Chinese) for walking into the man's legs. The three of them just laughed and dismissed his apology, saying a derogative term regarding his white ethnicity, which David didn't understand. He subsequently carried on walking, not thinking anything of it. He'd got a lot on his mind. David walked towards the Wusong river heading north-east, then phoned his mother using his mobile phone, giving her a very quick overview of his experiences thus far — no mention of Chynna — that will have to wait until ten o'clock Sunday evening (Shanghai time). David didn't look around, if he had've done, he would have seen that one of the group of three, was sixty metres behind him.

He followed the Suzhou River to where it met the Huangpu River, at the north end of the Bund. David sat on a riverside bench and mulled over the last few days, since arriving in China. He'd flown in on Saturday, the thirteenth of April, spent Sunday evening preparing for his first interview, which was ten o'clock Monday morning. He had his first date with Chynna, Monday evening. They went to a local restaurant by the Bund area. Chynna, as the headmaster's secretary, informed him on Tuesday, the sixteenth, that he was successful, and was required for a second interview on Wednesday, the seventeenth. David looked across the river and scanned the skyline of the tall modern buildings, then drifted back into deep thought. They went out for their second date on Tuesday evening, then went back to David's hotel to continue Chynna's tuition on the educational system, including the striptease. She didn't stay the night, but went back to her parents' house. They lived in the Jing An Temple, Shanghai residential area, to the west, a half-hour drive from the hotel.

He looked out over the river towards Pudong, but he didn't see anything, his mind was in a daze. He'd see Chynna again in the evening. After work she would go home first, finishing at five o'clock, driving west fifteen minutes to the Temple area, as the school was situated halfway between the hotel and where she lived. It started to drizzle, David decided to walk back to his hotel, spruce up, and wait for Chynna to pick him up at seven o'clock. Hopefully she might have an inkling of some good news for him. His 'shadow' wasn't far behind.

CHAPTER FOUR

David took a shower. Chynna soon joined him. It was now five forty-five on Monday morning, the twenty-second of April, his first teaching day. His mind was in a whirl, he started to think back to his short time in China. In just over a week, he had travelled over halfway round the world, sat two interviews, got the job, and met the woman he'd marry.

When Chynna phoned him from her office, the previous Friday, she teased him by saying, "I've got some good news and some bad news, which do you want first?" On the Wednesday evening of the second interview, she had hinted that the headmaster had taken a shine to him — no more than that. On Thursday the eighteenth, the interview panel met to make a final decision, it was between David and the American, who had followed David as the third interviewee. The principal of languages favoured David, whilst the director of academic affairs liked the American: the headmaster had the deciding vote. When she phoned him on the Friday, the nineteenth, he chose the good news option first. "You've got the job," she screamed down the phone.

"Well, what's the bad news?"

"You'll have to wait another night!"

They still hadn't gone all the way, it was driving David insane.

She told David on the Friday night over a meal, that, what swayed the headmaster, although he liked David, was the use of local nuances, and also, that he didn't knock other countries' variation of the English language, as the American had.

They met early the next day, Saturday, Chynna picking David up and taking him to meet her parents, who lived by the Jing An Temple. Her father was initially sceptical of David, her mother, however, thought he was wonderful. The four of them spent the day together, David having a tour around Yu Garden, Yuyuan Bazaar and the old city. By the end of the day, Chynna's father was walking arm in arm with David, showing him all the sights. "David, Yu Garden, means 'Happiness Garden', it is over four hundred years old, it was a private garden of the Pan family, from the Ming Dynasty." He even approved of her staying the night with him; her mother just laughed. David stood out in the crowd, as he was four inches taller than the average man, and also had blond hair. Easy for his stalker to follow.

On the Sunday, they spent the morning in bed, then walked to the Bund, which was crowded with locals and tourists. Chynna put her tour guide hat on. "This is a mile stretch of historical buildings dating back to the 1860s, bund means embankment. There are fifty-two buildings of various architectural styles, including, Baroque, Gothic and Neoclassical styles, being referred to as 'the museum of buildings'." David marvelled at The Hong Kong and Shanghai Bank building, roughly centrally positioned. "Built in 1923 and The Customs House next to it, built in 1927," his, tour guide pointed out. They waltzed along arm in arm, embracing every few minutes, manoeuvring around other people, blissfully unaware of a Shanghai 'undesirable' lurking in the shadows behind them.

"I'll ring my parents at ten o'clock tonight and tell them the good news," David whispered in Chynna's ear. "It will be three o'clock in the afternoon, back home, Sunday the twenty-first." They completed the Bund tour, turning at Suzhou Creek, heading back to his hotel. "I'll make the call when we are in my room, come on, we'd better get moving, I promised my mother I'd phone at three p.m. UK time, it will be the first time I tell her about my future wife."

***

"Come on dreamy, wake up." David felt a firm grip between his legs, the water from the shower raining down on him. It was six a.m. Monday morning, the twenty-second. David's first day at school.

"I was in a dream, thinking back about the last few days, it's been an amazing week."

Chynna manoeuvred David inside her. "Come on, we haven't got much time, it's your first day, you must be early."

They quickly ate breakfast at the hotel. It cost Chynna forty yuan. "Or Renminbi, which means, people's money," Chynna informed David, (although David knew), which he calculated as four pounds sterling. His breakfast was included in his tariff.

Chynna dropped David off, a couple of minutes' walk from the school, which was located between his hotel and her parents' house and continued her journey, parking in the school grounds. They wanted to keep their relationship secret for as long as possible. David walked the rest of the journey. It took five minutes to reach the school entrance gates.

He dressed casually smart, wearing a light blue blazer, white chinos, collar and tie, and brown loafers. He reported to the headmaster's office, where his two-day induction would commence.

The induction process involved familiarisation of the school building, room location, meeting other staff members and being introduced to his teaching groups.

Within two weeks, David was the most popular teacher in the school. The girls adored him as he was tall, good looking and had blond hair. They argued over whether he looked like Tom Cruise or Brad Pitt, either way, they giggled nervously whenever he spoke to them. They even formed a portmanteau of Brad and Tom's names calling David, 'Brom'. A couple of jealous boys reversed the portmanteau, referring to David as 'Toad', however, most of the boys liked him because he talked to them about sport, in particular football and had a flippant sense of humour. What they all liked was that he was very pleasant, approachable and used different accents and dialects, from not only the UK but worldwide. David purposely avoided seeing Chynna at school, maintaining the secrecy of their relationship. They would meet in their usual spot, making sure no one from the school was around.

David found a fully furnished apartment in Tongren Road, close to where Chynna's parents lived, and started renting it after his first teaching week. Chynna moved in with him after a few days, but they often went to her parents' house for their evening meal. Mr and Mrs Ling treated David as their son, and made a fuss of him every time he visited, as they had never seen their only child so happy. If she was happy so were they.

It was on the Wednesday evening of David's third teaching week, that Chynna told David about her previous boyfriend, Yuēhàn (John) Lee. They knew each other from school, lost contact, then Yuēhàn suddenly reappeared and started pestering Chynna for a date. Much to her parents' annoyance she relented and started seeing him twice a week. This 'romance' went on for a month, then Chynna finished it, because she detested him and was relieved it was over, emphasising to David there was no sexual intimacy. At best a 'peck on the cheek'. Yuēhàn, however, didn't see it that way.

CHAPTER FIVE

"They've just left her parents' house, like two 'turtledoves', I felt like throwing up. I followed them all the way back to his place." Zhān mǔ shì continued. "We can't let them get away with this Yuēhàn, we've got to teach her a lesson, she's taking the piss."

It was Wednesday evening, Yuēhàn and his brothers, Zhān mǔ shì (James) and Yuēsè (Joseph) were drinking coffee at a cafe not far from David's apartment. Yuēhàn, at twenty-two years old, was the youngest, Zhān mǔ shì, two years older, was the middle brother and Yuēsè, twenty-six years old was the eldest. Although Yuēsè was the oldest, Zhān mǔ shì was the leader of the Lee brothers, and was not happy about his younger brother's ex-girlfriend going out with another man, let alone a European.

"Let the 'slag' go with this blond ponce, Yuēhàn's better off without her!" Yuēsè snarled, slurping his coffee.

Zhān mǔ shi hit his elder brother with his right palm, against the left side of his head. "No, family honour has been mocked, if she thought dumping Yuēhàn was a joke, we'll teach her a lesson she won't forget."

The Lee brothers worked as track assemblers at a large car factory, on the outskirts of Shanghai. They'd not long come back from Hong Kong, trying to establish a link to a criminal gang, hoping to set up a satellite mob in Shanghai. It was just after they'd come back, that Yuēhàn started pestering Chynna for a date. During the previous ten years, they had been in trouble with the police for various petty crimes, ranging from burglary to assault, and so far had avoided a custodial sentence. The brothers were on a recruiting campaign to 'swell' their ranks, so they could pursue their goal of organised crime.

Yuēse, married for five years with one child, a daughter. He had a small scar on his right cheek, not from a knife fight as he told everyone, but from falling off a bike when he was younger. He was slight in build, of average height and looks, not very bright and lived with his wife and daughter in the slums on Shanghai's outskirts. He was the brother that followed David and Chynna 'on the bund tour'.

Zhān mǔ shì was the biggest of the Lee brothers, being above average in height and heavily built. He had a quick, violent temper, evil black eyes, and wore cropped hair, and was the 'brains' of the Lee brothers. He lived in the same location as Yuēse, with whichever woman he could intimidate into staying with him. He was the brother who looked at David and Chynna through binoculars at David's hotel, and also tripped David at the cafe.

Yuēhàn, although the youngest and still living at home with his parents, was ambitious and determined to be rich, 'by hook or by crook'. He would eventually usurp his older brother, and fancied himself as a 'big time' gangster. He was the best looking of the Lee brothers, just above average height, solidly built, wore a neat haircut and very sly. Yuēhàn had followed Chynna, David and her parents to the old city.

The brothers had taken it in turns to stalk, initially Chynna and now David, as they worked various shifts at the car factory. They kept in touch by mobile phone, as to where and what the 'love birds' were doing, hoping at the very least the relationship would finish. When they discovered that David and Chynna were living together in a rented apartment, they started to plot 'Chynna's lesson'.

CHAPTER SIX

David's life fell into a steady routine, he was certainly 'living the dream'. He loved his job, the pupils thought the world of him, and he got on well with his teaching colleagues and managers. He kept the relationship with Chynna secret, and avoided seeing her, if possible, whilst at school. They went to Chynna's parents' house most evenings for dinner, occasionally going out themselves or eating in. Mr and Mrs Ling always made a fuss of David, Mr Ling was interested in life in other countries, in particular the UK and USA, as he'd never travelled outside China. Chynna's parents spoke little English, and, although David's Chinese was greatly improving, courtesy of Chynna, she often had to be a translator. The weekend consisted of Saturday shopping and a meal out, and Sunday, breakfast in bed, then 'Mr Ling's tour'.

To celebrate the beginning of David's third month, as the summer term would be soon ending, Mr Ling organised a trip to the Shanghai Tower. Chynna and David walked to the Lings' house, in Yuyuan Road. Mr Ling then drove the four of them eastwards, to the sightseeing tunnel under the Huangpu river, the tunnel connecting the Bund and the Pudong financial quarter. They boarded the small train car for the five-minute, six-hundred-and-forty-seven-metre ride. David liked the tunnel's sound effects and light show, afterward they took a short taxi ride to the tower. Whilst they stood on one of the observation decks, on the one hundred and eighteenth floor, Mr Ling grabbed David's arm. "David, the tower is six hundred and thirty-two metres high, and has a hundred and twenty-seven floors. Its architectural design has the whole outer structure twisting upwards, so it looks like a great coil rising out of the ground, marvellous, absolutely wonderful. It is the tallest building in China and one of the tallest in the world."

Luckily the morning drizzle had stopped, thus David marvelled at the phenomenal view from the tower, as Mr Ling pointed out various interesting or historical landmarks. The complete 'tour' lasted a couple of hours, the party then decided to walk back to the tunnel, as it was now a warm, pleasant afternoon. They were just over halfway on the return journey, when Chynna's heart missed a beat. She recognised a car, and in particular the passengers, slowly drive past them. Consequently she squeezed David's hand and gasped. "What's a matter, Chy?" David asked.

"I feel sick, see that black car up the road," she pointed to it. Her parents who were walking ahead, now turned to see what was going on. "The guy in the back is Yuēhàn, his older brother is driving, and the front passenger is the obnoxious middle brother." The group watched the car turn at the top of the road and head back towards them. As it got closer, the vehicle, a black Honda, slowed down, then Zhān mǔ shì moved his index finger of his right hand across his throat as he glared at Chynna, simulating a throat cut. David put his arms around her in a protective gesture, not sure what else to do. Mr Ling, seeing his daughter upset, rushed towards the car, shaking his fist and shouting, the three just mocked him as the car slowly moved off.

David couldn't believe the character transformation of his future father-in-law, from being a calm, intellectual, smiling 'pussy cat' into a snarling aggressive 'tiger'. "Dad, calm down," Chynna whimpered. "Just ignore them, let's carry on as before, don't let it spoil the afternoon." Mrs Ling, who had rushed to Chynna, was still cuddling her daughter on the other side to where David was standing. She looked very concerned.

"I knew that Lee bloke would be trouble, I still can't believe you ever went out with him," Mr Ling said, his voice still trembling with anger, as he started to compose himself. "As soon as we get back home, I'm going to phone the police and report them for threatening behaviour."

Just to make matters worse, it started to lightly rain again, so the quartet quickly walked the remaining part of the journey to the tunnel. The topic of conversation revolving around the Lee brothers, and the threat gesture, what it meant, was it serious, and what they could do, if anything, about it. David, who had never had a fight in his life, felt helpless. It was very quiet on the journey back to the Lings' house. They had dinner, and gradually started talking about other subjects, and, by the end of the evening, things were back to 'normal', well, everybody pretended it was.

David and Chynna left Mr and Mrs Ling's house at nine thirty in the evening, resisting the offer to stay the night, 'just in case'. They started the short walk back to their apartment, initially in silence, before David tried to break the atmosphere. "I'll ring my parents and talk to my dad, he'll probably know what to do." They then discussed the imminent phone call, failing to notice a large black van, parked close to where they lived.

Mr Ling, due to his wife's protestations, did not phone the police that evening, something they would both regret for the rest of, what would be, their miserable lives.

CHAPTER SEVEN

"How did this guy take the break-up of your relationship?"

Chynna sighed, looked to the heavens. "It was only a brief relationship, I've no idea."

They were now only a couple of minutes from home, David wrapped his right arm around Chynna's right shoulder and pulled her snug. "Did anything happen?"

Chynna stopped, turned and slapped David gently on the side of his left cheek, with her right hand, and then softly kissed it. "David, you know you were the first and only one."

"I'm sorry, Chynna, I just got overwhelmed with jealousy, you mean so much to me."

Lightning struck the skyline, followed by the inevitable clap of thunder. "Just as well we're almost home, looks like a storm is brewing," David continued.

The black van, engine running, moved slowly towards them. Just as they reached the apartment, the side sliding door opened, out jumped Yuēhàn and Zhān mǔ shì. Yuēse, who was driving, stopped the van, but kept the engine running.

David and Chynna didn't initially realise what was going on. They were so engrossed in each other. Chynna was first to react. "What the hell do you two want?"

"Ah, our little 'Chinese chick' has spoken," mocked Zhān mǔ shì, as he swaggered towards them, arms wide open, in a mocking fashion. Both brothers were dressed all in black. They wore sleeved collared shirts, accompanying straight trousers and laced shoes; they could have been dressed for a funeral. Perhaps they were?

"Look, just leave us alone. Yuēhàn, what's going on?" Chynna asked.

Yuēhàn walked towards Chynna, both hands in his trouser pockets. He smiled. "I just had to see you my darling, I couldn't believe you were going out with this blond, American 'puff'. I'd like to rekindle our romance." Yuēhàn was laughing, looking at Zhān mǔ shì, who giggled insanely. He then moved closer to Chynna, grabbed her by the scruff of her neck, and kissed her aggressively on the lips. It started to rain lightly.

Chynna, with David's help, pushed him off. "Get off me you filthy pig," she snarled.

Zhān mǔ shì, who was hovering close, moved in quickly, raising his right arm, karate chopping David on the left side of the neck, forcing him slightly down and backwards, then turned and slapped Chynna hard across her face with the other hand. She also fell backwards and to the right of David. The brothers then grabbed Chynna by the arms, and threw her screaming body through the gap of the sliding door, into the waiting van. David, who had now recovered his balance, pitifully lunged at the brothers, not really sure what to do. Yuēhàn turned and kicked him hard in the stomach, knocking him to the floor. "Come on, grab this Yank, we'll take the pair of them for a little ride, it could be quite entertaining," Zhān mǔ shì snarled. The brothers picked the taller David up, and dragged him by the arms into the van, chucking him over Chynna, who was barely conscious. Yuēhàn slid the side door closed.

"Hit the gas Yuēse, we'll take them out of town," Zhān mǔ shì barked.

David tried to get up, but Zhān mǔ shì punched him several times hard in the head. He gasped as his head hit the side of the fast moving van. "Get the rope Yuēhàn, we'll tie him up, legs together, then loop round and tie his hands together behind his back. Every time he speaks, just hit him."

Yuēhàn rummaged around the back of the van, found the rope, and preceded to do what his brother had told him. David struggled in vain to resist; a couple of 'digs' in the ribs soon quelled him. David was positioned towards the back of the van, on the left-hand side, trussed and lying face down. He was bleeding from the mouth and head. He moaned quietly, he'd never been punched before, let alone beaten.

Chynna, in the meantime, started to recover from the initial slap and crash landing into the van.

"Ohh, what's going on? Where are you taking us? What's this all about Yuēhàn?

"Shush, my little chicken, we're just taking you and lover boy for a joy ride." Zhān mǔ shì moved closer to her and continued. "You've disgraced our family name, and the Chinese nation, by dumping my brother and going with a foreigner, especially a Yank. I hate those American bastards!"

Chynna, who sat towards the front of the rear compartment, on the right-hand side, focussed on David, and started to cry. "He's not American, he's from the UK. He's English!" she screamed at Zhān mǔ shì. "He's going back home soon," she lied. "Let him go, and I'll go back out with Yuēhàn."

David stirred, and just about raised his head off the van bottom, whispering, "No Chynna, I love you."

Yuēhàn, who was sitting in the middle of the van, hissed, "Shut the fuck up, you English wanker." He then slid his right foot out, and kicked him in the face. David's head jolted back and hit the side of the van; he shut up.

Chynna screamed, Zhān mǔ shì, who crouched next to her, slammed his right palm over her mouth. "Another peep out of you and I'll throw him out of the van." He then manoeuvred his hand, and squeezed her mouth into a round shape. "No, my cherub, you need teaching a lesson." Again he was speaking so close to her, she could smell his reeking breath. He'd recently had a skinhead haircut and looked even more menacing than usual.

She pushed his hand away with both her hands. "All right, you've made your point, at least let him go, besides, I was going to finish the relationship tonight, he was getting on my nerves."

Yuēhàn chuckled and then stared at her. "Yes, we could see how 'out of love' you were." He then sneered, "Do you think this little act is going to fool us, you 'white loving' slut!"

Zhān mǔ shì then rubbed Chynna's left breast with the outside of his right hand, poking his tongue at her. She instantly went to knock him off, but he anticipated this and grabbed her wrist with his left hand, squeezing it hard until she cried. He then slipped his right hand between her legs, and looked at her with his evil black eyes. "Feels a little tight, we'll have to do something about that." He grinned at her, and then started laughing, the other brothers joined in.

Yuēse spoke for the first time. "Where are we going, why don't we just dump the pair of them out of town, and go home?"

"Shut the fuck up and drive you moron, take us to a deserted car park, so we can pluck a few feathers from our little Chinese chicken." Zhān mǔ shì barked the orders. Yuēse lit a cigarette, blew out a thick cloud of smoke, stroked his thin moustache, then nodded in agreement.

"You fucking pigs, you're detestable, do want you want with me, just let him go." Chynna spat the words at both brothers in the back of the van.

Slap! Yuēhàn had lurched forward and hit Chynna hard with his right palm onto the left side of her face. "By the time we've finished with you, your tight little pussy, will feel like it's been gang banged by a heard of elephants!" This brought a rapturous roar of laughter from the other two.

David stirred. "You animals, I'll see you in h…" Yuēhàn leapt on him, grabbing David's throat with both hands, in a strangle hold. David was now gasping for breath. He went limp.

"Leave him," she screamed hysterically.

Slap! Zhān mǔ shì 'cracked' Chynna hard across the face and mouth, with the back of his powerful right hand. "I told you, not another peep!"

The force of the blow knocked Chynna backwards and to the left-hand side. She stayed in that position for a while, bruising and swelling about her face and head, blood dribbling from her mouth.

They continued to head north towards Baoshan Qu, a district on the south bank of the Yangtze River, close to the Huangpu tributary. There was little conversation. David lay quietly in a heap at the back of the van, Chynna just slumped lifeless against the van side. Yuēse concentrated on the driving, making sure he didn't speed to attract unwanted police attention. Zhān mǔ shì and Yuēhàn just glanced and gestured at each other, occasionally looking at their prisoners. The rain intensified; thunder broke the silence.

"This will do nicely." Yuēse broke the ice, he turned off the main road into an industrial area, and within minutes, found a quiet car park.

He parked the van in a darkened area of this large two-storey deserted car park. It was Sunday evening, nobody was about.

Yuēse got out of the van, walked around the side and slid the side door open, then quickly walked to the van rear and opened both doors. Yuēhàn, who exited from the side door, joined him. The pair of them pulled David's limp body out of the van, and dragged it to a nearby concrete stanchion. Yuēse tied his long hair into a ponytail, using an elastic band, then used the rest of the rope from the back of the van, to tie David securely to the stanchion. Zhān mǔ shì grabbed Chynna and dragged her out of the van, both exiting from the side door, almost simultaneously. She tried to resist, but he was far too strong and powerful, her strength and will were too weak.

He looked at the other two. "Right, who goes first?" Before either of them could answer, he continued, "I think Yuēhàn should have the pleasure, after all she's promised to go back with him." This was met with a chorus of sniggers. He didn't need telling twice.

The brothers quickly ripped Chynna's pink clothing off, she tried to kick out, and then grabbed Yuēse's leg with both hands and bit him on his left calf.

He screamed out. "You fucking bitch, you're going to regret that!" He pulled his leg free and then kicked her hard in the head with his other one. She yelped, then went quiet, barely moving.

Yuēhàn removed his trousers, raised her legs off the ground and forced himself into her. She almost buckled and cried out in pain. The other two held her arms down, not that she resisted much; he didn't take long. Zhān mǔ shì took her from behind, the other two holding her, stopping Chynna from falling flat on the concrete floor. Yuēse rolled her onto her back. She didn't need holding, she just cried and sobbed uncontrollably. There was little conversation during the gang rape, except for the occasional grunt or moan, apart from Chynna's weeping.

David, who was barely conscious, had watched the whole grotesque scene, he just cried and mouthed 'Chynna'. Worse was to come.

"I have an idea," Zhān mǔ shì said, "Why don't we take a 'hole' each, let's toss for choice." The other two grinned and nodded in agreement. It was quickly decided that Yuēse was to go 'in front', Zhān mǔ shì 'up the back' and Yuēhàn in the mouth. They manoeuvred

Chynna's body on top of Yuēse, he then pulled her down so that Zhān mǔ shì could penetrate her back passage; Yuēhàn, got on his knees, then pinched Chynna's nose to force her to open her mouth. After a few gyrating minutes, Chynna finally summoned the strength to clamp down hard on Yuēhàn's 'dick', biting it with all her might.

He screamed. "Look what the little bitch has done!" As he tried to free himself, but she wouldn't let go. Yuēse pinched her nose with his right thumb and index finger, finally she spat Yuēhàn's bloody 'dick' out. The atmosphere dramatically changed.

Zhān mǔ shì and Yuēse quickly finished and dressed, Yuēhàn was crying in agony, trying to staunch the blood loss from his manhood, or what was left of it. "Wrap this sock around it, we'll take you to a hospital as soon as we're finished," said Zhān mǔ shì.

"Yuēse get the machete out of the van, let's see if she likes English 'cock'?" Zhān mǔ shì ordered his brother.

Yuēse retrieved the machete from the front passenger side of the van, and gave it to Zhān mǔ shì, who was now standing by David. "Pull his trousers down, and get his white 'dick' out."

David, whose awareness was getting sharper, realised what was about to happen, and tried to struggle; it was a pathetic attempt, as he couldn't budge. Chynna, who was lying on the floor, head turned in David's direction, tried to scream, no sound came out. Yuēse held David's 'nob' out, Zhān mǔ shì swished down with the machete and chopped it off! David screamed with pain, blood spurted everywhere. "Put a sock in his mouth, and shut him up," Zhān mǔ shì ordered Yuēse.

Yuēhàn limped to where David hung, he stooped down and picked up the 'white sausage' lying on the floor. "Let's see if this bitch like sucking white 'dick'." He then limped the few paces to Chynna, stooped down, pinched her nose, and then shoved David's bloody manhood into her mouth. She gagged and spat it out. The rain was getting harder.

"Your fucking scum, a disgrace to your race, you need to be exterminated!" David had managed to spit out the sock. Phlegm was drooling from his mouth, his eyes were red with rage.

Zhān mǔ shì got a cigarette out, lit it, turning in David's direction. "We'll see who will be exterminated. You British think you're so high and mighty, 'Britannia rules the waves' and all that bollocks. Our forefathers died in the Second Opium War, in the 1850s, at the hands you lot and the French, here in Shanghai. Moreover, we also had to give sovereignty of Hong Kong to your empire, you Europeans make me sick." He then paced up and down in front of David. "You lot sailed all around the world, destroying everything in your path. Look what the Spanish did in Mexico and South America, the British and French in Africa and North America." He stopped pacing in front of David and shook the machete in his face. "What you Europeans did with the slaves was shameful!"

David, still writhing in agony, seized his moment, if he could reason with him he might be able to 'rescue' the situation. In desperation to try and distract Zhān mǔ shì he tried to debate with him about slavery. "Just hold on a minute, I agree with what you've said, but let's not forget who caught the slaves and then sold them to the Europeans — fellow Africans. Slavery has, unfortunately, gone on for several thousand years. Look what the Egyptians and Romans did with captives of war, enslaved them. Even today, slavery in Africa still goes on. Rival tribes raid each other's territory and take slaves, like they did thousands of years ago, you can't blame the Europeans for that!"

Unfortunately, David's plan backfired. "The British killed my great-grandfather." Zhān mǔ shì rolled his shirt sleeves up, revealing two tattoos, a tiger on the left forearm, a dragon on the right one, then continued. "Shot in the back of the head."

The rain was getting heavier, puddles were forming in the surrounding areas outside the car park. He now looked enraged and started hacking at David's body with the machete, chopping both of David's arms off at the elbow, right then left. Blood spurted like a fountain all over the concrete car park base. David screamed in agony as his forearms flopped to the floor, blood pumping profusely from his brachial arteries, he flinched in revulsion. David was losing blood at a critical rate, he started to feel faint, sheer terror was etched on his beleaguered face. *Things couldn't get worse, could they?*

"Hold his head back so I can get a clean swipe at it." He then looked at Yuēhàn. "Make sure she's watching." He nodded at Yuēsè, who obeyed. Yuēhàn made sure Chynna's face was looking at David's. David now knew that he was seconds away from death.

David, who was slipping in and out of consciousness, summoned his little remaining strength. "I love you, Chynna, the short time we spent together was the best period of my life." His voice was barely audible.

She looked at him, and sobbed. "I love you David!" Yuēhàn then slapped her hard across the face, holding it so she couldn't look away.

Zhān mǔ shì took a step back, raised the machete. Just then a lightning bolt lit the sky, the machete stood out in the silhouette. He turned ninety degrees, spun and sliced across David's neck, the tip of the machete cleanly beheading David. His blond hair seemed to flare up on the initial impact, blood gushed out of his carotid artery, his head fell to the floor, ironically rolling towards Chynna. She screamed for what seemed like an eternity, Yuēhàn pulled off his right shoe, took off his sock and rammed it in her gapping mouth.

Zhān mǔ shì, who now stood over Chynna, raised the machete and, with one swift blow, beheaded her. The area surrounding both bodies was awash with blood, forming one large red pool. Yuēhàn still holding his groin, retrieved his sock from Chynna's mouth, put it, and the shoe, back on. The storm increased in intensity, with lightning and thunder every few minutes.

Zhān mǔ shì looked around. "Let's put the bodies in the van, we'll dump them in the Yangtze. We'll get back home, clean up, get changed and then take you," he looked at Yuēhàn, "to hospital, we need to get that 'pecker' of yours stitched up. And make sure there's none of your blood on the floor, wipe it up with your shirt."

They quickly dragged and threw both the bodies into the back of the van. They gathered David's arms, and both his and Chynna's heads and nonchalantly chucked them in, followed by the rope and Chynna's pink clothes. Yuēhàn picked up David's 'nob' and then forced it into Chynna's mouth, laughing whilst doing so. "Take that 'cocksucker'!"

They double-checked the area for incriminating evidence, nothing was left except a large pool of blood. The three of them sat in the front of the van. Zhān mǔ shì drove as Yuēse's leg was still painful, and Yuēhàn was still in agony, and had lost a fair amount of blood. Both courtesy of Chynna's teeth. They took ten minutes to drive to the Yangtze River, avoided the port buildings, by keeping to the feeder track, then took another five minutes to find a dark, quiet spot to unload their 'cargo'. "Yuēhàn, you keep a lookout, Yuēse and me will throw the bodies into the river." They carefully dragged David's body out first, trying not to spill any blood on the riverbank. The rain made visibility poor and footing slippery, as they chucked his body as far away from the riverside as possible. The two of them repeated the process with Chynna's naked body, carrying her light frame slightly further down the embankment, then throwing it into the large river's estuary. David's arms and both their heads followed suit, and finally the machete, all thrown as far as possible from the river's edge. It was all done very business-like, with little or no respect for the people they were discarding. It was a question of getting rid of the evidence as quickly as possible. Any dripping blood was conveniently washed away, the rain also partially cleaned their bloody clothes. Not that it mattered. The pair had a quick check, all was clear, then the brothers set off, on the twenty-mile return journey, back to where they lived. The storm didn't abate.

CHAPTER EIGHT

Zhān mǔ shì drove the back routes on the return journey, mainly to avoid main road cameras, which could prove the location of Yuēse's van and possibly incriminate them. He and Yuēse each lit a cigarette and started to smoke. "When we get back, we'll wash the van out, have a shower and change of clothing, I'll then take your van and torch it. You will phone the police and report it stolen, before taking Yuēhàn to hospital in the black saloon, make sure you use a route without cameras."

"Can't we…"

"No, we do it tonight."

Nothing was said on the journey back, it was now in the very early hours on Monday morning. Each brother thought about how the evening had panned out. It was only supposed to be a bit of roughing up and groping, maybe rape at the very most. They were now facing execution, either by firing squad or lethal injection. If caught and found guilty.

They arrived back at the area where Yuēse and Zhān mǔ shì lived, quickly washed the van out, then showered at Zhān mǔ shì's flat. As he gathered all the clothes and footwear, he said, "I'll burn these along with the rope and Chynna's clothes, when I torch the van." He grabbed spare trousers and shirts from his wardrobe, for himself and the other two to wear. "Put these on, I know they're too big but they'll have to do for now." He then picked up a full can of petrol from his utility room. "Give me half an hour, then phone the police and report the van stolen, then take Yuēhàn to hospital, he looks ill."

He put on a fresh pair of trainers, put all the clothes in a black plastic bag, grabbed the petrol can and rushed out of the flat. He threw the bag in the back of the van, and placed the can on the passenger seat, then carefully drove to a rundown area about a mile away. The rain had conveniently all but stopped, Zhān mǔ shì turned the van lights off and killed the engine. He looked around, listened, and muttered, "Good, nobody about." He didn't have long, as people would soon be getting up and heading off to work. He grabbed the petrol can and climbed into the back of the van, spreading all the items of clothing around the van floor, thoroughly soaking them. He then splashed petrol all over the back of the van, finally dosing the seating area. He took the keys out of the ignition, pocketing them, then wound down the driver's window, struck a match, lit a cigarette then threw the match into the van.

Within seconds there was a 'whoosh' sound followed by a ball of yellow flame. Zhān mǔ shì sprinted for cover, he could feel the heat from twenty metres away. He kept running, the van could explode any second. He ran towards entries between blocks of flats, and then hid in the shadows. Two minutes past. 'Boom' the van 'blew'. He laughed to himself, and thought *job done, all evidence destroyed*. He knew the yellow glow and then the explosion would wake people, so he quickly walked off, keeping in darkened areas. It would take twenty minutes to walk back to his pad in Beishi Road, thus careful route planning was essential. The thought of facing a firing squad, sharpened his sense of direction.

Yuēse undid his ponytail and unruffled his long hair. It was now one thirty a.m., Monday morning. "Police please." He used his mobile phone to call their emergency number, one-one-zero. He explained to the police receptionist he'd just discovered that his van had been stolen. He gave his address and contact details then put the phone down. "Come on, I'll take you to hospital before that wound becomes infected, we'll go to my flat to get the car keys. I'll change into my clothes, these are too big for me."

They didn't disturb Yuēse's wife and young daughter, as he quickly and quietly got changed. He picked up the car keys, and the pair headed out to the Shanghai International Hospital, Pudong. They concocted a covert story that Yuēhàn had sex with a prostitute, and as she orgasmed she accidentally bit him. All very far-fetched. "No, I don't know her name or where she lives etc…" He had to give his personal details, and was seen within the hour. The medical staff looked at each other as he told his story, not sure whether to laugh or send for a psychiatrist. The treatment involved injections and ten stitches, all of which were very painful, and very embarrassing. He'd lost a fair amount of blood, and the doctor informed him that he was lucky to 'still be in one piece'. The nurse bandaged his 'appendage', he was given antibacterial cream and a course of antibiotics, then discharged. Yuēhàn would have to see a local nurse the following week, to have the stitches removed and the wound checked for infection. Yuēse smoked four cigarettes while waiting two hours in the car, whilst Yuēhàn was being treated. Yuēhàn, instead of returning back to his parents' flat, would stay at Zhān mǔ shì's flat for a day or two.

Zhān mǔ shì zigzagged his way back to his flat, making sure he kept to side roads and dimly lit streets, which took longer than a more direct, straightforward route. He got back before the other two, lit a 'ciggy', then started to plot their cover story. He knew that they would be the prime suspects. It would only be a matter of time before Inspector Chow and his buddies came knocking at the door. They must be fully prepared — he didn't fancy a bullet or injection.

CHAPTER NINE

"Hello, Mrs Ling speaking."

"Hello, Mrs Ling, sorry to disturb you, this is Alix, from school reception, is Chynna okay?"

Mrs Ling paused, what an earth is this girl talking about? It was ten o'clock Monday morning. "I'm not sure what you mean, of course she's all right, why are you contacting me?"

"It's only a courtesy call, as Chynna is not in work this morning, and she hasn't contacted us to let the school know. The headmaster has an end of term meeting and he wanted her there."

There was silence, Mrs Ling's head started to thump. *Chynna not at school, what's going on?* She thought "Em… well, she's now living on her own in an apartment nearby, have you called her cellular phone?"

"Yes, I tried that number first it didn't ring out, the battery must be flat."

Mrs Ling's head was now being squeezed by an invisible force, nausea was imminent. "Oh, I see, em… I'll go to her apartment and see if she is okay, and call you back."

"Thanks Mrs Ling, goodbye."

"Bye."

Mrs Ling put the phone down and rushed to the toilet, just making it before throwing-up. She freshened up, quickly tidied her hair then went to fetch her lightweight jacket, as it was overcast with a slight breeze. Ah Lam Ling was an attractive woman, typically Chinese in looks and build, was forty-eight years old, and worked part-time in a city centre shop. Her mind was in a whirl, should she ring Li Wei and disturb him at work. *No, I'll go to Chynna and David's apartment and see 'what's what,* she thought.

Ah Lam Ling walked the short journey to their apartment, she started to try and think positively. *Maybe the 'love birds' have got carried away and forgot to set their alarms* or *perhaps they're both ill*. A cloud then formed in her mind, the interaction with the Lee brothers only the day before, was still very fresh, was it merely a coincidence? Ah Lam Ling almost ran to David's apartment, her face contorted with anxiety. She seemed to have aged ten years in that many minutes. She knocked on the front door — no reply. She knocked again, this time harder. "Chynna, David are you there?" She prayed that the curtains would move or better still the door would open. Nothing. She dipped into her right jacket pocket and 'fished' for the spare key David had given her, as she volunteered to clean and tidy up for them when she wasn't working. Ah Lam Ling put the key in the lock, then carefully opened the door. "Chynna, David, it's only me." No reply, all was quiet. Nausea started to 'stir'. She walked into the bedroom, the bed hadn't been slept in, she started to breath rapidly. She noticed Chynna's cellular phone on top of the left-hand bedside cabinet. She checked it, it was flat. Her hands were shaking, she placed the phone in her pocket, then quickly, in vain, checked the rest of the small apartment. It was obvious to her, that Chynna and David had not been in the apartment since Sunday morning, to begin Li Wei's tour.

The sound coming out of Ah Lam Ling's mouth resembled a cat's when fighting, then she sobbed uncontrollably as she sat on a kitchen chair. *Where is her precious Chynna and lovely David?* Her thoughts were full of dread. She waited a few minutes and tried to 'pull herself together', pulled her cellular phone out and called the school reception.

"Hello, reception, Alix speaking."

"Morning Alix, it's Mrs Ling, I'm phoning from Chynna's apartment, she's not here, tell me, is David the English teacher in school?"

"Oh, you mean Mr Peters, no he isn't, he hasn't contacted us either."

"Okay, thanks, goodbye."

"Bye." Alix put 'two and two together', she wore a rye smile, so…

Ah Lam then called Li Wei. A brief phone call ensued, finishing with, "Call the police."

CHAPTER TEN

Detective Inspector Chow arrived at the Ling's residence mid-afternoon, accompanied by Detective Sergeant Wong. Mrs Ling made them both a cup of tea, all three sat in the living room, as she explained the past two days' events. The sergeant, who wore a grey suit, plus 'collar and tie', took copious notes as the detective kept questioning her, regarding the interaction with the Lee brothers. This, to him, was critical. He kept going over and over. Where? what? how? who? when? and finally why?

Mrs Ling was still wearing the same clothes, blue sweater and white bottoms, and explained the brief and unapproved relationship Chynna had with Yuēhàn, including how long it lasted. Was there any intimacy, was it a mutual termination? Mrs Ling tutted and gave Chow a disgusted look. "No, there was not anything of that kind, she's not that type of girl!" The police officers looked at each other, this wasn't the time for sly smirks.

Wong, in his mid-thirties, completed the notes on Chynna and Yuēhàn's brief relationship. He now braced himself for arduous scribbling, as the detective turned his attention to David. Chow, who always dressed very smartly in a dark blue suit, white shirt, mid-blue tie and black polished shoes, rubbed his chin for two seconds, "Mrs Ling, tell me all you know about David."

Ah Lam, sat back in her chair, brushed her hair with her hands and told the officers the full story, how they met at David's first interview, and were 'glued' to each other ever since. Chow asked about David's background, his character, and importantly, her 'gut' feeling about him. Mrs Ling didn't know a great deal about David's background. "British, well English, to be precise, single child, university educated, he worshipped Chynna." The questions kept coming. Chow, apparently, Ah Lam believed, thought that David was the prime suspect, she was wrong of course. He asked for photos of both of them. Mrs Ling sent him images via cellular phone.

"What were they wearing the last time you saw them, Sunday evening?"

Ah Lam, started to weep. "Chynna wore a pink top and skirt, David wore a black polo shirt and cream chinos."

Chow shook his head slightly as Wong was about to comfort Mrs Ling.

"Okay Mrs Ling, that's all for now, we'll be in touch shortly." Chow started to rise out of his chair, and as he walked towards the door added, "If you think of anything, let me know straight away — anything." He gave her his personal card.

Pleasantries were exchanged, Wong's wrist was aching, and Mrs Ling quickly closed the door. "Where to next Boss?"

Chow slipped his shades on, it was now hot and sunny. "Idiot, the school of course, phone them now and make an appointment with the headmaster, I must see him today." Detective Chow was in his early fifties: slightly above average height, solidly built, was very fit and trained most days; he wore his hair in a crew cut style. He had a reputation for dogged persistence and fearlessness, his nickname was 'Nimrod' — the Mighty Hunter.

They quickly arrived at the school, and showed their identification. The headmaster was in his office waiting for them. Chow got straight to the point; he was mainly interested in David. Wong's wrist wanted to 'wave the white flag'. The headmaster gave David a glowing character reference, everybody liked him. He is courteous, conscientious, an excellent teacher, the pupils adore him, in short, a lovely man. He was surprised, even astonished, when Chow informed him of the relationship between Chynna and David. "In a million years I never would have guessed they were an item, let alone living together, I can't believe it."

Chow dug into David's background, his parents, and their contact details, getting out of his chair, and started pacing around the office, rubbing his chin. The headmaster, who sat behind his desk, followed his movement. Chow suddenly stopped, shook the headmaster's hand. "Thank you for all your help." And he quickly walked out of the office, followed by a startled Wong. The headmaster sat in his chair and just stared at the wall, a tear trickled down his left cheek, he didn't move for some time.

They drove off, heading back to the police headquarters. Chow turned to Wong. "Well, Sergeant, what do you think?" Wong, whose wrist was throbbing tried to be clever.

"Well, they have probably run off together, maybe to get married, and then surprise everyone."

Chow, who was looking out of the side window, sighed, then cut Wong a killer look. "If that's the best you can offer, I'm going to transfer you to the dog patrol. It's obvious to the dumbest of 'cops' it's the Lee brothers." He then relented his attack. "Check the hospitals just in case they got run over, possibly hit and run, when we get back."

CHAPTER ELEVEN

"Right, everybody gather round, Sergeant Wong will brief you all." Chow, hands in pockets, addressed his small investigation team. When he 'barked' everybody paid attention. It was Tuesday afternoon at downtown police headquarters. The office was comprised of six desks, chairs and filing cabinets, each desk had a computer, which was linked to two printers, colour and black and white. Chow's office was at the far end of the room, his door was usually closed.

Sergeant Wong, average height, good looking with a slim to average physique, stood in front of a whiteboard, black marker pen in his right hand. He had a good head of hair, neatly groomed and was married with two children, twin girls. Chow leaned on a desk to Wong's right, dressed in his usual 'garb'. The team he was about to address, consisted of three men and two women, varying in age from mid-twenties to late forties.

Wong looked at Chow, he got the 'nod'. "This is what we know so far. Two people are missing, Chynna Ling and David Peters." He turned to the whiteboard behind him, at the top of it drew two boxes and put their names in it. He turned back and gave the team an overview of their backgrounds, adding scant detail underneath each name, linked with lines from the pen. He then described the relationship and interaction with the Lee brothers, he glanced at Chow, another nod. "The Lees are the prime suspects." He added their names and addresses with the pen, and turned. "However, we cannot rule out the following." Wong undid his shirt's top button and loosened his red tie, he took a sip of water from a glass, which was placed conveniently on a table next to him. He surprised Chow by asking for a volunteer to be his scribe whilst he continued with the briefing. A young male officer stepped forward, took the pen, and thought, *Ready teacher*.

Chow smirked inwardly *Wong's learning*.

"We are looking at all possible avenues of enquiry. The possibilities of: they eloped to get married; David has kidnapped or even killed Chynna; they were involved with a car, a hit and run; or they have been snatched by, probably, the Lees." He took another sip, 'inspected' his scribe's work *Not bad, not bad*, he thought. "I have contacted all the city hospitals, they haven't treated anybody that fits their description or name. However, Shanghai International Hospital, Pudong, informed me this morning that a certain Yuēhàn Lee checked in for a penile injury, a bite mark, in the early hours of Monday morning. Apparently he got it from a prostitute." Wong tried his best not to laugh, just about managing it, as Chow would have probably punched him. "Another important factor, Yuēse Lee's van had been reported stolen early Monday morning, it was found this morning burnt out, in an industrial area, within a mile and a half of where the Lees live." The whiteboard was now covered with black boxes, names and arrows. "Here is a photo of both missing persons and a description of what they were last known to be wearing." He handed out the photos to the team.

"Now, what do we know of the Lees? They live in the rough area on the outskirts of the city, their father is an opium addict, their mother is a part-time prostitute. They have a long list of convictions for petty crime, but yet to serve a custodial sentence." He handed his 'pupil' three photographs, who in turn, Blu-Tacked them to the board. He pointed to the first photo. "Yuēse is the oldest brother, he's slight in build, wears his hair long, married with a young daughter; he's the most dimwitted of the three. He then pointed to the second photo, took another sip, a quick glance at Chow, subtle nod returned. "Yuēhàn is the youngest, and was Chynna's boyfriend. He's good looking, neatly groomed and charming — don't let that fool you, he has aspirations." Wong then paused, took a depth breath, then pointed to the middle photo. "Zhān mǔ shì is the brains of the three and also the most dangerous. He is tall, powerfully built with short, cropped hair and unusually, has black eyes. He has a reputation for dishing out violence, rumour has it, he's trying to set up a satellite triad gang here, in Shanghai. All three have tattoos, and work at the SIAC motor factory." The sergeant stepped to one side.

Detective Inspector Chow stepped forward and addressed his underlings. "Thank you Sergeant. Let's give these boys a visit." He pointed to his officers."You two pick up Yuēse, you two pick up Yuēhàn, Wong come with me. You," he said, pointing to the youngest officer, "can man the ship."

CHAPTER TWELVE

"Turn the AC on," snapped Chow, it was a very hot July afternoon. Wong quickly did as instructed. They sped through the busy Shanghai traffic, Chow's patience was notoriously thin. Rumour had it, he had Japanese blood in him, although nobody ever dared mention it. His wife was his job, it was common knowledge that he had women scattered all around the city, although he kept his personal life private. It was well known in the criminal fraternity, that Chow didn't mind mixing it. He could certainly handle himself, because he studied kung fu during his teenage years, achieving black belt after four years of training, but never talking about that either.

It took half an hour to drive to Zhān mǔ shì's flat; they knew where the brothers lived as they'd been arrested from home many times. Wong knocked on Zhān mǔ shì's front door. A shuffling sound could be heard from inside and, to their surprise, Yuēhàn opened the door. "What do you want?"

Chow barged in knocking Yuēhàn out of the way. "Where's Zhān mǔ shì?"

"He's at work, doesn't finish till eight tonight."

"Mind if we have a quick look around?" Chow didn't wait for a reply. After a quick search, the pair of officers couldn't find any incriminating evidence. "You're coming with us."

"What for, I done nothing wrong?"

"Well, you've got nothing to worry about then have you?"

"Do you want the cuffs or not?"

"No, I'll just give Zha…"

"No you won't! Sergeant, ring Yuēhàn's 'taxi', when they get here, we'll go to the factory."

The two officers who had gone to the Lees' parents flat to pick Yuēhàn up, were met with a mouthful of abuse from his parents. Nothing new about that. They quickly travelled to the next block, to pick him up from Zhān mǔ shì's flat, after the phone call from Wong. "Keep them in separate rooms till we get back. Come on Sergeant, let's go and visit big boy."

Chow and Wong arrived at the SIAC factory, showed their identification to the shift supervisor, who immediately requested Zhān mǔ shì's presence in his office. Zhān mǔ shì, who was expecting an imminent police visit, acting all calm and innocent, and didn't resist arrest. "Of course Mr Chow, anything to help the police," were the only words he spoke, as they took him away.

With all three brothers in custody, Chow determined the interview procedure. Sergeant Wong assumed Zhān mǔ shì would be last, as usual, he guessed Chow wrong. Chow would like to have said, 'Idiot', but he never belittled his friend and close companion in front of anybody. "Whilst we interview Zhān mǔ shì, the rest of you get digging, if they are alive, which I doubt very much, we haven't got much time."

The interview with Zhān mǔ shì went as the Detective Inspector had envisaged. Sergeant Wong asked the questions. "No comment." Shoulder shrug, smirk. "No comment." He was locked back in an empty room.

Yuēhàn's interview went slightly better, he stuttered and stumbled about the injury, and admitted to seeing the Ling family Sunday afternoon. He then clammed up and was also locked back in an empty interview room.

"Okay Wong, let me take this one, go and get Yuēse."

The cigarettes were on the table, he advised him of his rights, and Wong switched on the tape recorder. "Well, Yuēse, you boys are in 'deep shit' this time. We've already talked to your younger brothers and they're pointing the blame in your direction."

"Bollocks, they wouldn't do that, do you think I'm that stupid as to fall for your bullshit Chow?" He leant back in his chair, then stroked his thin moustache.

"Have a smoke, Yuēse, if you cooperate I'll put a word in, it might save you the bullet."

Chow gave the packet of cigarettes to Yuēse, he took one. Chow lit it with his lighter, Yuēse took a deep drag.

"Okay, so we saw the Lings on Sunday afternoon, so what, that doesn't prove anything." He took a deep pull, took in all that lovely nicotine.

Chow sat quietly, Wong was itching to ask a question, but he thought better of it. "Did it get out of control, did Zhān mǔ shì lose his notorious quick temper, you didn't want them to be harmed, did you?"

Yuēse began to wonder what Chow knew. "Look, we played Rummikub all evening at Zhān's, had a few beers, that's it."

"Why did you torch your van?"

"I didn't."

"Ah, so you're blaming one of the other two."

"No, I don't know who did it."

"So, you played Rummikub all evening, just remind me, what's the difference with only three players?" This was a typical Chow 'red herring'.

"I don't fucking know." He looked agitated, took another deep pull.

"Tell me, Yuēse, how many tiles do you have with only three players, is it the usual fourteen?"

Yuēse started to relax. "Yeah, think so."

Yuēse fell for an obvious trap, even Wong knew there are fourteen tiles per player, regardless of how many play. Yuēse should have sidestepped this simple 'fish hook'.

Then Chow quickly switched tack. "Who fucked her first?"

Yuēse's face turned 'white', he felt like Chow had 'chinned' him. *What had the others told him? No, calm down, he knows nothing, they wouldn't drop him in it.* "Fucked who?"

"Was it David or Chynna who bit Yuēhàn's dick?"

"No, it was a prossy."

Yuēse was sweating, he couldn't look either officer in the face. They knew far too much for his liking.

He then went, "No comment", for the rest of the interview.

Chow ordered them to be released, he'd gleaned a lot from the interviews, much to his sergeant's astonishment. He deduced that they picked David and Chynna up in the van Sunday evening, with the intention of scaring them, possibly raping Chynna. For some reason it turned sour, Zhān mǔ shì probably lost his temper, sealing the fate of their victims. Wong just nodded, mesmerised with his boss' insight. Indeed, they were not the prime suspects, they were guilty, Chow now needed solid evidence to prove it.

He gathered his team together, stood in front of the whiteboard, and circled the Lees. Chow instructed twenty-four-hour surveillance on the brothers, then requested search warrants for their premises. He then demanded the torched van to be stripped and scrutinised, this was now key to the investigation. "Get all the CCTV footage in the vicinity of the Lings' residence and David's apartment, it should indicate the direction they took once they snatched them." He paused for a few seconds, chucked the board marker at the 'scribe'. "Give me the time line and get this right."

The team shouted out the known times. "Chynna and David left the Lings' at nine thirty p.m. It takes ten minutes to walk to their apartment, let's assume they arrived at nine forty p.m. The van was reported stolen at one fifteen a.m. Yuēhàn checked-in at the hospital at one fifty a.m. and checked-out at three fifty a.m."

Chow inspected the scribe's work, gave a nod, put his left hand in his trouser pocket. "This gives us an idea of the maximum distance they travelled. I must have the CCTV to get the direction!" He finished with, "We must find the bodies."

Chow stormed off to his small side office, slamming the door behind him. The team scrambled to their desks, who would earn brownie points by finding the van's direction first. Forty-five minutes later, "Ahh". One of Chow's underlings spotted the van on the north-south elevated road at 10.05 p.m. The rest of the team now focussed their search north of the city. "Got them, they were on the S322 at ten fifteen p.m. DI Chow was now prowling about the office, punching his right fist into his left palm. He quickly walked to the map of Greater Shanghai, which was pinned to the wall next to the whiteboard. He traced the roads with his right index finger, then snarled.

"Those bastards, they've dumped them in the Yangtze River. Quick, call the coastguard, get them to alert the local fishermen, we'll head up there first thing tomorrow morning." Chow pointed at members of his team. "You, keep the Lees under surveillance, you, do door to door. Where's those search warrants!"

CHAPTER THIRTEEN

Zhān mǔ shì lit another cigarette, scratched his shaved head. "Stop fucking going on about what we should and shouldn't have done, let's get the story 'water tight'." The three of them sat around his dining room table, it was Tuesday morning. "We can assume that they've scanned traffic cameras and probably picked up the van. Of course, we weren't in it." This brought a nervous chuckle from the other two. "You said," he pointed his index finger of his right hand at Yuēse, "we played Rummikub all evening." Yuēse nodded, he plucked out a ciggy, then stroked his moustache.

"Yeah, Chow was fishing for red herrings so I made out I took the bait." He smirked at the other two.

"How are we going to get around my bitten dick Zhān?" Yuēhàn looked at Zhān mǔ shì, who was sitting opposite him.

Zhān smiled. "You know the prossy junkie who lives in flat twenty-three?" They both nodded. "I popped around to see her last night, gave her fifteen hundred Renminbi, with another fifteen hundred to come, after her statement, plus a hit of top quality heroin."

Yuēhàn looked concerned. "What's she 'gonna' say?"

"Simple, really." Zhān leant back in his chair, pulled on his fag. "She came around here at nine p.m. Sunday evening, we were playing Rummikub, we took it in turns to fuck her, we then had a foursome, she orgasmed, and accidentally bit your dick, then went home."

Yuēse combed his long hair with his fingers. "Can she be trusted, if she fucks up, we've had it?"

"She's more frightened of me than Chow and his cronies. She knows I'll break her skinny little neck if she does, as you say, 'fuck-up'." He looked at the other two full of confidence, then put the cigarette out. "Besides, she's desperate for the money and score, we go back a long way, I'm her most regular customer."

"Fair enough." Yuēhàn rubbed his mid-section. "That Chynna bitch, good riddance."

"What about your wife, Yuēse, can she be trusted?" Zhān turned to his right looking at his older brother.

"She doesn't know anything, as you know, I often stay out all night, or even for several days. Chow could torture her, she couldn't tell him anything."

Zhān nodded, then changed tack. "Remember, you only discovered the van stolen, when you went to take Yuēhàn to the hospital, hence the phone call at that time." Another round of nods met this last bit of detail.

"Okay." Yuēhàn got out of his chair, wiped his hair with his right hand. "We must keep going over the story, it's got to be exactly the same, as you said," he looked at Zhān mǔ shì, "water tight." He then shuffled to the cooker. "Who's for chicken chow mien, I'm famished?"

They went over and over the story as they munched through their dinner, it was indeed becoming water tight. "If you can convince yourself, convincing other people is a cinch," Zhān said, spitting chow mien over his plate. "When I've finished, you two clean this place up, I've got something for our friend at number twenty-three. We must keep her sweet — for now."

CHAPTER FOURTEEN

It was Wednesday morning. Sergeant Wong was driving as fast as he could in the heavy peak time city traffic. "Can't you go any quicker, put the flashing light on the roof and use your horn, I wanna get there before midnight!" Wong did as instructed, bullying his way through. Chow was wearing his usual blue suit, freshly ironed, crisp white shirt and blue tie. Unbeknownst to Wong, and anybody else, Chow had spent the night with one of 'his girls'. This liaison put him in a slightly better mood than normal, although the sergeant would argue the case. It was a swelterer, the air conditioning was on full blast, hence Chow even undid his top button.

"When do you intend to contact the Lings and David's parents, Boss?"

Chow ignored the stupid question for a few minutes, Wong realised his error and prepared himself for the sarcastic reply. Instead, Chow, still benefiting from a rampant night said, "Well, Sergeant, when would you like me to?"

Wong inwardly sighed with relief, his boss had relieved some testosterone after all. "When you've got sufficient evidence, hopefully we'll get some today."

They headed out onto the north-south elevated road, then onto G1501 towards Baoshan port, Yangtze River. Little was spoken, Chow was deep in thought. They arrived at 9.12 a.m. Wong manoeuvred the unmarked black police car, to the port's headquarters and parked up. Security checked their credentials, they were then escorted to the harbour master's office.

They were cordially greeted by Mr Bo Zhang, a small, rotund, balding man, in his late fifties. DI Chow got straight to the point, Zhang had been informed of the impending visit. This wasn't a time for pleasantries. Zhang, dressed in traditional uniform, explained that, due to the storm and consequent very heavy rainfall, anything thrown into the river Sunday evening, would have been washed out into the Yellow or East China Sea. Chow had already deduced this fact. Bo Zhang also informed the police, that there hadn't been any report of unusual or suspicious behaviour in the vicinity, and as yet, no human remains or clothing had been found. The brief meeting finished with Chow telling Zhang, that he must be informed immediately if any fishermen found a Chinese female or white male in their catch. He also asked for permission, it was more of a courtesy gesture, to look around the vicinity. He instructed Sergeant Wong to give Mr Zhang photo prints of the two missing persons, then quickly left the office and walked off. The sergeant did as instructed, shook Bo's hand, thanked him and hurried out. *Now which way did Chow go?* he thought.

The pair spent several hours walking up and down the river embankment, looking for any sliver of evidence, even a crumb would have helped. "I know they dumped them here, I just know it. The heavy rain has washed away any sign of the Lees' presence." Chow looked out towards the estuary and Yellow Sea, he then pointed. "They'll be about there, I'll put my life on it."

Wong, dressed in his grey suit, looked in the direction of Chow's right index finger, made a mental note of the position — a stretch of water south-east of Hengsha Island. "Come on, let's get back to the office, I want another word with Yuēse." Ironically, as they made their way back to the car, they walked past the very spot the van had been parked. No tyre marks could be seen, everything looked pristine.

CHAPTER FIFTEEN

"Okay, so I forgot to mention our little gang bang, so what?" It was now Wednesday afternoon, Yuēse had been dragged in for questioning by two of Chow's team. He was still digesting his chicken chow mien. He'd had his rights read, refused counsel. 'I've got nothing to hide, I'm here to help,' bullshit. They'd gone through the notes from the first interview. Chow decided to work him in tandem with Wong.

Sergeant Wong looked at Yuēse, the previous interview notes in his hand. "What's this clap-trap, you said the three of you were playing Rummikub."

Yuēse threw them a dirty look, pulled on the fag he'd been given, blew smoke at Wong. "I've told you, we played Rummikub, had a few beers, this hooker came in, Zhāni had booked her, we had a turn each, then 'did' her together, she got carried away, then bit Yuēhàn's dick."

Chow sat silently, looking hard at Yuēse, who leant back in his chair, staring at the ceiling. He shook his long hair and pulled on the ciggy, blowing upward smoke rings. The sergeant cleared his throat. "I suppose this woman has a name?"

Yuēse kept staring at the ceiling. "Zhāni calls her Suzi, I don't know if that's her real name, I've never seen her before."

"Where does she live," Wong retorted.

"Not sure, I think she works out of flat twenty-three, not far from his dump."

"Tell me about the van," Chow chipped in.

"What do you want to know?"

Chow slammed his right fist down hard on the table, it made the other two jump. "Don't fuck me about, you know dam well what I mean, the missing phone call report!"

Yuēse sat back upright, composed himself. "I took Yuēhàn downstairs, then outside to the car, we then noticed the van was missing, as it was parked behind it. Cars are always getting nicked around there."

"What time was it?" Chow snarled.

"I not sure exactly, it was after midnight." All three knew the exact time, Yuēse was trying to be coy.

Chow got out of his chair and started pacing around the room, he then crept behind Yuēse and shouted in his left ear. "How do you think they got in it and then drove it off?"

"Not sure, I don't even know if it was locked as Yuēhàn used it last, besides those 'old tubs' are easy to open and start, I could do it in two minutes." He looked at Chow, who was now leaning against a wall to his right.

Chow left Wong to ask the next question, it was a good one. "Why didn't Zhān mǔ shì go to the hospital with you two?" Wong glanced at Chow for approval, Chow ignored him, the question was acceptable. Wong turned and glared at Yuēse.

Yuēse stroked his moustache, put his hands in his pockets, looked to his left. "He got rid of Suzi and then cleaned up the blood, besides it didn't take three of..." Chow 'flew' behind him.

"You liar, he was torching the van, wasn't he!" He almost bit Yuēse on the back of the neck, who straightened up in his chair, somewhat shocked at the attack.

"I've told you, you've got it all wrong, we played Rummikub all night, had a couple of beers, fucked Suzi, pretty boring night, really." He smirked when he said boring, then lit another cigarette.

Chow turned his chair around, so the back of it was facing Yuēse, then sat back down. Wong knew it was going to be a long session, Chow had got the bit between his teeth.

"Right, let's start from the beginning, you seen the Lings then..." The questioning went on for hours, over and over, Chow was relentless, he sent Wong for coffees on several occasions, more ciggies for Yuēse, the answers always the same. The Lees had practiced the impending interrogation on each other. One was the 'victim', the other two Chow and Wong, they then switched roles, until Yuēse was taken back in for questioning. Finally. "That will do for now, you can go." Chow, face like thunder. Yuēse smiled, prepared himself for his homeward journey. "To the cells, you're staying with us tonight, we'll have another little chat in the morning."

"You bastard Chow." He rushed at Chow, who half anticipated a tantrum, he stepped into Yuēse, blocked his flailing arms with his left forearm and grabbed him by the throat with his right hand.

"Sergeant Wong, take this piece of shit to the cells before I break his puny neck!"

Yuēse went quietly; he'll have porridge for breakfast. Chow for the first time that day, smiled. Well, only inwardly.

With Yuēse safely locked up, he went back to the main office and gathered his troops. "Two of you go and pick up Suzi at flat twenty-three, Block C, Beishi Road, her statement could send them to the firing squad. Have we got those search warrants yet?" He pointed at two officers, one of either sex. They rushed off.

"Yes, Boss, the search warrants came through an hour ago."

"Right, let's go, we'll do Zhān mǔ shì's first." Nimrod was out for blood.

Chow's team arrived at Beishi Road in the early evening, it was now pleasantly warm. Beishi Road was a depressing area, consisting of four, twelve-storey, large blocks of flats: A, B, C, and D. The flats each housed thousands of people, in pretty grim conditions. All the Lees, including their parents lived there. A surveillance team had been watching the brothers' activity, nothing suspicious was reported. Yuēhàn was back at his parents' flat, Yuēse was obviously in custody and Zhān mǔ shì was at work, due home soon. "To save hanging around, we'll visit Yuēse's flat, we can have a chat with his wife while we're at it," Chow begrudgingly instructed his team. He didn't expect to find anything incriminating but he had to be sure. "Sometimes criminals make silly mistakes."

The team quickly searched Yuēse's flat, his wife didn't know anything. "He often stays out for days, I wish he'd go for good." She looked older than her years, Chow nearly felt sorry for her. Chow's boys moved to the next block, B, and visited Yuēhàn's parents' pigsty. He was watching television with his father, who just sat there, glued to the

65

screen; the mother was nowhere to be seen. The search revealed nothing. Yuēhàn, wearing a black tracksuit, grinned as they left,

"Always nice to see you, Mr Chow."

They headed back to block C, Zhān mǔ shì was now back home from work. "Well this is a nice surprise, would you and your friends like to join me for supper?" He was quite an imposing figure, and carried an air of menace as he stood in the doorway. His left arm blocking the way, sneering at Chow, who stood looking at him, with hands in his trouser pockets. He wore denim jeans and matching denim shirt which was undone, revealing a tattoo of the large head of a snarling black panther, yellow eyes glaring, seemingly, at Chow. Sergeant Wong, who stood behind and to Chow's right, flashed the search warrant in front of Zhān mǔ shì's face. Before Wong could react, Zhān mǔ shì shot his right hand out, and snatched the paper out of his hand, screwed it up and threw it back at him. Chow had his full of these histrionics, and knocked Zhān mǔ shì's blocking arm out of the way, proceeding to barge his way into his abode, daring a retaliation. It didn't come. He had an inclination that if they were to find anything of worth, it would be there.

"Tear this shit hole apart, let's start with your Rummikub box." Chow stared at Zhān mǔ shì, holding out his left hand. His host swaggered past him, shoulder barged a young officer out of the way, and picked up a plastic bag lying by the lounge chair. The bag rattled as he handed it to the inspector. His body language had now changed from arrogance to annoyance. Chow took the bag. "You throw your weight around any more, and I'll book you for assaulting a police officer," he said, throwing him one of his killer looks. He checked the contents, then dropped it on the floor.

The team thoroughly and quickly tore Zhān mǔ shì's 'dump' apart. It didn't take long as it was, not only small, but sparse. Chow could have done it one his own in fifteen minutes. Whilst the search was being conducted, Zhān mǔ shì did his best to block and be as awkward as possible, he, and the police, knew he was a lot bigger and stronger than all of them, including DI Chow. The search proved fruitless. "Okay, let's go." He purposely waited until all of his team were safely out of the flat, just in case Zhān mǔ shì took a swipe at one of them. Just as he walked out of the door, he said, "Get me back to the station double quick, I'm looking forward to a little chat with Suzi Lay, from number twenty-three." As he said twenty-three, he cut Zhān mǔ shì a knowing look, it was returned with a look of hate.

"So, you say, you went to Zhān mǔ shì's flat, fucked them and then had a foursome." Suzi nodded at Wong. "Come on Suzi, do you expect me to believe that bullshit?"

Suzi Lay was small and painfully thin. Her youthful good looks had long gone, the hallmark of her lifestyle was clear for all to see. Wong thought *if she lives to thirty, it will be a miracle.*

Zhāni had drilled her with her part of the story, she just had to keep it together for a bit longer. She knew the brothers by sight only, she knew Zhān 'very well'. She crossed her matchstick legs, slowly, making sure any voyeur could see her red, lace thong. She had another drag, blew smoke seductively at Wong, then nodded. She wore a black mini skirt, red low-cut top and red high-heeled shoes, her hair was dyed peroxide blonde, her face covered with copious amounts of tacky make-up.

"Look, they gave me an extra five hundred Renminbi for a foursome, I couldn't turn that down, besides, I enjoyed it." She winked at Chow. "Do you fancy a threesome, detective." Chow felt like laughing, but this wasn't a laughing matter.

Wong was amazed at how Chow tried to charm Suzi, to seduce the truth out of her. He smiled, offered her another cigarette, lighting it for her first, although he didn't smoke. Suzi leant forward, pouted her lips. "Slip it in, Mr Chow." Chow did as instructed. Unfortunately for everybody except the Lees, she didn't fall for it like one of his girls, she was desperate for the extra money Zhāni would give her, plus the heroin. She doggedly stuck to the story: sex, beer, Rummikub, more sex, accident, home. Wong was persistent, trying to trip her up, finally Chow brought matters to a close.

"Okay Suzi, sign your statement, that will do for tonight." She signed the statement, picked up her red handbag, blew them both a kiss and walked out into the evening; she was in for a treat.

Chow and Wong walked back to the deserted office, the rest of the team had now gone home. "See you tomorrow, Sergeant, I'm having a coffee before I sign out."

"See you tomorrow, Boss."

Chow poured himself a coffee, sat in a chair looking at the whiteboard, took his tie and jacket off, undid the top two buttons of his white shirt, finally flicking off his shoes. He studied the whiteboard, looked at the map, had another sip of coffee, walked up to the board, picked up the felt pen and added the day's detail. He circled Suzi's name several times, sat back down, had another sip. Chow finished the coffee, put his shoes on and washed his cup, leaving it on the draining board, walked nonchalantly back to the board, studied it again. "Oh shit!" he muttered to himself.

He quickly put his jacket on, put the blue tie in his left-hand pocket, grabbed his police car keys and rushed out of the office.

Suzi caught a taxi back to her abode. As promised, Zhān mǔ shì was waiting for her outside her door. "How did it go, baby."

"All sweet honey, I think I gave Chowy a hard on."

They both laughed, she opened her door, invited him in, and closed the door. "Here's your money Suzi, and, as promised, the best 'H' you can get." He gave her the fifteen hundred Renminbi then pulled out a syringe from a small tin.

"Oh, thanks." She put the money in her red handbag, she was itching for a score. She walked into the lounge, quickly found an arm band, tightened it around the top of her thin left arm. She smacked the decimated veins, whilst sitting in an armchair, found the best one. "Okay, hit me."

Zhān mǔ shì gently pushed the plunger to squirt out the trapped air at the top of the syringe, inserting the needle into her arm and injected pure heroin into her. She undid the band, gasped, smiled at Zhāni, then slumped back in her chair. She was on her 'stairway to heaven'.

Zhān mǔ shì, quickly wiped his prints off the syringe, grabbed Suzi's right hand and pressed a couple of fingers onto it. He stole all the money in her handbag, wiped it, checked the scene and quickly left her flat. Zhān mǔ shì hastily got to his flat, closed the door, then heard the sound of a car outside, screeching to a halt. He listened as he heard a man rushing up the stairs, then banging on Suzi's door. The man then opened her door, walked in and yelled, "No, no, fuck, fuck, fuck." The man spoke on his cellular phone. "Ambulance, block C, twenty-three Beishi Road, hurry." All went quiet, Zhān mǔ shì recognised the voice immediately.

The ambulance arrived after fifteen minutes, the paramedics did their best to resuscitate Suzi. They put her on a stretcher, Chow accompanied them outside. He moved his other blue suit and spare white shirts out of the way, quickly got two evidence bags and crime scene tape, from the back of his car. Chow rushed back to Suzi's, carefully putting the syringe and red handbag in clear plastic evidence bags, locked the door and taped off the area. He waved the ambulance off, acknowledged the surveillance car, then turned and looked up to Zhān mǔ shì's flat, and thought, *I'll volunteer for the firing squad, you're going to hell, you evil bastard.*

Chow drove off, he'd had a unsatisfactory day that needed some relief. He headed to one of his girls' apartments, the same one as the previous night.

CHAPTER SIXTEEN

"What room shall we interview him in, Boss?" It was eight a.m. Thursday morning, and Wong felt that Chow was in a goodish mood.

"He's asking for representation, they're in his cell now, discussing his options." Chow pointed to the room at the far end of the corridor. "We'll use room one when they're ready."

Wong noticed a slight mark just peeping out of the top of Chow's shirt collar, a love bite. Chow's girls enjoyed his company, as he had a good physique, was of 'reasonable size' and knew how to 'use it'. He enjoyed giving and receiving pleasure, and liked 'jungle fucking', usually resulting in bite and scratch marks on his body. The girls also liked the presence of a powerful man, both physically and vocationally.

Whilst they were waiting to interview Yuēse, Chow instructed an underling to phone the hospital, to check whether Suzi was alive. "Unfortunately, she died in transit."

"Make an appointment for me at the hospital, I need to speak to someone about her death and Yuēhàn's injury, I'll be there ASAP."

"Okay Boss, sorted."

Wong walked into the office, looked at Chow. "They're ready."

Rights were read, the recorder switched on, introductions given. Yuēse, still wearing the same clothes as the day before, a grey tracksuit and black training shoes, went, "No comment", to every question. This irritated Wong, but really annoyed Chow, who thumped the table several times.

"Don't waste my fucking time." The interview was quickly concluded, the police had two alternatives: arrest or release. They didn't have enough evidence. "We'll get it" Chow snapped. So Yuēse was released. He shook his solicitor's hand, didn't look at Chow and Wong, then headed home.

"We'll get them, Sergeant, we'll get them", Chow said, loud enough for Yuēse to hear. "Let's go straight to the hospital, I need some good news." On the way, as they walked out of the police station Chow looked to the heavens. "Looks like a storm's brewing." Not bothering to look at Wong, he was right, both meteorologically and metaphorically.

Once they'd been ID checked, they met the doctor in charge of the A&E department, at the main hospital reception. After a quick introduction, she took them into her office and answered non-confidential questions, firstly about Suzi.

"Unfortunately, she died in the ambulance mid-journey, the paramedics did all they could to revive her, tragically, to no avail." She sat on a high-backed chair behind a desk, looking at both police officers, who were sitting on smaller plastic chairs, Chow to her left. "It was a heroin overdose, she injected a large dose of pure heroin into her left arm, resulting in respiratory failure." As she described what happened to Suzi, or Miss Lay, she spoke mainly to Chow, but also occasionally glanced at Wong. The doctor was in her late thirties, petite, nice looking and had a very matter-of-fact manner. She couldn't say whether or not it was self-induced, there wasn't a sign of a struggle or consequent bodily bruising. The topic then changed to 'the bite'.

Mr Lee had indeed been bitten on his penis, that was quite easy for the medics to deduce. "Could you tell if Suzi, or should I say, Miss Lay, had done it?" Chow asked.

"Too difficult to tell, certainly not now, as the victim has had treatment." The doctor folded her arms as she spoke.

Chow rubbed his right hand across his chin. "Was there anything unusual about the accident or the demeanour of Mr Lee?"

The doctor checked her notes. "Not really, we occasionally get patients who have 'got carried away' whilst having sex, you'd be surprised at what I've seen over the years."

That comment made Chow inwardly laugh, and he thought, *Yes I can imagine*.

She continued. "There was one thing." She looked at Wong. "He'd obviously had a shower and a change of clothes before coming to hospital." Then looked back at Chow.

"Why do you think he did that?" Wong chipped in, leaning forward slightly.

"Couldn't speculate, Sergeant, your guess is as good as mine." She then started to rise out of her chair. "Okay gentlemen, are there any further questions, as I've got a busy day ahead of me?"

Wong was about to say something, Chow gave him one of his killer looks. "No, thank you doctor, you've been a great help." Chow shook her hand, smiled then walked out, as did Wong.

They commenced walking back to their car. It started to rain, lightly at first, then intensifying. Chow sat in the passenger seat in silence, mulling over what the doctor had told them. Wong was about to give his opinion, Chow just waved his left hand in an upward 'shut-up' manner, so he remained mute. They arrived at the police station just as the thunder started. "Drop me by the door, I'll start the briefing once you join us."

Wong entered the office, put his umbrella in the hat and coat stand situated next to the door, and commented, "It's absolutely pouring down", to anybody listening and quickly walked to Chow's office. The rest of Chow's team were at their stations ready for the latest update from their leader.

"Right, everybody, gather round." Chow stood in front of the whiteboard, jacket off, shirt sleeves rolled up, wearing a look of determination. Wong stood to Chow's left. "Let's start with the door-to-door enquiries." He pointed to two of the team, one of each sex.

"Not much really, Boss," the male said. "The woman two doors up from David's apartment said she heard a vehicle door slam just after nine thirty, and what sounded like a bit of scuffling, nothing much really."

"What was her name and apartment number?" Chow turned to the whiteboard, pen at the ready. He received the details, putting them next to the estimated time, that David and Chynna would have arrived at his place.

The young female cleared her throat to gain Chow's attention. "An elderly man said he heard, what sounded like a young woman scream, and a bit of laughing by a couple of men. He said it was between nine thirty and ten p.m. He thought it was a bit of 'larking about', so continued watching the television." The officer gave Chow the man's details, he promptly added them to the whiteboard next to the woman's details.

Chow then turned to his underlings looking at the traffic CCTV. "What have we got?"

The officer closest to Chow said, "Unfortunately nothing else to report, Boss, the only sightings were on the north-south elevated road, and G1501 towards Baoshan port, they must have used the back roads back to the city, thus avoiding any cameras."

"What about identifying the driver."

The other officer chipped in. "It was too dark and wet, we could just about make out there was one person, the driver, sitting in the front. We couldn't even guess the driver's gender."

Chow nodded, gave Wong the pen to hold, took a chair, positioned it in front of his audience, placed his left foot on the seat, and proceeded to tell them what happened. Wong thought he was going to perform a trick. "Thanks for all your efforts everyone." He put his left forearm on his knee. "This is what happened."

Chow looked at everybody. "The Lees pulled up outside David's apartment in the van about nine forty p.m. They'd almost certainly been waiting for David and Chynna, that wasn't pure chance. A scuffle ensued, with two of them, probably Zhān mǔ shì and Yuēhàn, resulting in Chynna screaming before they threw or dragged her into the back of the van, via the side sliding door. It's difficult to know for sure whether they intended to take David as well. Once both of them were in the van they sped off, initially just driving out of the city randomly heading north." He looked at Wong and signalled he wanted a bottle of water. His sergeant rushed off and quickly returned with one. He gave it Chow, who acknowledged the fact, took a sip, keeping it in his left hand.

"I'm almost certain they didn't intend to kill them, at worst a 'kicking' for David and a sexual assault for Chynna, hence why they weren't over bothered about being caught on traffic CCTV. Something happened in the van to change their plans. Did they kill them in the van or stop somewhere, that's the key." He gazed at his team, looking right to left. "Chynna or even David was forced to perform oral sex on Yuēhàn, whoever it was, bit his dick. They then took the bodies to the Yangtze and threw them in, possibly, but highly unlikely, still alive. They then drove back to the city, now carefully avoiding any traffic cameras. One of them took the van, probably Zhān mǔ shì, drove it to a deserted

73

area and burnt it out, making sure any clothing was also destroyed in the resulting fire, that's why we couldn't find any contaminated clothes at their addresses. Once showered and changed, Yuēse took Yuēhàn to hospital for treatment, concocting this story about gang banging Suzi Lay."

He took another sip of water, changed legs on the chair. "They must have bribed her to testify, giving them an alibi, then quickly killed her, before we could squeeze the truth out of her." He then turned to the officers dealing with forensics. "Have you found anything incriminating in the van yet?"

They said, almost in unison, "Sorry, Boss, whoever did it made a thorough job of obliterating any evidence, it's completely destroyed."

"That's a pity," Chow retorted. "We need to find the bodies and the location, where the attack or murder took place, I don't think they did it in the van — too messy." He concluded his briefing with, "My guess is, that the Lees are going to remain very low profile until they think they've gotten away with it." He looked at the team. "Any questions?" None were forthcoming. "Okay, carry on looking for anything, somebody ring Bo Zhang, see if he's found anything, I'm going to ring the Lings to tell them 'nothing'." He grabbed his jacket and walked off.

DI Chow had telephoned the Lings every day, to update them on the investigation. He sat in his chair, putting his feet up on the desk, then undid his tie. It was the usual conversation. "Unfortunately nothing yet, I'll let you know as soon as we have something." This was followed by, "Have they been in touch with you?" This was Chow's way of placating the Lings. The phone call ended with, either Mr Ling's raspy voice or Mrs Ling crying. Either way, Chow felt sick. It was only a question of time, before the real bad news had to be delivered. He then had the dilemma as to when to contact David's parents. He looked at his office clock, two p.m. he calculated it would be five o'clock in the morning, UK time.

He had all the contact details in his drawer, retrieved from the school. He punched in the number. The phone rang seven times, he was about to put it down.

"Hello, Jeff Peters speaking." The voice sounded sleepy. Chow knew Jeff was David's father.

"Good morning, Mr Peters, sorry to disturb you, this is Detective Inspector Chow, Shanghai police." He took another sip of water, then sat up in his chair. He heard movement and whispering in the background.

"Hello detective, what's the problem?"

Chow could hear what he assumed was Mrs Peters in the background, she sounded slightly more alert. *Time for more placation* Chow mused. "Oh nothing really, Mr Peters, it's just that David seems to have disappeared and I wondered if, either he's back in the UK or you've heard from him?"

Chow heard voices. "It's the police, they're saying David's disappeared, and want to know if he's either here or has contacted us." The woman's voice in the background sounded anxious.

"No Inspector he's not here, and no, we haven't heard from him for several days, which is unusual. What's going on?"

Chow knew this was the critical moment of the conversation, he rubbed his chin with his left hand, imaginary tossed a coin. "It's probably nothing to worry about, David and Chynna Ling are missing; we assume they've probably eloped." Chow cringed when saying eloped. His command of the English language wasn't brilliant, so his pronunciation, he hoped, that Peters could understand him. "Don't worry Mr Peters, if we hear anything we'll be in touch." He threw in one of his red herrings. "If he contacts you, could you please call me." He gave Jeff Peters his contact details. "Goodbye, I'll be in touch."

"Goodbye Detective." As Jeff Peters put the phone down, Chow could hear Anne Peters crying.

Chow replaced the phone in its cradle, and just sat there, looking into space deep in thought. His door was knocked, it was Wong.

"Boss, we've just had a phone call from the local police up in Baoshan, somebody's reported a large pool of blood in a parking lot."

Chow jumped out of his chair, put his jacket on, tightened his tie. "Come on, let's get going, you can fill me in on the details on the drive up." The pair rushed down the stairs. "Get the car, bring it passenger side to the door, I don't want to sit in damp clothes."

Wong, brolly in hand, did as instructed; the storm was at its height. He avoided getting too wet, although his shoes were soaked. "Apparently, car drivers using the car park, noticed a pool of blood, when they parked Monday morning, but didn't think anything of it. They assumed somebody had cut up a pig, using the car park as a mini abattoir." Wong manoeuvred the car through the city traffic, driving was hazardous in the heavy rain.

"What made them report the blood pool?" Chow asked.

"The word got out that two people were missing, possibly cut up, so a woman reported it to her local police station, they still think it's nothing."

"Where exactly is this car park?" Chow had an inclination where it would be.

"Just off the S322, an industrial area."

Chow thought for several minutes. "This is it Sergeant, no doubt about it. The Lees pulled off the road, found an empty car park, away from any prying eyes. I bet the pool is in the far corner, on the ground floor."

"I think so, they didn't give specific details on the phone." Wong replied.

They arrived at the car park twenty minutes later, no further conversation ensued.

"Pull up over there," Chow pointed. "I want this area clear!"

Chow and Wong exited their car and took command of the situation. There had been a lot of footprints and tyre tread marks made, during the lapsed time between the murders and the reported phone call. He stopped Wong from rushing in and taking blood samples. "I want to survey this area first, without distraction." Chow walked all around the area, not in it, glancing one way then the other, then walked up to a concrete stanchion, carefully avoided stepping in any blood. He pointed to a scratch mark. "How tall was David?"

Wong checked his notes. "He was just under a hundred and eighty-two centimetres, about a hundred and eighty."

"What's the distance from the top of a head to the middle of the throat? And get me the tape measure from the back of the car."

Wong returned. "It's roughly twenty-two centimetres, depending on age , sex etc…"

Chow pointed. "With a pencil, put a mark a hundred and eighty centimetres from the floor on this stanchion, and then another one, twenty-two centimetres down from it."

Wong did as instructed; the scratch mark roughly coincided with the previous guessed measurement. The blood spray confirmed his suspicion. He then looked around the stanchion base and picked up minute rope fibres. "They tied David to this stanchion, then beheaded him." Gasps could be heard from the surrounding local police officers. "Okay, Sergeant, bag these rope fibres, and get your blood samples. I want them taken from various areas, make sure you label them from where you took them." Chow then continued surveying the scene, "I wouldn't be surprised if, after beheading David, they did the same to Chynna. The amount of blood would indicate it." He was looking for rope fibres elsewhere. "I reckon they killed Chynna here." He pointed to a spot. "She wasn't tied up, she was probably crouching or lying on the concrete floor." He kept the rest of the details to himself.

He continued to walk around the periphery of the kill zone. He'd got a very good idea of what had happened, the only gaps were why. "Take relevant photos of the area, Sergeant, I've seen enough."

Chow then turned to the locals, he snapped, "Keep this area clear, I don't want any further contamination."

"Yes! Mr Chow."

Chow stood by their car, waiting for Wong to finish photographing, then had a final look around, sat in the car and buckled up. He thought of the Lings and Peters, closed his eyes and rubbed them. Wong put the camera and evidence vials in the car boot, and jumped in the driver's seat. "Where to, Boss?"

Chow felt like saying, "To a bar, then a brothel."

"While we're up here, we might as well go and see Mr Zhang, see if he can pile more shit on us." They drove the short distance to the port, in virtual silence. The rain didn't abate. They parked the car outside his office, Bo Zhang came rushing down the stairs, brolly in hand. He'd seen them from his office window, and reached the passenger car window as Chow unbuckled.

"I've just had a call from a fisherman, they've found the right forearm of a white person, probably male, on the south-west shore of Hengsha Island. I've sent a small boat out to bring it straight here."

"Let's get to your office." Chow pointed up to it, grabbed his umbrella, and the three of them dashed to the harbour master's office. Safely inside, he didn't tell Zhang where they'd just been, or what they'd seen. "So Bo, can you give us any more detail?"

He was dressed in his uniform, he wiped the moisture off his forehead with a tissue. "Not really, they were fishing in the Yangtze estuary as it joins the Yellow Sea, when one of them spotted the forearm on the shoreline. They radioed me, I told them to wait by the area, so they could point out the location to one of my boy's. It won't take long, they'll be back in a minute or two. Do you want a drink whilst you wait? There's a drinks vending machine next door."

Chow nodded to Wong, who knew his boss' preference and returned with two coffees, giving one to Chow before he took a sip. There was now no doubting as to where the bodies were. "We're going to organise a full search of the area, this will include divers, drones, sonar and magnetometer equipment. Have you got the tidal map?"

The harbour master nodded in agreement, he then pointed to a large map on the far side of his office. The three of them walked to it. "Assuming they threw the bodies in Sunday evening, probably from this area," he pointed to the riverbank, "with the heavy rain and ebb and flow of the currents, I'd suggest we look in this area first." He pointed again, running his right index finger just south of where the forearm washed up.

Chow nodded, took a sip of coffee. "What's the furthest they could have washed out to?" He was pointing to various locations, even as far out as the East China Sea.

"Typical factors include size and weight, clothing, weather conditions etc… I would be extremely surprised if they, or one of them, got that far. Knowing these waters, I'd say they are here." He used his right index finger and circled an area just south of Hengsha Island, parallel to Shanghai Pudong International Airport. They heard an engine noise; he looked out of his window. "Here is the boat with the forearm, I'll tell them to bring it up."

Chow was on his phone to his office, barking orders as to what was required and where. "I want this area searched now!" One of Zhang's men, wearing yellow seafarers, carried the clear plastic bag containing the arm up the stairs to the office, and he gave it to his boss.

"Take the launch back out again, use sonar equipment and search this area." He pointed to the same spot that he'd just shown Chow and Wong. "We're looking for a white man and a Chinese girl, now shut the door, we all don't want to get soaked." The storm hadn't abated. Zhang's man rushed down the stairs, nearly slipping on the last tread. He shouted to his two colleagues on the boat. One jumped off and joined him, in getting the sonar equipment from a storage shed, located with other buildings twenty metres from the harbour master's office. The pair carried the equipment to the launch, which was idling by the quayside. Once carefully put on board, the launch sped off; time was of the essence. The boat bobbed about as the water was quite choppy, and made landing it reasonably difficult.

Harbour Master Zhang, holding the clear plastic bag with the thumb and index finger of his right hand, like it was an unexploded bomb, gingerly passed it to Chow. Chow held the bag up to the window and studied the contents, wearing an expression of despair. He was looking at David's right forearm, severed at the elbow. It was clear to Chow that the arm had been in the water for at least three to four days, by the wrinkling of the skin (housemaids' hands) and the start of *cutis anserina*, commonly known as goose flesh. The arm had been cut cleanly at the elbow, and evidence of 'nibblers' was apparent. *Small fish and crabs* Chow thought. "I'll take this and the glass vials back, I want forensics to examine them straight away." He turned to Wong. "You stay here, Sergeant, and organise the searching, keep me in the loop." He opened his left hand for the car keys. Wong immediately obliged, Chow put them in his jacket pocket. "Thank you, Mr Zhang." He nodded at Wong, promptly leaving with the plastic bag, vials and his brolly.

He was just entering the city when his phone rang. He looked at the number, accepted the call, and put it onto loud speaker. "Yes, Sergeant,"

"Boss, they've just found the other forearm, and…" His voice went dry. Chow knew the news was sickening. Wong gasped. "Chynna's head." Chow could hear Wong gasping in the background, he wondered if he'd been sick; it was certainly a sickening scene. Chow, although not astounded, was surprised at the butchery, and wondered if the Lees were capable of such an act. To go from petty crime to this, was a massive criminal jump, maybe they were telling the truth after all. No, he knew they were guilty, there was no doubt in his mind. "Boss, did you hear me?"

Chow was deep in thought, and momentarily forgot about his sergeant patiently waiting on the other end of the line. He didn't apologise though. "Bag the evidence, I'll send one of the team to pick you up." He then killed the line.

The rain was still pelting down and made driving hazardous, but he wasn't in the mood for sitting in heavy peak-time traffic, consequently turning his headlights on, fished out the blue light and put it on the car roof. With the extra help of his horn, he bullied his way through the traffic, driving somewhat dangerously. "Needs must, needs must," he kept muttering to himself. With this attitude, he soon arrived at the station, parking nonchalantly outside the main doors. He had telephoned ahead to get assistance. The female officer who helped him, cringed when she saw the severed arm. "Get this to forensics immediately, I need to be absolutely sure it's David's, I want the results within twenty-four hours, no buts!" Chow snapped, as he handed the bagged arm and blood vials over.

A member of Chow's team picked Wong up from Baoshan in the early evening, bringing the gruesome discoveries back to the department and straight down to the forensic team, who were checking the DNA from the arm and the blood samples from the four vials they already had. This procedure would normally take a couple of days, but the dioxyribonuleic acid (DNA) lead scientist, didn't fancy a visit from DI Chow.

Chow sat in his office, jacket off, tie undone, shouting on the phone at Mr Tai, the underwater search diver police supervisor. "I want a team of divers searching the area east of the airport and south of Hengsha Island, liaise with Harbour Master Zhang, he knows the exact spot, first thing tomorrow morning."

The dive supervisor, sitting in his office, held the phone at arm's length to avoid Chow's full blast. "We've got to check the area first."

"What the bloody hell for?"

"Sharks, these waters have many species of sharks, I don't want to put my divers at risk of an attack."

"Don't give me that, there's no sharks that would bother a diver in these waters, besides it's mainly in the river estuary."

The supervisor started to get irritated, he didn't like Chow's know all tone. "There's a white spotted seal colony just up the coast and you know what fish they attract, besides bull sharks swim up estuaries, and they're even more aggressive."

Chow wasn't in the mood for a fish quiz. "I don't know and, frankly, don't care!"

"The other being great whites."

This news surprised Chow, the last thing he wanted was divers being attacked by sharks, especially that breed. "Well make it quick, I'll see you first thing tomorrow morning!" He slammed the phone down, not waiting for a response. *White sharks what nonsense,* he thought. Wong knocked on his office door. "Come!"

"All the evidence is with the DNA team, is there anything else, Boss?"

"Thank you, Wong, you can get off home." Just as Wong walked off. "Sergeant, did you know that there are great whites in our waters?"

"Yes, Boss, they predate on the seal colony. Fishermen have often reported seeing them. Why?"

"Oh nothing, good night, Sergeant." Chow rubbed his eyes and pinched the top of his nose, deep in thought; it had been quite a day. He sat there for another fifteen minutes, not moving, almost in a trance, very deep in thought, he then headed off home. *Surely things couldn't get any worse, could they?*

CHAPTER SEVENTEEN

"Okay, this is how we're going to do it." It was eight a.m. Friday, in the harbour master's office. "We'll have a boat, tied to that will be a lead rope, fixed to a plastic tube forming a T shape, feeding four divers roped together, equally spaced at three metres apart. I want two launches either side, running parallel to the divers for added protection for my men, I'm not taking any chances, that's the deal DI Chow." Police Dive Supervisor Tai looked directly at Chow. He was small in height but stocky in build, mid-forties, pock faced, supporting a good head of black-greying hair, cut very short at the sides and back.

The storm blew out in the middle of the night, the morning sunshine started to dry the dockside area; it was going to be a hot day. Chow, who was leaning against the harbour master's side desk by the back window, unfolded his arms and nodded once. To his right, stood Wong, to his left and slightly closer to the speaker stood Zhang, all dressed in their usual garb. The dive crew were already on board their launches and boat, awaiting further instruction, as was the sonar equipment. Chow had demanded a drone to fly low over sea level, but it hadn't yet arrived. The dive supervisor left the office, descended down the stairs and jumped onto the lead boat, signalling the team to set off towards the search area. The other three stayed in Zhang's office — Chow didn't fancy a boat trip.

When they got closer to Hengsha Island one of the crew immersed the sonar probe into the water. Soon after, the dive boat stopped, the divers, already in their suits, rolled backwards into the water. They swam into formation, then submerged. The boat then slowly tugged the area, following a grid system decided by the supervisor. They would go in one direction for three hundred and eighty metres, sweep around then cover the next 'block', until that whole area was searched, then move on to the next search area and repeat the process. Once the lead boat moved off, the side launches positioned themselves either side of the diving group. It took twenty minutes to search the first three-hundred-and-eighty-metre 'block', the boat turned, dropped a marker buoy, moved to the next section as the dive supervisor instructed and repeated the process. Consequently, it took one hour to search the first area.

"Have you found anything yet?" Chow's voice crackled through the two-way radio.

"No, we've just searched area one, we're now going further out towards the airport and deeper water, to commence searching area two," answered the dive supervisor.

They were halfway through the third block. "What's that, is that the white guy?" One of the party on a launch, pointed to his colleague at something floating to the starboard bow, about thirty metres away from the vessel.

His colleague laughed. "No, you dumb cluck, that's a white spotted seal, look." He pointed further out. "There's another one, they must think we're a fishing boat, hoping for scraps."

"Will they bother the divers?"

"No, they won't," his more learned friend replied, with an ironic tone.

The crew member in charge of the sonar probe caught the supervisor's eye. "I've just picked up a large moving object."

Before the supervisor had chance to respond one of the middle divers released a small yellow buoy, a signal to stop; he'd found something. The boat stopped, the two middle divers pulled Chynna's naked, headless body out of the water. They put it in one of the launches, and covered it with a sheet. "Take this poor soul back to the harbour master's office." A look of general disgust and revulsion was shared by all. The launch sped off back to the harbour, leaving just one launch guarding the divers. The dive supervisor continued. "We'll do one more sweep then have a break." They'd just finished the final turn, ten minutes later, when another yellow buoy broke the surface. The right-side diver had found David, and his head.

The three divers started to pull him from the estuary bed to the surface. "What was that?" One of the team on the boat shouted. A large dorsal fin sliced through the water.

83

"Oh shit that's a shark, it's been attracted by the seals, it looks like it's going to take a bite out of the corpse," replied a panicked colleague.

Whilst the divers pulled the dead body to the surface, the three-metre bull shark tried to bite David's left leg, consequently the divers panicked and pulled themselves onto the remaining launch, whilst their colleagues tried to beat the shark off with two oars, which were placed either side of the launch bottom for rowing, in the event of outboard motor failure. When the last diver, who held David's head in his right hand, was being pulled onto the launch, the shark bit the end of his right fin completely off. Luckily it didn't touch his foot. The shark then circled around the launch before disappearing below the surface. There was a lot of yelling and screaming, the bitten diver fainted, letting David's head roll into the middle of the launch.

"Grab that dead man's body and pull it into that launch before it sinks again," Supervisor Tai yelled. Gingerly, two of his crew grabbed David's black polo shirt, whilst peering into the murky water ready for another attack, and, with a sigh of relief, they quickly pulled him out of the water. "Let's get back to the harbour and cover the victim with a sheet."

The diver who'd been bitten recovered after a few minutes, looking somewhat shaken. His colleagues, who had been chatting excitedly about the whole scene, helped him sit up. Once the search team was back and ashore, the remains were de-crabbed then wrapped in cling film for preservation and to slow down the decomposing process, which normally speeds up once flesh has been removed from water.

Chow, who had ordered a large van — ironically the same model as the one David and Chynna had been 'delivered in' — to transport their remains back to Shanghai, now gave the signal for the driver to manoeuvre it into position. "Get this van loaded, and treat the victims with respect." He stood at the harbour wall and water's edge, Chow's mind full of mixed emotions. Pleased that the dive had recovered both the victims, but repulsed at the barbarity of the attack. Zhang's harbour employees carefully loaded the van, with the assistance of the van driver, under Chow's beady eye. Wong walked quickly back from the harbour office, gave his boss another plastic cup of coffee, shaking his head in disbelief. The pair were soon joined by Bo Zhang and then the dive supervisor, all wearing a look of disturbance. "Get the victims back to Shanghai forensics sharpish." With that he waved the driver off.

Chow, right hand in his pocket, the other holding his coffee cup, looked out to sea, still slightly shaking his head in disbelief. He finished the coffee in one gulp, scrunched the cup, throwing it into the closest bin. He turned to Bo Zhang, who said, "What on earth possessed them to resort to this butchery?"

"I don't know Bo, but I will find out, come hell or high water." He turned to his right and thanked Dive Supervisor Tia for his help, finished by shaking his hand. He walked over to the divers, who were still de-rigging thanking them for their efforts. "Who's got the 'trophy'," he said, pointing towards the fins. The divers laughed, then one, who still looked shaken, held up the bitten fin, more laughter ensued.

He walked back towards the harbour master's office accompanied by Zhang and Wong, and turned slightly to Zhang. "If they threw the knife or machete into the water, where do you think they would have done it?"

Zhang, accompanied by the two police officers, walked past his office, then down a track and pointed to the area Chow and Wong had searched previously. "I'd say that they would have thrown the bodies and the cutting blade from the same place, if they did throw it in. So that area."

Chow followed his pointing finger. "Yes, that's what I thought. I'll ask the dive supervisor to take the team back out after lunch, to see if they can find anything." Chow took a final look at the area, and wiped the sweat from his brow. "Come on, Sergeant, let's get back to HQ, this heat is intense." As they walked back, Chow kept looking out onto the vast Yangtze River, almost in awe of it. *This is some river*, he thought.

They left with a handshake and he thanked Zhang. Chow had asked Dive Supervisor Tai a favour, as opposed to an order, to search the area where Zhang thought the weapon might be. He gave another quick wave to the divers, plus a nod to Bo. Chow undid his tie, placed his jacket in the back of the car. Wong was already in the car. "Hit the gas."

CHAPTER EIGHTEEN

On the journey back to central Shanghai, Chow sat quietly, deep in thought. The air conditioning vent angled to blow cool soothing air onto his troubled face. Wong didn't say anything, he knew better when his boss was consulting with himself. Chow looked out of the side passenger window, right hand rubbing his chin, thus, the search had 'delivered' and his suspicions confirmed. He now had the unenviable duty to inform both sets of parents the news they were dreading to receive; this troubled him most. Although he'd performed this task a few times before, it was never pleasant, but this would be the most challenging, especially the phone call. He would have a translator present in case of a communication misunderstanding. These thoughts put him in quite a melancholy mood. His phone suddenly chirped and Chow pressed the accept call button.

The phone was on loudspeaker, a middle-aged female voice came out of the speaker. "DI Chow, this is the head of forensics, Dr Huang, I have news for you."

Chow turned his head. "This is Chow, go ahead."

"We have examined the various blood samples from the vials you gave us yesterday."

About time Chow thought. "Well, what are they?" Chow and Wong glanced at each other: *here goes*.

"After examining the DNA from the white forearm, it matched the DNA from sample vial one. Vials two and three samples had this DNA mixed with it, however, the sample found in vial four did not contain any of sample one's blood, this vial matched only DNA from the female's head."

This information confirmed Chow's conclusion. Sample one was from the stanchion area, sample four was taken from the furthest pool from it, which he knew was Chynna's, the other two a combination of both blood types. "Okay, thanks, have you received the other body parts yet?"

"Yes, they've just come into the laboratory. Looking at the cutting marks, I'm certain that the white male had both his arms hacked off at the elbow and was beheaded. The female was also beheaded." There was a pregnant pause. "I'll cross-check the DNA to make absolutely sure, moreover, the cutting marks match, and so does the skin tone."

Chow and Wong were impressed with how quick the gruesome package had been delivered, the driver must have taken Chow at his word.

"Thank you very much. What cutting implement do you think did the damage?"

"Too early to say, at a guess, don't quote me, I'd plump for," there was a pause, "butcher's chopping cleaver or a machete."

"How long do you think the bodies had been in the water?"

"Can't say, I need to do more tests, I've arranged for a pathologist to examine the bodies, I'll let you know as soon as possible."

"Thanks, keep me posted."

"Bye." She finished the call.

Wong, who'd been itching to say something spurted out, "I bet it's the cleaver."

Chow, who still didn't want trivial chatter, tutted, cutting Wong a disdainful stare. "I'll hit you with a cleaver in a minute, it's obviously the machete. Now concentrate on your driving!" They continued the rest of the journey in silence, Chow putting all the pieces of the investigation together. The only thing he couldn't quite fathom out was, why such brutality?

They made their way through the afternoon traffic, the city heat was quite intense, arriving at the police station mid-afternoon. On Chow's instruction, they both went straight to the forensic lab. As they were about to enter, Chow's phone chirped.

"Inspector Chow, this is Dive Supervisor Tai, I have some news for you."

"Good." Chow could hear the seagulls in the background.

"We think we've found the murder weapon, it's a machete. I'll send it straight down to your station for forensic cross-checking."

Chow looked at Wong, nodded slightly. "Thanks Tai, where did you find it?"

"It was in the area Bo Zhang suggested, we found it on our second sweep."

"Thanks once again, bye." Chow pressed the terminate call button and continued walking into the laboratory. The smell immediately hit him.

The pair were greeted by a small, plump, bespectacled woman, Chow guessed about fifty-five years old. She was plain looking and had a pleasant, professional manner. He could see the evidence laid out on two metal tables, in the background behind the woman. "I'd like to introduce you to the pathologist, who's conducting the post mortem, I'm Dr Huang, I spoke to you earlier." She pointed to an elderly man poking at David. Well what was David.

Dr Huang then led the two police officers to the pathologist. "Dr Wu, this is DI Chow and DS Wong." Wu, a physician, was in his late sixties, stooped, balding with a few strands of grey hair, was painfully thin and small, with narrow, pincer like fingers. Wu wore a typical surgical gown, tight fitting gloves and face mask. Introductory nods were exchanged. Chow and Wong who were standing as far away from the corpses as possible, each placed a handkerchief over their nose and mouth area, sprayed with a light coat of Wong's eau de toilette, which, conveniently on this occasion, he always carried with him.

Dr Wu shuffled around the corpses, muttering to himself. He kept putting on, then taking off, wire framed readers, much to Chow's annoyance. Wu slid his mask down slightly. "It will require further detailed examination to be one hundred per cent correct, but I can say for certain the following." He then looked directly at Chow, as he shuffled to within spitting distance of the police officers. "Due to the blood coagulation here," he pointed to an area of David's right elbow, "the white male had his arms cut off before he was beheaded. Clotting starts almost immediately on bleeding. He was still alive when he was beheaded, he died, not surprisingly, from blood loss, in other words he bled out. However," he then looked at Dr Huang, "the arms, probably the right one, weren't the first thing that this man," he emphasised 'man', "had cut off."

Chow and Wong turned to each other, a look of disbelief on their faces. "When we examined the woman, we found this jammed in her closed mouth." Using a pair of forceps, he picked up off the table the remains of David's penis. "The killer or killers cut this off first." Chow had noticed that there appeared mutilation in that area on David's corpse, but assumed it was from fish or/and crabs. Both police officers winced, when Dr Wu picked up what was found in Chynna's mouth. "See these stripes on the man's upper body." Wu pointed to dark brown thin bruising, "This man was tied up whilst being cut up. He has stripes on the chest and upper arms, but not his back. This would indicate he was tied to," he paused, looked to the heavens, "a tree or concrete stanchion, something like that." He then pointed to other bruising on David. "He was also hit in the face, ribs and neck, the bruising is lighter indicating age, albeit only hours. He also has lighter bruising bands on his wrists and legs implying being tied, all before his death."

Before Chow had chance to stop him, Wong removed his handkerchief. "I thought the bruising would be dark purple." The smell hit him, he quickly regretted both the quip and the mask removal.

Dr Wu looked at Chow, raised his eyebrows, turned in Wong's direction. "Typical bruising on the living," he emphasised 'living', "changes in colour from pink-red to dark blue-purple then, after about five days, changes to pale green, indicating healing. The colour will then change to yellow-brown and then fade. Unfortunately, Sergeant, dead people don't heal."

Chow looked at David's naked, wrinkled body on the slab then glanced at the plastic bags with his clothing. He would wait for the appropriate time. "This man was put in water not long after death, I would say six hours maximum. Being immersed in water slows down the decomposing process, it also stops flies etc… from burrowing into the skin, especially this time of the year. However, due to the open wounds, fish and crustaceans have been nibbling at it." He second guessed what Chow and Wong were thinking and Wu continued. "The sagging and wrinkling of the skin, colouration and amount of nibbling, I'd say he's been in the water between four to six days." Dr Wu looked at both officers, they didn't react, then shuffled to the next table. Dr Huang remained silent.

Chynna's body looked, to Chow, as if it had more nibbling that David's, he deduced it was because she was naked when she entered the water. "Her bruising indicates this woman was beaten before she was beheaded." His spindly fingers pointed to her face, which was badly discoloured. Wu looked at Dr Huang, then turned back to Chynna. "Because of the severe tissue damage, she had been sexually assaulted with a truncheon or something, or," he looked at the police officers, "brutally gang raped." He paused, looked at Chynna's lifeless body. "Both vaginal and anal." Dr Wu then shuffled towards Chow. "She died of blood loss and was put in the water the same time as the man, both bodies have the same decomposition timeline, and yes," he looked at Wong, "the same weapon."

Dr Wu fiddled with his glasses. "Any questions gentlemen?"

"No, thank you Dr Wu, you've been most helpful," Chow mumbled through his handkerchief. He glanced towards Huang. "Dr Huang, have you examined the clothing you removed from David?"

Huang moved closer to Chow and Wong. "Yes, Inspector, I've only found their blood on his clothing, unfortunately any other useful information has been contaminated or destroyed in the water, but I will keep looking."

"Was there any semen in Chynna that could be DNA tested?"

"Unfortunately not, Inspector." Huang glanced at Chynna's brutalised body. "If there was any it has been washed away."

Chow had gathered all the information he needed and had now formed a complete picture of what had happened. He thanked both doctors and started to walk towards the door, then turned. "Dr Huang, the dive team found a machete, it's on its way here for forensic analysis, it might prove useful."

"Okay, I'll start the examination as soon as it comes in."

Chow took one final look at Chynna and David, he slightly shook his head in disbelief. "Thank you, goodbye."

There was no reply.

CHAPTER NINETEEN

The pair walked quickly away from the laboratory. Wong turned to his boss. "How can they stand that smell?"

"Beats me, I'm told they get used to it. The worst smell is, I think, cadaverine, produced by putrefaction, it reeks!" They got to the top of the stairs leading to their office. "Get the team together for a full update."

It was now late afternoon, early evening. Chow stood in front of his team, and gave the board marker to Wong. Jacket off — top button undone- tie loosened — sleeves rolled up — beads of sweat on his brow — an intense look — he wasn't taking prisoners. "This is what happened." He looked at everybody, nobody dared flinch. "The Lees grabbed Chynna and David, dragging them into their van. There was a bit of struggling, David had his hands and feet tied together, plus a few slaps to keep him quiet. When they arrived at the kill zone; the car park, David got tied to a concrete stanchion with rope, had his dick cut off, both his forearms, then was beheaded." Chow turned, looked at Wong's work on the whiteboard, a slight nod, then turned back to his audience.

"Chynna was striped then gang raped, more than once, in all orifices. She bit Yuēhàn's dick whilst being forced to perform fellatio, hence the reason why he went to hospital. Chynna was also beaten up, before being beheaded. Yuēhàn, as an act of revenge for the bite, shoved David's penis into Chynna's mouth, then shut it. It's either pure fluke or very good organising, that none of Yuēhàn's blood mixed in with Chynna's or David's." The last point seemed to irritate Chow, but he continued.

"They then put the bodies, her clothes, the rope and the machete into the van, leaving a large pool of blood, and drove to the Yangtze, where they chucked both corpses and the machete, in. Chynna's blood oozed onto David's clothing in the back of the van, during the short journey to the river." Chow took a quick sip of water from the bottle Wong had handed him, he looked at the whiteboard and continued.

"They took the side roads back to their flats to avoid traffic cameras. They showered, got changed into fresh clothes, Zhān mǔ shì took the van plus rope and all their clothing, including Chynna's, dumped and burnt out the van. The other two reported the van stolen, then went to the hospital. They got Suzi Lay to give them an alibi, then killed her with pure heroin." He abruptly stopped. "That's it in a nutshell."

The audience sat dumbfounded, as if they'd just been shown the best magic trick in history. Nobody moved for a few minutes. Chow checked the board for accuracy. "All we have to do is prove it, keep digging."

He summoned Wong into his office. "Sergeant, I need an interpreter for later on this evening, can you arrange it?"

"Yes, Boss, I'll phone down for one straight away, male or female?"

"I don't care, as long as they speak fluent English."

Chow then contacted Mr and Mrs Ling on their cellular phones, instructing them to be at home, as he was going to visit them with news about Chynna. "No, I can't discuss it on the phone, I need to tell you in person."

Wong came back into the office. "The interpreter, Miss Kim Lu, will be available later this evening, just call this number," he gave Chow a card with her cellular number on it, "when you want to make the call."

Chow then rang Mr and Mrs Peters on their cell phones, with the same instruction as the Lings, "I'll contact you later this afternoon, UK time."

"Come on, Sergeant let's get it over with. He buttoned his sleeves and top button, tightened his tie, before slipping his jacket on. He also wore a forlorn look.

They set off into the pleasant summer evening, arriving at the Lings at six thirty p.m. Pleasantries were exchanged, they'd met Mrs Ling before on the first day of the investigation, and Chow had spoken to them a few times on the phone, so there was a small degree of informality. Chow hadn't met Mr Ling before, he was typically average in height, build, and looks. He wore a good head of black hair, neatly trimmed with a side parting and was a quiet, serious man in his late forties.

Mrs Ling made them both a cup of tea, it went downhill from then on. Chow considered softening the impact of the news that Chynna's parents were dreading. *They drove up to the Yangtze River, walked hand in hand along the embankment, kissed and fell in, drowning.* The Lings sat on a settee, Chow on a chair opposite them, Wong, also sitting on a chair, to his left. Chow, when required, could be very empathetic, treading very carefully as he delivered the dreaded news. He kept roughly to the truth, but omitted the beheading and gang rape, replacing them with a stabbing and sexual assault, before slipping into the Yangtze. Mrs Ling started crying almost immediately Chow began talking. Mr Ling put his right arm around her shoulder trying his best to comfort her; he would fall apart later. Once the facts were told, including David's demise, Mr Ling asked questions about who and why. Chow fobbed him off with several don't knows. "It's under investigation."

Mr Ling mentioned the Lees several times. "I know it's them, I know it's them, I should have phoned the police Sunday evening."

Chow thought Mr Ling, understandably, looked more angry than upset.

The meeting finished with Chow hugging both parents. Wong noticed Chow's eyes had welled up. Chow's final comment was, "I'm sorry, really sorry, I'll bring the perpetrators to justice, if it's the last thing I do." Arrangements were made as to when they could see Chynna at the mortuary, it would also serve for absolute identification purposes. Wong shook both the Ling's hands, he felt sick to the stomach. The police then left the Lings to grieve.

Wong took his time driving back to the station, the atmosphere in the car was somewhat sombre. Neither spoke, words couldn't replace what they both were feeling. As they walked into the office, Chow fished out Kim Lu's card from his jacket pocket.

Wong, wearing a look of concern asked, "Do you want me to stay with you, Boss?"

"No Zìmò, you go home to your wife and two girls." Wong looked surprised, Chow rarely called him by his first name. Chow then patted Wong's shoulder. "Goodnight my friend, I'll see you tomorrow."

"Goodnight, Boss." It was Wong's turn to well up. As he exited the office, he turned to see Chow slowing walking to his small office, hands in pockets, shoulders slumped, head down, he'd never seen him like that before. Wong didn't notice the wetness of Chow's cheeks. Chow decided, before he rang Kim Lu, to have a quick drink. He unlocked his filing cabinet and took out a bottle of Báijiŭ, locally called 'white lightning', and a glass tumbler. He poured two fingers of the clear liquid into the glass, put the bottle back, then went to the general office fridge, placing one block of ice into his glass. As he walked the few paces back, Chow raised his glass. "Here's to you Chynna and David." Then he took a large gulp. He sat in his office chair, feet up on the desk, sipping his drink, looking out into space. He stayed like that for half an hour, finished the Báijiŭ, then replaced the glass back in the cabinet. Chow then called Miss Lu, who promptly joined him. Pleasantries were exchanged.

Chow explained the investigation, who and where the call recipients were. Miss Lu, who was in her late twenties, was of average height, good looking, long black hair, with a nice figure, nodded understanding. "This is how it's going to play out. I'll put the phone on loudspeaker, then introduce you to Mr and Mrs Peters. If I don't understand what they're saying, I'll nod at you for either, interpretation or for you to talk to them."

Kim, who sat on a chair within arm's reach of the phone, nodded. "Okay, Detective, I'll watch for your signal."

Chow rang the Peters' number. It was answered by Anne Peters on the second ring. After the initial introductions, Chow explained Kim's role, she said hello and so the harrowing experience was repeated. Chow's version of what happened was similar to what he told Mr and Mrs Ling, this time with David as the lead person. "He was stabbed defending his girlfriend." That was all. A couple of times during the conversation Kim had to interject, at Chow's behest, as Mrs Peters spoke too quickly or mumbled, but by and large he managed very well. As earlier, the phone call finished with condolences and sincere apologies. "Let me know which flight you are on, yes, I'll meet you at the airport, once again, I'm so sorry."

Chow heaved a sigh of relief, he felt emotionally drained. "You did well, Detective, is there anything else I can do?" Kim acknowledged.

Chow was deep in thought. *He picked Kim up, lay her on his desk, pulled her legs up onto his shoulders, and gave her a good seeing too.*

"Detective Chow, did you hear me?"

Chow snapped out of his trance. "Oh, sorry Kim, I was miles away." He then shook her hand, thanked her for the help and said, "Goodnight." He hoped she couldn't mind read. Chow waited five minutes after Miss

Lu had disappeared before having another glass of Báijiǔ, this time three fingers and two ice blocks. Chow sat at his desk, feet back up on it, mulling over his next step. Hopefully the machete would have DNA evidence or fingerprints on it, that would conclusively tie the Lees to the murders. His case was based on supposition; he needed a break to crack his nutshell. He took another sip, made a mental note to contact the embalmer in the morning, to get the bodies presentable for their parents' viewing. His thoughts then went back to the parents, he could only imagine what hell they were going through. The lasting sound of Anne Peters screaming down the phone would stay with him forever.

CHAPTER TWENTY

The Peters sat holding hands on their settee, waiting for the phone call from Detective Inspector Chow. It was Friday afternoon, UK time. DI Chow had rung them at work, on their mobiles, asking them to go home as soon as possible, as he had news of David for them. It took Jeff just under half an hour to rush home from the engineering factory where he worked. The couple weren't sure of the exact time the inspector would ring, the waiting around was starting to niggle Anne, subsequently, she let go of Jeff's hand, stood up and started pacing around the room.

"How much longer is he going to be, I wish David had never gone to, bloody, China." She then looked at Jeff. "It's your fault, encouraging him, chumming up to 'that' girl's parents."

"Don't be like that Anne, they're a lovely family." Jeff shook his head. "You enjoyed the Skype chats just as much as I did."

The Skype chats were David's insistence, with both parents being initially, very sceptical. He suggested it to Chynna, the pair then badgered their parents, David via telephone. David set it up the fourth Sunday he was there, calling home via his iPad, in the evening local time, the afternoon UK time. After having a basic chat with his mum and dad, he then introduced Chynna for a quick chat, then swung the iPad onto Chynna's embarrassed parents, Ah Lam and Li Wei.

"Good afternoon, I mean evening Mr and Mrs Ling," Jeff said.

"Hello Mr Peters, please, call me Ah Lam, this is Chynna's father, Li Wei."

Jeff smiled. "Pleased to meet you both, I'm Jeff and this," pointing to Anne, "is Anne, David's mother."

They chatted for a few more minutes, the typical pleasantries, then said their farewells. The conversation was stilted as Jeff and Anne couldn't speak any Chinese whilst Li Wei and Ah Lam spoke a smattering of English, courtesy of David and Chynna. After this initial meeting, this became a regular thing with both parents looking forward to it, the two families clearly getting on with each other, arrangements were being made for a visit, firstly with Jeff and Anne travelling to Shanghai and later in the year the Lings visiting the UK.

Jeff suggested to Anne about going to night school to learn Chinese, she wasn't remotely interested, so he enrolled on a basic conversation course at the local college. The parents also had things in common. Jeff and Li Wei both worked at a factory and were interested in engineering, particularly cars and motorcycles. Anne, who worked in the city centre as an accountant's secretary, and Ah Lam, were both interested in animal conservation and painting. Chynna told David that he looked like his mother, she had long blonde hair, blue eyes, good looks, reasonable figure, being just above average height for a female..

Jeff and Anne's life continued in the same routine after David had gone to China. Due to the time difference, the phone calls were at the weekend, although he often sent a text message in mid-week, accompanied by a photo. Chynna was always with him. Jeff enjoyed his job, a design engineer at a large car factory and tinkered with an old motorcycle he'd owned for years in his spare time. The tennis season was in full swing, his game was in good stead, he wasn't particularly bothered that his 'after match practice' with Rosemary had fizzled out. Life was good for the Peters. That all changed after the first phone call early Thursday morning, from Inspector Chow.

Jeff took the first call, as the upstairs phone was on his bedside set of drawers. They were both half asleep when the phone rang. The gist of the call was that David was missing, was he back in the UK, and not to worry too much. The moment Anne heard the possibility that David was missing, she immediately panicked and, being a pessimist, starting crying, presuming he was dead. Unfortunately she was right. Jeff, ever the optimist, calmed her down. "He's probably ran off with that girl, you know what a dreamer he is." He then put his pyjamas and slippers on, and went downstairs to make them both a cup of tea. Beneath the veil of calmness Jeff was also worried sick. He had always said, "If anybody ever harms David, I'll kill them," as a throw away comment, but nobody ever took nice Jeff seriously. The Peters, over the cup of tea, then discussed their dilemma. They thought about ringing the Lings, and then decided against it. With a lot of ummimg and ahhing, they both decided to carry on as normal and go to work, and hope for the best. Due to the early time, Jeff even suggested a quick bit of rumpy pumpy to pass the time away. Anne, of course, was disgusted, and hit him over the head with her pillow, nearly knocking his empty tea cup over. They struggled through the rest of Thursday and Friday until the phone call on their mobiles from DI Chow, telling them to go home at the first opportunity, as he needed to speak to them there.

Anne arrived home first, followed a few minutes later by Jeff. Making them both a cup of coffee, they then sat on the settee, praying for good news. They didn't speak to one another, just held hands. Anne had got her handkerchief at the ready. They'd been waiting nearly half an hour when the phone started ringing. They both looked at it with terror. Anne was trembling, Jeff picked up the receiver, putting it on loudspeaker.

After the initial introduction, the police inspector informed Jeff that a translator was present, if he struggled with their English. Jeff thought the inspector was pleasant, polite and succinct in his delivery of horrendous news. The interpreter cut in on a couple of occasions when Jeff or Anne spoke too quickly. After the bomb had been dropped, as the inspector gave his sincere condolences and signed off, Anne exploded with grief. Their world would never be the same again.

The initial sobbing and grief lasted the rest of Friday, they didn't eat that evening, instead they got drunk on gin and tonics, trying to drown their sorrows. Anne eventually staggered upstairs for a quick bath, before bed. As she lay in the piping hot water, she could hear Jeff crying and then swearing loudly, shouting all sorts of drunken threats, before he threw his glass against the lounge wall, smashing it to pieces.

They struggled through Saturday due to a combination of grief and a hangover. Anne began the process of applying online for a Chinese visa. Luckily, she'd watched David when he applied for his, hence it was still relatively fresh in her hazy mind. Jeff, when he eventually got up, was as much use as a chocolate fire guard, and just moped about all day, starting to drink in the afternoon. Due to the urgency of the situation, on completion of the online form, the Peters could go to the Chinese embassy Monday morning and have their visa expedited, at an extra cost.

Saturday night went pretty much the same as Friday, they pecked at their evening meal, scampi and chips, which was washed down by several large glasses of gin and tonic.

On Sunday afternoon, with Anne's insistence, Jeff went to the tennis club. He wasn't in the mood for the usual banter and supported a terrible hangover, his breath also smelt of stale liquor. Jeff certainly wasn't his usual jovial self, Rosemary asked him if he was all right, but he fobbed her off. He thought about leaving early before they played 'smart Alec' Tony Jacks and 'drama queen' Lol Carun, as he wasn't in the right frame of mind for their antics. It didn't take long before Jacks started his sarcastic remarks, mainly due to Jeff's poor play. Jeff initially ignored the sarky digs, but then became more aggressive. "If you open your big gob again, I'll ram your racket up your big fat arse."

Rather than take heed of the warning, the 'smart Alec' just laughed. Sure enough, halfway through the next game, he called, "I've seen snails run quicker." Jacks and Carun just fell about laughing.

Jeff charged around the net, yelling and screaming at Jacks, who wisely ran off, with Jeff in hot pursuit. Jeff didn't have a prayer in catching Jacks, as snails don't run very fast, so he threw his racket at him, catching him on the back. Jacks yelped and kept running. Jeff stormed off the tennis courts, retrieved his clothes and went straight home, without showering, changing or talking to anybody. It was the talk of the club for weeks. Jeff didn't mention it to Anne, and made a lame excuse for being home early and not showering, Anne knew something was wrong, but didn't press it.

They contacted their respective employers, informing them that they would be absent from work for a while, due to family issues and would take compassionate leave and owed holiday time. Anne and Jeff then travelled to London, Monday morning, to complete the visa process. The Chinese visa took a couple of hours to complete, using two pages of their passports. Once home, Monday afternoon, they booked online the next available direct flight to Shanghai. It flew from London, Wednesday afternoon, arriving in Shanghai, Thursday lunchtime. Jeff, who wasn't drinking as much as he had been, phoned DI Chow, Wednesday morning, making arrangements to meet him at the airport, on arrival. Anne then booked hotel accommodation, initially for three days. The Peters jointly decided to contact the Lings once they arrived in China. The time from the initial call from Chow to boarding the aircraft was just a blur, a feeling of numbness for Anne and Jeff.

CHAPTER TWENTY-ONE

"Make sure you hold the sign the right way up and at their eye level, so they can see it easily." Chow was giving Wong instructions as they walked through the arrivals area of Shanghai Pudong International Airport. He had the spelling checked before they left the office, PETERS in large capital letters using a black felt pen on a white background, printed on thick cardboard. He didn't want any silly, unprofessional mistakes. Chow triple checked the arrival time the plane from London, UK would be landing. He had an inclination as to what Jeff and Anne looked like, as Jeff had roughly described his and Anne's appearance when he rang Chow Wednesday afternoon, Shanghai time, to inform him of the flight number, date and times. "They've both got blonde hair, Anne's is long, Jeff's is short. To be candid, a middle-aged white couple, slightly above average height for us with blonde hair, are you paying attention, Sergeant?"

Wong, who was now standing in the arrival greeting line, holding the name sign above his head, felt like hitting his boss with the said sign. "Yes Boss." He then stood on his tiptoes, whilst turning to his right. "This could be them, there's a white couple approaching the arrival sliding door." He pointed to the stream of arrivers, with his right hand.

Chow tutted. "They're elderly and 'wear' white hair, not blonde."

He was about to admonish Wong, but Wong called, "I can see them, Mr Peters is wearing a blue polo shirt and Mrs Peters is wearing an orange top."

When Jeff and Anne passed through the arrivals sliding door, Anne spotted a youngish, smartly dressed man in a grey suit, holding a sign above his head. "There they are Jeff," she said, pointing to where the police officers were standing.

The two pairs acknowledged each other's presence. Jeff and Anne continued to walk out of the arrival group, Jeff pulling just the one suitcase. With a look of regret, Chow put his right hand out. "Mr Peters, I'm Detective Inspector Chow," he said, shaking Jeff's hand. "Mrs Peters." He then shook Anne's hand. Chow then introduced the sign bearer. "This is Detective Sergeant Wong." Wong shook both their hands, trying his best not to smile. The quartet quietly made their way out of the terminal, Chow leading the way, nobody spoke. The police car was parked directly outside in the special area. Luckily it wasn't too hot with a light breeze.

Jeff's first impression of Chow was that he had an air of authority, a no-nonsense man. They were roughly the same height and build, but Chow was more powerfully built.

"Here we are." Chow pointed to the car, removing a police notice from the windscreen, whilst addressing the Peters.

Wong opened the car boot. "Let me take that Mr Peters." He picked up their suitcase and put it in the large boot.

Chow and Wong then opened the rear passenger doors. "Would you like to go to your hotel to freshen up?" Chow asked, as his guests were seated.

"No inspector, we want to see our son," Anne replied, somewhat curtly. Chow nodded to Wong, as the hosts buckled up. There was an air of tension in the car, nobody spoke, not even to each other. Chow had anticipated that there would be a good chance that the Peters would want to see David as soon as they arrived, so he had the embalmer get his body prepared.

Under Chow's instruction, David's body had been moved from the morgue to the mortuary, then placed in an adjoining reflection room, in preparation for the Peters' visit. He had gone through a similar experience the previous Saturday with Mr and Mrs Ling, not something he was looking forward to again. Chynna's body was resting back in the morgue. Chow had also arranged for an interpreter to be present as he had envisaged his or Wong's, although better than his, command of the English language, would not suffice. A particularly awkward moment could be if the parents wanted to touch their son, which they couldn't, as his death was still under investigation, and they might contaminate evidence. Chow wanted all eventualities covered.

102

Wong, dressed in his usual work outfit, wore a black tie, as did Chow as a mark of respect, drove very carefully from the airport to the mortuary, which was an adjoining building to the police station. When the car came to a gentle stop, Anne began to softly weep, and Jeff tried his best to comfort her. Chow and Wong felt like hearse drivers as they got out of their police car, carefully opening the rear passenger doors, leading the bereaved parents towards the reflection room entrance door. Anne and Jeff huddled together, both now weeping. The interpreter, Kim Lu, stood next to the front door, hands clasped together, head slightly bowed. Chow, walking slightly in front, introduced Kim to the Peters, who acknowledged her with a slight nod. Kim, who was formally dressed, opened the entrance door to allow the party to enter the mortuary. Chow then lead the Peters down the corridor to the reflection room, Kim and Wong following behind Jeff and Anne. Chow opened the reflection room door.

Jeff and Anne slowly walked in. Anne's legs wobbled as she saw David, laid out on a wooden table, a white sheet covering his body from the neck down. The room, about the size of a large bedroom, was pleasantly decorated with pastel colours, including the thick floor carpet, flowers adorned all of the walls. Chow decided to play safe and instructed European classical music to quietly play in the background. Jeff held Anne as she steadied herself; they looked as white as David's sheet. Anne then rushed towards David, wailing, "My son, my son, what have they done to you?" Chow quickly moved by the corpse, just in case Anne tried to touch David.

Chow thought the embalmer had done an excellent job, David looked 'alive' but asleep, as did Chynna, previously. "Please, Mrs Peters, don't touch David, thank you."

Jeff shuffled to join Anne. "Please, Detective Chow, can we have a few moments alone with our son, we won't touch him?"

Chow looked at Miss Lu for confirmation he understood the request, Kim quickly whispered the translation. "Yes of course, we will wait outside." Chow then gave a slight head movement, and they left the room. As Chow was exiting the reflection room, he slightly turned to see what looked like Jeff whispering in David's ear.

The three stood on guard outside the reflection room, listening to the Peters talking to their son, between loud sobs and screaming. Chow didn't have a time frame for the visit, he decided to play it by ear. They stood quietly, not looking at each other. Wong looked close to tears, Chow assumed it was because he had children, probably, but not necessarily. Eventually he heard movement towards the door, it had been about half an hour. He opened it to allow the Peters to stagger out. As he closed the door, he noticed a small, blue, baby hat, placed mid-point, on top of the sheet.

After a very brief discussion, it was agreed to take the Peters directly to their hotel. They would see Chow the following day to discuss the investigation. Chow thanked Kim, asking her if she was available for future meetings — she was. After dropping the Peters off at their hotel, which, at Anne's insistence, was the same one as David had stayed in, the police headed back to their station. Chow wanted a team meeting. He thought about the two reflection experiences, the only difference being the background music played, both sets of parents acting very similarly, with sorrow but dignity. It hardened his resolve to prove the Lees guilty, and he wanted to be there when they 'took the bullet'.

Jeff and Anne checked in. They had booked the same room that David had stayed in. Over their evening meal at the hotel, they discussed the events on arriving in China. "David looked presentable, the police officers were polite, when shall we meet Chynna's parents." That was about it. They both nibbled at their meals, then went back to their room, showered and then went to bed, slept — or tried to.

Sergeant Wong picked the Peters up at ten thirty a.m. Friday. Pleasantries were exchanged. "Inspector Chow will meet you in his office." Jeff was wearing light cream trousers and a black polo shirt. Anne dressed in a light blue top and white bottoms sat in the back of the police car. Nothing was said. During the evening, whilst in their room, Jeff had uploaded a translator app onto his mobile phone, ready for when they met Chynna's parents. Over breakfast they decided to contact the Lings once they'd finished the meeting with Chow.

"This way Mr and Mrs Peters." Wong made his way up the stairs to the main office. "Through the doors, be careful with the door, that's

Inspector Chow's office at the far end of the room." Wong pointed it out to Jeff, as they entered the main office of Chow's team.

Chow had briefed his team that they were getting visitors. "Look busy, avoid staring, smile if looked at, etc..." He also told one of the team to cover the case evidence whiteboard with a black sheet, to avoid possible embarrassment. He put out his hand, as, firstly Anne, then Jeff entered his office. After hand shaking and salutations he reintroduced Miss Lu, who nodded and smiled in acknowledgement. Anne and Jeff declined the offer of a cup of tea. Wong placed the Peters in comfortable chairs, opposite Chow, the other side of his desk, he then left, closing the door behind him.

Chow, with the occasional assistance from Kim, glossed over the investigation, thus avoiding the full grisly details, he didn't want to put David's parents through any more anxiety and misery. He explained that they were looking into all possibilities, and had narrowed down potential suspects. "I'm sorry, I can't divulge any names at this stage." They then discussed when the coroner would release David's body. "As soon as all evidence has been obtained, and hopefully the case will be solved." He immediately regretted saying hopefully. The meeting continued for forty-five minutes, culminating on an agreement to visit David before they flew back to the UK, arrangements being made at their convenience. Both parties shook hands, said their farewells. Wong was waiting to drive them back to their hotel. Just as Jeff and Anne started to walk away from Chow's office, a gust of wind from a side window blew the sheet up covering the evidence whiteboard. It was flapping about long enough for Jeff to spot the details as to David's demise, and photographs of who the suspects were. Although the notes were in Chinese, Wong had drawn a silhouette of a male and female, showing the cut marks on them. One of Chow's underlings jumped out of his chair to pull the sheet back down, leaning another chair by it, to keep it against the whiteboard. Jeff looked at Chow, Chow knew that Jeff was aware of his deceit. Chow expected a reaction, but they just stared at each other for a couple of seconds, then Jeff nodded slightly, and walked away to catch Anne and Wong up. Immediately after the Peters had exited the building, Chow held an enquiry as to how the sheet blew up. A young woman admitted to opening the guilty window to allow fresh air to circulate, as it was quite stuffy in the office. The look on Chow's face said it all. Miss Lu quietly left the main office.

Chow moved the chair, and pulled the sheet off the wall staring at the whiteboard, arms folded across his chest. Unfortunately for everybody except the Lees, the machete didn't reveal any compelling evidence. The surviving blood samples on the machete, tested by forensics, matched both Chynna and David's DNA. It was also confirmed as the murder weapon. Dr Huang couldn't find any fingerprints, paint or fibres to tie the machete to the van. Her team had stripped the van and drawn a blank, consequently the police didn't have any concrete evidence to arrest the Lees, it was all circumstantial. The Lees, since their release, had kept a very low profile, which in itself, Chow thought, indicated guilt. Chow then paced slowly left and right, whilst his eyes were glued to the whiteboard, if he didn't get a breakthrough soon, the coroner would release the bodies for burial. Another experience he wasn't looking forward to.

He sighed, then slowly walked back to his office, sat in his chair and mentally compared the two victims' families. Apart from the obvious ethnic differences, they were very similar in many ways, including how they'd conducted themselves at the mortuary. He was shaken out of his reflection by Wong, who knocked on his door.

"Do you want me, Boss?"

"Yes, Sergeant, let's line the Lees up and shoot them." If only.

CHAPTER TWENTY-TWO

"Thank you, Sergeant." Jeff waved Wong off, as Anne walked towards their hotel entrance. They sat in the foyer. "Right Anne, you ring them, I'll have my translator app open."

"Let's leave it a minute Jeff, I don't know if I could face them."

"You can't blame them Anne, they're nice people, besides they probably feel the same."

The blame game, for both couples, had started the moment they were aware of their respective child's disappearance. For the Lings it was less than twenty-four hours. They initially blamed each other, Li Wei for allowing Ah Lam to talk him out of phoning the police, that Sunday evening, once Chynna and David had left their abode to walk home. Ah Lam hit back by saying, "You should have insisted." The subject never completely went away. What they both conveniently agreed on was that if Chynna hadn't met David, she, no mention of him, would still be alive. In moments of desperation and anger, Li Wei would rant about getting the Lees. He, along with Chow, was one hundred per cent certain it was those fucking pigs who killed them. In a more thoughtful mood, they lamented David's death, in a matter of weeks of meeting him, they also loved him, in particular Ah Lam. They also liked David's parents. Initially sceptical, they looked forward to the Skype meetings although they couldn't properly communicate. Ah Lam warmed to Anne and Li Wei had a lot in common with Jeff. Once it was obvious something was seriously wrong, they considered ringing the Peters but, mainly due to the communication issue and the awkwardness of the circumstance, they put it off. They were aware that Anne and Jeff would be coming to Shanghai to see David, courtesy of Inspector Chow, who mentioned it when they visited Chynna at the reflection room on the Sunday, a week after last seeing her. Ah Lam hoped that David's parents would contact them, Li Wei wasn't so keen; he still held deep resentment.

Jeff took another sip of his tea, pondering over what he'd seen on the whiteboard. He hadn't mentioned the full circumstances of David's execution to Anne, he'd have to pick the right time, if indeed, there ever would be a right time. It was approaching lunchtime, he could smell the food being prepared in their hotel kitchen, however, he didn't have an appetite. Anne, sitting in an adjacent foyer chair, suddenly turned to him. "Let's get it over with, they might not even be at home." She dialled the number David had given them. Jeff had his app open. The phone rang four times.

"Hello, Mrs Ling speaking."

Ah Lam heard what she assumed was English voices, then a robotic, "Hello, this is Jeff and Anne, shall we come and visit you?" Jeff waited for the translator app to decipher Ah Lam's response. He heard background mumbling.

"Yes, do you know where we live?" Ah Lam and Li Wei had their house phone on loudspeaker listening to Jeff speak to a translator.

A few seconds passed. "Yes, David gave us your address, we will come now, if that's okay?"

"Yes, we are just about to have lunch, you can join us."

Jeff was struggling with the translator, so kept his answers brief. "Thanks, we'll be at yours shortly."

The Lings weren't quite sure what he meant but still answered. "Okay, bye."

"Bye."

The Peters went to their room, freshened up, ordered a taxi at the hotel reception, held their breath and set off.

The Lings, who hadn't been to work since Chow's visit, welcomed the Peters with hugs, handshakes and tears, both speaking to each other without knowing what was said. Once inside, Jeff started using his translator app, which helped the communication. Li Wei then uploaded one onto his cellular phone so the conversation became normalish but disjointed. Over lunch, which was a fish salad, they just talked about David and Chynna, how in love they were and what a tragedy their deaths were. The atmosphere could have gone from warm to very cold with the mention of the Lees, but Ah Lam changed the subject quickly, muttering to Li Wei, so that Jeff couldn't use his translator. He didn't need it for that, it was pretty obvious. Anne and Jeff spent most of the afternoon with the Lings, parting warmly, with a promise to keep in touch, especially now they had the translator app.

CHAPTER TWENTY-THREE

The next few days passed uneventfully for the Peters, they just meandered about the area close to the hotel, roughly where David walked when he first arrived in Shanghai. They didn't do the sightseeing they had planned on doing with their first visit, they weren't in the mood for it. They had agreed with DI Chow, to visit David again, which they did. He informed them that they could either collect David, or he would organise David's transportation as soon as his body was released by the coroner. Hopefully very soon.

Ah Lam and Li Wei insisted on taking Jeff and Anne to the airport, both parents keeping a stiff upper lip. They took with them David's suitcase and personal items, after visiting the apartment he had shared with Chynna, on the day of departure. They also visited the school where David and Chynna worked, it was now closed for the summer holiday, en route to the airport.

With a promise of keeping in touch, both parents went home.

CHAPTER TWENTY-FOUR

It was the middle of August when Anne received the phone call from DI Chow; the coroner had released David's body. Arrangements were made for Anne and Jeff to meet the hearse at Shanghai airport, to fly David back home. They decided to escort the body back to the UK on a passenger plane at an extra cost. They arranged for a hearse to transport David to their mortuary, the planned funeral for the day after arriving back.

The month and a half between the journeys to China, had dragged for both Jeff and Anne. They went back to work on the Monday, following their return from the first visit. Life was pretty mundane, Jeff hadn't bothered going to the tennis club, he instead just tinkered with his old motorbike, and drank a lot. Anne, who had her hair cut slightly shorter just existed: work — lounge about — drink — watch telly — go to bed. Jeff enrolled on a Chinese course for beginners at the local further education college, and he supplemented it by buying a CD language programme, which focussed on listening and speech. He was determined to have basic communication skills the next time he flew to China. Anne thought he became obsessive trying to learn Chinese, *at least it stopped him watching too much television*, she mused.

Chow had also informed them that, unfortunately, no arrests had been made. "But, rest assured, the investigation will never close, I will not rest until justice has been done." Jeff thought that Chow was a sincere man and meant what he'd said.

The Lings and Peters, as they had promised, did keep in touch, a quick phone call once fortnightly, with the aid of the translator app. Anne and Jeff decided to go to Chynna's funeral on the begging of her parents, which would be held on the day after they arrived in Shanghai, as her body was also released by the coroner the same time as David's. They couldn't return the compliment, as it would've taken too long to get a visa to the UK.

Ah Lam informed Jeff, that Chynna's body was being kept in a coffin in their front room. They took it in turns to perform 'shǒu líng', which she enlightened him, means 'keeping watch besides a coffin'. Jeff asked her what colours to wear at Chynna's funeral. "Plain white, please, and no jewellery, thank you."

Li Wei met the Peters on a wet Wednesday afternoon at Shanghai airport, driving them to their hotel, the same one as last time, but a different room, as theirs was booked. The Lings wanted Jeff and Anne to stay at their place, but Anne didn't fancy it, especially with Chynna's body being there. Mr Ling noticed a difference in his passengers since their last visit. Jeff's hair was longer, he'd got a paunch and had aged, Anne's hair was shorter, she also had aged, but seemed to be holding up better. Li Wei, however, was impressed with Jeff's rapid progress on speaking and understanding Chinese. Jeff informed Li that he had enrolled on a 'learn Chinese in twelve weeks' beginners' evening course at the local college. He also practiced every night, listening and speaking with the aid of a CD language programme. With the aid of the translator apps and Jeff's linguistic skills, Li Wei gave Jeff the time and address for Chynna's funeral, Thursday morning. They would have to order a taxi to take them there. A quick shake of hands. "See you both tomorrow." Jeff hoped it would be at least dry.

Once checked into their hotel, Jeff Peters arranged a meeting with DI Chow for late Thursday afternoon, as they didn't intend to stay too long at Chynna's wake. He didn't speak any Chinese, the conversation was in basic English, finishing with, "We will make our own way to the police station."

Jeff ordered the taxi via the hotel reception, after breakfast, on a warm, dry, Thursday morning. He spoke as much Chinese as he could. 'Slowly speak', Anne noticed, was the most frequent phrase used. Jeff wore a white polo shirt and chinos, Anne dressed in a white blouse and cotton bottoms, both wore beige, lightweight, summer footwear.

Being Buddhists, the Lings held Chynna's funeral service in a Buddhist temple. Jeff noticed the burning of joss paper, which he later learned, ensured Chynna had a safe passage to the netherworld. Fake paper money and Chynna's favourite household items, plus a photograph of David was also burnt, believed to follow her into the afterlife. After prayers and a brief eulogy, Mr and Mrs Ling distributed to all their guests, a red envelope with a coin inside, ensuring they return home safely. The guests were also given a piece of red thread, which should be tied to their front doorknob to repel evil spirits, Li Wei informed Jeff in one very brief personal moment. They also pinned a black cloth band on their right sleeves, this showed a period of mourning for a deceased female.

The small family procession then followed a marching band to the crematorium, playing loud music to ward off evil spirits. The hearse, containing Chynna's body, adorned with a large portrait of Chynna hanging in the windscreen, slowly drove behind. The rest of the procession, with Jeff and Anne at the end, walked after the hearse. After the cremation the mourners dispersed as there wasn't a wake reception, the wake was held pre-burial. Mr and Mrs Ling briefly thanked Jeff and Anne, wishing them luck. "Keep in touch."

The Peters went back to their hotel to freshen up, before popping in to get an update from DI Chow. The experience of Chynna's funeral had left them emotionally drained; it was a taste of things to come. Jeff had a quick shower, then slipped on a fresh dark blue top, and the same trousers and footwear that he'd worn in the morning. After her shower, Anne wore a black top and the same clothes she wore earlier. They'd both avoided bright colours as a mark of respect for the Ling family.

The meeting with Chow didn't last long, as the investigation, although ongoing, was no further forward. "All stones will be unturned." Chow was inwardly impressed with Jeff's attempts at speaking Chinese, but wasn't surprised at both parents' haggard look. The arrangements were finalised for transportation of David's body, firstly from the mortuary to the airport, and then the placing of the coffin onto the passenger aircraft. Chow would meet them at the airport, prior to embarkation. Hands were shaken. Jeff gave Chow a knowing look. "See you both tomorrow." Was Chow's closing comment.

Anne and Jeff hired a taxi to follow the hearse from the mortuary to the airport. Luckily, the imminent rainfall kept off during their last few hours in China. Chow and Wong met them at the airport. With the aid of airport officials they made sure procedures went smoothly. With a final farewell, the Peters 'family' departed China.

On arrival back in the UK, David's coffin was removed from the airport passenger conveyor belt, then carried by bearers to a waiting hearse. The coffin was then driven to the mortuary, ready for his funeral the following day.

CHAPTER TWENTY-FIVE

David's funeral was a quiet, sombre affair, with only a few very close friends and family present. The vicar delivered the eulogy prior to the cremation. Jeff placed a scarf of David's favourite football team and photo of Chynna in his coffin, before it was finally sealed at the mortuary. The Peters decided not to hold a wake reception, they, under the circumstances, didn't think it was appropriate. Anne made the decision to leave David's room as he'd left it, as a form of memorial; at least until his murderers were found and brought to justice.

Once Jeff and Anne arrived home from the service, Jeff changed out of his black funeral attire into casual clothing, then got blind drunk, much to Anne's annoyance. Their relationship had not been particularly close since 'that' first phone call from Chow. They both suffered from depression and grief resulting from, not only David's death, but by how it happened. Consequently Anne bickered at Jeff because she blamed him for supporting and, in her words, encouraging David to go and stay in China. The physical side to their relationship had also dried up. In general, they were getting on each other's nerves.

The months after David's funeral followed much as those before it. Both Anne and Jeff drank too much, they continued to go to work, and Jeff beavered away learning Chinese, much to Anne's irritation. Although Jeff had his hair trimmed for David's funeral, he let it grow again, shaved once a week and continued to put weight on, in short, in Anne's opinion, "He was a scruffy, fat, slob".

Things came to a head in October, on David's birthdate, when they had the mother of all rows. They were both drunk, Anne slurred, "David would be ashamed of you, you're a pathetic, useless, fucking tramp, either, get a grip or get out!"

Jeff stormed off, he felt he needed a walk in the fresh autumn air, to clear his head and weigh-up his options. He could not dispute Anne's accusations regarding his physical appearance, what she didn't seem to realise was, that he was dying inside, as far as he was concerned, he was a walking dead man.

Jeff walked aimlessly, oblivious to where he was going, deep in thought. If he didn't get a grip, he knew Anne and he would definitely split up; he had to channel his grief and anger in a positive direction. When he crossed a road, he was so engrossed in his planning, he almost got run over. "Look where you're going, you fucking twat," was the unsympathetic driver's pleasantry.

Startled, he stopped walking and looked around to get his bearings, he was almost lost, but managed to follow the main road back into his neighbourhood. From there he knew his direction back to Burlington Road. The walk had not only sobered him up, he now had a plan. "I'm not doing this for you, Anne, I'm doing it for David," he muttered to himself, as he walked through his house front door. The red thread was still tied to it, given to him by Li at Chynna's funeral. He didn't explain his plan to Anne, she would know sooner or later.

"Well, what are you doing, Jeff."

"You'll find out!"

CHAPTER TWENTY-SIX

The following night, after tea, Jeff started browsing the web. "This will do," he said to himself. His plan, as Anne would soon find out, consisted of joining the local gymnasium and a martial arts class, the closest being a beginners' class in ju-jitsu; he would have preferred judo, which derived from ju-jitsu, but the dojo was too far away. Jeff did a bit of research before his first class. Ju-jitsu, a Japanese martial art, founded in the eighteenth century, is a rough version of judo. He didn't really like the sound of the adverb 'rough'. The night before Jeff's first ju-jitsu session, on the way home, he decided to have a haircut at the local barbers. On a whim and a moment of madness, he told the clipper, "Crew cut". He was virtually unrecognisable, it looked more like a skinhead. Anne had a double take when he walked through the front door, she'd never seen him with his hair worn so short.

The ju-jitsu sessions were held twice weekly, Tuesday and Thursday evenings, from seven p.m. to eight p.m. at a local sports centre, a small side room allocated as the dojo. On Jeff's first session he wore his tennis tracksuit. The instructor or sensei, bowed on entering the dojo, put Jeff with the other beginners, whilst the better, more experienced players, fought at the other end of the dojo. After the warm-up, the sensei demonstrated, with the aid of a volunteer, a move that he wanted his students to practice. Within ten minutes Jeff was puffing for breath, he was surprised just how unfit he was. His practice partner grabbed Jeff and with a swift leg sweep, took him down. Other moves followed including: choke holds, joint locks, throwing, striking and kicking. At the end of the first session, Jeff felt like a rag doll and could hardly walk to his car. As he was leaving, the sensei advised him to buy a 'gi', which, white in colour, comprised of loose-fitting cotton trousers and top, which in turn was held together with a double wrap-round belt, also white. The sensei, a sixth Dan, who was roughly Jeff's age, a short man, but very broad, thanked him. "See you Thursday."

By the time Jeff drove the short journey home, he was as stiff as a board. He walked into the house, straight legged, crawled upstairs and soaked in a very hot bath for a good half hour. This was the start of his new life: ju-jitsu twice a week, the gym three times a week, Chinese language course, plus continuance with his language CDs. He, as did Anne, still drank too much. It took until Christmas before Anne noticed a difference in Jeff's physique. Although he was still overweight, he had firmed up due to the combination of the gym work and the ju-jitsu training. She also noticed a gritty side to Jeff, that she'd never been aware of before. She also picked up on that he'd lost his blue-eyed sparkle, his eyes now had a cold, death stare. When they occasionally went out, he wasn't his old affable self. It was as if his tolerance of people was diminishing, which she partly liked, as she previously thought Jeff was a bit of a soft touch.

The Peters didn't celebrate Christmas, well not in the true sense anyway. They made a toast to David, and Chynna, that was it. They Skyped the Lings, at dinner time, who commented on Jeff's command of their language. Ah Lam informed them that the investigation, although still open, hadn't bore any fruit. DI Chow visited them once a week, her impression of him was that he was determined never to let it go, she, as did Li Wei, even warmed to him and his sidekick, Sergeant Wong. The Skype meeting finished as usual. "Keep in touch."

Jeff's routine continued through the winter, he'd enrolled on the intermediate Chinese language course, the ju-jitsu was getting better, as was the gym training. Anne was pleased that he'd also cut down on his drinking, although he still drank too much. Jeff decided to keep his hair shortish. She was surprised that he never mentioned Hiltin tennis club; he also hadn't renewed his membership, for the first time since he initially joined. She thought, in some ways, Jeff was becoming a bit of a bore, as all he thought about was getting fit and learning Chinese. The ju-jitsu training progressed, Jeff learnt dirty tricks, like gouging, biting, hair pulling and strangulation techniques all of which, strangely, he seemed to relish. He continued to visit the gymnasium, concentrating on light muscle development and stamina building.

One Thursday evening at the end of February, the sensei stopped Jeff as he was leaving the dojo. "Jeff, there is a grading next week, I think you're ready, are you going for it?"

Jeff pulled his gi jacket tight, as he started to put on his jacket, it was dark, cold with light snow outside. "Thank you, sensei, no I'm not grading, I'm mainly training to keep fit, I don't intend to become a black belt." He looked at his instructor, gave him a slight smile. "I didn't think I'd enjoy it, but I do, I'm still amazed how somebody small can use a bigger person's force to such effect."

The sensei, who was nearly as wide as he was tall, nodded his head in agreement. "Glad you enjoy it, Jeff, you've got a good attitude, see you Tuesday." With that Jeff walked off, it was the first time for a while he felt pleased with himself. He inwardly smiled for a milli-second, outwardly he looked as miserable as sin.

Life in the Peters' household continued to roll along, through winter into spring. The Lings informed them that, after a recent visit from the police, the investigation was no further forward. The Lings told DI Chow that they kept in touch with Jeff and Anne. He sent his best. The Peters tried to keep themselves together, luckily, they had their jobs to distract them.

One mid-April, overcast Sunday morning, out of the blue, Jeff received a phone call from his old tennis partner, Rosemary Shaft. She retrieved his tennis racket after he'd thrown it at Tony Jacks, keeping it in the back of her car, expecting Jeff to return to the club the following week. After an initial chat, it was agreed that he would nip around just before Sunday dinner to collect it.

Rosemary greeted Jeff with a gentle hug as they met on her house doorstep, then invited him in for a quick coffee and catch-up. Sitting in the Shaft's front room, she informed him that Geoff and the girls wouldn't be home for hours. Rosemary told him, that initially after the incident, the 'smart Alec' and 'drama queen' had everybody's sympathy, which they, of course, milked. However, some weeks later, once the news got out about David, the sympathy switched sides, with Jacks and Carun being ostracised. Jeff took another sip of his coffee, just nodding as Rosemary updated him on Hiltin T&S Club's news. Just as she handed Jeff his tennis racket, she stroked his right-hand index finger with hers, saying how much she missed their after-match practice. She then 'accidentally' dropped her phone, bending down to pick it up, making sure Jeff could see she wasn't wearing any underwear under her skirt. Jeff immediately knelt before her, gently lifted up her skirt, put his tongue in her 'mouth', quickly kissed her on the 'lips', then got to his feet, saying, as he walked off laughing, racket in hand, "never mind Rosemary, never mind.". That was the last time they ever saw each other.

The months dragged by. Jeff had enrolled on the advanced Chinese course, and continued keeping fit at the gym and dojo. He decided to keep his hair short and had it cut with an old-fashioned short back and sides style. He was reading the daily paper one mid-week evening, when he spotted an advert for a part-time worker at the local morgue and mortuary. Jeff took the details down, and secretly emailed the coroner in charge, and received a positive reply the next day.

The following day, Jeff approached his manager at work, applying for a change in working hours, from five days to four, with his salary being adjusted, pro rata. His manager, an old friend, knew of Jeff's personal grief, and wrongly assumed he wanted a reduction in hours to spend more time with Anne. Jeff's request was granted, starting forthwith. His interview for the new job was arranged the following Friday; he took time off in lieu to attend it.

Although it was a part-time, temporary post, Jeff thoroughly prepared himself for the interview, the first one he'd had in years. He discovered that mortuary, evolved from the fourteenth century Anglo-French word 'mortuarie', which meant 'gift to a parish priest from a deceased parishioner', which evolved from the Latin word 'mortuarius', which translates as 'pertaining to the dead'. Jeff read on, intrigued. He found that the term, 'morgue' is fifteenth century French, meaning to look solemnly or defy. He then turned his research to the storage of the dead. He read on and discovered there are two types of mortuary cold chambers: positive temperature and negative temperature. Bodies kept in positive temperatures, of between two to four degrees Celsius for a few weeks, decompose at a lot slower rate than at room temperature, whilst negative temperature storage of between minus ten to minus fifty degrees are completely frozen. Jeff's research continued. Negative chambers are used for forensic examination, or if the body hadn't been identified.

Jeff then researched the role he was applying for, a basic mortuary assistant, the lowest position held. Other more important and qualified positions, were that of a mortician and diener. He looked up the term diener, he learnt, it derived from the German word 'Leichendiener' which translated as 'corpse servant'. The tasks of a mortician or diener required skills and qualifications, ranging from assisting pathologists, reconstructing cadavers, to washing and cleaning bodies and preparing them for burial.

Jeff made brief notes as he researched his chosen subject, summarising in bullet points. Anne enquired as to what he was doing. "Oh, nothing, just checking the football results." She thought that was strange, as she knew he already knew them. *Maybe he's on a dating agency* she mused.

The interview, timed for ten o'clock Friday morning, was held at the mortuary where Jeff hoped to be working. Jeff had booked the morning off, taking half-day annual leave. He dressed formally and was neatly groomed. *No point taking any chances*, he thought. Anne had left for work at eight thirty a.m. so Jeff sneaked back home to get changed, as he'd left home to drive to 'work' earlier. As he sat outside the main mortuary office waiting to go in, he took a last look at his notes.

At exactly ten a.m. the receptionist called him. "Mr Peters, you can go through now."

Jeff walked into a small office, typical in layout and furnishings. His interviewer greeted Jeff, the pair sat around a coffee table, the lounge chairs positioned at forty-five degrees to each other. Due to the type of vacancy, future employees' responsibilities and temporary position, the coroner authorised an informal style interview, with the diener as the interviewer. This type of interview technique on the surface, seemed laidback as it relaxed the candidate, who potentially dropped their guard. Jeff was aware of this.

His future boss, Mr Micary, was of mixed race, fifty-five years old, tall and slightly overweight. He wore black framed glasses, was completely bald and spoke with a Welsh accent. After the initial introduction, Micary, who was casually dressed, asked Jeff why he wanted the job. Jeff gave him a cock and bull story that he'd always wanted to be a mortician, with the recent loss of his son making it more

121

poignant. Micary then asked more profession based questions, the roles of the mortician, diener and coroner. Jeff went into detail about each role, clearly showing background knowledge and understanding. He was careful not to overdo it, he didn't want to be too clever for his menial role. The interview then directed towards his role as a mortuary assistant. Micary outlined Jeff's duties, which were mainly moving corpses and cadavers to and from the mortuary, morgue and laboratory. He would also assist Mr Micary in basic cleaning preparation, as and when required. Micary then gave Jeff an overview of his working conditions. Sometimes he would have to work long hours, possibly without a break, due to the urgency of a pathology report or forensic examination. The job could also be emotionally draining, due to either the condition of the corpse, or the age of the deceased. Micary then threw Jeff slightly, by asking him about his private life. He gave a succinct answer. Finally, Mr Micary asked Jeff if he had any questions. Jeff anticipated this standard interview question, thus avoided the cheesy type questions, so, asked about particular clothing or equipment he might need.

Micary smiled, he liked the question. "No, Mr Peters, all clothing and equipment is supplied by us, you will arrive dressed as you please, change into a white boilersuit, plastic shoes etc… shower and change back before you leave, gloves and masks are provided as required."

"Thank you, I think everything else has been covered, I'm looking forward to starting."

With that, Micary stood up, put out his hand. "Right, I'll contact you tomorrow to let you know if you've been successful, and if so, your start date."

Jeff shook his hand and thanked him. When Jeff walked out of the building, a smartly dressed, middle-aged woman, walked in, he rightly assumed, his rival. He drove back home, got changed and then went to work, for his afternoon shift.

Mr Micary's secretary, as promised, sent Jeff a text message the following day.

Congratulations Mr Peters, you start work with us next Friday. Please reply to this message for confirmation.

Jeff would be joining the coroner's team the last day of June.

In July, to 'celebrate' David's and Chynna's deaths, the Peters lit two candles and made a toast. After all, they felt they had nothing to celebrate, their son was dead, he'd been murdered and the perpetrators were still unaccounted for. Ironically, it fell on Jeff's second day at the mortuary.

On his first day, he was shown around his new work buildings by the diener's secretary, Mrs Hunter. He was also introduced to his work colleagues. Hunter, off the record, informed Jeff that what swayed his successful application, was his question at the end of the interview. His competitor, the woman, asked about holidays and salary. Mr Micary, apparently, wasn't impressed. He was taken to a changing room, where he put his outer clothes into a pound coin locker, putting on the white boilersuit and galoshes. Hunter waited outside. Hunter then led Jeff to the mortuary where he would be working, assisting the full-time mortician assistant, Miss Jones. Clare Jones was in her late thirties, small in height, of average build, plain looking with short brown hair. Jones explained Jeff's duties, initially he would be transferring corpses on a wheeled stretcher to and from the morgue, mortuary, laboratory and finally funeral parlour. He would also be liaising with the funeral assistant, who placed the dead body in the coffin, prior to burial or cremation. The undertaker, who undertook the responsibility of funeral arrangements, was based at an adjacent building, close by.

At the same time as Jeff started his new job, he set up, online, a new bank account, under a false name. Due to the lack of identity evidence, he had limited banking facilities, consequently he could only deposit money, and withdraw money from that account. There would be no borrowing or overdraft facility, with a minimal interest rate of one per cent. Due to his 'no fixed abode' persona, he insisted on collecting, in person, his cash point card and personal identification number (pin). Once the account was set up, he started transferring money to it from one of his current accounts. Anne would be none the wiser because they had separate bank accounts, as Jeff paid for the holidays and household bills, whilst Anne paid for the shopping, furniture and fittings.

CHAPTER TWENTY-SEVEN

July proved to be a relatively pleasant month, weather wise. Nice and warm, not much rain. Jeff continued with his Chinese course. Much to Anne's amazement, he was now proficient in speech and understanding. He could communicate quite comfortably with the Lings during their fortnightly brief Skype meetings. Although it was always tinged with sadness, both sets of parents rallied round and seemed to enjoy each other's company. There was always a quick update on the investigation, Chow kept in touch with a weekly, very brief visit. Still nothing conclusive, but we will keep investigating, was always his departing comment. Nimrod would never give up.

Jeff continued his keep fit campaign, visiting the gym and attending the dojo. Due to the training, he was back to his best, even getting rare praise from Anne. Unfortunately, they both still drank every night, and their relationship was hanging by a thread. Although Jeff looked physically very good, his face had aged, he, as did Anne, looked haggard and haunted. At least his activities took his mind, just for a few seconds, off thinking about David.

Work wise, Jeff adapted nicely to his four-day week at the engineering factory. The reduction in his salary wasn't that noticeable, as his wage for the part-time post, although half his daily factory rate, compensated it. With the tax reduction, it worked out only a few pounds less a week.

Jeff was surprised how quickly he adjusted to his new job. Initially quite squeamish, he found it quite relaxing and to a point enjoyable — well sort of. He went to the mortuary in the same clothes as he wore to the factory, also leaving at the same time, to keep up the veil of secrecy. He kept his sports bag in the car, for a fresh change of undergarments after his shower, on finishing his shift. As his competence became apparent, he was trusted to help clean and prepare corpses ready for examination or autopsy. This task involved carefully washing the body with a cloth dipped in water, and a small amount of soap. The cleaning started from the head down, closing the eyes and mouth before rigor mortis, from two to seven hours after death, sets in. Jeff noticed that Clare often talked to the corpse, whilst cleaning and preparing the body for viewing from grieving relatives. Hair would be combed, teeth cleaned, men shaved, the body then wrapped in a sheet or dressed, depending on viewing or the funeral arrangements. Jeff discovered the wearing of gloves, masks and an over-gown was essential.

He also helped Clare with the embalming procedure, if the body was being kept in the mortuary for more than a few days. She injected embalming fluid, which consisted of preservatives, disinfectants, sanitising chemicals into the arterial system of the body. The chemicals used included formaldehyde, glutaraldehyde and methanol, which slowed down the decomposition rate and improved the appearance of the corpse. Clare informed Jeff that the mixture would be stronger if the body was with them for longer periods.

Jeff became friendly with the lads working at the funeral parlour, as he often wheeled bodies from the mortuary to the parlour, prior to a funeral or cremation. One old boy who had worked in the business since he was a lad, often quipped, "Which one on the Fs are you in today Jeff?" Jeff gathered what he meant: the morgue meant 'freezer', the mortuary meant 'fridge' and the other 'F' referred to fire, the crematorium. He occasionally had to move bodies from the morgue, which were stored at negative temperatures to the laboratory, for pathology, or medical students to study anatomy.

These corpses were known as cadavers, he wasn't very keen on doing this, and, when asked if he'd like to help in the lab said, "No thanks".

In the morgue, the bodies were placed in three rows of what, to Jeff, looked like large vertical freezers. The corpse was wrapped in a white sheet or shroud, and put on a horizontal sliding metal tray for easy accessibility, as the wheeled stretcher or gurney could be adjusted for height to accommodate the particular row required. Jeff noted some of the corpses remained in the morgue for months, he rightly assumed that's where David had been most of the time.

The majority of Jeff's time was spent in the mortuary, where bodies were kept at a positive temperature of three degrees centigrade. Corpses were placed in two rows of, what Jeff thought, looked like large fridges, on sliding metal trays, the same as in the freezer. The mortuary was where most of the work was carried out as bodies were transferred from the morgue to the mortuary then to the funeral parlour. As the weeks progressed, he was entrusted to prepared bodies for funerals. He quickly picked up certain codes the undertaker's staff used, as to whether the body was going to be cremated or buried, and whether or not it needed preparation for viewing by grieving friends and relatives. On a couple of occasions, relatives were allowed, with special permission, to clean and dress their loved ones, in preparation for their imminent departure to the afterlife. What impressed, and slightly surprised Jeff, was the dignity the staff at the morgue, mortuary and funeral parlour had for their customers. There were no shortcuts, everything was carried out with the utmost respect.

On one occasion, whilst helping Clare embalm a body, she informed Jeff that some corpses were taken straight to the small cremation building, at the rear of the funeral parlour. "This furnace is called a cremation chamber or retort, which reaches temperatures of two thousand degrees Fahrenheit." Jeff tried to calculate what that was in centigrade, he 'guessed' at one thousand and ninety-four degrees C. "There is no need for a funeral director to get involved, as a funeral is not being held, the corpse doesn't have any friends or relatives of concern. The cremation takes between one and a half hours to two hours, depending on the size of the person being cremated."

Jeff thought, *that's some fire.*

Clare cleared her throat. "Once the cremated remains have cooled, a large magnet is wiped over them to pick up any metal left behind, this could be coffin hinges or metal body pins. The remains, which still have small bones in them, usually from the shin or hip," she looked at Jeff who obviously gave off a surprised look, "are ground to dust by a cremulator. Ironically younger bones are stronger and reduce less easily." Jeff frowned, not sure whether he wanted to hear any more, however, Clare was on a roll. "All the incinerated remains, which includes the body, clothes, casket or coffin etc... are commingled to form the cremains, what the general public refer to as the ashes, gritty in texture and blackish-brown in colour, which are put in a plastic bag, then usually into an urn."

Jeff had never thought too much about cremation before Clare's overview, he made an effort to sound interested. "How much do…"

Clare was reading his mind. "Anything between three to nine pounds, depends on the size of the person."

Big person, big urn, thought Jeff.

They'd finished injecting the embalming fluid. Clare had made an incision in the femoral artery in the groin area, Jeff knew this avoided potential visitors seeing the incision. "Right Jeff, the diener is coming in to drain the blood, temporarily remove the organs, then remove the contents of intestines, bowel and bladder, would you like to assist him?" Clare knew the answer.

"No thanks Clare, I'll leave you and Mr Micary to it." Jeff then busied himself by tidying up, moving bodies between the morgue, mortuary and parlour. Once the body came back from the lab, Jeff helped Clare prepare it for visitation. He noticed, due to the injected chemicals, that the body had a bit more colour and was more lifelike. Jeff cleaned and trimmed the fingernails. He had wrongly assumed that the nails and hair continued to grow for a short time after death. Clare, a few weeks previously, had informed him that the skin retracts, making the nails appear longer.

"It's a bit like teeth, Jeff, as a horse got older their gums recede, making the teeth look longer, hence the phrase 'long in the tooth'."

Jeff instinctively wiped his teeth and gums with his tongue. *I'm still youngish*, he thought.

"Here's another thing, Jeff." Clare nudged him to get his full attention, she didn't have to as she already had it. "Did you know that most people who die of natural causes, pass after their birthday or another special occasion, like Christmas or a grandchild being born. It's as if they struggled on, you know, like a marathon, just exerting enough energy to finish, then collapsing." Jeff looked at Clare, not sure whether to believe her, then grabbed a handful of cotton wool.

They continued with the preparation, Jeff put cotton up the body's nose, to stop any fluid leakage. Other areas of the body that could leak, had incontinence pads placed around them. Clare positioned plastic half-moon caps under the eyelids, so that they would keep their shape. The eyes were then closed. Micary had already put cotton down the throat to avoid seepage, and around the mouth, to pad it out. He had also stitched it closed from the inside. Jeff added a touch of make-up to take away the waxy look. The hair which Jeff had previously washed and dried, was then combed neatly. Finally, the pair dressed the body in clothes that the family left at the funeral parlour. Jeff then wheeled the body to the parlour ready for viewing, as two of the family would be visiting the chapel of rest later in the day. The funeral director collared Jeff as he started to walk back to the mortuary, asking him if he could give him a hand as he was short on manpower. One of the lads was, ironically, at a funeral. Jeff obliged, pushing the wheeled stretcher into the chapel of rest. Together they placed the body in a casket, then put the casket on a decorative, wooden framed platform, called a catafalque. Flowers adorned the tables positioned at the corners of this small, serene room. Jeff felt faint, he had to leave quickly.

As time progressed, Jeff became the utility man, he would work in any department, helping out as required. He was also popular when it came to moving bodies as he was quite strong, due to the keep-fit campaign. He knew every inch of the premises and, more importantly, where all the security cameras were, both internally and externally. Every Friday morning, on arrival, he would purposely park his car in different positions, so a parking pattern wasn't apparent. He eventually began parking closer to the area close to both the mortuary and the funeral parlour, always reversing into the parking slot or bay. He monitored every corpse coming and going, noting, rather conveniently for him, that most of the deceased males were his height and build, after all he was average in both. Once he was established as a member of the team, he was entrusted to prepare, on his own, a body ready for cremation, sometimes, obligingly, working into the evening. Jeff was so popular due to his work ethic, that the diener considered making his part-time, temporary post a permanent one, as the woman he'd filled in for was coming back from her pregnancy leave.

It was the anniversary of David's birthday, in October, that Jeff decided to act.

CHAPTER TWENTY-EIGHT

The Peters held a vigil on the Thursday evening of, what would have been, David's twenty-fourth birthday. A sombre evening, looking at past photographs followed by a tidy up of his bedroom, which had remained as he'd left it. Due to the commemorate, Jeff didn't attend the dojo that evening, a rare miss for him. They received a text message from the Lings, the English wasn't perfect, but the words and thoughts were.

Jeff drove to the mortuary in a more depressed mood than usual, and had to, ironically, raise his spirits considerably to appear normal. *It was time*, he thought. His car boot was filled with all the requirements needed for this particular part of his journey. Bones from the butcher for his fictitious dog, bags of sawdust, thick oak logs, drill, screwdriver and wood glue. He parked his car, reversing into the slot by the doors closest to the mortuary and parlour. The rear half of the car was out of camera range. If the opportunity arose he would strike in the evening.

It turned out to be a busy day for Jeff, moving bodies to and from the morgue, for pathologist examination and student experimentation. He helped Miss Jones prepare two average sized males for cremation, one was for viewing, the other wrapped in a shroud. He noticed it didn't have any pockets, the body was going to be cremated unusually, first thing Saturday morning. The funeral parlour got quite busy in the afternoon, Jeff volunteered to help out into the evening, as a gesture of good will, nothing unusual about that. When the funeral director left to go home, he instructed Jeff to put the body for cremation in a basic wooden coffin, as he informed him, surprisingly, it burned quicker than the cardboard ones, due to the wood retaining a slow even heat. The coffin would be then left, ready for immediate incineration in the morning. All the staff drifted off home, leaving just Jeff and the diener, who was working in his office at the far end of the building. He was always last to leave after locking up. Jeff took the identification tag off the man's foot, 'Mark Ian Kurt Ellis'. Jeff called him Mike.

Mr Micary doing his rounds, popped down to see Jeff, who was placing the pocketless shroud-wrapped body into the coffin. "How much longer will you be Jeff, as I want to get off soon?"

"Oh, not long Mr Micary, half hour tops."

Micary replied, "I'll give you a hand if you want?"

Jeff thought quickly, this could ruin his chance. "No it's okay Mr Micary, I enjoy doing this on my own, it brings back memories." He played his emotional card.

With that Micary walked off, rubbing his bald head. "Okay, don't take forever, I've got an engagement tonight, and I can't be late." Jeff then weighed the coffin on the scales placed in the corner of the mortuary, tying Mike's ID tag to the coffin handles.

Jeff placed the coffin on a wheeled stretcher, and manoeuvred it to the open doorway. He thought, *good, it was now dusk*, then quickly pushed the trolley to the back of his car, opened the boot, and took the body out of the coffin, placing it into his large car boot. He put the bag of sawdust, drill, oak, screwdriver, glue and bones into the coffin, closed the boot, and quickly pushed the stretcher to the parlour.

Once safely inside he took out the glue, drill and screwdriver out of the coffin, placing the oak logs where the arms and legs would be lying, put the bones in the hip area, then emptied most of the sawdust around the logs and bones, for extra weight and to stop them moving. He then weighed the coffin, on the scales, placed just inside the funeral parlour door. It was still too light, so he added more sawdust, weighed it again, this time too heavy, so he scooped some out, spilling it on the floor, the weight was now near enough. He wiped wood glue all around the edge of the coffin lid, and placed it on the coffin. The lid was secured with ten screws, four each side and one either end. After tightening the screws, he drilled the heads out, so that they could not be removed. If the undertakers wanted to remove the lid, they'd have to smash or cut it off. He wiped around the lid edge, removing any residue glue that squeezed out. All done, he pushed the stretcher into position, moved the coffin onto a table, ready for dispatch.

He heard Micary's footsteps walking into the parlour, so he quickly hid his tools and equipment behind a pedal bin, but noticed sawdust on the floor. Just as Micary walked through the door, he saw Jeff calmly sweeping up. "I thought I'd tidy up for the lads, save them a job tomorrow morning."

"I wish everybody had your work ethic Jeff, I, for one, will be sad to see you go: are you sure you don't won't to stay on?"

Jeff continued sweeping. "Yes Mr Micary, I've got to move on, thank you anyway." He manoeuvred himself in front of the bin, surreptitiously placing his equipment in it. "I'll empty the bin before I go, it's rather full."

Before Micary could argue, Jeff picked up the bin, walked to the large waste container and tipped the contents into it, making sure they were scattered and not particularly visible.

"Jeff, I've got to lock up, I'm afraid you won't have time for a shower, sorry about that."

"Don't worry Mr Micary, I'll have one when I get home, I'll quickly change, get my bag and go out the front door, as you start locking up."

Jeff rushed off. Micary thought, *what a great guy, always goes the extra mile*, as he commenced his locking up, lights out routine.

"Hold your nerve Jeff, hold your nerve," he said to himself, as he walked quickly to his car. He checked around the car boot area, in case anything incriminating was left on the floor or hanging out of the boot. It was now dark, so he used the torch on his phone. "All clear," he muttered. When he started to drive off, Micary came rushing out of the building towards him. "Oh shit, what does he want?" he said to himself.

Micary waved at Jeff. "Thanks once again, Jeff, I'll see you next Friday, for your last day, have a nice weekend."

Jeff just smiled, partly in relief, and calmly drove off, if you can drive calmly with a corpse in the boot of your car. He drove steadily home, the last thing he wanted was to be stopped by the police for a trivial traffic violation. Jeff made a lame excuse for arriving home late. Anne noticed a strange smell on him as he brushed past her. "Jeff, you smell like a pickled onion."

Jeff laughed, falsely. "Ha, ha, one of the lads gave me a Russian cough sweet, it's got a weird mixture, smells like formaldehyde to me."

Anne just looked at him confused. *Is Jeff going off his rocker*, she thought, what a load of old claptrap.

"Let's have a drink, I've had a hard day," he said as he poured them both the first of a few gin and tonics.

CHAPTER TWENTY-NINE

Jeff, dressed in scruffs, spent most of Saturday tinkering with his car, particularly in the area around the petrol tank. It was a cold, damp day. "Needs must, needs must," he kept saying to himself. He very briefly peeped into the boot, muttered, "Yes Mike's still there." Anne asked him what he was doing, as he hadn't fiddled with his car in years.

"There's a wire loose," he lied "I think it's affecting the rear light."

More claptrap, Anne mused.

What Jeff was in fact doing, was loosening various wires close to the petrol tank and then starting the engine to see which loose connection caused a spark. After several attempts, he found one, then wrapped blue electrical tape around it, not for repair, as it might appear, but for identification purposes.

After changing back to his normal gear, following their evening meal, Jeff told Anne he was going to the gym to warm-up, as he'd frozen his nuts off repairing the car. He went upstairs, filling his largest sports bag with a couple of sets of clothing, as well as his usual gym sundries. Anne was watching television as Jeff walked into the living room. "I'll be off then Anne."

She barely looked up. "See you later Jeff."

Jeff walked over to where Anne was sitting, leant down and hugged her. "You know I love you Anne."

"Of course you do, now get off to the gym." Anne looked at Jeff, there was something odd about him, she just couldn't put her finger on it.

Jeff rubbed Anne's shoulder, gave it a gentle squeeze, had a good, long look around the room, and mumbled, "Goodbye love". He picked up his sports bag then walked out of the house, rubbing the red cotton thread that Li Wei gave him at Chynna's funeral. He looked up to the clear, dark sky, the evening was cold but dry.

Jeff drove out of town, eventually stopping at a petrol station, where he filled his car, bought and filled two plastic fuel cans with petrol. He drove for another eight minutes finding the location he was looking for, a waste area, renown for stolen car burnouts, parking his car in a location not easily seen from the road. Fortunately, there wasn't a soul about, he turned the engine off and waited for a few minutes, rationalising his proposed next actions. He still had the opportunity to stop this lunatic idea. *To hell with it*, he thought, *in for a penny, in for a pound*. With that, Jeff got out of his car, walked to the boot and gently lifted Mike out. He laid him by the side of his front driver's door. He then slid under the rear of the car. Using his phone's torch, he quickly located the blue taped wire and disconnected the electrical fitting. He carefully unwrapped the shroud from Mike, stripped his tracksuit off and slid it onto Mike's decomposing body, which whiffed a bit. He removed his sports bag from the passenger seat and dressed in one of his casual outfits, placing the bag to one side. Jeff thought he heard a noise, he froze and looked about. Much to his relief, he saw a fox sniffing about, he wondered if Mike's whiff had attracted it. He placed Mike in the driver's seat, threw the shroud onto the passenger seat, took the petrol cans and a spanner out of the opened boot. Jeff tapped Mike's front teeth with the spanner, smashing them. "Sorry 'Mike'," he said a few times. He wasn't sure if the teeth would remain, so he wanted to impair dental record checks for identification purposes. Jeff forced Mike's rigor mortised mouth wide open, which took some effort, removed the cotton bung, then shoved the funnel of a petrol can in it, proceeding to pour petrol into Mike's throat, filling him with petrol. Jeff then soaked Mike, pouring petrol from the other can over him, the shroud, and the driver's area. He placed the two empty cans by the driver's control pedals. Jeff took out his wallet, removed most of the notes, his plastic bank card that he'd recently set up, and placed it and his mobile phone in the glove compartment, closing it. Jeff scoured the area, all was quiet, he started the engine, closed the driver's door, and picked up his sports bag placing it ten metres away. Jeff walked around the passenger side of the car, opening the door. He lit a match, throwing it at Mike, closed the door and ran. He heard the whoosh then felt the heat as he got to his bag, picking it up whilst still running. Once he'd cleared the combustible area, Jeff stopped running, turned his head to see a yellow ball of flames. He continued to run out of the area making it on to the main road. It was then that he heard an almighty explosion, the car, full of fuel, was a petrol bomb.

It took Jeff two hours to walk to the nearest bus stop, waiting a further twenty minutes for one to arrive, which terminated in the town centre. Keeping in the shadows, wearing a woollen hat and jacket turned up at the collar, he walked to the railway station. Next stop, London.

CHAPTER THIRTY

Jeff hid behind the settee, he could hear the footsteps getting closer. "Jeff, I'm coming for you." He could hardly breathe, he closed his eyes, the end would be soon. "Look at me Jeff, look at me!" The voice was only centimetres away from him, he opened his left eye, he screamed. It was Mike, skin singed, hair smouldering, wearing Jeff's tracksuit.

"I'm sorry Mike, Mike forgive me, Mike." Jeff started to crawl away from the settee, not daring to look behind. He smelt Mike's burning flesh. He made a dash for the stairs, his legs felt like lead. Mike was closing in behind him.

"Why me Jeff, why me, what have I done to you?" Smoke came out of his mouth as he spoke. He reached out to Jeff.

Jeff tried to scramble up the stairs, it was as-if his slippers were glued to the tread carpet, "I had to do something Mike, you fitted the bill," Jeff pleaded.

"Stop calling me Mike, my name's Mark." Smoke blew in Jeff's direction, suddenly Mike's right eye popped out.

"It was a nickname, an acronym," Jeff was shaking, he couldn't move.

Mike closed in, cooked flesh dripping on the stair carpet, smoke coming out of his mouth and right eye socket. He reached out with his left hand and grabbed Jeff's right shoulder. This was the end. "No Mike, no Mi…"

Jeff felt a hand shaking his right shoulder, he suddenly woke up, with a start.

"Who the hell's Mike?" It was the train attendant, checking that passengers had bought a ticket and paid the correct fare.

Jeff was still in a daze. "Eh… What? Where am I?"

"Look mister, you've had a nightmare, you kept calling out Mike, now where's your ticket?"

136

Jeff was on the ten past twelve, midnight, train to London. He sat in an unoccupied compartment, which was relatively easy, as there were only a few passengers on board. He'd put his sports bag on the baggage rack above his seat, within minutes he was fast asleep, having nightmares. He gathered himself, fished out his ticket bought at Chelsham railway station and handed it to the conductor, who punched it and gave it him back.

"Enjoy the rest of your journey," the conductor muttered as he walked out, closing the door behind him.

Jeff was still recovering from his nightmare. It was so realistic, it gave him the creeps. He decided to try and keep awake for the remainder of the journey; he didn't fancy another visit from Mike.

The train pulled into King's Cross railway station at two o'clock Sunday morning. The first thing he had to do was get accommodation and then buy a throwaway mobile phone, as his exploits were relatively unplanned. He'd done a bit of basic research on bed and breakfast establishments in central London, and decided on staying in the Camden Town area. He walked the two miles from King's Cross to central Camden Town, then looked for somewhere open and with a vacancy. After walking about for forty minutes, he spotted a B&B in Buck Street, that suited his situation. The receptionist commented on the unearthly hour of Jeff's request, which Jeff thought was ironic, as there were still a lot of bars, clubs and shops open, after all London, like New York, never sleeps. Mrs misery guts gave him his key, took a swipe of his card, then pointed to the stairs. "First floor, turn left at the top of the stairs, down the corridor, and be quiet!"

Jeff thanked her and started walking off.

"Breakfast is eight thirty to ten a.m. Sunday morning, any later and you miss it."

Jeff opened the door to room number nine, taking his woollen hat off as he walked through the door. He quietly put his bag in the corner of his single bed accommodation, stripped and tiptoed into the shower, trying to be as quiet as possible. After a quick shower, he got into bed, setting the alarm on the bedside radio to eight forty-five a.m.

Jeff had a restless night's sleep, he found the bed uncomfortable and missed Anne's company, even if it was just her back. He wondered what was going on back home as it would now be obvious to her that something was amiss. He'd just started to doze off, when the alarm went off, making Jeff jump. He felt groggy and was tempted to go back to sleep. "Needs must," he muttered to himself, forcing himself out of bed. Jeff rubbed his eyes, and opened the curtains to let in some natural day light.

He could now see the full extent of his room, in short, a pokey little dump. Jeff guessed it was about two and a half metres wide by three and a half metres long, with an en suite shower, basin and toilet. The carpet was typical of this type of establishment, multicoloured to conceal all sorts of stains. The wallpaper, woodchip, was covered with magnolia matt emulsion paint, the ceiling, decorated with woodchip paper, painted matt white. A small wardrobe stood against the opposite wall from his bed, which was of the large, single variety. Jeff scratched his head, yawned a couple of times then ambled to his feet.

He removed his under garments and stumbled into the shower, he needed to freshen up quickly. Once showered, he towel dried his hair, so it was just damp, wrapping the towel around his waist. He walked to his sports bag, which wasn't very far away, taking out a small tube of black hair dye, that he'd bought at the small chemists at King's Cross station. He squeezed just enough dye out to temporarily darken his hair, then rubbed the dye onto his head, making sure it was completely and uniformly covered. As his hair was relatively short, this didn't take long. Jeff waited fifteen minutes then rinsed his head under the shower. He then took the hair drier out of the second drawer of the drawer cabinet by his lumpy bed, plugged it in and quickly dried his hair. Jeff looked in the bathroom mirror, combing his new hair in a different style to his normal parting, thinking, *not bad for first attempt*, although it looked more dark brown than black. He'd decided to change his hair colour and style as a disguise, just in case the police put a missing persons report on the news, showing a photograph of him. Jeff pulled up a fresh pair of jeans, followed by a T-shirt, socks and shoes, it was now nine thirty a.m. Time for breakfast.

Jeff quietly walked five paces down the corridor, turned right on the landing, descended down a flight of stairs to the ground floor. The dining room was to his left, facing to the front of this three-storey building. With three paces, he opened the single latched predominantly glass door and walked in. He assumed rightly, he was one of the last to eat. Jeff made his way to a single corner table, sitting with his back to the rest of the room. A few minutes passed. As Jeff was studying the menu, the waitress, a young, black, tall, attractive woman, asked him what he wanted. Jeff ordered a full English, toast and tea.

The dining room was quite large with a high ceiling. The floor was finished with a mid-grey carpet, the walls papered with a yellow-grey diamond pattern on the main feature wall, plain light grey paper on the other walls, and the ceiling consisted of smooth plaster, finished with matt white paint. Three mid-sized windows gave a road-side view. Whilst Jeff sat waiting for his breakfast, he put his hands under his chin, keeping his elbows on the table, deep in thought, seemingly oblivious to the other guests having their breakfasts. An elderly German couple sat two tables away from Jeff, they looked like they were almost finished, an Asian man occupied the end, window table, opposite Jeff's; he was halfway through his breakfast. Fifteen minutes later, the waitress came in with Jeff's breakfast and pot of tea, he thanked her and got tucked in. She came back a few minutes later, enquiring if everything was okay. It was as Jeff had almost polished the full English off. The room was now empty, Jeff seemed to relax slightly, he wondered if his apparent demise might be in the papers, with a photograph, hence his quick hair colour and style change. Jeff drank his second cup of tea, wiped his mouth with a napkin and walked back to his room. He freshened up, went to the loo, grabbed his jacket, locked his door and was off for the day.

CHAPTER THIRTY-ONE

Jeff walked down Buck St onto the main road in Camden, the A502. He turned left at that junction heading south. Within ten minutes he found a mobile phone shop, buying a cheap burner phone and a second-hand iPad. The phone was a pay as you go basic mobile, just to make and receive calls, text messages and camera/video, no identification was required for purchase. Jeff bought the iPad for research and enquiry purposes. Jeff exited the shop and headed north into Camden Town centre, as he needed more clothes. He went into a clothes store and bought a few more garments of full outfits, from underwear, shirts, black and blue trousers, to shoes. With two shopping bags full of clothing, Jeff decided to go back to the B&B and drop them off.

Just as he walked past reception, he heard, "Mr Smith, could you leave your key?"

Jeff carried on walking, he was preoccupied and temporarily forgot his pseudonym, Thomas Smith.

"Mr Thomas Smith," the receptionist shouted.

Jeff suddenly stopped, realising she was talking to him. "Oh sorry, I was miles away, I'll leave my key with you when I go back out, I'll only be a few minutes."

He dropped the shopping in his room, put the iPad on charge, keeping the phone in his jacket pocket. Jeff didn't bring any extra clothing with him when he left home as it would've aroused suspicion and an investigation; at a reasonable glance his wardrobe at home would have appeared normal. "That'll do for now, I'll tidy up when I get back," he muttered to himself.

Jeff, or Thomas Smith, handed his key into reception, followed by heading to Camden Town tube station. Paying by swiping his new bank card, he boarded the Northern line southbound into central London. Ten minutes later he walked out of Leicester Square station and continued on foot to Soho. Jeff knew roughly where he was going, finding the consultancy he'd seen on the Internet Friday evening. The receptionist, a well-groomed Asian male in his early thirties, invited him to sit and wait for the consultant, as he was advising a potential patient. It was warm in the shop, so Jeff removed his jacket and browsed a magazine whilst waiting.

Twenty minutes later, a Chinese male in his mid-fifties approached Jeff. "Mr Smith, you can come through now." Mr Cheng, wearing a white medical coat, ushered Jeff into a consultancy room. Cheng was small and slim with receding black hair in a combed-back style, he wore thick black framed glasses almost concealing hazel coloured eyes. Jeff thought that Cheng hand very small effeminate hands. They sat in typical office chairs, opposite each other. Jeff explained that he wanted to look more oriental, as his new girlfriend was Chinese. Cheng did not believe him, but that didn't matter. Cheng went on to describe the basic procedure, it involved rhinoplasty and blepharoplasty. The rhinoplasty would make Jeff's nose smaller and flatter with a rounded tip, as his was long, straight and pointed: typical Caucasian in appearance. His eyelids would have the creases removed to give a single eyelid, and also close up the inner corner, giving a 'slant eyed' look. Cheng commented on the irony, as thousands of young Chinese people are having the reverse procedure, making themselves look more European, with wider eyes and bigger pointed noses. They talked at length about the procedure, intertwined by Cheng showing Jeff photographs of previous clients, most of them were oriental with a European look. Cheng proceeded to take photographs of Jeff from the front and side, loaded them into a computer, pressed several buttons to demonstrate the surgery, then sat back. "This is what you'll look like after the surgery."

Jeff stared at the image and didn't like what he saw. His good looks, or what was left of them since David's demise, had certainly gone. He also looked older. Cheng took his glasses off and cleaned the lenses, he could tell by Jeff's expression, he didn't like what he saw. "That's it I'm afraid, Mr 'er' Smith, you'll also have to get brown contact lenses, and," he looked again at Jeff's head, and smirked, "keep dyeing your hair, I suggest black." Cheng, whose breath smelt of garlic, slid his chair away from Jeff, putting his small hands in his jacket pockets. Jeff sat looking at the image, it reminded him of an ugly version of DI Chow. *Perish the thought.*

Cheng coughed, then mumbled, "You will also have to apply a skin cream, to get the proper look."

Jeff scratched his head, it didn't itch, but he felt like he needed to do something. Eventually he turned to face Cheng. "How much and when?" Cheng looked surprised, he told Jeff that it was a simple, quick procedure, he would do it, as a favour, for three thousand pounds, if he agreed to have it done straightaway, paying before he left the shop. Cheng said that he had a vacant slot Wednesday morning, performing the operation under local anaesthetic. He also explained, that Jeff would have to lie down in a resting room to recover, and be issued with painkillers. The bandaging around the nose, could be removed after a couple of days. Bruising will last about a week, but it can be carefully covered with coloured face make-up. Cheng made it sound very matter-of-fact.

"The nose is too flat, it'll have to be a better shape." Jeff turned to face Cheng.

Cheng shrugged his shoulders. "You can have whatever shape you want, but if you want the authentic look…"

"Yeah, but let's not go to that extreme." Jeff looked back at the screen. "Show me what a slightly different shape will look like."

Cheng combed his hair back with his right hand, slid his chair back to the desk, punched in a few codes, and the nose shape changed slightly. "There, that's slightly better." He half looked at Jeff. "Let's add brown contact lenses." Cheng nodded at Jeff, Jeff nodded back. Cheng blackened Jeff's hair and eyebrows, and light-yellowed his face. After three minutes of fiddling, he said, "That's what you'll look like, due to your height, build and skull shape, you will be taken for mainly Chinese and a bit of Anglo mixed race. You will also have to use mascara on your eyebrows and lashes to complete the look." Cheng took his glasses off, whilst he gave Jeff a printout of the image.

Jeff stared at the screen, and the printout, the transformation was startling, he didn't recognise himself. His head started to pound, Jeff got out of his chair, he looked at the floor, then shook his head a few times. He could still reverse the situation, he could turn up, out of the blue, claim amnesia, maybe kidnap, and go back to being, good old Jeff, and stop this insanity. He started to walk towards the door. There, in a moment of madness, he said, "Wednesday morning it is."

Jeff shook hands with Cheng, his normal man's size hand swallowed Cheng's, proceeding to walk out of his consultancy room. The receptionist was waiting for him. He swiped Jeff's card, well Thomas Smith's. "See you Wednesday morning, ten a.m." He smiled and gave Jeff his card back. "Bye."

Jeff walked out of the consultancy, his mind was spinning, he felt nauseous. He stood and looked at the images adorning the glass front windows of Cheng's consultancy. *'We specialise in Chinese-Anglo plastic surgery, you can change your look from this to this!'* He admitted to himself, that the images, in his opinion, had improved in looks, he wondered what other Chinese people thought, was this a reflection of that race. He thought of Chynna, she was beautiful, and her parents, Ah Lam and Li Wei, were good looking. He knew a lot of white people that weren't attractive, by any stretch of the imagination, perhaps they should all go under the knife. He shrugged, good, bad and ugly in all races, then started humming the theme tune for the spaghetti western of that film title. Jeff stood dithering, he started to get cold, he zipped his jacket up, turning the collar up around his neck. The weather, although dry, was cold, with a northerly breeze. Jeff needed to get moving, the last thing he wanted was a dose of flu.

Jeff walked back to Leicester Square tube station, took the northbound Northern line to Camden Town, back to Buck Street. When he grabbed his room key, he asked the receptionist for the B&B Wi-Fi code, and she informed him it was in his room, at the bottom of the 'dos and don'ts' sheet.

He closed his room door and locked it. On the way back from Camden Town tube station, he had nipped into a chemist and bought a packet of headache tablets. He pinched two out, grabbed a glass from the bathroom, and swallowed the tablets with the aid of a couple of mouthfuls of water. Jeff took his jacket off, hanging it in the wardrobe, spending the next ten minutes tidying his room, and putting his new clothes in the wardrobe and drawers. He took the iPad from the top of the bedside cabinet, grabbed the dos & don'ts sheet, flicked off his shoes and sat up on the bed, leaning against the headboard. The iPad was fully charged, so he typed in the Wi-fi password, it was typical, a combination of numbers and letters, some capitalised. Luckily the Wi-fi signal was strong in Jeff's room, he went onto the Internet, searching the dark web.

It didn't take him long to find what he was searching for, and was surprised at how much selection he had, or seemed to have, after all he was dealing with unscrupulous people. He found a couple of suitable sites and began messaging — the other side. Messages went backwards and forwards, the content based around how long, cost and authenticity, with examples readily to hand. Finally, he agreed to meet The Scribe, Monday evening, in a central London pub, The Slaughtered Wolf, at nine o'clock. Details were exchanged as to what Jeff would be wearing, his blue zip-up jacket, he would have to wear a white cap and sit in the bar, close to the door leading to the toilets. The Scribe would find him, both then signed off, Jeff as James Bond's moniker — Lone Wolf.

Jeff felt exhausted and generally unwell, he closed the iPad and drifted off, into a deep sleep. A couple of hours later he woke with a jolt, he'd another visit from Mike, this time he was in Jeff's car boot, banging on the boot door, demanding to be let out and put back in his coffin, strangely wearing Jeff's tracksuit. Once he woke, Jeff was gasping for breath and felt sick, so he staggered to the bathroom and freshened up. It was now early evening, he decided to go to a local pub and have a pub meal, supplemented with a much-needed drink. He hadn't had one for a day, the first time he'd missed a drink since Chow's phone call.

Jeff walked the short distance to a traditional pub, The World's End, on High Street, in seven minutes. He hadn't bothered changing his clothes, just freshened up, with added deodorant and a splash of cologne. He managed to get to the pub just before it started raining, which was lucky, as he hadn't an umbrella. He ordered a drink at the bar, quickly studied the menu, added scampi and chips and paid in cash, taking his wooden table number spoon with him. Jeff made his way to an empty table in a quiet area of the establishment. As he sipped his pint, he took out a vintage motorcycle magazine he'd bought from a newsagents in Soho, and browsed through it, thus avoiding conversation, wanted or unwanted. The pub was half full of customers and had a lively atmosphere and music, which Jeff liked, blasting out from many speakers. The hostelry was a nice distraction for Jeff, it took his muddled mind off matters both past and present; he nearly felt normal. He removed his jacket, placing it on the back of an adjacent chair, one of four surrounding his table, just before his meal arrived, which was served twenty minutes after being ordered, by a fat, grumpy, toothless, waitress, who didn't hang around for questions. Jeff enjoyed the meal, drank another pint of ale and headed back to Buck Street, getting wet, as it was still raining.

He hung his wet clothes on an old-fashioned radiator to dry, jumped in the shower to warm up, standing under it for twenty-five minutes, *perhaps it would wash his troubles away*, he thought. Jeff, now in bed, switched his iPad on, found his favourite Chinese language site and practiced conversation, something he still enjoyed, for just under one hour. Feeling tired, he switched the room light off, put the iPad down, and tried to get some kip. He wondered what was going through Anne's mind.

CHAPTER THIRTY-TWO

Anne looked at her watch, it was ten thirty p.m. Saturday, she wondered where Jeff was, as he was normally home from the gym by this time. *Perhaps he's gone for a drink with someone from the gym*, she thought. She turned back to watching the news on television, took another sip of wine from her glass, thinking she'd finish that and go to bed. *He should be home by then, after all, the football will be on TV*. She eventually polished off the bottle of wine, it was now eleven fifteen p.m. She yawned, didn't bother to put her hand over her gaping mouth. *Where the 'bloody hell' is he?* she wondered. She got out of her chair, checked her phone for messages or missed calls — nothing. Anne placed her wine glass on the kitchen worktop, put the empty bottle in the recycle bin and went upstairs, quick teeth clean, then bed. Anne, partly due to the wine consumption, went into a deep sleep and didn't stir till eight a.m. Sunday. She felt for Jeff with her right hand, nothing there and, for the first time, she started to worry.

Anne sat up in bed, wiped the sleep out of her eyes, re-checked her phone, still nothing. She rang Jeff's number, it was dead, her worry, went up a notch. She went downstairs to see if he'd got in late and fell asleep on the settee, nobody there. Anne made herself a cup of tea, and went back upstairs to bed, to drink it, mulling over what, if anything, to do. Once fully awake, she decided to ring the gym and see what time Jeff left there.

It took five chirps for the gym reception to answer Anne's call. "No, we haven't seen Jeff for a few days, bye."

So, he didn't go to the gym, he fiddled with his car, he gave me a hug before he left, he's up to something, she mused. Anne finished her cuppa and weighed up her options. *Has he gone off with another woman* — possibly, she couldn't think of any other possibilities. Anne checked the wardrobe, all of Jeff's clothes were there, if he went off with another tart, he left empty handed. Anne got dressed, washed her face and cleaned her teeth, before going downstairs for breakfast. She kept her powder dry — for now.

The fire engine arrived at the scene in the early hours of Sunday morning, a passing motorist having reported seeing a burning car. "It was like an inferno." The fire crew quickly subdued the fire, the car was completely burnt out, with only minimal parts remaining. The driver was burnt to cinders, with just part of their charred skeleton remaining. It was difficult to identify what sex the said driver was, at that stage. The fire crew alerted the police as to the car registration number, as the rear numberplate was still readable. Once the burnout was cool enough, they checked the inside of the car, nothing of significance was found.

The fire service notified the police, who then arranged for a forensic team to inspect the site as the remains of a body was in the car, to ascertain whether or not foul play had occurred. The police checked their vehicle registration database to find the vehicle owner, it belonged to a Jeffery Alan Peters, twenty-five Burlington Road, Chelsham. The forensic team inspected the surrounding area, there didn't appear anything of significance to suggest foul play. Photographs taken, the vehicle was transported to a police holding warehouse for closer examination, by both them and the fire brigade. The vehicle owner would have to be notified as soon as possible.

Anne was in limbo not sure whether to prepare the Sunday dinner or leave it until Jeff got home, she certainly was going to give him what for when he walked through the front door. She busied herself with the housework, vacuuming the house from top to bottom. She was about to turn on the washing machine when the house phone rang. She answered it on the third ring.

"Where the bloody hell have you been?"

There was silence at the other end.

Anne wasn't in the mood for one of Jeff's silly antics. "You better have a good excuse for not letting me know what's going on?"

"Hello, is that the Peter's residence, this is the police."

Anne heard a female voice, she guessed about thirty years old. *Did she hear right, the police*? She sat down, her face flushed with both embarrassment and worry. "Yes, this is Anne Peters speaking."

"Sorry to bother you, Mrs Peters, is Mr Peters there, Mr Jeffery Alan Peters?"

Anne's mind was racing, obviously Jeff hadn't been arrested as he'd be in police custody. *What's he been up to* she thought. "No, Jeffery," she looked out of the front window, "Jeffery is not here, what's this all about?"

"It's probably nothing to worry about Mrs Peters, we've just picked up a car registered to your husband." The female police officer didn't elaborate on the details, this could go one of several ways. "Where is Mr Peters, we need to speak to him?"

Anne explained the situation, as it stood, she also wanted to speak to Mr Peters.

The call closed with, "If you see or hear from him, he must contact the police immediately, if we hear anything we will be in touch."

Anne was worried sick. *What on earth has happened to Jeff?* She changed tack, from annoyance to sympathy. *Poor old Jeff, where is he?*

Sunday morning passed into Sunday afternoon, still no sign of Jeff, by this time Anne was beside herself with worry. Jeff hadn't come home, he hadn't contacted her, his mobile was dead, the police were looking for him. *What on earth is going on* she worryingly thought.

Anne rang the police late Sunday afternoon, firstly to enquire as to whether or not they had found Jeff. The conversation developed far beyond Anne's imagination. Jeff's car had been found, burnt out, in a derelict area on the outskirts of the town. The police would not divulge any further information, but enquired into Jeff's physical description, in particular, his race, height, build and age. Anne quickly gave the officer those details, then probed the police officer she was talking to. He wouldn't confirm if a body was found in the car, being a pessimist, as far as Anne was concerned, Jeff was dead, probably burnt alive!

The car, now in a police crime investigation warehouse, was searched Monday morning, after it had cooled down sufficiently enough. The surviving skeletal remains were carefully removed, being laid out on a table in close proximity. A pathologist was present, placing bones in their position, rebuilding the body's frame. Due to the intense heat and the consequent explosion, there wasn't a great deal of material to work with. Bones had scattered about the front driver's area of the car; the smaller thinner ones had been completely burnt to dust.

Part of the skull, right humerus, pelvic girdle, both femur and the right tibia were the main bones partially intact. She was placing surviving fragments in their envisaged position. It wasn't until Monday mid-afternoon, that she concluded in her preliminary report, due to the shape of the skull and pelvic girdle, the victim was Caucasian, male, medium build, between five feet eight inches to five feet ten inches tall, probably middle-aged.

The investigation team were informed of these details, mapping them to the ones Mrs Anne Peters had given them regarding her missing husband; they were close, very close. One of the team searching what was left of the car, found the smouldered remains of a mobile phone and a wallet in the passenger glove compartment. On careful examination, the bottom half of a partially melted credit card revealed Jeff's name. It was time to visit twenty-five Burlington Road.

Anne had a restless night's sleep, Sunday evening, fearing the worst about Jeff. She hadn't contacted any of Jeff's family, mainly his elderly parents and sister, so as not to alarm them for, possibly, nothing. She phoned her workplace when she got up Monday morning, informing her manager that she wouldn't be at work, possibly Tuesday as well. She made herself a cup of coffee, taking two headache tablets with it and went back to bed, feeling like, death warmed up. She wished she was a bit more like Jeff, his glass was always half full, he planned for the worst but hoped for the best, whereas Anne's glass was almost empty, preparing for the worst. Anne spent most of the morning moping about, occasionally raising her depressed spirits enough to think that Jeff would walk through the door, with another claptrap story. This time she would hug, then admonish him. It was late afternoon, she'd just made herself cheese on toast, when the house phone rang. She knew it would be the police; she was right, they were on their way.

She stood by the front window, wearing jeans and a sweater, looking out onto the road, waiting for the police car to arrive. Fifteen minutes had past, when it pulled up onto their drive. The officers, dressed in uniform, one of each gender, methodically walked to her front door, the male carrying objects in a clear plastic bag. Anne greeted the officers, who

149

introduced themselves showing their identification, business was conducted in the front living room. Anne sat in a single seat, the two officers sat on the settee. The police, being professional, and not having the absolute proof, aired on the side of caution, therefore explained what evidence they had, taking it in turns to emphasise certain points. They had the remains of a body, probably male, who roughly fitted Jeff's profile, but nothing was being ruled out. The police were softly dropping the bomb on Anne, by being purposely evasive.

The male, a sergeant, slipped on skin tight, clear gloves, took out the remains of the mobile phone found in the glove box, held it up so Anne could see it, asking her if it could be Jeff's phone. Barely audible, she said, "It could, it looks like the same make, model and colour." It was the phone's cover that gave the game away as it was his favourite football team's colour, with their logo in the corner. The officer then placed the remains of the phone back in the bag, then pulled out the wallet, and repeated the process. All Anne could do was nod, the meltdown had started, tears followed then the howling hysterically. The female officer rushed over to Anne, placing a comforting arm around her shoulder; she didn't say anything. The police officers looked at each other, the sergeant phoned for medical assistance, they needed to sedate Anne and have a nurse stay and keep an eye on her. The medical team arrived twenty minutes later, two females, one a doctor, the other a nurse. The doctor spoke to Anne, then administered a tranquillising injection. They helped Anne to her feet and up the stairs to bed, putting her in it, clothes and all. The nurse then nipped downstairs, grabbed a kitchen chair and put it in the bedroom. She would stay with Anne until it was decided the next, if any, course of action. The doctor left another tranquilliser and a pack of sedatives to be used at the nurse's discretion. The police and doctor departed from the house, leaving the nurse and a sobbing Anne. "Why Jeff, why?" Was all she could slur.

The police, although all the evidence pointed to Jeff being the victim in the car, couldn't, at that stage into the investigation, rule out the body being someone else. They decided to leave the case open and wait for either Jeff to turn up, or a report of someone missing, fitting the pathologist's profile. The decision would be conveyed back to Anne; she was obviously hoping for the former.

CHAPTER THIRTY-THREE

Jeff caught the ten past eight tube into London from Camden Town tube station; he didn't want to be late for his meeting with The Scribe. He'd spent most of Monday walking around Camden Town, as it was a dry, sunny October day, albeit cold. He bought the white cap as instructed, it was folded and in his blue jacket pocket, blue jeans, black polo shirt and jumper and black lace up shoes completed his attire. Jeff had his evening meal in The World's End pub, lasagne and chips washed down with just the one pint of ale, prior to catching the Northern line into London, getting off at Embankment, transferring to the District line, and disembarking at Blackfriars tube station. The short walk to Queen Victoria Street put another eight minutes on his journey time, totalling twenty-three minutes. consequently the time was eight forty-five p.m. as he walked through the main door of The Slaughtered Wolf public house.

The Slaughtered Wolf, positioned just off Victoria Street, near Puddle Dock, was typical of an old London town drinking establishment, being built in the early nineteenth century, towards the end of the Georgian period. It was of solid wall, dark red brick construction, all the openings were finished with a segmental arch, the ground floor windows were of bow style, supported on a bow brick wall. The windows were of leaded glass design, the front door of solid dark oak. Jeff slipped his white cap on and made his way to the toilet area of the pub, which was at its far end. Once located, he went to the bar, bought a pint and sat in a large leather chair, in the designated area, facing outwards, so he had a good view. The interior of The Slaughtered Wolf comprised of a lot of nooks and crannies with alcoves leading to small rooms, each small area was sectioned off from its neighbour. Jeff got the impression *a person could easily hide in this place*. The lighting was dim and ironically, shadowy, small wall lights adorned the walls, radiating minimal light. The walls were finished with a dark red blown vinyl wall paper, the pub floor with matching carpet, worn in places. Jeff noticed a couple of wolf pelts hanging from the two side walls, one slightly darker than the other. A head of a large black wolf was fixed to the wall above the bar, its yellow eyes seemed to glare at Jeff, so he thought.

Customers' furniture was a mixed bag of tables and chairs, varying in shape and style which, Jeff thought, gave it a quaint feel, the only consistency were the settees around the perimeter of the main section of the bar. Bar stools were positioned here and there next to the bar, which was slightly curved in shape. There weren't any television screens on the walls, the only music being played was classical of a low volume. Jeff tried to categorise the pub clientele, he couldn't, like the seats and tables, a real mixture. He looked around trying to make out The Scribe, it could've been anybody. There were city types, typically booted and suited, and at one end it looked to Jeff, like a small biker gang, half a dozen men, cladded with leather jackets, with 'colours' which appeared to Jeff, like, coincidentally, a howling wolf on the back of their jackets. The rest of the customers' dress varied from smart to casual to scruffy, matching their hairstyles and general appearance. Jeff noticed that there weren't any young clientele, the youngest, in his opinion, being late twenties and also women were scarce, just a few elderly 'old gals'. A smartly dressed, neatly groomed, middle-aged man in a blue suit, with dyed blond hair, on his own, sitting at the bar, kept looking at Jeff. Was this The Scribe? Jeff took another sip of ale, it was eight fifty five. The man winked at Jeff, Jeff winked back. Smiling, he walked the four paces to where Jeff was sitting, sat next to him; it was The Scribe.

"My name's Charles, you can call me Chas," he said as he sat down. He then slipped his right hand onto Jeff's inner left thigh.

Jeff jumped in shock. "Get your hand off me, now bugger off."

Chas stood up. "Oh suit yourself, prick teaser." He then walked, mincey fashion, back to his bar stool, snubbing Jeff.

Jeff felt uncomfortable, he wondered if the pub was a pickup joint, he certainly didn't wink at anybody else. He took another sip, and continued to scan people coming and going, avoiding Chas at all costs. As he was close to the toilet area, this was the busiest place. He wondered what The Scribe would look like, *maybe dressed all in black, plus a fedora and cape*. A youngish couple casually dressed, in their early thirties, sat at the table next but one to his, quietly chatting to each other. The bikers were laughing, joking and generally messing about, the rest of the clientele were talking quietly to each other or, if on their own, reading the daily newspaper. It was now nine twenty p.m. still no sign of The Scribe. The pub was half full, Jeff took another sip, he'd never drank so slow. A few minutes later, the youngish couple both went to the toilet area, the man carrying a small suitcase, closing the door behind him, Jeff took no heed of them. Five minutes later the woman, suitcase in hand, returned sitting back down, continuing her drink; she didn't look very happy, Jeff wondered if they'd had a tiff. A few more minutes passed, then a strange looking character, dressed in a pink suit, walked all around the pub, as if he was looking for somebody. *This must be The Scribe*, Jeff assumed. A few seconds later, bizarrely, Jeff noticed the stranger walking out, arm in arm with a grinning Chas, *who walked even mincier*, Jeff thought. Jeff smiled to himself, looked at his watch, it was now nine thirty in the evening. Jeff made his mind up, he'd finish his pint and go. He looked to his right and noticed an old man coming out of the door leading to the toilets. *Strange he didn't recall seeing him come in, he must have entered the pub through the small rear exit, leading to the river Thames,* he thought. The old boy looked around then shuffled towards Jeff. He looked about seventy years of age, stooped over with a walking stick for support, his hands were gloved. He had a thick grey beard and moustache, a good head of silver-grey hair, gold round-rimmed glasses, and wore a long brown overcoat, dark brown trousers and shoes; he could have been taken for a tramp.

"Is this seat taken?" He spoke in a hoarse, strained voice, pointing to the chair opposite Jeff.

Jeff eyed him up. "Yes it is, and I don't want company, now goodnight."

The old man stood his ground. "Are you waiting for somebody?"

Jeff started to get irritated, this was a distraction, what if The Scribe came in and caught him talking to somebody, it could jeopardise everything. "I am, as a matter-of-fact, but not you, now clear off." Jeff finished his pint and started to get up to leave.

The old man sat in the chair opposite Jeff's. "Sit down, Lone Wolf, I'm The Scribe!"

Jeff took a double turn, either it was an old man or a fantastic disguise, Jeff wasn't quite sure. "Now, what can I do for you?"

Jeff described what he wanted, preferably a USA passport, a UK one would however suffice. He gave The Scribe the name Peter Jeffreys, which in Chinese was spelt, Bídé Jié fú lísī, the rest of the details he would leave with The Scribe. The Scribe needed a current photo, Jeff gave him the one Dr Cheng printed out, he put it in his right coat pocket, it now came down to the costs. "It'll cost ya five grand, half before, half on completion."

Jeff balked at the cost, he didn't think it would cost that much. The Scribe' sensed the resistance. "As a special favour I'll do it for, four thousand five hundred pounds, take it or leave it."

Jeff nodded in agreement. "How long will it take?"

The Scribe started to get out of his chair. "Three days, meet me here tomorrow night at twenty-one hours with a better photograph and," he looked Jeff in the eye, "two thousand two hundred and fifty pounds, in twenties." He started to slowly walk off, back the way he came, through the entrance door to the toilets. Jeff sat in shock, he decided he needed another drink to calm his nerves. The same barmaid who served him earlier did the honours. As he got back to his seat, he noticed the young woman had drunk up and gone, her boyfriend's drink was still at the table. *He must have stormed off in a right old tantrum,* he thought. Jeff removed his cap, placing it in his inside jacket pocket, took a large mouthful of ale and thought about The Scribe. He tried to work out if he was in disguise, if so, what did he really look like. Soon after Jeff thought about his next plan of action, he had to somehow get a decent photograph from Dr Cheng, that might be easier said than done. His main concern, however, was, could he trust The Scribe, what guarantees had he once he handed over his deposit. In short, none. Jeff pondered over his pint, he was going round in circles, so he quickly finished it and headed back to Buck Street, *Tomorrow's another day.*

Jeff had a restless night's sleep. Concerns over The Scribe, getting another passport-sized photograph from Dr Cheng and worrying about Anne, in addition, he also had another visit from Mike. Mike refused to leave the mortuary, the pair 'sword fighting' with a broom handle and a mop handle. The fight being broken up by Micary, who ordered Mike, wearing his shroud, to get back into his storage fridge. Micary then told Jeff, who was wearing his tracksuit, to report to the morgue, he took both their 'weapons' after admonishing the pair.

Jeff sat in his usual spot for breakfast, thus avoiding as much contact with other guests as possible. If somebody did pass an innocent remark, like, the weather, Jeff just nodded his head and then ignored them rudely, thinking, *needs must, needs must.* On the way into London, he sounded out a launderette in Camden Town, as he needed to wash his depleted wardrobe, and he didn't want to buy more clothes. He was wearing the same clothes he had worn the previous evening, except for undergarments and the white cap. Jeff walked into Dr Cheng's consultancy at ten forty-five on Tuesday morning. The same receptionist greeted him, thus, he would have to wait an half hour or comeback, as Mr Cheng was busy.

Jeff decided to wait, he sat in a comfortable chair and pretended to read a magazine he picked up from the small room table, purposely put there for that reason. He felt himself drift off, his eyelids felt heavy, the room was warm and snug against the autumn cold. He decided to rest his eyes. He could hear background movement, he slowly opened his eyes. Dr Cheng was talking to a young Chinese female, from the gist of their conversation, Jeff deduced she'd had her surgery bandages removed and Cheng was giving her last-minute instructions. As she walked past Jeff, he took a good look at her, she was slim and very attractive, and bore an uncanny resemblance to Chynna. She glanced at Jeff and smiled, he noticed her eyes were wider than normal, and her nose was narrow and pointed, typically European. She said her goodbyes and walked out of the consultancy. Cheng spotted Jeff and waved him into his office.

They sat in the same chairs as their last chat, pleasantries were exchanged. Dr Cheng could read Jeff's mind, he showed him a photo of the beauty prior to her surgery, the transformation was a sight to behold. Her nose looked like that of a boxer's which had been hit far too many times, her eyes were like slits. Cheng explained that some Orientals had a single eyelid crease, for this young woman, he created a double eyelid crease, making the eye look bigger, and more alert. Jeff nodded in agreement, and soon after they got down to business. Jeff explained to Cheng that he was applying for a passport and couldn't wait for the surgery to completely heal before taking a photograph, so he requested a copy from him. Cheng responded by explaining that this would require special gloss photography paper and better imagery, as he'd been asked to perform it on a couple of previous occasions. It would cost Jeff fifty pounds for two passport-sized photographs, so he reluctantly agreed.

Cheng tidied Jeff's hair with a comb, added black mascara to Jeff's eyelashes and brows, and thereon took a few frontal photographs of Jeff with a high quality digital camera. He loaded the images onto a computer, opening them with a photography software program. He selected the most appropriate photograph then started to alter it, using a digital pen as skilfully as his scalpel. Cheng zoomed into the nose area, removing and adding pixels, called airbrushing, often used to enhance models' body shapes, Cheng informed Jeff.

Once satisfied with the nose and eye shape, he then slightly darkened Jeff's skin so it was a light yellow-brown colour. He explained to Jeff that the Chinese skin colour can vary from pale white through to light brown, forming a yellow shade. Cheng went into more detail on the skin colour subject. "This would depend on whether they are from the north or south China, and also what type of life they led, either farmers or city folk and that females have lighter skin than males." With this new information, it was followed by a deep discussion about skin colour. Jeff recalled how the middle and upper classes in Europe would avoid direct sunlight, so that their skin wouldn't get sunburnt, as it was related to working class outdoor workers, white skin being associated with wealth and purity.

"The all over tan eventually became popular after the Second World War, being associated with expensive luxury holidays and a healthy glowing look, consequently, tanning shops sprung up everywhere. Too much exposure to the sun highlighted the risk of skin cancer, so some people avoided the sun or used very high factor sunblock or sunscreen."

"What's the difference between sunblock and sunscreen?" Jeff asked, trying to sound interested, in Cheng's lecture.

Cheng put his small hands together. "Screen is the more common sun protection, it filters or screens some of the UV rays, but allows some in, whereas," he looked at Jeff with his hazel coloured eyes, expecting a comment, however nothing was forthcoming, "block, reflects and blocks the UV rays, acting as a physical sunscreen, utilising titanium oxide or zinc oxide, resulting in a thick paste." He again looked directly at Jeff, pushed his glasses firmly onto his face. "Some people consider it unsightly."

They then discussed skin whitening, a treatment to reduce the amount of melanin concentration in the skin. Discussion over, Cheng used software to coloured Jeff's eyes brown, and blackened his hair, as it looked dark brown. He called Jeff to look at the image, Jeff nodded his approval. Dr Cheng then loaded his high definition colour printer with a sheet of gloss photography paper and printed two passport-sized photographs, thirty-five millimetres wide by forty-five millimetres tall.

Dr Cheng handed the photos to Jeff for examination. He was impressed, bizarrely he also looked younger due to the removal of his baggy eyes, which had increased in size since David's demise. His nose was smaller, being rounded. Cheng, to Jeff's surprise, then revisited the skin colour subject again and advised him to, tone up, to see what kind of reaction he gets from the general public, as he would look North Indian without the oriental surgery.

"You see, Mr Smith, you can easily tell from where people originate, by how dark their natural skin colour is, for example, in the north of India, the skin colour is light brown, in the south, say, Sri Lanka, it is very dark, almost black. The same scenario applies in Africa, the closer a country is to the equator the darker the people's skin colour will be. In China, further north than Beijing, the people are a lot lighter than folk in the south, by Hong Kong. You will be taken for a mixed-race man, that in itself will have issues, due to acceptance, or not, of both Chinese or white Caucasian people."

Jeff hadn't considered racist issues like acceptance or bigotry, and then recalled a discussion he had with Anne regarding that very subject, if David and Chynna had children, what would they look like. They discussed eye colour would it be blue or brown, hair colour, black or blond and then general appearance, white Caucasian or Chinese oriental, or the obvious mixture. Much to Jeff's surprise, he discovered that the Chinese were less tolerant of mixed ethnic relationships than the British, especially from the elder generation and rural communities, and their consequent mixed race, offspring. He reflected what Ah Lam and Li Wei thought about it all. It wouldn't have mattered to Jeff, he wasn't bigoted, he'd have loved them regardless. It reminded Jeff that he would never be a grandfather, something he was really looking forward to. It was all irrelevant now, it made him more determined than ever.

He had a friend who had children with a mixed-race partner, one of the girls was very light, the other was dark. He told Jeff in confidence, that some of his family rejected the lighter skinned girl, because she had too much white blood in her. Jeff decided to experiment with the colour issue, once he left Cheng's.

He paid Dr Cheng fifty pounds in cash, who flashed his small right hand out, pocketing the notes in his trouser back pocket. Jeff nodded, putting the photographs in his jacket inside pocket, and they shook hands. "See you tomorrow morning."

"Goodbye Dr Cheng."

Jeff waved at the receptionist as he walked out of the consultancy.

"See you tomorrow morning, Mr Smith."

He left Cheng's, turned to the left, walked across the road towards a large bank, because he had to withdraw cash from it to pay, The Scribe. Jeff had to use a bank, as the maximum amount of cash he could withdraw from an automated telling machine (atm) was four hundred pounds. He took a few deep breaths, he felt strange, as he'd never been nervous about walking into a bank before. He wondered if this was how bank robbers felt before holding up the bank. Jeff admonished himself, he wasn't doing anything wrong, he wasn't committing a crime, although that could be argued. His main worry was that he didn't have any identification, except for his bank card, which could prove awkward. He walked through the bank's main entrance doors, turned slightly to his right, heading towards a shelf with cash withdrawal forms on a rack. He stood and filled the form in, using a ballpoint black ink pen, fixed to a chain, which in turn was secured to the shelf edge. He calmly, lightly whistled to himself a made-up tune, he was calmness personified. He signed the slip *Mr Thomas Smith*. Jeff walked with a deliberate, confident stride to the end of the queue waiting to see a cashier.

He stood behind four other people, three middle-aged women and an elderly man, who was in front of Jeff. Two cashiers were on duty, both in their late twenties, one male the other female. The queue in front of

Jeff went down, he was next but one, two men joined the queue, waiting behind Jeff. The elderly man was served by the male. "Next please," said the young woman.

Jeff said, "Hello", smiled and gave her his card and the cash withdrawal slip. She read the withdrawal details, then asked for further identification.

Jeff explained that he didn't have any to hand, she told him to wait there. She then walked to a side office and spoke to a middle-aged, bespectacled man, wearing a grey suit. Three minutes later, she returned to her post and informed Jeff that he would have to wait, as a search for a missing card would be generated. She pointed to an area at the far end of the bank, where he could sit comfortably in one of six lounge chairs, and await the outcome, either way, she kept the card. Jeff asked the reasoning behind this search, and how long it would take. She informed him that the card could be stolen and it would take an hour, or so.

Jeff sat in one of the black lounge chairs for three-quarters of an hour, pondering on recent past and present dilemmas, when 'grey-suit' introduced himself. "Sorry to have kept you waiting, Mr Smith, but we had to do several security checks, I'm sure you fully understand." The bank manager stood just under six feet tall, was stout in build, topped with a balding head with dark grey hair around the ears and neck. He wore black, square framed glasses, Jeff guessed he was mid-fifties in age, and spoke with a neutral accent. Jeff noted his name on a badge on his jacket breast pocket, Mr T. Bates. He wondered for a second what the 'T' stood for.

"That's fine, all good, I assume?"

Grey suit sat opposite Jeff on one of the other comfy chairs. "I need to ask you security questions, because you don't have any identification." He looked directly at Jeff, trying to mind read him. "I assume that will be all right?"

Jeff shrugged his shoulders. "Of course, I'm all for extra security checks," he replied, in an almost patronising tone.

The bank manager referred to a clipboard with a questionnaire attached to it. "Thank you, I will go through a couple of questions, it won't take long, and then I'll sanction your request." He bounced back Jeff's patronising manner.

Bates went through the questions. Security numbers, when the account was set up, by whom, how much was the recent payments, was there any withdrawals. These were typical questions: the standard bank security checking, all of which Jeff easily answered. The bank manager then asked why Jeff wanted the money and why in cash. Jeff explained that he wanted to surprise his wife with a secret present and that she often scrutinised his bank accounts, hence the reason for cash. Grey suit then asked Jeff why he didn't have any proof of identification.

"My wife keeps all our identification documents in a safe, mainly for security reasons, but also for safe keeping, and it was a last-minute decision, you could say, a rush of blood."

Bates almost laughed, *what a load of bullshit,* he thought. "Okay Mr Smith, you've answered the questions satisfactorily, I'll sanction the transaction, will fifties be okay?"

"No, I'd prefer twenties please, I don't like carrying large denominations."

More cods wallop, Grey Suit thought. "Okay, go to cashier one, he will complete the transaction." With that, the bank manager got up, didn't bother to shake Jeff's hand, walked through the dividing door separating staff and customers, then talked to the cashier and walked back to his office, looking somewhat suspicious.

Jeff waited for Grey Suit to disappear into his office, then confidently walked to the front of cashier one's queue. He handed the withdrawal slip to the young man, who, on his manager's instructions, counted out two thousand, two hundred and fifty pounds, in twenty-pound notes, plus one ten-pound note. He handed the notes to Jeff and wished him a good day. "Next customer please."

Jeff put the money in an inside jacket pocket, the same one as Cheng's photos, zipped it up, had a quick look around, then turned left out of the bank. He walked a couple of hundred metres to a large chemists, rather unusually for a man, heading straight for the make-up section. He bought a tube of medium white to light brown skin cream. After purchasing the cream, he then went back to the make-up area, squeezed out a two centimetre length and rubbed the cream all over his face, paying particular attention to his hairline, with the aid of a large mirror, making sure he had an even covering all over. It took fifteen minutes to get it right, rubbing the residue onto the top of his right hand. He took a good look in the mirror, initially not recognising himself; if it wasn't for his blue eyes he thought he looked North Indian. A couple of customers gave him a quizzical look as they walked past, he heard them whisper to each other, assuming Jeff was an actor in a West End show, perhaps playing an Egyptian in *Joseph and the Amazing Technicolour Dreamcoat*. Whilst he was walking back out of the shop, he stumbled across a notice by the eye care section, '*Change your eye colour*'. Jeff stopped in his tracks and found the new product, eye drops that gradually transformed the colour of your iris. He picked up a bottle of blue to brown. "That'll save me the problem of keep buying brown contact lenses," he muttered to himself, as he picked up a box of thirty brown daily lenses, then walked back to the cashier to pay. She gave him a funny glance, he didn't think she liked his 'North Indian' look, or was it that she thought it odd, that a light brown skinned man had blue eyes. Jeff didn't know or care.

Jeff turned right as he exited the chemist, heading back to the tube station; it was time to experiment. He crossed the road at a set of traffic lights, into a busy pedestrian area, purposely bumping into people, of all ethnicities and both genders, apologising as he did, with a slight Asian ancient, or his best interpretation of one. Jeff continued his experiment, on the tube journey and also the walk back to his B&B, purposely choosing both men and women of different races, ethnicities and ages. It was a mild distraction to his other business, and was fascinated by the outcome. *I could write a book about this,* he thought, as he digested the results of the Jeffery Alan Peters social experiment.

Jeff categorised the reaction of people he bumped into three main groups: non-reaction, aggressive and racist. He found that most people, after he apologised, didn't really react, maybe the odd comment such as, "Watch where you're going". A couple of men and one woman were a bit more aggressive, and swore at Jeff, and only three people used racist language: a white man, a black woman and a mixed-race young woman. He wondered what the reaction would be if he was Chinese, it wouldn't be long before he'd find out.

Jeff put the thoughts to the back of his mind and prepared himself for another meeting with The Scribe. Jeff powered up the iPad and quickly booked himself into a Travelodge, situated in Lupus Street, Pimlico, as he didn't want to be disturbed for the first few days after surgery, plus, Pimlico was slightly closer to the city centre, being on the Victoria tube line. He would check out of the B&B in Buck Street, first thing after breakfast, taking his few belongings to the Travelodge, then head to Cheng's. Jeff closed the iPad and took a quick shower, then lay on his bed, resting his eyes. He decided to repeat the same process as the previous evening, a meal in The World's End, then the tube journey into London, finishing in The Slaughtered Wolf.

Jeff woke from his power nap, freshened up, and prepared himself for the evening ahead. It was now six thirty p.m. Jeff dressed in jeans, black polo shirt, blue jacket, pocketing the white cap in the inside pocket of his jacket. He checked the money and photographs were where he'd left them, double-checked the room and then headed out.

The World's End was relatively quiet for a Tuesday evening, he had the pick of tables to sit at, but decided on the same table as the night before, as it gave him a good all round view of the pub. Jeff ordered his meal, scampi and chips, at the bar, whilst ordering and paying for his lager shandy, being served by a young, good looking bar maid. He decided on the shandy as he wanted a clear head and his wits about him, as he felt very uncomfortable carrying any amount of cash over fifty pounds. For this reason, he also kept his jacket on, constantly feeling the bulge in his inside jacket pocket. To a keen-eyed pickpocket, this action would have immediately given the game away, luckily for Jeff, the pickpockets were elsewhere. Whilst he was waiting for the meal to arrive, a tall, big busted, dark haired, middle-aged 'woman' approached him, and, with a deep voice, asked him if he wanted company. The lady who had thick bright red lipstick and copious amounts of make-up on, was about to pull up a chair at Jeff's table; he didn't need this distraction.

"Sorry love, I'm waiting for my wife, thanks for the offer though," Jeff said, with a wry smile, and a slight dismissive wave of his right hand.

"Are you sure baby, we could have a real good time?" she said, breathing vodka smelling breath over Jeff, whilst nearly popping out of her tight fitting catsuit.

"I'm absolutely positive, now please go," he said, with a tone of assertion.

Red lips stood, hands on hips, not sure whether to pursue this punter, when Jeff got rescued by the waitress, bringing his meal. The fat, toothless, ugly, grey haired, miserable hag, slammed Jeff's scampi and chips onto the table, barging red lips out of the way.

"Fuck off Roger, leave this man alone. Go do your business elsewhere, or I'll throw you out of the pub."

With that, both Roger and miserable hag walked off, in different directions, Roger blowing Jeff a kiss as 'she' walked out of the pub. Jeff splashed vinegar on his scampi, sprinkled salt on the chips, and sighed with relief, for all he knew, Roger could have robbed him and blown the whole plan. *I'll have to consider whether to continue going out,* he thought to himself, as he tucked into his meal, gently touching the bulge in his jacket pocket. Jeff took his time eating his dinner and only drank the single pint of shandy, furthermore, he didn't have any more uninvited company. He looked at his watch, it was now seven forty-five p.m. Time to head off and meet The Scribe.

He purposely sat in a near empty carriage on the southern bound tube journey into central London, Jeff was paranoid about getting pickpocketed, or worse, mugged. He walked out of Blackfriars tube station and headed towards Queen Victoria Street, making sure he kept on the path with good street lighting. It took him nearly one hour from leaving The World's End, before he walked through the front door of The Slaughtered Wolf.

Jeff slowly made his way from the front door to the toilet area, trying to subtly observe the evening's clientele. Light, quiet classical music played in the background, Wolfgang Amadeus Mozart's, *Overture to Don Giovanni,* Jeff thought, although he wasn't quite sure. The lighting was dim and shadowy but, unlike The World's End, the pub was busy. Jeff stood at the far end of the bar, avoided looking at the black headed wolf's head, ordered and paid for another pint of lager shandy, then sat at the same seat as the previous evening, slipping his white cap on as he did so. He took a sip of his drink, then took in the rest of the pub's customers, whilst looking for The Scribe.

Jeff heard a cackle to his left, he turned, it was the bikers fooling about. There was a lot of laughing and joking and general piss taking, with one in particular being the brunt of it. Jeff noticed he had 'prospect' on the back of his leather cut, and didn't have any club colours. The prospect seemed to be constantly at the bar buying the full members drinks, and fetching cigarettes for them to smoke outside. Jeff counted six full patched members, varying in age from late twenties to early fifties, all heavily tattooed, three had long hair and beards, two were crew cut with goatees and one had his head completely shaved, wearing a 'handle-bar' moustache. When one of the gang turned his back to Jeff, he noticed the club's colours: a black snarling wolf's head, not a howling one as he originally thought, with blood dripping from its fangs, the eyes were glowing bright amber, and the ears were pinned back. Jeff made out the letters W.O.R.A.D. shaped like an arc, above the wolf's head, and London Chapter, with a small MC below it. Jeff just about read the words, 'Wolves Of Rage And Destruction', on the front of another member's jacket, underneath another patch, 'Sergeant at Arms'. Although the group was jovial, they had an air of invincibility. Jeff noticed all the pub clientele gave the group a wide berth — he didn't blame them.

The rest of the customers were similar in mixture to the previous evening. Jeff glanced slightly to his right. Chas, dressed in a tight-fitting red suit, was sitting on a bar stool, drinking a cocktail. Jeff guessed Sex on the Beach by the look of it and the added accompaniment of an orange wedge and umbrella. Chas slipped Jeff a sly look, then quickly turned away, his eyes focussed on the door, and in particular who was entering the pub. Jeff took another sip of shandy, slipped his cap back slightly, whilst tapping his right middle finger on the table, to the music. Ludwig Van Beethoven's *Fifth Symphony*. It was now 8.55 p.m. when close movement caught his eye — it was the same young couple as the previous night.

This time, they stood by the bar opposite to where Jeff was sitting, both with a drink in hand, which they'd purchased from the other side of the bar. They whispered to each other whilst furtively looking at Jeff, then the woman walked off to the toilets, carrying the same case as the man had previously, leaving the young man drinking on his own at the bar. Jeff took another drink, put his glass down on the table and looked around for The Scribe. Ten minutes passed, the door to the toilet area opened, and The Scribe shuffled into the pub, dressed in exactly the same clothes as the previous night. He sat on a chair with wooden hand supports, opposite Jeff. He got straight to the point.

"Right Lone Wolf, have you got the reddies?" he whispered in a hoarse voice, holding out his left hand. In it was a folded newspaper.

"I have, but what proof have I that you won't just do a runner?" Jeff replied, holding out both hands as he spoke in a questionable fashion.

"Don't fuck me about," he snapped, his voice sharper and clearer. "And you don't," he added. "Now, do you want the fucking passport or not?" The Scribe looked Jeff in the eye, through his gold rimmed glasses, his expression was one of a cross between assertion and aggression.

Jeff reached inside his jacket pocket, quickly looked around, grabbed the money and swiftly put it in the fold of the paper. The Scribe slipped the paper inside his coat, Jeff presumed into a large inside pocket.

"Aren't you going to count it?"

The Scribe gave Jeff another dirty look. "If it ain't all there, you won't see me or the money again, now stop acting like a prick," he said, without moving any part of his body except his lips. "I'll have the photos now."

Jeff dipped his right hand into his inside jacket pocket, and pulled out the two photographs Cheng had printed for him earlier in the day, which now seemed a long time ago, and slid them across the table, towards The Scribe's waiting right hand. He picked them up, took out a magnifying glass from a right-side coat pocket and scrutinised them, making a few inaudible noises whilst doing so. Jeff felt like he'd just handed in his homework, for his tutor to give a quick once over check. The music playing was now Ennio Morricone's *Once Upon a Time in America*, a tune which Jeff particularly liked, so he started to hum along with it whilst The Scribe checked his 'homework'.

"For fuck's sake, stop that fucking humming," was his friendly quip. "Okay these will do." He placed the photos in a top inside pocket. "Meet me here on Friday night, same time, with the rest of the dough." With that, he got out of his chair, stroked his beard, then slowly shuffled back out the way he came, his brown brogues hardly leaving the carpet. Jeff followed his movement whilst taking another swallow of shandy. Jeff turned slightly to his left, and noticed Chas walking out of the pub with a mid-twenties, good looking black fellow. He then turned to his right, to see the young man disappearing through the toilet entry door, both his and his girlfriend's drinks remained on the bar.

Jeff sat in a state of shock, just looking down at a worn section of the red carpet, his right hand under his chin rubbing the underside of his bottom lip, as he comprehended the change in The Scribe's attitude. From quite amiable to hostile. He took the white cap off, and brushed his hair with his right-hand fingertips, then placed the folded cap in his left-hand jacket pocket, still deep in thought. *I hope I haven't fucked this up,* whilst having a quick left to right scan of the pub. Jeff took his time drinking, taking a mouthful, then looking around the pub at the customers and the fixtures and fittings. *It was certainly a real mixture,* he thought, *the most characterful place I've ever been in, although the carpet needs replacing.* And he would change the wallpaper. Jeff studied the bar with more intent, noticing quite a variety of draught beers and lagers plus a good selection of spirits, in particular many types of gin. The music was just audible above the chitter-chatter, he couldn't quite make out the composer. He turned to his left and noticed the bikers suddenly drink up and rush out with a fair degree of purpose, barging past any unfortunate customer in their way, without apologies, the prospect being the last to leave. One old gal shouted her disapproval as she got shoved out of the way — she was ignored. Jeff drank up as a middle-aged couple sat in the next adjacent seats. He slowly walked to the main door, taking a quick glance into the alcoves as he made his way out, he noticed couples of various genders holding hands and whispering to one another.

Once outside, he zipped up his jacket, it was a cold dark October evening. *At least it's not raining,* he thought, as he briskly walked back to Blackfriars tube station, a lot lighter in pocket than the inward journey. There weren't many passengers on the tube, at least he didn't have to worry about pickpockets. He just made it back to the B&B in Buck Street, when it started to lightly rain. Jeff picked up his key from reception, passed evening pleasantries with the young receptionist and headed for his room, hoping for a peaceful night's sleep. It was now eleven o'clock. He closed the room curtains, hung his clothes up and jumped into bed. His last thoughts as he drifted off, were about Anne and how she was getting on.

CHAPTER THIRTY-FOUR

Anne slept, with the aid of sedatives, through Monday, eventually waking Tuesday lunchtime, in somewhat of a daze. "Where's Jeff, what time is it, where's Jeff?" she hoarsely said to the nurse, sitting at her bedside.

The nurse, a mature, experienced woman, asked Anne if she wanted a cup of tea, adding, "The police are still looking for him, all eventualities are being investigated." She knew full well that Jeff, or what was left of him, was burnt to cinders.

Anne, after agreeing to the drink offer, sat up in bed, resting two pillows behind her back, whilst the nurse popped downstairs to make them both a drink. Hers was coffee. She took the drinks back to the bedroom, offering Anne another sedative, however, she declined it. They then commenced a discussion as to what the police had or hadn't discovered, and to where the investigation into Jeff's whereabouts was; the nurse fobbed Anne off with a lot of white lies. The nurse then quickly changed direction, focussing on Anne, and whether she felt like going to work, so as to keep her mind occupied, or stay with a relative. Anne mulled over the nurse's suggestions whilst sipping her tea, not really sure what to do, as the shock of Jeff's sudden disappearance had numbed her brain. She wrongfully assumed Jeff would either just turn up, or she would be informed he was in hospital due to an accident; she couldn't come to terms with the thought of him being dead. The discussion closed with the nurse telling Anne that she would have to go, and whether or not Anne needed company for support, and if so who. She told the nurse that she'd sort things out herself. She had her family for support if needed, as her sister would stay with her, plus she had to contact Jeff's family and work, for the obvious reasons. Satisfied, the nurse left, seeing herself out. Anne took a quick shower to freshen up — she'd got phone calls to make.

Once showered and dressed, Anne made herself a light lunch of a cheese and tomato sandwich, then phoned Jeff's parents, only informing them that he'd disappeared, no other details were discussed, and she expected him to walk through the front door any minute. Anne made a quick call to her employer, telling them she would be in work the next day, as she'd been poorly, a follow up call from Monday. She then phoned Jeff's employer, telling the personnel officer that Jeff wasn't feeling very well, and wouldn't be at work until further notice. She was somewhat taken aback when informed that Jeff was only working four days a week, recently changing his working conditions, having Fridays off. The personnel officer was also surprised that Anne didn't know. Once the call was terminated, she sat in the living room, finishing the second sandwich, whilst mulling over this new information, concluding that Jeff was up to something, but what? Anne looked out of the front window, it had started to rain slightly. She felt cold and put a cardigan on, wondering how the police investigation was going.

The police were no further forward solving the case regarding Mr Jeffery Alan Peters. All their evidence indicated that Jeff, consumed with grief at the death of his son, cremated himself in a moment of madness. Close circuit television from a garage on the outskirts of the town, revealed that Jeff had filled his car with petrol. He also bought two plastic Jerry cans and filled them with petrol, thirty-five minutes before the passing motorist reported seeing a blazing car on waste ground. The recording also showed that Jeff was on his own, and seemed to be acting normally, thus almost certainly ruling out kidnapping or somebody else driving Jeff's car, although every eventuality was being considered.

The initial pathologist's report indicated that the few charred remains from the burnt out car, were from a Caucasian male, of average height, but that was all. This was deduced from the partial remains of the skull shape and size and the charred remains of the various bones, which had been placed in their previous skeletal position. The police forensic team were in the process of taking a sample of bone for a DNA profile, and then comparing it with that of Jeff's mother's and father's DNA, to make absolutely sure.

The investigation team hadn't had a report of a missing person, or Jeff being found either wandering about mentally confused or being hospitalised. They decided not to put out a missing persons' report to the media, for another day and then only after permission from Anne Peters, who would have informed all other relevant close family and friends. Although the majority of the investigative team were convinced it was a suicide, purposely or accidental, one officer, a sergeant wasn't quite so sure, because of where the mobile phone and wallet were found, and that there wasn't a suicide note left in close proximity to Jeff's car. The rest of the team dismissed this doubt, as some of them put their own valuables in their car glove compartment when driving, for security reasons.

Anne made herself another hot drink, turned the central heating on low, then walked back into the living room, sitting in an armchair deep in thought. There was no doubt in her mind, that since David's death and consequent funeral, Jeff's personality and character had changed. He seemed obsessed with learning Chinese, trained at the gym and went to ju , didn't bother with the tennis club he'd been a member of for years, and also drank a lot. She then took into account his personality change, from affable, amiable to intolerant and slightly aggressive, he certainly wasn't the soft touch of old. She took a large gulp of coffee. *What was he up to with the car, fiddling around with the boot area, on Saturday,* she thought. *And he smelt odd on Friday, no, this didn't add up.* Anne had another sip of coffee, looked at the photo on the mantlepiece, of the three of them when David graduated, then looked out the front windows. *He's either incinerated himself in a moment of insanity, or,* she thought, *still be alive, and, if so, where?*

CHAPTER THIRTY-FIVE

Jeff woke up with a jolt, it was six thirty Wednesday morning, and he'd just had the worst night's sleep of his life. The nightmare involved The Scribe and a meeting with Jeff in The Slaughtered Wolf.

The Scribe started taunting Jeff about the money, laughing like a madman, and throwing the twenty-pound notes like confetti around the pub. When Jeff protested and started picking up his money, The Scribe turned violent and attacked Jeff, who tried to run away, with The Scribe in hot pursuit. The Scribe was being egged on by the young couple, who strangely were the only live customers in the pub. Jeff tried to hide in the alcoves but The Scribe always found him, and so the chase continued. The rest of the customers were blurred out and seemed oblivious to the pursuit and Jeff's predicament, and his consequent cries for help. The Scribe's hair was flared out, thus joining his beard, looking more like a lion's silver and grey mane, his eyes glowing amber with rage. He had a demonic facial expression as he chased Jeff, cackling like a lunatic. Just as The Scribe was about to bludgeon Jeff with his walking stick, there was an almighty explosion coming from the front entrance door of The Slaughtered Wolf. It was Mike riding through the doors on one of the bikers' Harley Davison's, into the pub, completely engulfed in flames.

Mike was wearing Jeff's tracksuit, which, although alight, strangely didn't burn. Bright yellow flames were coming out of the tracksuit's openings from his head, arms and legs. His head was surrounded with large yellow and orange flickering flames, ironically having a lion's mane appearance, his being yellow not silver, like The Scribe's. Mike screamed at The Scribe to leave Jeff alone, as it was his destiny to kill him, smoke coming out of his mouth as he shouted his demand. The Scribe, taken aback at this rude intrusion, told Mike to fuck off, as he raised his stick to bash Jeff with it. Mike roared the Harley at his competitor, slamming the front wheel full on into The Scribe's left leg, knocking him off balance, and into a small adjoining alcove. Jeff seized his chance to escape and quickly scampered away on all fours, not daring to look behind. If he had, he'd have witnessed the most bizarre cat and mouse chase around the pub, with The Scribe leaping from table to table. The Scribe was being pursued by the Harley riding Mike, weaving around punters, tables and chairs with incredible riding skill. When Jeff finally made it to the entrance, he hit his head on the front door of the pub. He awoke, covered in sweat.

Jeff had just bumped his head on the headboard of his bed and, for a second, looked around his room, looking for The Scribe and Mike, and, with a sigh of relief, realised he'd just had a horrible nightmare, although all nightmares are unpleasant. He looked at his watch, which was on the small bedside chest of drawers, it was 6.35 a.m. Jeff yawned two or three times, stretching his arms out in between each one, scratched his head, then decided to get up and have a shower, switching the water temperature to cold to freshen up. It certainly did the trick. By the time he stepped out of the shower cubicle he was fully switched on. He looked in the mirror and noticed the beginnings of his blond-haired roots showing, something that he'd have to be aware of in the future. *But it didn't matter too much for the time being,* Jeff thought. Once shaved, Jeff dressed in the same clothes he'd worn the night before, and went downstairs for breakfast, being surprised to find an elderly couple already waiting to enter the dining room, as it was early. Pleasantries were exchanged, Jeff waited for the couple to take a seat, then sat as far away from them as possible. He didn't need the everyday polite chat.

Breakfast consumed, he put his belongings in his bag, checked the room twice, then went downstairs to check out at reception. Next stop, the launderette. He washed and dried all the soiled clothes he'd worn since Saturday evening, having help from a middle-aged Asian woman, on how to use both the washer and spin drier, then headed for the tube station. He wanted to check-in at his next place of abode, before going to the bank, and then to Cheng's.

Jeff walked the short distance from Pimlico tube station to the Travelodge in Pimlico. He quickly checked in, using Mr Smith's card as a guarantee, then dumped his bag in his room, which was on the second floor of the three-storey hotel. Jeff thought that the room decor, size and furnishings were better than his previous one. Consisting of a: dark grey, short pile carpet, white emulsion painted walls and ceiling, finished with mid grey paintwork on the skirting and architrave. The bathroom was neat and tidy and typical in size and layout, as was the main room, having a king-sized bed, centrally placed. *Yes, this will do nicely, very nicely,* he thought, then put a splash of aftershave on, before he closed and locked the door, placing the key in his inside jacket pocket. Jeff decided not to use the tube, but walk the short distance to the bank, as it was a cold but dry October morning. *Besides the fresh air and exercise will do me good,* he thought, as he headed for the bank entrance doors.

The bank had only just opened, as it was five minutes past nine, consequently there was only one other customer being served by the solitary cashier. Jeff quickly completed the cash withdrawal slip whilst waiting, he was then called. "Next."

Jeff exchanged morning pleasantries with the smartly dressed, early thirties, young female, who informed Jeff that the bank manager would have to counter sign the acceptance slip, as Jeff couldn't produce identification. She quickly walked to Grey suit, who, Jeff thought, was lurking in the shadows. A quick chat resulted in Jeff once again having to speak to the manager, thus the cashier pointed Jeff to the comfortable waiting chairs. "He'll be with you shortly," was her parting quip.

Jeff sat in a comfy chair, and whilst he waited, he looked around the bank, trying to give off an air of confidence. The small bank, being built in the mid-sixties, was typical in size, layout and ambiance of its period, decorated in light shades of beige and pictures of pleasant seaside harbours. Jeff heard Grey suit's footsteps approach him from his left-hand side. He purposely ignored them, acting, or trying to, nonchalant and carefree.

"Sorry to keep you waiting Mr, er, Smith." Jeff thought that Bates almost laughed when he said, Mr Smith. Grey suit stood directly in front of Jeff, clipboard in hand.

Jeff deliberately paused, before he turned to the bank manager. "That's okay," he replied, with a casual tone. He noticed that the manager was wearing a clean, crisp white shirt and a dark grey tie, tied with a Windsor knot, the tip of the tie finishing in the middle of his black trouser belt.

The bank manager sat opposite Jeff, and quickly got straight to the point. "I've ran security checks on your account, consequently I need to ask you a few questions before I can sanction the cash withdrawal, is that okay, Mr Smith?" He pushed his black framed glasses back with his right middle index finger, so they were tight to his face. Bates crossed his legs, then he looked Jeff directly in the eye, and started asking Jeff questions he already knew the answer to.

Bates looked at the clipboard he held in his lefthand. "Who set up your account, when and why?" He sat back in his comfortable chair, put his right hand under his chin and waited, this was round one of a 'title fight'. He knew Jeff would know the answers, he was testing his mettle.

Jeff smiled at Mr T Bates. *Is Batesy playing games* he wondered. Jeff knew that Bates knew that he knew the answer. "My close friend Jeffery Peters set up the account for me, the other details are private." And *none of your fucking business.* Jeff felt like saying, "Strictly private." Jeff kept his tone friendly but felt he needed to illustrate an air of confidence, rather than cow towing to the bank manager.

Grey suit gave a slight nod in acknowledgment, "We'll check with Mr Peters, I'll ring him now on his mobile phone." He then looked at Jeff for a reaction — there wasn't one. "Just to make sure everything is in order," he said with an air of condescension.

Jeff knew that Bates was playing games with him, as this was unusual behaviour for identification checking, as he'd already given the bank all relevant cross-checking detailed information on the previous withdrawal. "Fair enough," he replied, with a slight shrug of his shoulders.

The manager looked at the notes on his clipboard, touched the Windsor of his grey tie, then pulled out his mobile phone from his right-hand jacket pocket. He dialled Jeff's mobile number, then held the phone to his right ear. What Jeff didn't know, was that Bates was trying to ascertain whether or not money laundering was afoot, hence his charade was to try and flush out and panic Jeff. The phone was dead. "Em, it looks like Mr Peters is unavailable, not to worry."

That's a shame, I wanted a nice chat with him, Jeff was tempted to say, but remained silent, looking at Bates' name badge, trying to guess what the T stood for, and keeping an air of nonchalance.

Grey suit's bluff hadn't drawn any reaction, and he knew that he couldn't refuse Jeff's withdrawal request, as he'd already given all the relevant security information on his previous visit. *Still it was worth a try,* he thought. *Besides it makes a change from the usual day-to-day stuff.* He decided to have a parting swipe at Jeff. "On this occasion I'll sanction your request," he said with a haughty tone.

"Thank you so much," Jeff replied, in a camp, patronising manner. He stretched his legs out, hoping to trip the bank manager up, as Bates got out of his chair and started to walk towards the counter and offices.

Mr T Bates stepped over Jeff's outstretched legs, just clipping Jeff's right shin with the heel of his right shoe. Jeff winced slightly, Grey suit had the last laugh after all. He didn't apologise. "See the cashier for your money," he quipped, without looking at Jeff. "You'll have to join the back of the queue, I'm afraid." Returning Jeff's camp, patronising tone, pointing to the end of the queue, still without gaining eye contact, as he made his way back to his office.

Jeff thought he heard Batesy whisper, 'lying tosser' when he first moved out of his chair, but he wasn't absolutely sure. He rubbed his right shin a couple of times with his right palm, then sauntered off to the end of the queue, which was now four strong, glancing to his left, watching Bates disappear into his office. Bates never looked back, wearing an expression of smug satisfaction. The queue, comprising, in order: an elderly lady, a young woman in her mid-twenties, and a suited and booted man in his late thirties, soon went down. Jeff just looked around the bank, taking in the decor and general ambience. *I wouldn't like to work here for long,* he thought.

"Next please." The cashier broke Jeff's thoughts. He was just about to develop a plan of action to liven Grey suit's establishment up.

He handed the female cashier his withdrawal slip. "All in twenties please." The young woman flicked her long brown hair off her shoulders, then proceeded to put a bundle of twenty-pound notes into a banknote counter. Jeff noticed the counter had ultraviolet ink, magnetic ink and strip counterfeit detection. The machine quickly counted out the one hundred and twelve notes. Once collated, she added the single ten-pound note for a total of two thousand two hundred and fifty pounds, handing it over to Jeff with a slight smile. "Thank you," Jeff said, as he relieved her of the cash. She put the remaining twenties back in a cash drawer.

"Next please." Jeff was dismissed. He grabbed the cash with his right hand putting the money, which was in a white envelope, in the same jacket pocket as previously, zipped it up, partially zipped his jacket up and started to walk out of the bank, acknowledging the woman as he did so with a nod. Jeff walked the few paces to the main entrance and exit doors, then turned his head in the direction of Bates' office. Grey suit was watching him. The pair stared at each other expressionless, for, what seemed like ages, but was only five seconds, nobody blinked, before they both looked away at the same time. Jeff exiting the bank, whilst bank manager of a small branch, Mr T Bates, instructed another member of his team to open another service window. Jeff walked out of the bank, completely zipped up his jacket, as it was dry but cold, crossed the road and headed towards Dr Cheng's.

It didn't take Jeff long to walk the short distance to Dr Cheng's establishment. His head was pounding with indecision. *He could just forget the whole stupid idea, forgo all the money he'd spent, and go home to Anne and normality.* He was still pondering as he arrived at Cheng's clinic, when he looked up at photos fixed to the glass frontage of post-operative attractive Chinese women. Consequently, this reminded him of Chynna, and inevitably David and furthermore, the fact that he'd never have grandchildren — he opened the door and walked in.

The female receptionist greeted 'Mr Smith', then guided Jeff to the operating room, which was at the back of the clinic, next to the consultation room. She opened the door. "Mr Smith, Mr Cheng," she said, ushering Jeff into the room, closing the door behind him, and quickly returning to the reception.

"Mr Smith, good morning, Linlin will be helping me today, strip to your underwear and put that gown on." Cheng, dressed in typical surgery scrubs, greeted Jeff with a half-smile, nodded in Linlin's direction, then pointed to a patient gown, hanging on a medical privacy screen, to his left. Jeff nodded in acceptance, walked around the operating table to where Linlin was waiting, holding the gown over her left arm.

Linlin smiled at Jeff. "Stand behind this medical privacy screen please, hand me your clothes, I'll put them on clothes hangers for you."

Jeff nodded, and started to strip, taking in the room's detail, starting with Cheng's assistant.

Jeff guessed Linlin was about thirty years old, and from northern China, as she had a light skin tone. He had been paying attention to Cheng's explanation of skin colour depth. She was attractive, small and typical in build, having her long black hair tucked in a surgery hair cap. Jeff noticed she had hazel coloured eyes, which enhanced her look. Linlin thanked Jeff every time he handed her an item of his clothes, neatly putting it on a clothes hanger, then hanging it on a clothes peg on the wall. Jeff continued to scan the room.

The operating room, Jeff thought, was about the size of an average house bedroom, the walls, as was the ceiling, were finished in white matt paint, the floor, with pinewood panels. The room was sparsely furnished, the only items being tables laid out with operating tools and equipment. Once he'd finished undressing, Linlin handed Jeff a hospital patient gown to slip on. "Could you put this gown on, Mr Smith?" she said with a smile.

Jeff finally spoke. "Sure, no problem." Whilst Jeff struggled getting into the gown and tying it up from the back, he glanced to his right to see what Dr Cheng was doing. Cheng was busying himself by laying out various surgical equipment, including different sized knife blades and forceps, clamps, scissors, hooks, adhesive tape and dressings, muttering to himself as he did so. "Okay, I think I'm ready," Jeff said, as he stepped from behind the screen.

"Excellent," Cheng replied. "Mr Smith, can you lie on the operating table, we will commence immediately." Jeff did as instructed, positioning his head so it was directly under a bright, adjustable light. "Now," Cheng leaned over Jeff, giving him a half-smile, "I will talk you through the process as I perform this operation, if at any time you feel a bit of pain, just tap the table, okay, Mr Smith?"

Jeff had closed his eyes, as the overhead light was blinding. He just about understood what Cheng was saying, as he spoke through his mask. "Yes, that's all right with me, you'd better start before I come to my senses."

Cheng tittered, then said, "I'm going to inject anesthetiser into your eyelids first, then your nose. once it has worked we will commence. I'll start with your left eye. Linlin, the needles please." Cheng proceeded to inject anaesthetic into Jeff's eyelids and nose, waited a few minutes, then pinched his left eyelid. "Can you feel anything, Mr Smith?"

Jeff muttered, "No."

Cheng then scratched his eyelid. "And now?"

"No."

Cheng slipped on his binocular loupe magnifying lenses, then commenced the surgery. As he started to talk Jeff through it, Jeff imagined that Cheng imagined, he was lecturing learned scholars. "I'm making two incisions in the top eyelid, thus removing the saggy, aged flesh, forming an eyelid without folds." *Cheng looked at his audience, who were in awe at their master.* "Many western women have this procedure to enhance their looks, what they don't realise is that, in effect, when they feel tired, their eyes look like slits." *The audience applauded Cheng's observation.* Cheng then clicked his fingers to Linlin to hand him the needle and nylon. "This is the most important role, Mr Smith, anybody can use a scalpel, suturing, the medical device used to repair wounds, requires skill and patience — my forte. On your eyelids I will suture using a non-absorbable, small diameter, point seven, nylon thread, which is a natural monofilament, stitching continuously, over and over style. This helps distribute tension along the single length of your stitched cut." *The audience cheered Cheng as his performed this delicate procedure, using a small needle with superb skill.* He then made a slight cut in the left-hand corner of each eyelid. "I'm making a slight cut, and then I'll stitch the wound, this will encourage the eyelids to close slightly, again enhancing the 'squint eyed' look." Cheng, looking through his magnified lenses, inspected his work. "Yes, it's looking very good." Cheng then repeated the same procedure with Jeff's right eye. The blepharoplasty took one and a quarter hours.

Cheng then started the rhinoplasty. "I'm going to just shave a fraction off your nose bone, just to reduce it slightly, then change the shape cutting and shaping the lower end, the lower lateral, consisting of cartilage and tissue." Cheng made an incision and proceeded as he described. "It's a shame, Mr Smith, as your nose, which is straight, called Greek, is considered the most attractive, I'm changing it to a snub shape. Most of my rhinoplasty for European people is reshaping a Roman nose, also called an aquiline or eagle or a hook shape. I perform surgery on a few Nubian noses, to reduce the base width and raise the nasal bridge." *The audience cheered their master's skill and knowledge.* Cheng, with Linlin's occasional assistance, continued to manipulate and shape Jeff's nose, his fingers scampering over Jeff's face. Jeff thought they felt like the pads of a tarantula's feet. Cheng completed the surgery with neat stitching, this time using interrupted separate stitches. On inspecting his work, he said, "Right, Mr Smith, the surgery is complete, Linlin will clean the area and then I'll finish the procedure." *The audience stood and applauded Cheng, who waved at his adoring fans.*

Linlin, cleaned Jeff's face, using disinfectant wipes, removing the smears of blood, then asked him how he felt. Jeff, who had hardly spoken since walking into Cheng's establishment, whispered, "Not too bad." The truth was, he felt terrible.

Cheng, who had stood to one side, returned to the table. "I'm going to protect your nose by placing a metal nasal splint on it, and then finally bandaging the area." He proceeded, finishing by taping the bandages to Jeff's cheeks. Jeff had been in 'theatre' for three hours in total. "That's it Mr Smith, I'm very pleased with the operation. Before Linlin takes you to the recuperation room I must insist on you doing the following." Cheng, who had removed his binocular loupe, hair cap and gloves, stood, arms folded, looking directly at Jeff, who, by this time, was sitting on the operating table.

He took a sip of water. "You must avoid blowing your nose and have a bath, not a shower. You should eat a high fibre diet so as to avoid," he coughed, "constipation, and clean your teeth gently. Please wear front fastening clothes and avoid glasses and the sun." *Cheng's adoring fans stood up and applauded their master, who had delivered an expert performance, from the first injection to the post operation aftercare explanation.*

Jeff nodded slightly in agreement. Linlin helped him to his feet, as he shuffled to the screen to remove the gown and get dressed, again with her assistance. Linlin gently held Jeff's right arm. "I'll take you to the recuperation room now, Mr Smith, are you sure you're okay?"

Jeff, who had a splitting headache, and, although he wasn't in pain, felt like he'd been in a car crash. "Yes, I feel all right, just a bit groggy, that's all," he lied. "Can I please have a drink of water?"

"Of course, first, let's get you to the recovery room, where you can lie down, then I'll get you a drink, are you sure you don't want a cup of tea?" Linlin helped Jeff through a door at the back of the room, which led to a staircase to the first floor of the building. Jeff held the banister and slowly ascended the stairs. Linlin climbed behind him, just in case he lost his balance, making reassuring comments. "It's the first door on the right, it's open, go straight in." The room, which was one of four on the first floor, was typical in size and layout of a small bedroom. A large single bed was placed centrally against the main wall, which was decorated with beige emulsion paint, next to it was a small cabinet; they were the room's only furniture. A large window, positioned opposite the door, radiated daylight. "I'll close the blinds for you."

Jeff walked three paces to the bed, took his shoes off, then lay on it, resting his head on two thick pillows. "I'll get your drink now, and then leave you to rest, you've had quite an ordeal." She walked out, returning with a glass of cold water, placing it on the cabinet. "Take small sips, I'll come and see you in a while, if you need painkillers, just shout, I'll be in the next room."

"Okay, thanks." Jeff took a sip of water and watched Linlin leave the room. Jeff put the glass down, and laid on the bed, closed his eyes and tried to sleep, dreading the pain once the anaesthetic had worn off. Whilst resting his head on the pillows, he tried to kid himself that he was in a nightmare, and would wake up, either at the Travelodge, or better still, at home in Anne's arms: after several minutes, he dozed off.

Jeff eventually went into a deep sleep, a consequence of the anaesthetic and the anxiety of the operation, plus his jousting with Mr T Bates. When he eventually awoke, Linlin, who unbeknown to him, had been occasionally popping in to see if he was comfortable, greeted him with two painkillers and a fresh tumbler of cold water. "Take these Mr Smith." She placed the capsules in his left hand. "Do you feel up to going home?"

Jeff swallowed the painkillers, one at a time. "Yes, I think so." She assisted him putting his shoes and jacket on, then guided Jeff down the stairs and eventually out of the clinic. Linlin handed him a packet of extra strong pain relief, and an instruction sheet with the aftercare operation guidelines, the written version of what Cheng had barked at him. "Thank you, Mr Smith, be careful, and we'll see you in five days, to have the stitches removed." Linlin started to close the door. "If you need anything, just call," she said, in an offhand tone. With that she was gone.

Jeff slipped his cap on, luckily he'd left it in his jacket, positioning the peak to cover the top half of his face. He decided to walk back to Pimlico for two reasons. One, he wanted the fresh air and exercise, and two, he didn't want nosey parkers staring at him on the tube. It took him forty minutes to walk the two miles back to the Travelodge, fortunately it wasn't sunny or raining, but overcast with a slight breeze. Jeff initially struggled to keep his eyes open. *It's like peeping through a narrow keyhole,* he thought. His breathing through his nose felt strange. Once in his room, he lay on the bed to rest his eyes and then practiced Chinese using the iPad; he didn't have an appetite for a meal. Jeff started to feel slight pain at nine thirty in the evening, mainly, but not solely, to his nose bone, so he pinched two extra strong painkillers out of their wrapper, and swallowed them with a glass of water. The pain faded after fifteen minutes. Just before going to bed, he carefully dabbed around his face with a damp face towel. Then, for the first time since cleaning his teeth that morning, looked in the mirror, noticed the bruising around his eyes and cheeks. *Fuck me, I look a mess,* he thought.

The following two days quickly went by, the only time Jeff ventured out was for his lunch, a takeaway plus fruit, his only meal of the day, which was consumed whilst walking along the river Thames. He followed Dr Cheng's post-operative advice, as and when applicable. He handheld the shower head to wash his body, taking care to keep his face dry. Jeff noticed the pain intensity ease slightly by Friday afternoon, consequently he decided to reduce the amount of extra strong painkillers to one and try and ride out the discomfort. He spent most of his time in the room, intensifying his Chinese understanding and speaking, in particular listening and talking fast. His eyes still irritated him, Jeff felt like he was squinting and where Cheng had stitched the corners together, it tugged. *I must speak to Cheng about this,* he mused, whilst getting ready to go out. It was eight o'clock Friday evening, time to meet The Scribe.

CHAPTER THIRTY-SIX

Martin (Marty) Dereks hummed away to the track being played on his turntable, looking in the mirror, whilst adjusting his wig. He preferred listening to vinyl, and always played his favourite LP, *Dark Side of the Moon*, by Pink Floyd, before meeting his customers. Marty was forty-two years of age, just above average height and medium build, with blue-grey eyes and a good head of dark brown hair, cut short. Dereks had a good physique, working out daily in his abode, was reasonably good looking, and could 'handle himself' if required — which was rarely.

Marty lived alone in a first floor flat in Soho, central London. He worked for many years, and still did occasionally, as a hair and make-up specialist for film and television actors; his specialty was make-up. His father, 'Phil the Lip' taught him his other trade when he was a young lad, as 'the Lip' was one of the top forgers in London. Consequently by the time Marty was fourteen years of age, he was already competent at forging currency, in particular twenty-pound notes. Marty lost his father when he was seventeen, as Phil, living up to his name, was overheard in a pub, bragging about forging fifty-pound notes for a well-known East End gangster family, who, on finding out, shot him, and threw the Lip's dead body into the Thames. Marty, whose mother left him and his father when he was a toddler, due to the Lip's criminal activities, had been on his own ever since.

On leaving school, Marty pursued a career in acting, enrolling on a drama course at a local college, but became more interested in the production side of acting. He was fascinated by the transformation of actors after visiting the hair and make-up team, in particular the make-up. Eventually, after two years of drama training, he transferred over to the hair and make-up course, thus being a competent hairdresser but became a very good make-up artist.

Whilst attending the college course, he continued to develop his forgery skills, and started to build up a client base, initially for easily to forge documents, then to currency and passports. Contacts were made on the web. Marty, using a variety of pseudonyms, would eventually meet his clients in disguise, once he'd triple-checked their credentials. Consequently nobody knew what he really looked like, including the police, or where he lived — he didn't want to go 'swimming with the fish' in the Thames. Due to his reputation for attention to detail and extreme skill level, he soon became a sought-after forger, therefore, mixing with high level criminals, who were both wealthy and dangerous. Marty always met his clients in a variety of public places, and paid different lookouts to 'scout ahead', before he made a quick, brief entrance and departure, insisting his clients were easily recognisable and alone. If potential clients didn't like his modus operandi, he didn't work for them, regardless of any monetary persuasion. It was Marty's way or the highway.

Once Marty completed his diploma, he worked as a freelance hair and make-up contractor, travelling wherever he was requested, working on a variety of productions, from major films, to dramas and soap operas. Although the earnings weren't high, and the hours were long, he enjoyed his work, especially if an actor, or extra, required transforming, either to a grotesque disfigurement or extra-terrestrial. He also occasionally stepped onto the other side of the camera, if one of the actors, or background artists didn't show, as assistant directors knew he had acting experience and training. In his mid-thirties, Dereks joined an amateur dramatics group, as he still enjoyed working on the stage, whilst helping out with the hair and make-up for his fellow thespians. Marty had never married, nor had ever had a steady relationship, he preferred one-night stands, very often paying for it, and of course, he'd be in disguise. His life had always revolved around his three passions: working for film production in the hair and make-up department; amateur dramatics; and his main income — top-notch forgery.

Dereks tapped his right foot to the beat, the black vinyl shining as it spun around the turntable at thirty-three revolutions per minute. He was now pressing the beard and moustache firmly onto his face, making sure all the adhesive he'd previously brushed on was covered. Once secured, he moved his mouth to mimic talking, looking in the mirror for any loose fitting, then smiled — all good so far. Marty then smeared ageing cream on his face, purposely creating wrinkles by grinning and frowning, then put a squirt of cream on the back of his hands, rubbing them together to produce the wrinkled effect. Once satisfied, he then took a brush and small tub of tooth dye from the middle drawer of his make-up desk, and coloured his brilliant white teeth to look unhealthy and rotten, continuously looking in the mirror whilst doing so. He rechecked his silver-grey-haired wig, making sure the securing clips were hidden, pushed his thick grey beard and moustache against his face, looked in the mirror, then muttered to himself, "Time to put the rags on."

He methodically and carefully slipped his costume on, which was neatly hung on a clothes rail fixed to the back wall of the room, with the rest of his other costumes, all neatly separated from one another. First on was a black shirt, then dark brown corduroy trousers, supported by braces, followed by a dark brown knitted jumper. He then slipped on a pair of dark brown brogues, slightly oversized, so he couldn't walk properly, this enhanced his shuffle gait. Dereks then put on his long, mid-brown overcoat, reached for his walking stick, which had a heavy, chrome plated capstick handle. Marty converted the end of the cane, by inserting a sharp, steel point, covering it with a rubber end cap. He took the plain glass, gold rimmed spectacles off the dressing table, and slipped them on, making sure he didn't disturb his hairpiece. Dereks then shuffled around the room, bending forward, muttering to himself in a hoarse voice, then checked his pockets to make sure all that he required was in its place. He was almost ready.

After a few minutes of rehearsal, he walked to the table and picked up a passport, putting it carefully into his deep, inside coat pocket. The passport, a United Kingdom one, proved quite a challenge to Marty, due to mainly forging the Chinese visa, but also in scanning the photographs he'd been given to by the client. Marty bought the original passport off Roy 'Fingers' Brant, who pickpocketed an unsuspecting traveller at Heathrow airport, leaving it in an agreed location for Marty to pick up — in disguise of course.

Dereks looked in the mirror for one final check, he half smiled to himself, he was ready. Marty turned the turntable off, and commenced to leave his accommodation, mobile phone in hand as he did so. He called a taxi company to pick him up, it was now eight forty-five p.m. It wouldn't take long to drive to the pub. The taxi quickly arrived, Marty gave the driver the destination, then made another call.

"Is he there yet?"

Ryan answered his phone. "No."

"Okay, I'll be arriving soon, message me as soon as he arrives."

"Will do." Ryan looked at Olivia, they were standing in the bar of The Slaughtered Wolf, close to the toilet area.

Marty was paying them one hundred pounds to perform a simple but important role. His instructions were to go into the pub, buy a drink each, once the punter was spotted, one would walk to the toilets with a small suitcase, phone Marty, then open the fire exit door. Marty had met the pair on London Bridge, offering them one hundred pounds for five minutes' work, as long as they followed his instructions explicitly. He was, of course, in disguise. He contacted them by using a burner phone, which he would throw away later that evening. Marty's phoned pinged. It was time to meet Lone Wolf.

CHAPTER THIRTY-SEVEN

Jeff, dressed in black trousers and shirt, walked at a steady pace. He'd gauged the timing of his journey, as to arrive at The Slaughtered Wolf just before nine o'clock in the evening, meet with The Scribe, then go straight back to his accommodation via the tube. He'd worn his cap every time he went out, with the peak purposely pulled down, to cover most of his face. The last thing he wanted was stares from nosey parkers, looking at his bruises and nose bandages. Jeff approached the front of the pub and glanced at his watch, he was relieved to note it was five to nine, *just right* he thought. He turned to his left and noticed more motorcycles outside the pub than his two previous visits, they were being, what Jeff thought, *guarded by the prospect.*

Jeff entered The Slaughtered Wolf, unzipped his jacket, walked head down, heading straight for the agreed meeting area, almost bumping into one of the WORAD chapter. "Watch what you're fucking doing, now fuck off," was the Sergeant at Arms' friendly snarl. Jeff, due to the lowness of the cap peak, couldn't see clearly in front of himself in a crowded area. He had to be more careful. Jeff noticed that there were a lot more bikers in the pub than before, and the atmosphere seemed strained and somewhat aggressive. He carefully manoeuvred himself around the group, surreptitiously glancing at them as he did; he didn't like what he saw. Some of the group were cut and bruised, to various degrees of severity, they all seemed 'tooled up' with hammers, heavy chains and metal bars, hanging from their belts, partially hidden from view. *It looked like a war party!* Jeff thought.

The pub was busy, it was a typical Friday night atmosphere, plenty of chatter and good humour — except for the WORAD chapter. Jeff wormed his way to the designated meeting area without further ado. Unfortunately all the seats were taken, so he stood by the toilet entry doors, next to Olivia and Ryan, who'd just put his phone away. They were standing in their usual position, both with a drink in hand, Ryan had the same suitcase as before. When Jeff arrived, Ryan instantly walked out to the toilets, Olivia remained at the bar, next to Jeff, who didn't bother ordering a drink. Ryan opened the fire exit door and waited for The Scribe to shuffle into the pub, he then stood by the door as The Scribe entered the bar, and quickly spotted Jeff.

"Follow me," he hissed. "We're not doing business here." The Scribe, on seeing there wasn't any seating available, shuffled back out into the toilet area, followed by Jeff. Olivia remained in the bar, seemingly to block the doors. "I see you've had the 'op' then."

Jeff, not in the mood for wisecracks, replied, "Let's get this quickly over with, here's the rest of the money." He reached into his inside jacket pocket and took out an envelope, passing it to The Scribe.

The Scribe took the envelope, but this time he counted the cash, making sure it was all there. "Excellent Lone Wolf, here's your passport." Whilst holding the cane with his left hand, he took the passport out of his inside left coat pocket, and handed it to the somewhat bemused Jeff, whilst replacing it with the money. Olivia, followed by a biker, walked through the door leading to the toilets, stopping by Ryan, who still held the fire exit door open. The biker, with an expression of suspicion, looked at the four of them, then continued to the male toilets.

Jeff checked his passport. "Um, looks very good," he said, looking The Scribe in the eyes as he commented. "I'll follow you out that door, let's go." Jeff started to walk towards Ryan, putting the passport in his inside jacket pocket.

The Scribe stuck his cane out. "No you fucking won't," he snarled. "You'll go back through the pub and exit from the front, fucking door, now fuck off." He threw Jeff a look of sheer disdain, then pointed his walking stick towards the toilet's entry door.

Just as Jeff was about to challenge The Scribe, the biker walked out of the men's toilets. "What the fuck's going on here?"

Jeff noticed the biker's patch: Sergeant at Arms, more worryingly he had an axe on his left waist, wedged between his belt and jeans plus he'd a black eye and a front tooth missing — things could go awry. The biker, six foot three inches tall and weighing two hundred and twenty pounds looked menacing. *This guy could take us all out,* Jeff thought. *No problem.* It was a tense moment.

"Oh nothing, thank you," The Scribe replied, in a pleasant friendly tone, smiling whilst doing so. "See you my friend." He pointed to Jeff with a slight wave. "Come on you two let's go," he said, shuffling towards Ryan and Olivia. The three of them started to walk out of the fire exit door, Jeff took the hint and moved, following The Scribe's instructions, opening the toilet's entry door for the disgruntled biker, who walked through it without thanking him.

Jeff continued to walk through the crowded bar, keeping his left hand close to his face shielding it from mainly accidental knocks, but also from casual gazes. He didn't have to worry about the onlookers, as other customers were engrossed in their own conversations. They weren't remotely interested in a strange looking man wearing a white baseball cap, with his left hand shielding his face. Jeff exited the pub, zipped his jacket up to his neck and headed for the nearest tube station. It was a cold, late October evening, he didn't want to hang about. He wouldn't venture out again, apart from buying his daily meal, until Monday, to have his stitches removed.

The Scribe shuffled towards the waiting taxi, having already paid Ryan and Olivia their one hundred pounds; they would never see him again. He instructed the cab driver to take the long route back to his flat, so he could check if they were being followed, by constantly looking out of the rear window. Once satisfied there were no tailers, he told the cabbie to pull over close to where he lived, within a couple of minutes' walk, or shuffle in his case. He waited for the cab to drive off, had a quick glance about. He then pulled out a pair of black ballet shoes, from deep inside his right jacket pocket, flicked his brogues off and quickly put them on. Dereks picked the brogues up and briskly walked to his flat, his cane under his left armpit. He could now run if he had to.

CHAPTER THIRTY-EIGHT

Anne Peters was at her wit's end, it was now nearly a week since she last saw or spoke to Jeff, she was beginning to fear the worst. The police had kept her up to date with the investigation, unfortunately, all their news was not what she wanted to hear. She had pinned her hopes on a DNA test, on the remaining cindered bones from Jeff's incinerated car. Unluckily, the forensic scientist couldn't get a proper profile, as the bone samples were too badly fire damaged, consequently the police didn't pursue DNA testing from Jeff's parents. They informed her that the vehicle inspectors, after a thorough check, discovered loose electrical wiring by the petrol tank, which, more than likely, caused a spark to arc across and ignite the tank. Anne recalled that Jeff was fiddling with the back of the car, the Saturday his disappeared. *Was he repairing or damaging the wiring,* she mused.

The inspector who kept her updated, was quite candid with the results of her investigation, although nothing was conclusive. All findings pointed towards Mr Peters, in a moment of overwhelming depression due to the death of his son, filled his car with petrol, drove to a desolated place, then ignited it. She informed Anne that it could well have been an accident. He could have changed his mind, but it was too late, with the fire consuming him before he had chance to get out of his car. No one will ever know for sure. The other factor was the body, if it wasn't Jeff, who was it? Nobody had been reported missing, and, what's more, Jeff had disappeared, leaving all his belongings either in the car or at home, plus the CCTV footage showing Jeff, alone, filling his car and jerry cans with petrol. What was strange a couple of officers thought, was when Jeff put the cans of petrol into the boot of his car, he seemed to pause, carefully placing them, so as not to disturb something. The angle of the garage camera was such that it only showed the front of the car.

"I'm sorry to say, Mrs Peters, but all the evidence indicates Mr Peters died in the car. We will not be pursuing the investigation further," was the last thing she said to Anne.

Anne, an intelligent woman, knew it was the obvious conclusion, and was relying on the DNA testing to finalise the report. She now had the arduous duty to inform family and close friends of Jeff's death, then arrange his funeral. Her nerves were being tested to the limit.

CHAPTER THIRTY-NINE

Micary looked at his watch, it was nine thirty a.m. Friday morning, Jeff hadn't turned up for work or informed him that he was sick. *Most strange and out of character,* Micary thought. He was hoping that Jeff would change his mind and stay on at the mortuary, because he thought quite highly of him. He reflected on Jeff's last day, the previous Friday, and how conscientious Jeff had worked. It seemed to Micary that Jeff was a happy, contented employee. He was impressed by how Jeff volunteered, without any persuasion, to get the corpse ready for the incinerator, on Saturday, the following day, working overtime without extra pay, then tidied up and drove home without having a shower. *What a great guy,* Micary thought. Micary then reflected on the cremation of the corpse that Jeff had prepared, it burnt rather quickly, but unusually left a couple of large bone fragments that required grinding to dust.

Micary decided to ring Jeff on his mobile phone, to find out if he's coming to work, or if he's decided to finish and go elsewhere. Not surprisingly, Jeff's phone didn't ring. *Strange,* he thought. *Very strange, perhaps he's decided to get another job, or has gone on holiday. Ah well, it was good while it lasted, I'll miss him though.* His thoughts about Jeff were interrupted by the mortician, who needed a hand in the laboratory.

CHAPTER FORTY

Jeff felt upbeat for the first time in a long while, as he briskly walked to Cheng's for the removal of his stitches. It was lunchtime Monday afternoon. He'd spent the vast majority of his time since the operation in his room, practicing Chinese, plus the occasional dabble at using chopsticks to pick objects up off the table. He only ventured out for his lunch and the visit to The Slaughtered Wolf.

He reflected on the last time he met with The Scribe and wondered whether or not he was in disguise; he still couldn't make his mind up. One factor that gave Jeff second thoughts, was how The Scribe's body posture seemed to change, just for a few seconds, when he stopped Jeff from going outside. It was that of a younger, fitter man. He deduced that, although The Scribe was an articulate, clever man, he could also be a nasty piece of work, plus he looked like he was quite prepared to use the walking stick as a weapon if necessary. Jeff had plenty of time in his room to examine The Scribe's workmanship, concluding that he was a master of his craft; the fake passport was a work of art. Jeff's thoughts about The Scribe were disrupted, squinting through his eyes he could see Cheng's clinic. *I can't wait to get these bandages off,* he thought.

Jeff was greeted by the female receptionist as he breezed into the clinic. "This way Mr Smith, Mr Cheng is waiting for you." She escorted Jeff into the same room as the operation. Cheng greeted him, wearing a mask plus the binocular loupes, which were positioned on his forehead.

"Good to see you, Mr Smith, how have you been feeling?" Cheng said, with a faint smile, he didn't offer his diminutive hand for a shake. "I hope you've heeded my advice regarding the post-operative procedures, in particular," he quietly coughed, "your dietary needs."

Jeff looked around the room. Linlin wasn't present, however, he noticed the door leading to the first floor was slightly ajar. Jeff gave

Cheng a quick glance and nod, slightly changing the subject. "My eyes are still irritating me, I'm struggling to see through them."

Cheng, wearing a white laboratory coat and black flannels, returned Jeff's nod, whilst pointing to the operating table, his expression was neutral. "I'm not surprised, it will take another week before your new eyelids build up enough strength to fully open. Now please lie on the table, let's get these sutures out."

Jeff took his cap off, did as instructed, lying on his back, his head on one pillow. "Em, I'll start with the eyes first, you shouldn't feel any pain, it might be slightly uncomfortable, that's all," Cheng mumbled through a health face mask, slipping on his binocular loupes. "I must first check to see if the wound is fully healed, as it's been only five days, the minimum time for sutures to be removed after surgery." Cheng peered intensely at Jeff's eyelids. "You see, Mr Smith, we remove the stitches from facial surgery as soon as possible, to avoid scarring and stitch marks, however, the wound must be completely healed, regardless."

Jeff, although appreciating Cheng's professional knowledge, was dreading another lecture from 'Professor Cheng'. He felt like shouting, "Just get on with it Cheng, cut the cackle out." But instead, meekly replied, "Is it looking okay?"

"Perfect, now keep still." Carefully using tweezers and minute scissors, he gently pulled the nylon knot with the tweezers, slipping the scissors underneath, cutting the stitch, followed by pulling the nylon through the skin. Jeff felt a tingling sensation as the thread wriggled through his left eyelid — first stitch out. Cheng proceeded to remove the stitches at the corner of his left eye, repeating the process to Jeff's right eye, placing all the nylon in a small stainless steel tray. "Excellent, you can now blink."

Jeff blinked three times. *Yes, that does feel easier and more comfortable*, he thought.

Cheng put the scissors and tweezers down. "Now let's get these bandages off, and have a look at your new nose." Cheng gently pulled at the plasters that were keeping the bandages in place. Jeff felt a very slight tugging sensation. Once all the bandaging was removed, he carefully took off the protective metal splint. "Taking shape nicely," he muttered blandly, putting the bandages, plasters and splint into the tray. He proceeded to remove the nasal stitches. "Some of these are individual, so it will take a moment longer." A few minutes later, he declared, "That's it, Mr Smith, all done."

Jeff instinctively twitched his nose, whilst starting to rise from the table. Cheng stood back, removing the binocular loupes at the same time. "The bruising is now yellow-green, it will gradually fade over the next few days. Within another week the surgery will be unnoticeable — from a distance anyway." Cheng pointed to a mirror, fixed to the main wall. "Have a look at your new face, Mr Smith, I'm pleased with the outcome. What do you think?"

This was the moment Jeff was dreading. As he walked a couple of paces to the mirror, he initially closed his eyes, gradually opening them, squinting at first. His nose, as described by 'Professor Cheng' was flatter and wider, he'd definitely lost the Greek look. Jeff moved his face closer to the mirror. *I don't like the look, but he's made a good job of the surgery, I'll give him that,* he thought.

Cheng, who was oblivious to the real reason Jeff had the surgery, was a bit more upbeat. "Once you put the make-up on, brown contact lenses, not forgetting the black hair dye, you'll definitely pass as partly Chinese, make no mistake about it."

Jeff continued to study his uglier face. "That's the main thing, I guess," he replied, in a somewhat half-hearted tone, whilst admiring Cheng's handiwork. *He certainly knows how to stitch,* he thought. He then turned to Cheng, and they shook hands. "Thanks, I'll be on my way."

"Smear a small amount of petroleum jelly on the wounds to avoid them drying out, thus improving the healing and eventual appearance," Cheng said, as Jeff started to leave the room.

"Will do, goodbye."

Jeff nodded at the receptionist as he walked out of Cheng's. At last he felt 'normalish', it was a relief. Jeff, deep in thought, started the walk back to Pimlico without feeling conscious of people staring at him, although he still kept his cap on. *Passport, surgery, I'm all set, let's get this nightmare over with.* Once back in his room, he powered up the iPad, searching for cheap flights to Shanghai.

CHAPTER FORTY-ONE

Jeff was feeling nervous, he felt a similar sensation to when he entered the bank for his first joust with Batesy. He held his passport in his right hand, tapping it nervously against his right leg, pretending he was drumming to a favourite tune, whilst trying to look calm. The couple in front of him moved to the check-in counter, it wouldn't be long now, he was next.

Ten minutes later. "Next please," the Chinese airline check-in assistant said, looking straight at Jeff. Jeff dressed smart casual, wearing trousers and shirt, walked the three paces to the check-in desk, wearing a pleasant smile. "Boarding pass and passport please," she said, holding out her left hand. Jeff guessed she was in her early thirties, she had her long black hair tied up, and was typical in size, stature and looks for a northern Chinese woman. She checked the boarding pass first. "That's okay," she said giving it back to Jeff, who kept his pleasant demeanour, trying to look nonchalant. She then scrutinised his passport, or Peter Jefferys (Bídé Jié fú lísī), as it was written by the Home Office officials, or The Scribe in Jeff's case. Her facial expression changed from professionally warm, to concern, she was looking at Jeff's photo. "Em, wait there Mr Jié fú lísī, I won't to a minute." She took the passport to a senior looking man, who was hovering in the background a few paces behind her. They started muttering in Chinese, whilst looking at the photograph and Jeff simultaneously. Jeff couldn't quite make out what they were discussing. Their conversation went on for a couple of minutes, and Jeff's nerves were being tested. Finally she came back, her supervisor stood just behind her. "When was this photograph taken, Mr Jié fú lísī?"

Jeff, trying to act blasé, joked, "It was taken in one of my better moments." He chuckled after he said it.

"This is no laughing matter Mr Jié fú lísī, this photo looks years younger than you look now." Her tone was one of bemusement. "Can you please answer the question?"

Jeff started to sweat, he hoped the face cream he'd applied a couple of hours previously didn't smudge. "It was taken at the same time I applied for the passport, eight years ago," he replied, keeping the friendly facade going. "Unfortunately I had a slight motorcycle accident last year, plus my wife recently left me, it's clearly taken its toll, as you can see." *Go for the sympathy factor,* he thought. Jeff had overlooked that the computer image Cheng created was too perfect, not having the 'lines of life' that he now had.

You can say that again, she thought. "I suggest you get this passport renewed as soon as possible, with an up-to-date photograph. Now, let me check the visa."

Jeff's split-second moment of relief over the photograph was soon forgotten; he was hoping, or inwardly praying, that The Scribe's workmanship was as good as he thought it was. What seemed like an eternity, but was in fact thirty-five seconds went by, she then closed the passport, giving it and the boarding pass back to Jeff. "Have you any luggage to check-in?"

"No, just this carry-on bag."

She glanced at the bag sitting to Jeff's left and shrugged. "Have a nice flight."

Jeff, still with a certain amount of external calmness, felt like wiping his forehead with the back of his right hand whilst saying 'phew', however, replied, "Thank you." He put the documents in his inside jacket pocket, picked his bag of hand luggage up with his left hand, and casually walked off, giving the woman a slight smile in the process. Jeff, or Mr Jié fú lísī, negotiated airport security without an issue, eventually arriving at gate three, terminal five, London Heathrow Airport. He'd got forty-five minutes to wait before boarding his flight to Shanghai.

Jeff sat as far away from the other passengers as was possible, placing his bag on the seat next to him to act as a barrier. He wasn't in the mood for idle chat. Whilst sitting in the departure lounge, his mind drifted back to the recent events since leaving Cheng's, ten days previously.

He'd spent most of his time practicing Chinese, in particular, polishing his local Shanghai accent, speaking and listening intently; he was now fluent. Jeff could also write Chinese to a competent standard but found that part of language a bit monotonous. He stuck to his one large midday meal, enjoying various takeouts plus fruit, consuming it whilst ambling along the Thames, weather permitting of course. Jeff kept up the practice with the chopsticks, not only picking small items up with them, but placing them by his mouth, mimicking eating. He took Cheng's advice regarding the petroleum jelly, buying a small tub from a general store on the return journey from the plastic surgeon's, applying it every time he gently washed his face. The bruising took another five days to completely disappear once the stitches had been removed.

Jeff had practiced putting the brown contact lenses into his eyes, two days before his flight. It took him forty minutes to perform this thirty-second task, mainly due to the narrowness of his eyes in addition to lack of practice. Every time he got the lens near his eye, he instinctively closed it. Eventually, once he slipped the lens onto the bottom of his right eye, he then manoeuvred it onto his pupil by closing his eye and 'feeling' it into position through his bottom eyelid — which wasn't easy. Jeff discovered wearing the contact lenses was uncomfortable, so he nipped out and bought lubricating eye drops, which semi masked the irritation. *Needs must, needs must,* he kept muttering to himself, as he practiced a few more times. It took him five minutes to insert the lenses prior to leaving his abode to catch the tube on the Piccadilly line to Heathrow.

Jeff booked the flight, an indirect one as it was a lot cheaper, the day before he flew out. It would stop in Hong Kong, before continuing northward to Shanghai. Once the flight was confirmed, he booked a cheap hotel within ten minutes' walk from where the Lee brothers lived, as he knew their address courtesy of Chynna's father, Li Wei. The price of the flight and hotel reflected Jeff's financial standing, in short, he was running out of money. The cost of the surgery and passport had used up most of the money he'd transferred into Mr Thomas Smith's account, he had to be frugal from now on.

Jeff's thoughts were temporarily interrupted. "We are now boarding the flight to Shanghai, please have your boarding passes ready," the boarding gate receptionist said, over the intercom. Jeff snapped out of his preoccupation, and looked around the departure lounge, noticing it was nearly full of fellow passengers, the vast majority of them being of Chinese origin, who now started to queue at the check-in gate. Jeff waited, he was in no rush.

His mind went back to his previous thoughts, reflecting on recently dying his hair, which he performed carefully the previous night, this time making a lot neater job. He wondered if Cheng would have approved. The last thing he did before leaving the Travelodge was to apply skin cream to his face, neck, ears and hands. He now smirked to himself thinking how effeminate he felt, massaging the ultra-light tan coloured cream onto his skin, in particular gently on his nose and top eyelids. He had to admit it, Cheng did a very good job, the surgery scars were hardly noticeable. With the cream applied, they disappeared. He felt slightly unmanly while applying the black mascara to his eyelashes and brows. *What the hell,* he thought. Jeff was once again abruptly woken from his daydreaming.

"This is the final call for the flight to Shanghai, the departure gate will close in five minutes."

Jeff, deep in preoccupation, was now the last passenger to board the aircraft, quickly picked up his travel bag, walked the three paces to the check-in desk, and gave the receptionist his boarding pass. "Thank you," was the last time he spoke English, he would converse in Chinese from the moment he boarded the aircraft. He took one final look out of the glass windows of the airport, it was pouring with rain. He wondered what the weather would be like in China, mid-November. He had twelve hours before he found out.

CHAPTER FORTY-TWO

The flight was relatively uneventful. Jeff just had the one mid-flight meal, and he tried to sleep as much as possible. His seat was towards the rear off the plane, starboard side, the seat next but one to his was occupied by an elderly Chinese man, who, Jeff deduced, was also a solo traveller. They didn't converse. When the plane landed in Hong Kong, all the passengers had to disembark. Jeff joined his fellow onward journey passengers in the departure lounge, embarking again after two hours, being accompanied by a few new travellers. His journey was completed when he passed through Chinese passport control, who scrutinised his photo in a similar manner to the check-in woman at Heathrow. The mid-twenties male kept looking at the photo in Jeff's passport, then at him, eventually stamping it, with a slight shrug of his shoulders, muttering to his male colleague. Jeff could just about make out what he said, the gist was similar to his Heathrow counterpart, referring to his present-day haggard look. Jeff, bag in hand, walked out of Shanghai International Airport at 2.23 p.m. hailing a taxi to his new accommodation. Jeff hoped it would be better than the reviews — he would be disappointed.

The journey took three-quarters of an hour, with the taxi weaving its way through the mid-afternoon traffic, which although busy, was not as bad as peak time. The driver tried to pass the time with everyday chat, but Jeff fobbed him off, preferring to gaze out of the rear right-hand passenger window, sitting diagonally opposite him. He felt quietly smug with himself though, as he could easily converse with the male driver, he even dropped in the odd slang word. He paid the driver one hundred and ten Renminbi, which included a tip, grabbed his bag and headed for the hotel reception. This would be his living quarters for the foreseeable future.

Jeff took his jacket off, and slipped his sunglasses on, as the weather was warm and dry. Shanghai had similar weather to Spain as it had the same latitudinal line, both being just north of the Tropic of Cancer.

The hotel receptionist, a man in his forties, greeted Jeff requesting his passport whilst exchanging everyday pleasantries, also handing Jeff a pro forma to fill in. Once all documentation had been completed satisfactorily, he returned Jeff's passport, whilst simultaneously giving him his room key, number thirty-four, which was on the second floor. Jeff noted the man didn't even look at the photograph, he just jotted down the number and expiry date. Jeff picked up his bag, put his jacket over it and proceeded to walk out of the foyer to the stairs which were to his right; this gave him a chance to give the hotel a quick once over. The Golden Flower, positioned midway along Guchuan Road, was built in the nineteen fifties, consisting of five floors, each having twenty-eight rooms. The decor was tired and required serious revamping. *Or better still, knocking down and rebuilding*, so Jeff thought. It had a feeling of being dirty and smelly. *I've been in smarter youth hotels.* Jeff slowly ascended the stairs, further taking in his new accommodation, nearly bumping into a fellow guest as he rounded the corner of the staircase to the first floor, which split into two corridors with fourteen rooms each. Jeff ambled along the west winged corridor, his room was approximately halfway down it. He put the room key in, then held his breath.

His initial thoughts were *what a dump.* The room was small to average in size, consisting of one single bed, a small wardrobe, shower and toilet, all of which had seen better days. The walls and ceiling were finished with magnolia matt paint, the floor with green linoleum covering, the external wall had one medium-sized window. A large photograph of Chairman Mao hung on the back wall, placed centrally above the bed. Jeff now wished he'd put more money into Mr Smith's account so he could afford at least a three star hotel's tariff, but that could have aroused Anne's suspicions, the last thing he wanted.

Jeff took a pace forward, he heard a crunch under his right shoe, lifting it to reveal a small cockroach, which he scooped up with toilet tissue, binning it — he looked at Mao for inspiration — he didn't get any. He emptied the contents of his bag onto the bed, hanging trousers, shirts and jacket in the wardrobe, undergarments and T-shirts on the bottom shelf. One thing that he had overlooked was his dress code, as it was obvious to any keen observer, that he wore western clothes, which wasn't what he desired; that had to be rectified immediately. Jeff stripped, taking a quick shower to freshen up before setting off on a quick shopping trip. The shower, much to his surprise, worked fine, he was careful not to get his face too wet, as to wash off the medium-olive skin toning cream and black mascara. He used the solitary towel to dry down, dressing in cream chinos, white short sleeved shirt and blue loafers. Jeff added a dab of cream to his arms, to conceal the white skin, then checked himself in the mirror, smearing a small amount of cream on a small white patch on his neck, which must have wiped off on the flight. He then put two eyedrops in both eyes, as the lenses were irritating his eyes; he couldn't wait to get them out. Another quick once over, touched up the mascara. *That'll do,* he thought.

Jeff descended the steps from The Golden Flower, turned right, heading for a shopping mall which he could see in the far distance, observing what other men wore on the journey. He found an appropriate general clothes shop, purchasing a light-coloured pair of flannels and two pastel coloured long-sleeved shirts, one light yellow the other beige, all clothing locally made being obviously Asian styled. On leaving the shop, Jeff decided to stretch his legs and have a good walk around; he needed to get his bearings as quickly as possible. He enjoyed the walk, the weather was dry, as it was midway through the Chinese dry season, the late afternoon temperature was a pleasant eighteen degrees Celsius. He kept his route simple and straightforward, walking in blocks, eventually coming back out onto the main road then repeating the tactic for another block, mentally remembering his route. Although Jeff was fractionally taller than the average Chinese male, he didn't stand out, seeming to blend in with the local population, who were milling around, going about their daily business, nobody staring at him or even giving him a second glance. It was quite obvious to anybody who did study his face, that he wasn't one hundred per cent Chinese, because of his skull shape, being Caucasian instead of Mongoloid. Jeff turned right at the next junction, he was now on Beishi Road, in the area where the Lee brothers lived. *So this is where those scumbags live,* he thought to himself.

Jeff slowly cased the area. His initial thoughts were, *fuck me, this is a right dump.* The four large blocks of small flats reminded him of a pigeon coop, the inclusion of litter strewn about the place made it look worse, if that could be possible. Jeff strolled along the road, eyeing all the many comings and goings. He felt sorry for the people that had to suffer living in this type of squalor. Just as Jeff was about to cross the road and take the next left junction, he noticed a couple with their daughter, struggling with their, what he assumed, was weekly shopping expedition. Feeling sorry for them, the woman in particular, he rushed towards them to give a helping hand. "Do you folks need help?"

The woman was about to accept this stranger's offer, when the man replied, "Fuck off, no we don't."

Jeff, slightly taken aback at such rudeness, just stood and gawped at this guy, the woman looked somewhat embarrassed. Jeff gave the man a good look over, there was something familiar about him, he was slight of build, had long hair tied in a ponytail accompanied by a moustache plus a small scar on his right cheek, plus a large tattoo of a cobra on his right forearm. Jeff guessed he was in his mid-twenties. His thoughts were abruptly broken.

"I told you pal, fuck off, I won't tell you again."

Jeff took the hint, the last thing he wanted was his new nose rearranged, consequently he started to walk away, heading back towards The Golden Flower. The woman cussed the man, calling him by his name, Yue, telling him the stranger was trying to be kind. He just shrugged his shoulders. "Fuck him, interfering busybody."

Jeff continued his journey to his hotel, racking his brain's about the man, he'd seen him before, but just couldn't place him. No he wasn't on the plane, no he wasn't at the shopping mall, he was just about to let it go when it suddenly dawned on him. *Yes, yes, it's got to be him*, he thought. He remembered where he'd seen the man's face, it was pinned to Inspector Chow's investigation board. He'd just met Joseph (Yuēse) Lee.

CHAPTER FORTY-THREE

Detective Inspector Chow was in a particularly sombre, remorseful mood as he walked to his car; he'd just had his weekly meeting with Mr and Mrs Ling. After the initial greetings, Mrs Ling made Chow a cup of tea. The three of them sat in their living room, Chow giving the couple an update on the investigation, which unfortunately was very brief. He gave Li Wei and Ah Lam an overview of how it had progressed, which unfortunately for them, the Peters and the police, was that it hadn't.

Chow visited the Lings in his own time, at eight o'clock every Wednesday evening, something they appreciated, in particular Mr Ling, who had grown to like DI Chow. The meeting usually only lasted twenty minutes, finishing with a gentle hug for Mrs Ling and a firm handshake from Le Wei. "I'll never stop hunting for your daughter's killers, never stop," was always his closing words. He never felt happy after this visit, but this particular Wednesday was different.

Ah Lam had given him the horrific news, that Mr Peters, in a moment of overwhelming depression, had committed suicide by setting light to his car, thus incinerating himself. Chow, who removed his tie on these meetings, asked how the Lings knew of this tragedy. After taking a long sip of tea, Mr Ling told Chow that they kept in touch with the Peters, Jeff doing most of the talking as he spoke reasonable Chinese. The last time they Skyped each other was the previous Sunday afternoon, when Anne broke the terrible news to them. She used a language app on her phone to help with the translation, as she only spoke a couple of Chinese words, breaking down when she realised that the Lings had understood her. They understandably were full of remorse, both openly weeping. The brief Skype meeting was then terminated.

Chow took the news very badly, partly blaming himself for Jeff's death, because he felt he should have arrested the Lees and held them on remand, as their alibi was far from watertight. He wanted to, but his supervisor argued there wasn't enough cast iron evidence. Chow being threatened with disciplinary action if he didn't stop ranting and raving at him. Chow didn't like not getting his own way and stormed off from his last supervisor's meeting.

He threw his suit jacket into the back of his car, he needed sustenance tonight, a couple of slugs of white lightning followed by a visit to one of his girls. He had a particularly dirty one in mind, hopefully that would do the trick, he thought. Chow drove off heading for the hovel where the Lees lived. He regularly dropped by outside their flats, purposely parking so that they, and in particular Zhān mǔ shì, knew he was there, staying for half hour or so, hoping to get on their nerves — he at least succeeded in that. After hanging around for forty-five minutes, Chow drove off with a slight wheel spin, glancing up at Zhān mǔ shì's window as he did so. Their eyes met for a second, hate in both pairs.

Chow clenched his steering wheel as he drove through the evening traffic, stopping at an off licence for the bottle of white lightening, then continued to his chosen lady's apartment. She was in for rough night — lucky girl.

CHAPTER FORTY-FOUR

Jeff zigzagged his way back to The Golden Flower, his mind deep in thought. He got temporarily lost on a couple of occasions, taking a right turn too early, but quickly rectified the situation, coming out of a junction more or less opposite to his hotel. He decided to take a nap, removing the lenses beforehand as his eyes were now very sore, and go back out again for his evening meal, then take another walk to where the brothers lived. The hotel receptionist gave him a cursory nod as he entered the hotel, he returned it, heading quickly to his room. It took several minutes to remove the lenses, discarding them into the toilet. *What a relief to get them out,* he thought, it had been the longest period of time he'd worn them. *I think I'll get a pair of tinted glasses first opportunity.*

Jeff, fresh from a couple of hours' kip, slipped on one of his new shirts, accompanied by the new flannels, then came the dreaded new contact lenses insertion. A quick check in the mirror thinking, *yes the make-up and mascara is holding out,* he then grabbed his jacket and headed out. He headed to the large shopping mall, his first stop would be a general store for the tinted glasses. He bought a pair of aviator framed, light brown tinted non-prescription spectacles, gingerly trying them on, as his nose was still very sensitive to the touch. Jeff had gotten used to the shape of it, but nevertheless he detested it, it felt like a blob to him. He put the glasses in his shirt chest pocket, then walked a couple of minutes to a restaurant translating as Happy Duck, finding a table in the far left-hand corner. Jeff ordered Sichuan pork with accompanying vegetables, washed down with iced cold water. Jeff glanced around the Happy Duck, it was, like the mall, quite busy, with a mixture of couples, families plus a few solo diners. He was inwardly pleased that nobody gave him a second glance, he certainly had no problem with the language, speaking quickly and fluently to whoever he conversed with. Jeff enjoyed the Sichuan pork, but not the accompaniments. His use of chopsticks was still slightly clumsy, and he also had to get used to eating more over his plate, scooping his food in, rather than sitting more upright. Jeff stayed in the Happy Duck for fifty minutes, paid and exited, slipping his jacket on as he left, as it was now a bit chilly. He headed into the dark evening towards the Lees' living quarters.

He walked at a brisk pace to keep warm, keeping the route simple and hopefully easy to remember the return journey. Jeff belched a couple of times as he crossed a road, bringing up the flavour of his meal in doing so, which he promptly spat out, first making sure no one was too close. He didn't particularly enjoy all of his meal, moreover, wasn't overly keen on Chinese cuisine. It was his least favourite foreign dish, preferring Italian or Indian. He continued his route, heading down Lanxi Road, which connected Guchuan Road and Beishi Road, as they ran parallel to each other, albeit some distance apart, turning sharp left at the bottom of it. Zipping his jacket up whilst crossing, he was now in their neighbourhood — Beishi Road.

Jeff knew were the Lees lived due to two reasons, the quick glance at Chow's investigation board when the sheet blew off it, and from Li Wei. During a Skype conversation, just before he and Anne travelled to Chynna's funeral, Li Wei let his feelings be known about who the suspects were and, importantly, where they lived, but not their exact flat number. That is except John's (Yuēhàn's), who lived with his parents in Block B. Chynna had told her parents where he lived, and roughly where the other two did, when she briefly went out with him. Jeff, on learning this, made a mental note, writing the details down as soon as the Skype meeting finished, fobbing Anne off with a jumbled answer, when she asked what he was writing down. At the first opportunity, he opened his laptop to a map of Shanghai, and started to draw a picture in his mind of the area he was now in, refreshing his memory by studying the map regularly. Jeff knew the area was sandwiched between two parallel major roads, Caoyang Road and Daduhe Road, with the smaller Lanxi Road situated roughly central to them, forming three equidistant parallel roads. Beishi Road and Guchuan Road were at ninety degrees to them at either end, with several other small roads forming a small network. This was to be his stomping ground for the foreseeable future, so he had to know it like the back of his hand.

Jeff slowly walked along Beishi Road, looking up at the flats within this tenement, thinking how miserable it must be living in there. He ambled past block A, then slowed down when he got to B block, checking all the exit and entry points, continuing unhurriedly to block C, scanning the block, then crossed the road and reversed his walk, back towards block A. Jeff had to have his wits about him, as this was a rough part of Shanghai, he wondered what he would do if he was confronted, being a stranger in the neighbourhood. He continued his reconnaissance, mentally noting the tenement design, before heading back up to Guchuan Road, via a couple of side roads. He was surprised that there were still plenty of people about.

Jeff returned to The Golden Flower at 10.40 p.m. and nodded to the receptionist. Once in his room, he quickly took the contact lenses out, flushing them down the loo, followed by wiping off the toning cream. After he hung his clothes up, Jeff lay on his bed contemplating his predicament. Now that he was in Shanghai, he hadn't a plan of what to do. Ten minutes past, he still wasn't any the wiser, so he switched the small television on, located on the wall opposite the photo of Moa Tse-tung, also being in about the same position. Jeff navigated the remote control to the BBC world news channel, to check on the latest developments back in Blighty. The newscaster was describing a disturbing new trend, where young women who were out at night in bars and clubs, were being drugged by another person, presumably male, injecting their drink with a drug, thus leaving them vulnerable. The newsreader went into more detail about the attacks. Jeff's mind started to whirl — a plan was hatching.

Jeff's alarm on his iPad went off at eight o'clock in the morning, he woke with a jolt as he'd been dreaming about Mike, who visited him for the first time in a while. Mike, dressed in Jeff's blazing tracksuit, was ridiculing him over his surgery, whilst flicking small chunks of pork at him, forcing him to eat it or he'd tell Anne where he was. The alarm rescued Jeff, who instinctually rubbed his stomach. *At least it wasn't a nightmare,* he thought, with a sigh of relief. He then sat up in bed, powered up the iPad and started researching the web. Research completed, he jumped in the shower, treading on a cockroach in the process, as it was running across the bathroom floor. Jeff then went through his now daily ritual of carefully toning up his face, neck and hands, thoroughly checking that the coverage of the cream was complete and even — this job couldn't be rushed. Then came the arduous task of slipping the brown lenses in, he still struggled with this, partly due to the narrowness of his slit-shaped eyes. Finally, he used black mascara on his fair eyebrows and lashes. Jeff wore the same clothes he'd worn the previous evening, putting his sunglasses in his shirt breast pocket before heading out for the day; he'd have his breakfast en route.

It didn't take too long to find the chemist in the local shopping mall, it was situated at the far end next to a small cafe and butcher's shop, which Jeff thought smelt disgusting. Jeff waited behind an elderly woman and, after a few minutes, the assistant asked him what he wanted.

"Gamma hydroxybutyrate acid please, in liquid form, plus a needle and syringe," he said with a charming smile.

The chemist's assistant, a mature woman replied, "What do you want that for?" She looked somewhat surprised.

Jeff, relying on his recent research responded, "I have terrible insomnia, I've tried sleeping pills, GHB is the only thing that will cure my sleep deprivation."

"Why do you need the needle and syringe?" she replied with a hint of suspicion.

Jeff anticipated this question. "As I said, the pills have little effect, I find the quickest and best treatment is injecting the drug, I've been using it for some time." He chanced his arm, adding the last bit.

"Em, I haven't seen you before, where do you normally get your dosage?"

Jeff kept the calm pretence, although he felt the same as he did in airport check-in. "No I haven't been here before, I've travelled from Hong Kong on business, could you give me one week's supply?" He was tempted to add more information, but thought better of it.

"I'll have it ready for you this afternoon, come back at one thirty p.m. Mr…"

"Thank you, that will not be a problem, my name is Mr…" Jeff thought for a second, he didn't know many Chinese surnames, "Flowers (Huā, Mr Huā)." He took the name from his hotel, The Golden Flower. Jeff bluffed a smile. "Thank you once again." With that he walked out of the chemist, heading for Lanxi Road. He carefully put his sunglasses on, it was a dry, warm Thursday morning. Time for a Lee visit.

Jeff came out of the junction of Lanxi Road and Beishi Road close to the end of block B, scanning the blocks whilst slowly walking one way then the other, trying to avoid looking suspicious, which was something he felt he might look. He had to come up with a better idea. He wandered around the area for another forty-five minutes, then headed back up Lanxi Road. *He'd have his breakfast in the cafe by the chemists,* he decided. Jeff was about a quarter of the way up Lanxi Road, when he noticed two solid looking young men walking towards him, heading in the direction of the tenements.

The men were oblivious to the middle-aged man walking towards them. Jeff could make out they were talking about DI Chow, the bigger one bragging to his companion how he would love to give Chow a good kicking, eventually killing him, if he could get away with it. Jeff was so preoccupied with studying them, that he lost his balance slightly on a broken paving slab, just as the two groups crossed, consequently brushing the younger man's right shoulder with his right shoulder. Jeff immediately apologised, however, the other man, wearing very short hair, turned around grabbing Jeff by the neck.

"Watch where you're walking old man, now apologise again to my brother," he spat, his right palm squeezing around Jeff's neck, his right forearm revealing part of a dragon tattoo.

Jeff started to panic, this altercation could ruin his plans. "I'm sorry, really sorry," he grovelled. "It was an accident, I lost my balance, sorry, sorry."

"Don't start Zhān mǔ shì, leave it, besides there are too many people about," the younger man suggested.

"Okay little brother, you're right, there are too many witnesses around." Luckily Zhān mǔ shì let Jeff go, but slyly shoved him in the process, resulting in Jeff falling over, much to the amusement of the brothers, who proceeded with their journey laughing out loudly, not bothering to see if Jeff was okay.

Jeff sat on the paving watching the brothers continue their journey. It wasn't what he'd hoped for, but he sighed in relief because it could have got a lot worse. A passer-by, one of many, as Lanxi Road was a busy road, asked him if he was all right, offering a helping hand, which Jeff accepted. The elderly man helped Jeff to his feet, they exchanged pleasantries, the man obviously knew the Lees, as he quietly cursed them by name. Jeff continued northwards towards Guchuan Road gently rubbing his neck, deep in thought.

Jeff quickly realised who they were, the bigger meaner looking one with short, cropped hair was James (Zhān mǔ shì) Lee, the better looking, neater groomed companion was his younger brother John (Yuēhàn) Lee. Jeff wondered what he would do if he randomly bumped into the Lees. He felt a mixture of emotions, full of hate and fear, he'd now met all three and thus agreed with Mr Ling's opinion of them, in short, detestable.

Jeff carried on walking up Lanxi Road, weaving in and out of the human traffic, it was now mid-morning, and the weather had stayed dry and reasonably warm. Just as he got near the junction with Guchuan Road, he spotted something out the corner of his left eye, an idea immediately sprang to his mind. *That might be the answer,* he was thinking. *Yes it could do the trick.* He half turned to his left, almost barging into a mid-seventies couple. He quickly apologised, and continued towards a small car rental shop, which apparently, according to the sign he'd just read, was offering excellent, unbeatable hire rates. He walked in.

The office was about the size of an average kitchen, finished in matt white paint. A man in his fifties, with long, slicked black hair combed back and styled to reveal a widow's peak, sat behind a desk, smoking a tipped cigarette. "What can I do for you, my friend?" he asked, in a confident tone, pointing to an empty chair opposite him.

Jeff accepted his gesture, pulling the seat back as he sat on it; he didn't want smoke puffed all over him. Jeff explained he wanted to hire a car, asking the man what his best rates were as he couldn't afford anything too expensive.

The man, who was dressed in a light grey suit, chuckled, and blew smoke up to the ceiling. "I'll beat any rates you can get, business is not so good this time of the year," he replied, waving his right arm about.

The discussion went on for a few more minutes, 'toing and froing' between the pair, who eventually agreed a price. "Bring your driving licence later on today, say five p.m.," he said whilst blowing out a lung full of smoke, and flicking ash on the floor.

Jeff shook his head, as he started to get off his seat. "I told you, I haven't got my licence, I left it in Hong Kong, I only have my passport for identification." He started to walk towards the opened door of Joni's Car Rentals. He wasn't sure if Joni was his first or last name.

Jeff walked three strides. "Okay, okay my friend." It was Joni walking quickly to him. "On this occasion, I'll grant this special favour, bring your passport and," he paused, "the cash, later on this afternoon. I'll have that car," he pointed to a small silver saloon, in his car lot, "ready for you."

Jeff turned, looked at Joni, then the car. "Okay, see you at five p.m." he said, proceeding to walk northwards. From the quickest of glances, Jeff could tell the car was several years old, a very basic Nissan. *Probably a sixteen hundred cc,* he guessed. *It will do.*

"Scrambled eggs on brown toast, plus a pot of tea please," Jeff said, to the young waitress, ordering his breakfast, although the time suggested brunch. He decided to sit near the side window of the café. He translated it as Red Cow, the cafe that he spotted first thing, next to the chemist. He pulled out a free daily newspaper he'd picked up in the mall, casually reading it whilst surveying his surroundings. The Red Cow, he considered, was typical of a small cafe, consisting of eighteen tables with accompanying chairs, most of which were occupied. It had a nice buzz to it, plenty of chitter-chatter, his fellow customers eating a variety of breakfast foods. Jeff turned a page of the paper, pretending to read it, whilst mulling over his altercation with the Lees. It had certainly shaken him up, in particular how strong and aggressive Zhān mŭ shì was, which instinctively made him rub his neck.

His thoughts were broken by the arrival of the breakfast. "Here you are sir," the very pleasant waitress said, placing the plate of scrambled eggs on brown toast in front of him, accompanied by a pot of tea, cup, saucer plus a small jug of milk. "Is there anything else I can get you?"

Jeff surveyed the items the young woman had put in front of him. "No, that's fine thanks," he said, commencing by sprinkling pepper on his eggs, followed by pouring himself a cup of tea. *Not bad, um, not too bad,* he thought, but *not anywhere near as good as Anne's.* He devoured a mouthful of the breakfast, which he thought, had a slightly different presentation and taste to what he was used to. *At least I don't have to use the chopsticks.* He slowly ate the breakfast, intermittently having a sip of tea, whilst looking around the cafe, in particular how people behaved and whether anybody stared at him — they didn't. Jeff took his time in the Red Cow, he ordered another pot of tea, much to his surprise he started to read the free newspaper, trying to show partial interest in the local news. After spending just over an hour in the Red Cow, Jeff paid his bill, exited, deciding to have a good look around the mall, before going back to the chemist. It was a good opportunity to see what other amenities were available.

Jeff spent a couple of hours slowly ambling about the mall. He came to the conclusion that pretty much everything he would require was obtainable, which, considering the close proximity it was to his hotel, was convenient. Two shops that gave him particular interest were the general hardware store and the launderette, places he would be visiting soon.

"I've come to pick up my order please," Jeff addressed the same assistant as he'd spoke to before. It was now two o'clock in the afternoon.

She had the package of gamma hydroxybutyrate placed in a paper bag, readily to hand,. "That will be two hundred and fifty Renminbi please," she said holding out her left hand whilst holding his package with her right one.

Jeff fished the money out of his wallet, giving her a three one hundred Renminbi notes. "There you go."

She handed him the change plus his package. "Be very careful with that stuff, if you get the dosage wrong it could be lethal, make sure you thoroughly read the instructions," she instructed, without smiling.

"Will do, I've used it before, I know what I'm doing," Jeff lied. "Thanks." Jeff was about to leave, when a thought suddenly dawned on him. "Can I also have a packet of smelling salts plus cotton wool pads please?"

The assistant gave him a look of surprise. *What an odd fellow,* she thought. *There's something peculiar about him.* She walked to a shelf, found the salts and cotton wool, bringing the items back to the counter. "That'll be ninety Renminbi please," she said, holding out her left palm.

Jeff, paid, putting all the items in one package, confidently strolled out of the shop, and headed back to his room in The Golden Flower. He needed to get clued up and thoroughly read the instructions, as the woman advised.

Once safely in his room, Jeff tipped the contents of the package onto his bed: syringe, needles, plus small bottles containing GHB. The instructions advised the user on the required dosage, depending on their physical size, as well as how long they wanted to sleep, warning the user that overdosing could be lethal. Jeff's hands trembled slightly as he finished reading the guidelines. He put the contents back in the package, placing that in his zip-up side pocket of his bag, which also contained black hair dye plus skin toning cream. He didn't want a nosey parker cleaner finding his 'special things'. Jeff took the lenses out of his eyes. *Glad they're out.* He decided to take a quick cat nap before visiting Joni's. He got his passport ready, just in case he might have forgotten it, before lying on his bed.

After a couple of hours nap, Jeff took a quick check in the mirror. *Yep, still covered,* he muttered under his breath, checking the toner. Jeff put his passport in his back trouser pocket, gently slipped on the tinted aviators, then headed out to the mall to withdraw Joni's cash from an atm. Jeff's eyes almost popped out of their sockets, when he saw his balance after withdrawing the cash. *Luckily I didn't have the lenses in or they might have flicked off,* he bemused. There was less than eight hundred pounds in his, or Mr T Smith's account. After putting the Renminbi in his wallet, he headed to the car rental, thinking about his options. *I might have to get a job at this rate, shudder the thought.*

Joni was sitting behind his desk, hiding behind a cloud of thick cigarette smoke, feet up on his desk, leaning on his chair. "Take a chair, we'll do the paperwork now." Joni was his surname, he stood five feet one inch tall, being very thin in build. He removed his feet from the desk, offering Jeff the same chair as before, wearing a blank facial expression. He took another drag of his ciggy, whilst running his left palm through his widow's peak.

Jeff sat down, taking the passport out as he did so and placing it on the table in front of Joni, who picked it up. "And the cash please," he asked with the faintest of smiles. He flicked the cigarette stub into a bin, blowing the last drag to his left-hand side. Joni proceeded to fill the hire form in using a black biro, whilst Jeff counted out the cash. "Right Mr," he looked at the passport, "Mr Jié fú lísī, two weeks' hire, a full tank of petrol on return, okay?" He looked up at Jeff. "Now sign here, Mr Jié fú lísī," he said pointing to a dotted line at the bottom of the pro forma.

Jeff leant forward, trying his best to avoid Joni's smelly smoky breath, who was busy lighting up another smoke, striking a match on his desk, blowing out the first drag through his nostrils. He handed Joni the cash, which he calculated as ten pounds sterling per day, whilst retrieving his passport.

Joni leant back on his chair, picked off a set of car keys from a keyboard behind him. "All's good, let's go and get your car," he said, sliding the cash into his back trouser pocket. Jeff followed the diminutive, skeletal smoking Joni out of his office, placing his passport where he'd got it from.

Joni walked around the car, pointing out to Jeff the odd 'little love bite' on the battered, ten-year-old Nissan. "There you are Mr Jié fú lísī," he said, handing Jeff the keys. "Remember, Mr Jié fú lísī, we drive on the right here, not on the left like they do in Hong Kong."

Jeff couldn't recall telling Joni he'd come from Hong Kong, perhaps it had slipped out in conversation, or maybe he'd spotted it stamped on his passport. "No problem, see you in two weeks, I might have to extend the hire time, we'll see." He fired the car up, put it in first gear, and drove off, removing his aviators once he was safely behind the wheel, into the heavy late afternoon traffic. Joni just watched him leave, tidied his widow's peak, pulling on a smoke like his life depended upon it.

Jeff drove slowly, quickly adjusting to driving 'on the wrong side of the road' as he'd driven many times abroad, on holiday with Anne and David — in the good old days. The gearbox, a typical four speed, was crunchy, especially in third gear. Jeff also deduced the clutch was slow, but overall he thought it drove reasonably well, considering its age, condition and mileage, which was quite considerable for a rental car. *No wonder it was so cheap,* he considered. He decided to take the car for a spin around the local vicinity, mainly to get used to its nuances, but also to get a feel for the city's driving style — a bit frenetic. The drive reminded him of when he drove in Italy, what seemed like a lifetime ago.

After driving for half an hour criss-crossing the neighbourhood, he parked up outside The Golden Flower, put the aviators back on, locked the car, not that anybody would pinch it, then headed back to the mall. More shopping was required.

Jeff knew exactly what he wanted. It was a hare-brained idea he'd hatched, but he couldn't think of a better one, except maybe buying a self-loading rifle and shooting the Lees to smithereens. He walked around the small, cluttered hardware store, picked up: two medium length black tie-down straps, a packet of long nylon cable ties, and walked up to the counter. "Can I also have a small penknife please?" The old man, whose shop it was, stood behind the counter, smoking, whilst reading a magazine, more or less ignoring Jeff.

"Can I..."

"What size knife?" Without gaining eye contact, he spoke very quickly and used a slang word Jeff had never heard before.

Looking puzzled Jeff asked, "What size what?"

"Knife," the man growled. "Knife." He gave Jeff the impression he couldn't care less whether he served him or not, he came across rude, bordering on obnoxious. The owner, Mr Maye, wasn't very tall, of plump build, topped with a fat, round, balding head, with a few grey hairs surrounding his ears. His vulgar mouth consisted of a few stained teeth, for, as like Joni, he was also a chain smoker.

"Oh knife," Jeff chuckled. "Yes of course." He tried to bluff he knew all along what was said. "Only a small one."

Maye tutted, half turned, took a small penknife off a cardboard wall fastening, chucking it on the counter in front of Jeff.

"That'll be one hundred and eighty Renminbi," growled Maye.

Jeff counted out the notes from his wallet, placing them in his waiting fat sausage-like fingered left hand, his other one pulled on a non-tipped ciggy, his toothless mouth blowing smoke all over Jeff.

"Can I have a bag please?"

Maye reluctantly gave Jeff a plastic bag, put the receipt in it, almost throwing it at Jeff in the process.

Jeff grabbed the bag, put the items in it, threw Maye a disgusted look, thinking, as he walked out of his store, *what an obnoxious so and so.*

Maye shrugged his shoulders, not bothering to look at his last customer. *Fuck him*, he thought, *disturbing me, I should have charged the pleasant wanker for the bag, some people are far too happy.*

Jeff briskly made his way to the Lucky Duck for his evening meal, to get his sustenance out of the way. He'd decided to put his hare-brained plan into operation that very evening. He struggled to find an empty table, as the restaurant was very busy, eventually, with the assistance of a waiter, sitting down near the door, on the right-hand side. He ordered Peking roasted duck and vegetables with an accompanying jug of cold water. Whilst he waited for his meal to be served, Jeff considered what he knew, with help from Chow and Mr and Mrs Ling.

The Lings described the first encounter with the Lees, the Sunday of the attack on David and Chynna, when they drove past making a threatening gesture, in the black car which Mr Ling guessed was a four-door, mid-range Honda. Li Wei also told Jeff (and Anne) that the brothers not only shared the car, but also job shared at the local SIAC car factory working a variety of shifts, both day and evenings. He also told Jeff, via one of DI Chow's visiting chats, that the brothers, although keeping a low profile since the murders, were trying to set up a local criminal gang, with links to Hong Kong. How Chow knew that, Mr Ling wasn't sure. So, Jeff knew they worked shifts and drove a black, four-door Honda saloon. It was now a waiting game.

CHAPTER FORTY-FIVE

Jeff slotted the silver Nissan into first gear, pulling off the kerb outside his accommodation, taking the first right turn onto Lanxi Road. It would only be a matter of minutes before he arrived at his destination. Since leaving the Lucky Duck, he had gone back to his digs, taken a nap, freshened up, touched up his make-up before heading out into the cool Shanghai evening, tightly holding the bag containing the goodies he'd bought earlier.

Jeff slipped the aviators off, putting them in his shirt breast pocket, glancing to his right at the bag on the passenger seat. At the bottom of the junction with Beishi Road, he turned left, always more difficult than a right hander, especially for drivers who normally drive on the left, like most of the 'old empire' countries, plus, strangely Japan. The traffic was light, typical for late evening. Jeff noticed a scattering of pedestrians rushing in both directions to their 'pigeon hole'. He parked the car in the shadows, on the opposite side of the road, adjacent to block C, scanning the few parked cars outside the block for a black Honda saloon. He couldn't spot one, *one of those bastards must be at work*, he assumed, driving their car to and from the factory. Jeff turned the ignition off, grabbed the newspaper he'd picked up in the mall before going into the Lucky Duck, which was also on the passenger seat, proceeded to open it, feigning reading, and using it as a prop. The casual passer-by probably thought he was either waiting for a, 'lady of the night', or was an undercover cop. Jeff glanced at his watch, noting the time, it was ten thirty. *This could be a long night,* he mused, *a very long night.*

Jeff waited for what seemed like an eternity, but was actually two hours, before deciding to take a quick stroll, to freshen up thus sharpen his concentration. He locked the car up, and quickly looked around, before heading down Lanxi Road, doing a few stretching exercises in the process, returning after twenty minutes. A few more hours passed. Jeff started to doze off, when he was woken by the screech of a parking car's brakes. He jolted up in his seat to see what unthoughtful person was driving like a lunatic, he looked at his watch, it was two o'clock in the morning. The car's lights were still on, which made it easy to identify. Jeff held his breath, it was a black, saloon Honda. *But was it the Lee's car*, he wondered. The driver opened his door, blew out a puff of smoke, undoing his pony tail at the same time, looked around, then leant back into the car to pick something up off the back seat. Jeff was about to drive off, panic overcoming him, as he only intended to survey the scene. Bizarrely, however, Jeff suddenly changed his mind in a rare moment of bitterness. *Fuck it, in for a penny, in for a pound,* or, as in his case, nine Renminbi. He picked up the syringe, which was half-filled with GHB, pulled the needle out of the vial containing the drug, put the penknife in his back trouser pocket, and threw the bag onto the back seats before getting out of his car. Jeff had left the needle in the vial, as he wasn't sure who, if any of the Lees, would show up first, measuring half a syringe full for a medium person, who he calculated as Yuēse, three-quarters full for a large person (Yuēhàn), and a full syringe for a very large person, as he considered Zhān mǔ shì to be. That was according to the dosage recommendations he'd read the previous day, for a good night's sleep.

He slipped out of his car, quietly closing the door, looking about the street for people, as he crossed the road. "Yuēse, my friend, can I help you?" He approached the black Honda, still not sure if it was his intended target. If it wasn't, he intended to apologise, returning to his car. Jeff held the syringe in his palm in such a way as to conceal it. He was getting closer to the Honda.

Yuēse gathered the items he was rummaging for in the rear of the car, consequently, and conveniently for Jeff, his arms were full of clothes. He heard 'the friend' say something behind him. "What the fuck do you want?" he said as he exited the Honda, still puffing on his ciggy.

Jeff honed in. *Yes it was Yuēse,* he confirmed to himself. "Let me help you."

Yuēse was trying to close the driver door with his right foot, spat the cigarette out, and half turned to 'his friend'. "I told you, fuck off."

Jeff got within strike range, slipped the syringe from his palm to his fingers, then rammed it into the unsuspecting Yuēse's left buttock, injecting the drug instantaneously.

Yuēse jerked in shock, dropped his work clothes, half spinning around, snapping the needle in the process, threw a punch at Jeff's head with his right fist. "You bastard, I'll kill you for this, what have you done?"

Jeff, using what little skill he'd learnt on his ju-jitsu classes, ducked the punch, quickly lunging at Yuēse, who now started to wobble; the two were grappling. The drug had taken a couple of minutes to work and was now 'running' through Yuēse's body. He started to go limp, he couldn't stand properly. Jeff grabbed him by the shoulder, wrapping his arm around his right shoulder, placing Yuēse's left arm around his left shoulder. "Come on, my friend, I'll look after you." If an onlooker had been watching, it would have appeared as if two friends, one very drunk, were staggering to their waiting car, which was exactly as Jeff intended it to look like. Jeff strapped him in with the passenger seat belt, then rushed around to the driver's seat, doing his seat belt up as he drove off, looking to see if anybody was about. *Good, no one.*

Jeff drove at the correct speed of forty kilometres per hour, as he didn't want to attract police attention. His heart was racing ten to the dozen, his hands were trembling. Yuēse, by this time, was completely comatose, sitting slumped in the passenger seat, dribbling from his mouth, occasionally moaning. Jeff decided to drive slightly out of town, getting a reasonable distance from Beishi Road, just in case Yuēse's wife, or anyone else, had raised the alarm. He needn't have worried, she was fast asleep and didn't expect or want to be disturbed. After driving for fifteen minutes, he found a quiet, dark location. *This will do nicely*, he thought.

He pulled the Nissan over, into a factory car park, there weren't any street lights, and the area was deserted. Jeff undid his seat belt, leant into the back seat, picked up the bag he'd received from Maye, pulling out the tie-down straps and the cable ties. He slipped one strap over Yuēse's head, and the back of his chair, sliding it down to his waist, slid the plain end of the strap into the metal fastener, then pulled it tight. Jeff repeated the process with the other tie-down strap, this time to Yuēse's chest, again pulling on the metal fastener for a tight fit. He then secured Yuēse's legs with cable clips; he was trussed up like a chicken. Jeff double-checked all fasteners, once satisfied, he took the smelling salts out of the bag, pouring the clear to white ammonium carbonate onto a cotton wool pad, placing it firmly against Yuēse's mouth and nose. He shook, spluttered, then slightly opened his eyes. Jeff put the cotton wool pad back onto his mouth. Yuēse flinched his head back, he was starting to come around. He tried to move his arms, but he couldn't as they were tightly strapped to his torso.

Jeff put the smelling salts pad on the car dashboard and turned to Yuēse. "Now tell me what happened," he said slapping him hard twice across the face.

Yuēse gasped, he was still half conscious, it was as if he'd been woken from a deep sleep, which, in reality, he had. "What, who, where am I?"

Jeff slapped him hard on his left cheek, with the palm of his right hand. "I won't ask you again, what happened?"

Yuēse yelped, he was now fully aware of his surroundings. "What the fuck are you talking about?" He turned his head to his left. "And, who the fuck are you?"

Jeff, full of rage, slapped him very hard on the face. "What did you and your brothers do to Chynna, and her boyfriend?"

Yuēse struggled to free himself, but it was helpless, he couldn't move. "Okay, I'll tell you what happened, as long as you promise to let me go, all right?"

"Fair enough, don't lie to me, or else." Jeff took the knife out of his back trouser pocket, holding it in his right hand.

Yuēse realised, as he came out of his drug induced sleep, was in deep shit. "You promise, okay."

"Of course, now get on with it." Jeff took the mobile phone out of his jacket pocket, set it to video, reversed the camera, switched it on, and placed it on the righthand dashboard in front of his passenger.

Yuēse told Jeff the full story, of how the brothers picked David and Chynna up in his van, from outside their flat, then drove to a deserted car park, raped Chynna killing them both, before throwing the bodies in the river. Jeff clenched the steering wheel, tears dripping from his face.

Yuēse, tactically emphasised that he had no part of any of it, he was simply the driver, the other two did the raping and killing, in particular Zhān mǔ shì.

"Let's get this right, you kidnapped them from their flat, drove to a car park, butchered and raped, before dumping their dead bodies in the Yangtze River." He turned to his right. "Have I got that right?"

Jeff, full of emotion, asked Yuēse where the car park they killed David and Chynna was located. He told him the directions, hoping it would save his lying neck.

"Yes, that's it," Yuēse was pleading. "But I had nothing to do with any of it, please let me go." He looked at Jeff. "Who are you?"

Jeff looked him in the eye. "I'm the father of Chynna's boyfriend." He punched Yuēse hard in the face with his left fist. "You killed my son, why?"

Yuēse peered at Jeff, suddenly realising that the person talking to him had blue eyes. "But you're Chinese," he spluttered out. "He was white, blond headed, we thought he was a Yank."

"But why?" Jeff asked again.

"It started as bit of a joke, to teach Chynna a lesson." He turned to Jeff. "For going out with a white guy, it wasn't planned, it just got out of control."

"One last time, Yuēse, did you have anything to do with the rape or killing?"

Yuēse, realising he was in the 'deepest of shit', pleaded, "No, it was the other two, please let me go." He spluttered, "I'll go to the police and confess to everything." That was the last lie he'd ever tell.

Jeff shook his head. "I've given you the opportunity to be truthful, you're just a lying, piece of shit." Jeff got close to Yuēse. "Have you heard the expression, 'what goes around, comes around'?"

"Ah, eh, what?" Yuēse was shitting himself.

Jeff shot both his hands out, grasping Yuēse's neck, squeezing it as hard as he could, trying to strangle him. Yuēse flinched, rocked his head from side to side, gasping for breath.

"Ah, ah," he wheezed.

Jeff squeezed with all his might, this struggle went on for several minutes, Jeff just couldn't finish him off. He looked around the car. *That might do,* he thought, looking at the plastic bag that Maye gave him. He let go of Yuēse, leant into the back of the car, grabbed the bag with his right hand, shaking the contents out of it at the same time.

Yuēse took a few deep breaths, he thought the worst of his ordeal was over, he dared to open his eyes, but then he wished he hadn't. "What the…"

Jeff pulled the plastic bag over Yuēse's head, picked up a cable clip off the car floor, slipped it around the bag and his neck, pulling it secure and airtight. Yuēse started to breath rapidly, his open mouth sucking in the plastic, within a few minutes, the bag stopped moving, his head slumped forward.

Jeff looked outside, checking if anybody was about. He turned the phone off, pocketing it. He left the bag on Yuēse's head, whilst he tidied the car, placing all his former bag's contents in a neat pile in the rear footwell. He checked for a pulse. *Good,* he thought, there wasn't one. He took the penknife out of his rear trouser pocket, opened the small blade, carefully cutting the cable clip around, firstly Yuēse's ankles, then the clip around his neck, putting both with the pile in the rear footwell. Jeff released the two holding straps, firstly pulling the loose strap through the metal clasp around his waist, followed by the other one around his chest, again placing the straps with the rear footwell pile. Finally, he carefully pulled the bag off Yuēse's head. Once completely free, he put that on top of his rear well pile. Unfortunately for Jeff, he didn't realise the receipt for his items he had bought in Maye's, slipped out of the bag, sliding into the gap between Yuēse's neck and shirt, resting halfway down his back. Jeff gave Yuēse the once over, took another quick look outside, satisfied all was clear, started the car up, and carefully drove back into Shanghai. Yuēse, was still strapped in by his seat belt, remained motionless, his head slumped forward, as if asleep.

It took Jeff twenty minutes to reach his next destination, the early morning Shanghai traffic was minimal. He slowly pulled up outside Chynna and David's former apartment, killing the engine carefully exiting the Nissan. He walked around the rear of the car, looking about to see if anybody was in proximity. He spotted a young man in the far distance walking in the opposite direction, other than him nobody, therefore the coast was clear. Jeff quietly opened the passenger door, undid Yuēse's seat belt, put his arms around his body, carefully pulling him out of the car, dragging him to the boundary wall of the property, methodically leaning his back against it, making sure Yuēse's legs were stretched out forward. He hoped it gave the appearance to a casual passer-by, that the person slumped against the wall had drunk too much, consequently falling asleep on the floor. Jeff took another quick look around, all was quiet, he closed the passenger door, jumped in, slipped the car into first gear, and steadily drove back to his digs.

Initially, after dropping Yuēse off, Jeff felt quite pleased with himself, as he calmly drove back to The Golden Flower. Towards the end of the journey, the realisation of what he'd done started to dawn on him. Racked with guilt, he suddenly started to feel nauseous, he pulled the car over, opened the door and was violently sick. Jeff sat, wondering what on earth possessed him to kill Yuēse; he'd never killed anything before, let alone a human being. *Why didn't I take him to the police station?* he considered. *Too late, you idiot.* He waited a few more minutes before continuing, only to stop and throw up again — his conscience wasn't going to let this go easily.

Once he'd parked the Nissan outside his digs, he carefully put all the contents from the rear footwell into the plastic bag; he could still smell Yuēse's breath in it. Jeff turned the lights off, locked the car, then took the bag out, furtively looking about, whilst walking unsteadily into the hotel, not feeling well at all. He dumped the plastic bag on his room floor, before rushing to the toilet to be sick again. Jeff swilled his mouth out, spitting out the last food remnants, most of it was now bile, followed by a quick teeth clean. Although he didn't feel particularly tired, he thought it would be better if he had, or tried, to have a sleep, deciding to close the small window curtains, as it wouldn't be long before daylight.

Surprisingly Jeff did sleep, he went into a very deep slumber. In addition he also had the worst nightmare of his life — thus far. Typically Mike made an appearance, accompanied by the recently deceased Yuēse, who still had the plastic bag secured to his head. Jeff was stripped to his underwear, strapped to a dining chair, in the middle of a deserted car park. Mike, dressed in his shroud, stood diagonally opposite Yuēse, the pair of them walked, in unison, around Jeff, pointing an accusing finger at him, whilst shouting. Yuēse called Jeff a murderer, Mike named him a body snatcher. This went on for some time, and Jeff's head started to spin. They then turned on one another, Mike blaming Yuēse and his brothers for his predicament; if they hadn't murdered David, Jeff wouldn't have snatched him from the morgue. Yuēse retaliated by reminding Mike that he was going to be cremated the following morning of the snatch. The barracking continued on and on it went, before they both turned back on Jeff. Jeff's head was constantly moving from right to left, then back again, he felt nauseous, he was going to be sick. He woke in a daze, rushed to the toilet and puked.

CHAPTER FORTY-SIX

"Put your foot down, Sergeant, I want to get there before the area gets contaminated," Chow snapped at Wong. The police had been informed of a dead body being found in the Jing An Temple area, the phone call coming from a young man on his way to work early in the morning. He told the police emergency receptionist that he initially thought the man was drunk, because he was sitting on the pavement, slumped against the wall, eventually falling asleep intoxicated. Feeling sorry for the drunk, he shook his shoulder to try and awaken him, quickly realising he was seriously ill or possibly dead, maybe dying from alcoholic poisoning or hypothermia, but that was just a guess. He phoned the emergency services, firstly the ambulance, then the police, leaving his name and contact details, before continuing his journey to work.

Wong could tell his boss was in an irritable mood, he knew Chow liked to be at a crime scene before all the other idiots destroyed vital evidence, as Chow described everybody else. Wong's life at work had been nervy since the case against the Lees had been put on hold. The death of Mr Peters had exacerbated the situation, and he knew Chow had taken it particularly badly, partially blaming himself. Chow had informed Wong, in confidence, a couple of days after he'd been told by the Lings. It was the most depressed he'd seen his boss since the murders of Chynna and David, his mood a consequence of it. Wong, wearing one of his three identical grey suits, white shirt, black socks and shoes, hoped this case would give his boss something to get his teeth into. Chow, dressed in his standard royal blue suit, crisp white shirt, black socks and brogues, tapped the dashboard in frustration; he couldn't understand why the traffic didn't give way to Wong's police car.

"Use that horn, bully these idiots out of the way," he snapped at Wong, whilst touching his blue tie, tied in a half Windsor knot.

Wong observed that the colour of his boss' tie often matched his temperament, wearing either blue or yellow, most of the time it was blue. Chow had ordered forensics and pathology to get to the scene forthwith, he also wanted the crime scene, if indeed it was a crime, sealed off, until further notice. Wong could see the Jing An Temple in the distance, consequently he knew they were now only minutes away from Tongren Road. *Thank Buddha for that,* he thought.

Wong pulled up sharply at the address given by the young man, a small crowd of onlookers were hanging around. Chow, who leapt out of the screeching car, soon got rid of them — not many people argued with DI Chow. Once the scene was cleared, the pair took a closer look at the unfortunate drunk lying on the floor. Realising who it was, they looked at each other in unison and shock. Forensics arrived soon after Chow and Wong. Chow ordering them to take all relevant photographs, whilst also looking for any clues as to the dying or the dead man's reason for demise. The pathologist's assistant appeared seconds later, temporarily taking charge of the scene, quickly deducing the man was, in fact, dead, but couldn't expand further as to the reasons. Her guess, she emphasised guess, was not from natural causes, she would give Chow an initial report as soon as possible. The only information she could give Chow with certainty was that he'd been dead less than twelve hours and, crucially, he didn't die where he was found. Chow thanked her as the ambulance arrived, the paramedics carefully removing Yuēse's dead body, taking it to the morgue's laboratory for a full post mortem.

Chow stood motionless, arms folded, looking intensely at the building where Yuēse's body had been placed, wearing a puzzled expression. Wong knew the relevance, Chow didn't believe in coincidences. Chow instructed two of his team to make house to house enquiries, only in the immediate area, for now. Once satisfied that all the evidence had been gathered, Chow emphasised all, he opened the area back up for public use, as they'd blocked off the pedestrian thoroughfare, causing potential accidents plus inconvenience. "Come on Zìmò, let's get this over with."

Zìmò Wong tidied his red tie, his boss hadn't called him by his first name for some time, he sensed something wasn't sitting right with Chow. "Where to first, Boss?"

Chow felt like cuffing his sergeant for asking such an obvious question, but he relented, as his mind was troubled. He ordinarily would have been over the moon with the news of the death of a Lee brother, however, the placing of the body could bring a cloud of conflicts, which he was reluctant to follow. The cloud he was worrying about involved the potential suspects, some of whom he particularly liked. He finally answered. "Yuēse's wife, followed by his parents then the brothers." He wasn't expecting a welcome.

Wong headed the unmarked police car towards Beishi Road. Chow looked out of the passenger window at the building where Yuēse's body had been found, hoping he was wrong in his assumptions. Chow's envisaged welcome from the Lees went as he thought; the only person who didn't seem too upset was his wife, although she did shed a tear or two. Yuēse's kin, typically, demanded a full police investigation, with no expense spared, if, as they and Chow suspected, he'd been murdered. The family thought something was wrong, due to his clothes being found on the road by the Honda; the fact that he hadn't gone home didn't raise immediate alarm. Chow and Wong left his parents' and brothers' flats with sarcastic and snide remarks thrown at them. Chow for once, let it go.

The drive back to the police station was somewhat sombre, neither man saying anything. Wong didn't want to put his foot in it, Chow pondering on his options, hoping his hunch wouldn't bear any fruit. Wong concentrated on his driving, enjoying the mid-November dry weather, wondering what the autopsy would reveal.

Chow, with Wong in tow, headed straight for the mortuary laboratory on arrival at their base, initially being greeted by Dr Huang, the head of forensics. She worked in unison with the pathologist, Dr Wu, who was taking notes as they walked in. Dr Huang did the introductions. Chow, eager to ascertain critical information, asked Wu what his examination revealed.

Wu scratched his thin, balding head with his pincer-like fingers and turned to Chow. "I haven't completed a full post mortem yet, however, I can tell you the following." He shuffled his small thin frame, closer to the police officers. "He died of suffocation, probably from a plastic bag, after an attempt at strangulation."

Chow frowned, almost in disbelief. The police officers looked at each other, before returning their gaze to Wu.

"There is bruising present in two places on the victim's torso, probably from some kind of strapping." Wu paused, looked at the corpse. "And thinner, deeper bruising on his ankle area and his neck, my guess would be cable ties or something similar." Wu picked up a plastic tray from off a near side table. "I found these items, one inside him, the other down his shirt." Wu firstly showed Chow and Wong the snapped off needle, then picked up the receipt. "You'd better take this, Inspector, it might help with your investigation."

Wu put the evidence in a small plastic bag, giving Chow the receipt, who promptly glanced at it, slightly nodded before showing it to Wong, then pocketed it. "Have you a time of death, Doctor?"

Dr Wu, turned slightly towards Yuēse. "Somewhere in the region between midnight and six o'clock this morning." He moved his old, thin, balding head towards Chow. "I'll have a more precise time for you when I open him up." Wu's stooping frame seemed to be wilting, and he sat on a close chair, almost slouching in it. "Another important factor, Detective, he didn't die at the scene, but shortly beforehand, as," he seemed to gasp, "minimal rigor mortis had started, his muscles had begun to stiffen." Wu was about to go into the six various stages of rigor mortise, Chow cut him short.

"Thank you, Doctor, you've been of great help." The pair started to leave, nodded at Wu. Dr Huang intervened, looking slightly disappointed.

"I've run blood tests on the victim." She looked at Chow patronisingly. "Do you want to know the results?" She folded her arms across her small, plump frame; her usual pleasant smile had vanished.

Chow realised his mistake in taking Huang for granted. "Apologies Doctor, I was preoccupied, forgive me." He looked at her, and opened his arms. "Yes please."

She'd made her point and nodded. "I've discovered gamma hydroxybutyrate acid, known as GHB in his blood." She nodded to the snapped syringe needle in Wu's tray. "Injected by that needle." She looked back at Chow. "It's been in his bloodstream less than twenty-four hours." Chow and Wong glanced at each other. "I also found traces of ammonium carbonate, known as smelling salts, in his nasal and throat passages."

Chow nodded gratefully at Dr Huang. "Thank you Doctor, is there anything else?"

Huang removed her spectacles, her pleasant demeanour returned. "That's all for now, I'm checking his clothing for fibres. I'll let you know if I find anything of significance."

Chow, eager to get the intriguing investigation moving, thanked both doctors and turned to Wong. "Get the team together for a briefing." He took one final look at Yuēse's dead body, before rushing out of the laboratory. Wong had already disappeared.

Chow held a black whiteboard marker in his left hand, the top was still on it. His audience held their breath as their master was about to deliver his expert opinion; they were under his spell. Chow, jacket-less, shirt sleeves neatly rolled up to the elbow, stood in front of his team, tossed the pen to Wong, and commenced his revelation. "Yuēse arrived home from work at his block in the early hours of this morning — parked up — he was attacked — injected with GHB — put in a vehicle, which drove off." He looked at Wong's line diagram, turned back to his team. "He was strapped to an object, probably a chair of some sort, his legs were tied together, whilst in a state of induced slumber. Yuēse was brought around by smelling salts and probably a few hard slaps to the face. The attacker, or attackers, tried to strangle him — stopped, placed a plastic bag over his head causing suffocation." Chow looked at his underlings, who sat at their desks captivated. "His dead body was placed against the wall and on the pavement in Tongren Road, a few hours later." For a few seconds, the room remained silent.

Chow pointed to a couple of his team. "Any joy with the house to house?"

In unison they replied, "No, Boss."

Chow nodded slightly, as if he already knew the answer. He quickly stepped to his jacket, put his hand in a pocket, taking out the small plastic bag. "This receipt was found between Yuēse's shirt and back," he said, holding the bag in the air. "The items listed on it are: tie-down straps, cable ties and a penknife." He paused, and his team looked at each other. "I'll be visiting Maye's hardware store forthwith."

Wong continued to add all the details on the whiteboard, he knew what was coming next, and consequently started a new box. He wrote in it *suspects.*

Chow put his right foot on a nearby chair. "Let's now look at suspects and motive." Chow took a sip of water from a bottle on the table. "The Lees could have many enemies, but at this stage, none that we know of." He took another sip, placing the bottle back on the table. "Is the positioning of Yuēse's dead body of significance?" He opened his arms, at the same time taking his foot off the chair and turned to look at Wong's scribing. "Could the Lings have anything to do with it, as it was outside their daughter's apartment?" He gazed at everybody. "One person we can rule out is Mr Peters." His team looked at each other. "He's dead." Chow picked up his jacket. "Come on, Sergeant, we've got some visiting to do."

CHAPTER FORTY-SEVEN

Jeff eventually got out of bed just after midday, the day after the killing, deciding to take a long shower to get his 'shit together'. *Why didn't I take the recording of the confession to the police, Yuēse said he would confess and tell the whole story.* Jeff pondered on that thought. *There again, he could've denied it, saying he was coerced into confessing, I would then be charged with kidnapping, maybe even trying to kill him by drug inducement.* Thoughts, mostly negative ones, were swirling around inside Jeff's head, which was aching. *Think, Jeff, think.* The hot water was showering down on him, he liked the feel of it on the back of his head and neck, he wondered how other people felt after they'd killed somebody, especially for the first time. Strange, very strange. Jeff had never killed anything before, let alone another mammal, least of all a human being. *I didn't intend to go through with my hare-brained plan, it was a moment of shear idiocy, I only drove to their flats to get the lie of the land. Typical beginner's luck.* He reflected back to a time he had taken David fishing for the first time, every time David cast in, five minutes later, he reeled in a fish. Bizarrely, the few times after that fishing trip, he never caught another fish, consequently he soon lost interest; they always joked it was beginner's luck. Jeff still couldn't quite believe he had acted out his plan, executing it in more ways than one. *I've got to come to terms with what I've done, in addition, the consequences of my actions, if I'm caught, regardless of possible sympathy, I could be executed.* Jeff had to face that daunting prospect, he was now a wanted man. He now had to be very cautious, his next decision would be vital. *I could cut and run, get out of China, back to sunny Blighty, tell Anne I had a severe car crash, and work hard to make it up to her.* He now stood in front of the shower, hot water raining down on his face. *No, I made a promise to David, I've stepped over the line, I might as well get hung for a sheep as for a lamb.* He turned the shower off.

Jeff felt a lot better after the very long shower, although his nose was still sore as he'd been sick both nasally and orally. He looked in the mirror, he looked awful. Jeff checked his hair, deciding the roots needed colouring, as blond/grey hair had started to show. Colouring satisfactorily accomplished, Jeff dipped his left hand into his bag, replacing the hair dye with skin toner, carefully applying it in the usual places, before putting the brown contacts in. After a thorough check in the mirror, Jeff dressed, deciding to wear a cream pair of flannels, beige shirt plus the loafers, and he headed out for a light, plain lunch. His stomach couldn't take anything greasy or spicy.

Jeff walked casually to the shopping mall, it was a pleasant autumn day, the early morning drizzle had stopped a couple of hours earlier. He ordered scrambled eggs on plain toast, accompanied by a pot of tea, sitting in the front window of the Red Cow, which was three-quarters full of fellow customers. Whilst waiting for his lunch, Jeff tried to put himself in Chow's shoes. He rightly assumed the police had found Yuēse's body. *Chow would link the dead body position to Chynna and David, that was a certainty.* Jeff now questioned himself as to whether that was such a good idea; he deduced the idea was good, but maybe not complying with it. *Water under the bridge.* He assumed Chow would have knowledge of, at the least, a basic autopsy report, detailing the use of GHB plus the smelling salts, in addition, the probable bruising caused by the straps and cable ties.

"Here's your eggs and pot of tea." The young waiter broke Jeff's preoccupation. "Is there anything else?"

"No, and thank you."

Jeff poured himself a cuppa, sprinkled pepper on his eggs, and thus preceded to slowly eat his lunch. He looked out of the cafe window whilst munching, still deep in thought. *So, Chow will know about the drugs and ties, but he won't know where I purchased them from, that information will take time, once he's found the chemists and hardware store, the person who served me will give Chow my description.* Jeff, of course, didn't know about the hardware receipt that Chow had in his possession, if he did, he wouldn't have stomached his meal. Jeff continued to deliberate his options, concluding that the police would probably stakeout the Lees' living area just before they returned from work, in case the attacker struck at the same time. *That's it, I'll go after one of them as they prepare to leave for work, they won't expect that.* Another one of Jeff's bright ideas.

For the first three days after killing Yuēse, Jeff kept a low profile, going for long walks, avoiding Beishi Road and Tongren Road. He rightly assumed they would be busy with police presence. Jeff, on one of his 'clear his head' walks, discovered another shopping mall which, although further than his local one, he decided to frequent. Thus, consequently keeping clear of the chemists and hardware store, just in case he was spotted by the person serving him when he bought his 'goodies', and possibly reporting him to the police.

He parked the silver Nissan in the dimly lit small hotel car park, which was at the back of the hotel, an eight-minute walk to the main entrance, just in case a witness mentioned seeing a car fitting that description. He wasn't taking any chances. On the fourth evening after the killing, he drove to the Lees' area, parked up and waited, purposely not taking his 'killing kit' just in case the opportunity arose. He had to be patient this time, he'd got away with his beginner's luck. He sat and watched the parked Honda, till two o'clock in the morning. Nothing happened, this was now a waiting game — he had to hold his nerve. The same pattern continued for another couple of days, however, on the third evening, at eight o'clock, Yuēhàn, walked out of block B, warily looked about, before jumping in the Honda on his way to work. Jeff double-checked the time, waited a few minutes before heading back to The Golden Flower, and parking in the hotel car park. Jeff repeated this pattern of behaviour for the next few days, noting that Yuēhàn left within a few minutes either side of eight o'clock in the evening. *Tomorrow night's the night,* he thought, as he drove off.

CHAPTER FORTY-EIGHT

Wong was trying to second guess Chow as to who his boss wanted to visit first, he was trying to avoid asking, "Where to Boss", so consequently headed for the mall where Maye's hardware store was located. Chow looked at him with a wry smile as they pulled up. Wong looked up to the sky, although the weather was still pleasantly warm, a few mid-afternoon clouds were forming. Within fifteen seconds they entered Maye's, Chow almost kicking his door in.

Chow entered first, reversing the open sign on his shop door to closed. Maye ignored his potential customers, not bothering to look up from reading his paper.

"I want to know who recently bought these items from your shop," Chow growled, holding the receipt, still in the plastic evidence bag, and walking towards Maye.

Maye continued to read the paper, whilst puffing away, ignoring Chow.

Nothing irritated DI Chow more than being ignored. Wong braced himself. Chow hit the shop counter hard with the palm of his right hand *Wham*. Maye jumped. "Now." He simultaneously grabbed Maye's newspaper with his left hand throwing it on the floor.

Maye looked up, blowing smoke in Chow's direction, his ugly fat face full of disdain for the men standing in front of him. "Why should I help you?"

Chow felt like grabbing Maye around the neck, however he refrained. "If you don't, I'll get a team in here and take this dump of yours apart, no doubt we'll find opium hidden away somewhere. You're renowned for selling the odd ounce here and there."

"You bastard, Chow, you're trying to fit me up." Maye's right middle sausage was pointing accusingly, whilst blowing his smelly smoky breath over both police officers.

Chow folded his arms. "Look at this receipt and tell me all you know about the person or persons you gave it to." Chow shoved the receipt in front of Maye's ugly mug.

Maye peered at the receipt through the plastic bag. "Yes I remember him." He lit another ciggy up. "He's a bit different."

Chow was losing patience, but he didn't show it, he wanted to keep 'sausage fingers' talking. "Tell me about him."

Maye pulled heavily on his smoke, paused for a couple of seconds before purposely blowing smoke all over Chow, his fat, ugly, toothless face grinning. "He was about your height, similar build." He looked to the ceiling, shook his head. "I reckon he was mixed race and," he took another drag, "he's not a local."

Chow put the receipt back in his pocket, he was now intrigued. "Mixed race, what do you mean?"

Maye knew he'd got Chow hooked. "Why don't you buy something, Detective?"

"Don't fuck me about." He snatched the cigarette out of Maye's mouth with his right hand, rubbing it out in his left palm, before throwing it on the floor, not flinching as the hot ash touch his skin. "I won't ask you again!"

Maye knew of Chow's 'hard man' reputation, and he considered, *you don't get reputations for nothing, even if they might be exaggerated.* "I would guess he was Chinese-Caucasian, probably white as opposed to Indian."

"That's better," Chow said, almost patronisingly. He looked at Wong for a second, who was scribbling copious notes. "Why mixed?"

Maye lit another ciggy, this time blowing smoke upwards. "His face wasn't Chinese shaped, his cheek bones were too high, his chin was too angular." He held the cigarette in his two right hand middle sausages. "One hundred per cent not pure Chinese, definitely not."

Chow moved on. "Fair enough, now, what about not being local?"

Maye was starting to lose patience, his shop had been closed for fifteen minutes. "He spoke too perfectly, like received pronunciation, he didn't have any accent, of course, he could be university educated." He looked at Chow. "He didn't know the slang word for knife, although he made out he did, very strange, yes it was strange." He looked at both police officers. "That's it Mr Chow, I can't give you any more information." He walked towards the front door, reversing the door sign back to open.

Chow nodded to Wong. "Okay, thanks for your help, if this guy comes in again, ring me straight away," he said, placing his card in Maye's left hand, before walking back to the car.

Maye waited for the car to start up before throwing the card in the bin. "Fuck you, Chow." He picked his arse with his middle right sausage, smelt his finger, he reacted as if it was like snuff, belched, farting as he waddled back to his counter. "You can get fucked Chow." He smelt his middle sausage again. "Well and truly."

Wong headed the car towards Yuyuan Road, located in the Jing An Temple area. He again rightly assumed they were going to interview the prime suspects, Mr and Mrs Ling, Mr Ling in particular. Chow, preoccupied, looked out of the passenger window, he was somewhat relieved at the description the obnoxious Maye had given him. He was dreading it to be similar to that of Li Wei. The man Maye described wasn't necessarily the killer, he could just be the errand boy. Chow had to be absolutely sure Li Wei wasn't involved in any way. Hopefully the forthcoming little chat would clarify his gut feeling, he wanted to be at his tactful best.

"Good evening, Mr Chow, what a pleasant surprise, Sergeant Wong is with you." Mrs Ling greeted the pair with her usual charm. "Come in, come in." Ah Lam showed the pair of police officers into her living room. Mr Ling, who had only just got home from work, stood and greeted them with a firm shake of his right hand.

"Tea as usual, Detective, what does Sergeant Wong want to drink." Ah Lam walked back into the kitchen to make them both a cup of tea, leaving Chow to talk to Li Wei.

Li Wei sat back down in his chair, nodded at Wong, smiled at Chow. "Have you got some good news for us Mr Chow?"

Chow sat on the settee close to Li, Wong sat at the other end of it. Mrs Ling brought the refreshments in, placing the drinks plus biscuits on the small coffee table, within arm's reach of her guests. Chow played a coy hand. "How are you both?"

The Lings looked at each other, their faces etched in grief. "We're just about surviving, every day seems to drag, I was hoping you had some good news about the investigation." Li Wei spoke for the couple.

Chow took a sip of tea. "I'm sorry to say that there haven't been any further developments." He put his cup back on its saucer, he was trying to tease something out of Li Wei.

Mr Ling suddenly stood up, his face distorted. "Those bastards, I hate them, I hope they rot in hell!" He sat back down again, trying his best to hold back the tears.

Ah Lam comforted her husband. "We pray every morning and evening that you will catch them, Mr Chow." She stroked Mr Ling's greying, black hair. "We know you'll never give up, we're absolutely certain of that."

Chow nodded in acceptance of the compliment, casually saying, "Have you ever considered taking the law into your own hands?" He nibbled on a biscuit. Wong sat in silence, trying to fathom out his boss's tactics.

"We're not that kind of people, besides we assume it's the Lee brothers, but it might not be, we're hoping justice will be done," she replied.

Li Wei Ling moved his wife's hand from his head. "I'd like to kill them, I know it's them, I just know it." He started weeping again.

Wong glanced at Chow, he took his notebook out of his suit jacket pocket. Chow gently shook his head, he raised his eyebrows at Mrs Ling, with an expression of empathy. He chuckled. "Just as a point of interest Li, how would you do it?"

Mr Ling blew his nose. "Oh I don't know, a slow painful death, something that would knock the smug expressions of their faces." He looked at Chow. "Put them in a cage with a tiger, before throwing them into a pit full of cobras." He nodded to himself. "Yes, I like the sound of that."

The three men laughed quietly. Ah Lam wiped a tear from her eye as she walked head down, slowly back to her chair. "Nothing will ever bring Chynna back." She paused. "Or David."

Chow knew the Lings initially blamed David for Chynna's death. "If he hadn't come here, if he hadn't worked at that particular school, if, if, if." Chow wondered if the Peters felt the same.

Mrs Ling continued. "Poor Jeff, he must've been out of his mind." She wiped the wet residue from her eyes. "And Anne, she must be…" It was Li Wei's turn to do the comforting, getting out of his chair, putting his left arm over his sobbing wife's shoulder. The atmosphere in the room was somewhat sombre. Chow and Wong half glanced at each other.

Chow took another sip of tea, purposely taking his time. Whilst the cup was in his hand, he said, "I do have some news for you both." He took another sip, before replacing it on its saucer.

Ah Lam stopped weeping, the Lings looked at Chow. Li Wei stayed by his wife.

Chow wondered whether or not the news of a dead body being found in the neighbourhood had reached the Lings. "Have you heard the news about a dead body being found on Tongren Road?"

In unison they both replied, "No."

Chow nodded slightly, he gave Wong a knowing look. "The news I have for you, is that," he paused, "Yuēse Lee was found dead this morning."

For a couple of seconds the room was stony silent, suddenly Mr Ling raised his arms and cheered. "That's the best news I've heard in a long time." He cheered again. "How did it happen?" Li Wei was full of excitement, he sat back down in his chair, clearly delighted with the news.

Chow looked at them both, firstly Ah Lam, before turning to Li Wei. "We don't know yet, they haven't completed the post mortem," he 'white lied'. "I thought you should know, due to the circumstances." Again 'white lying'. Chow studied Mr Ling, who looked both surprised and pleased. "We must now be going." He started to get out of his chair. "And leave you in peace." The police officers commenced to leave the room. "Thank you Mrs Ling, for the hospitality." He gave Ah Lam, who looked in shock, a hug. Mr Ling showed Chow and Wong to the door, still clearly chuffed with the news.

Wong thanked the couple, said his farewells before walking back to their car. Mr Ling shook Chow's hand, leant slightly forward, and whispered in Chow's right ear, "Thank you for considering me a suspect, I'm honoured." Chow kept a straight face, gave the pair a final farewell, then slowly walked back to the waiting Wong, who was sitting behind the steering wheel, the engine ticking over.

Chow surprised Wong as they drove back to the police station. "Well, Sergeant, do you think he had anything to do with the killing?"

Wong, who had made a couple of good decisions regarding who to visit, felt it was a reward being asked by his boss such a critical question, and carefully thought out his answer. "No." He was going to elaborate, but he didn't want to push his luck.

Chow nodded at his sergeant's reply, then he continued to look out into the now, dark, dry evening. Chow was convinced the positioning of the body was significant. *If the Lings had nothing to do with the killing, who was it?*

CHAPTER FORTY-NINE

Jeff freshened up. He decided to wear both black shirt and trousers and had a quick check in the mirror. *Yep, that'll do.* He gathered his 'tool kit', thus was all set; it was seven thirty p.m., time to meet Yuēhàn Lee. His tool kit consisted of the tie-down straps, cable ties, smelling salts, GHB including a newly inserted needle as the first one had snapped off, plus a blue thick tipped felt pen, walking stick and small conical hat. He had bought the thick tipped felt pen from a newsagent, to alter the numbers and letters of his car registration, as he assumed he would be seen due to the time of the attack.

The walking stick and hat were bought from a general store, Jeff intended to mimic an elderly man, hoping it would catch Yuēhàn off guard.

Jeff put his bag in the back of the Nissan, after firstly taking the blue felt-tip pen out, took a quick look about before covering white parts of the letters and numbers, hence, the letter E was changed to an F, B to a P, number eight to a three, altering the rear plate first. He'd used his phone torch for lighting as it was a dimly lit area. He killed the light, took a couple of paces back to check his colouring in, concluding it would cause confusion — job done.

Jeff arrived outside block B at seven thirty-five, parking as close to the Honda as possible. He turned his head one hundred and eighty degrees. *Good, not too many people about.* It was a quiet, cold, dry evening, just a gentle breeze. He injected the new needle into the bottle of GHB, filling the syringe to three-quarters full, placing it on the passenger seat, before leaning into the rear of the car to retrieve the hat and walking stick, putting them with the syringe. He sat as still as possible, hoping the black shirt would blend in with the darkness. He wasn't wearing the aviators or contact lenses, he found them both too uncomfortable in the evening.

Jeff sat and waited, concentrating on the job in hand. His stomach was churning, it was the same sensation as going into the bank for the first time. He looked at his watch, it was five minutes to eight. *Any minute now, any minute now, hold your nerve, you can do it.* Eight o'clock came and went, ten past eight, still no movement from block B. Jeff checked his watch, it was now twenty-two minutes past the hour. *Perhaps he's not working tonight,* he thought. All of a sudden Jeff heard the front exit door crash open. Yuēhàn had just kicked it, he was in a rush, being late for work.

Jeff quickly got out of the car, grabbed the stick, put the hat on, slipped the syringe into his right palm, then limped towards the preoccupied Yuēhàn, "Yuēhàn can I have a word?" he croaked.

Yuēhàn ignored the old man limping towards him. *I bet he wants money, probably a street beggar,* he thought. Just as he got to the car, the old man lost his balance, consequently tripping him with his walking stick. "You clumsy old twat."

Jeff leapt on the grounded Yuēhàn, ramming the needle into his stomach, quickly releasing the drug.

"What are you doing?" he gasped. Jeff dropped on top of him, pinning him down. The pair struggled for a couple of minutes, Yuēhàn tried to punch Jeff off by hitting him in the ribs with both fists. Jeff held him in a headlock, one that he'd learnt in the dojo; the punching gradually ceased. Jeff retrieved the syringe, grabbed his 'drunken' friend, 'helping' him to his car. He left the hat and stick on the ground by the driver's door of the Honda. He'd just opened the passenger door and was halfway putting Yuēhàn in, when he heard footsteps.

"What's going on?" It was a neighbour, a small man in his mid-thirties.

"I'm taking him to the hospital, he's been drinking too much, give us a hand." Jeff tried the bluff, if that didn't work, he'd have to take more drastic action. "Come on hurry up."

"Oh, okay." The pair quickly strapped the slurring Yuēhàn into Jeff's car. "Who are you?"

"Friend of the family." Jeff purposely didn't gain eye contact with the neighbour, squinting as much as possible, now wishing he'd put his lenses in. Jeff closed the door, rushed around to the driver's seat. "Thanks, must go," he said, before starting the car up and driving off.

Jeff drove for a few minutes, saw a quiet, dark area and pulled over, proceeding to cable tie Yuēhàn's ankles together followed by pulling his arms behind the passenger seat, cable tying them behind his back. Jeff headed north out of the city, towards the Yangtze River, he was looking for a quiet car park in the Baoshan Qu area. He roughly knew where to go, courtesy of his 'friend' Yuēse, eventually finding the particular car park his was looking for. After driving around the locality for eight minutes, he manoeuvred the vehicle to the far end of the car park. Jeff waited for a young courting couple to leave, it looked to Jeff like she was adjusting her top as they drove off. At one time, he would have laughed at that. After waiting for several minutes, he got out of the car, grabbed Yuēhàn, pulling him off the chair, which was a struggle, and dragging him to a concrete stanchion. He rushed back to the car, picked up his tool bag, which was in the passenger foot well. Jeff took the hold-down straps out, wrapping one around the stanchion and Yuēhàn's chest, pulling it tight. He pulled out the smelling salts, poured the whitish liquid onto a cotton wool pad, before smothering it onto Yuēhàn's nose and mouth — he flinched. Jeff repeated the process, followed by a few hard slaps to the face. He started to come round, another whiff of salts — he opened his eyes.

"Where am I, who are you?" he slurred, looking around, whilst trying to get up, pulling at the hold-down strap with his chest. His arms and shoulders ached due to his hands being tied behind his back. He looked at Jeff, who slapped him hard across his face. "Ouch."

"Do you remember this place, you fucking bastard." Jeff knelt in front of him, looking him in the eye.

Yuēhàn didn't like what he saw. "You've got blue eyes, who the fuck are you?" He struggled again, the strap holding him firm against the stanchion. "Let me go, when Zhān mǔ shì gets hold of you, you'll regret it." He thought the threat of his older brother might frighten his captor. "Let me go, what do you want?"

Jeff pulled out his mobile phone. "Tell me what happened that night."

The two men glared at each other; their faces were close enough to smell each other's breath. "What night, what are you talking about?" He struggled again, his wrists were very sore.

Jeff slapped him twice, hard across his face. "You know dam well what I mean, I won't ask you again, start talking." Jeff switched his phone on to video record.

Yuēhàn whimpered, thus the sorry tale was repeated, very similar to Yuēse's, typically blaming the other two. He of course, just stood and watched, claiming all innocence.

Jeff slapped him. "Do you expect me to believe that pack of lies?"

Yuēhàn looked Jeff in the eyes, snarling. "Who the fuck are you?"

"Have a fucking guess." Still holding the phone, he undid a couple of buttons on his shirt, revealing white skin.

"Shit, you're white, but, but, you look partly Chinese." Yuēhàn looked confused, not quite sure quite what he was seeing. "You killed Yuēse didn't you."

"Tell me again, the truth this time, what happened?"

Yuēhàn repeated the story, this time admitting to one rape only, again blaming the other two, in particular Zhān mǔ shì, whilst also protesting his complete innocence of the killings, making out he suggested letting them go, in particular David.

"You lying piece of shit, do you expect me to believe that, you've one last chance, to admit your part in it."

Yuēhàn stuck to his version, hoping it might give him a reprieve. "I'll go to the police, I'll tell them everything, take me there now, I'll confess, honest." He looked beggingly at Jeff.

"All you've said is to try and save your scrawny neck, gutlessly blaming the other two, you haven't once shown any remorse." Jeff moved his face close to Yuēhàn's, eyeballing him. "You and the other two are the scum of the earth."

Jeff switched his phone off. "Have you heard the expression, those who unsheathed the sword, die by it?" He nodded at Yuēhàn. "You know who I am don't you?"

"Eh, what?"

Jeff reached into his toolkit, grabbed the penknife, opening the longest blade with his right index finger and thumb. The blade was three inches long and, being new, was very sharp. Jeff held Yuēhàn's head by the scruff of his hair with his left hand, raised his right arm slashing down on Yuēhàn's neck, cutting the carotid artery. Blood started to squirt out. He repeated the process, this time making a deeper cut, and oxygenated blood pumped out. Jeff let go of Yuēhàn's hair, standing clear of the bloody mess.

Yuēhàn initially screamed, his eyes were wide open, the scream became a gurgle, and his head drooped slightly. He struggled in vain. Jeff ripped his shirt open, feeling Yuēhàn's ribcage, counted down to the third rib, held the point of the blade in the gap between the ribs, glanced at Yuēhàn, before ramming the blade into his heart. Yuēhàn slightly lurched forward, gasped a moaning sound. Jeff pulled the blade out, which was followed by a narrow jet of bright red frothy blood. He had to quickly step to his right to avoid the red jet. Yuēhàn started to shake, he was gasping short breaths, his eyes rolled back, he was bleeding out. Jeff wiped the bloody blade on Yuēhàn's shirt, closing it once he was satisfied it was clean, putting it back in his toolkit.

Jeff left Yuēhàn dying, as he quickly walked back to the Nissan, putting his bag in the back of the car, before wiping the blue felt-tip off the number plates. He surveyed the area, which, although dimly lit, he might still have been seen. *Good no one around.* He took one last look at the dying youngest Lee brother, slipped into the car, slowly driving off without switching his lights on. Yuēhàn, head down, still strapped to the stanchion, shuddered for the last time. He died as Jeff turned onto the road.

Jeff turned the car lights on after driving a couple of hundred metres. He made sure he kept to the speed limit, carefully and methodically driving back to his hotel, parking in the rear car park, where he was promptly sick, for the first and only time, thereafter, gathering his bag of goodies. Once safely in his room, Jeff noticed he'd got blood on his clothes, consequently he threw them in the shower whilst also having one, leaving the clothes in the shower tray while drying off, thinking, *I'll check them in the morning, I'll probably throw them away.*

Jeff lay on the bed reflecting on what he'd done. Although it sickened him, he was satisfied that he'd achieved his goal. He started to think about how to complete his overall aim, killing the last and most dangerous brother — Zhān mǔ shì.

CHAPTER FIFTY

Yuēhàn's disappearance was reported to the police by Zhān mǔ shì later in the evening. He noticed the Honda was still parked outside on returning home from a night out, and quickly phoned his dad to see if, indeed, Yuēhàn had left for work. Once he knew the answer, Zhān mǔ shì phoned the police to report Yuēhàn missing, fearing the worst after Yuēse's abduction and consequent execution, thereafter, driving around the neighbourhood in the Honda searching for him.

The police, who had, as Jeff assumed, been keeping a vigil every night, just before a brother returned home from work, arrived at the scene of abduction at ten thirty the same evening. An enquiry was made as to whom the walking stick and conical hat, found at the scene, belonged to, subsequently, both were bagged as possible evidence. The man, Jeff's helper, Fing Yuck, on being made aware of why there was a police presence in the area, came forward, giving a brief statement to the police; he would be helping them with their enquiries the next day. DI Chow, who was unavailable, would be taking charge of the case first thing the following morning.

Chow arrived at the police headquarters early the next morning, having spent the night with one of his lady friends, thus was in a goodish mood, for him anyway. He took a brief overview from the officer in charge of the previous evening's enquiries, including most importantly, Fing Yuck's brief statement. Chow wanted to see him as a matter of urgency. He quickly briefed his team as to their duties before heading to Beishi Road. He intended to speak with the Lee family first, before meeting Mr Yuck; the information gathered from him would determine in what direction the investigation would go.

The meeting with the Lees followed a similar pattern as when Chow and Wong visited them regarding Yuēse's death. What are the police doing? Why weren't the police present when Yuēhàn left for work, not just when he arrived home from work? Typically of criminals, the police should drop everything, their needs must and should come first. Chow let the family including Zhān mǔ shì, who was with his dysfunctional parents, rattle on, closing the meeting with, "We'll do all we can".

Fing Yuck was expecting a morning visit from the police, being instructed to stay in his flat until they arrived, furthermore, not to speak to anybody about his involvement in Yuēhàn's disappearance. Yuck, who lived on his own in block C, was a small, slim man in his mid-thirties greeted the police. He was obviously expecting their visit, offering the pair of officers refreshments as they entered his 'pigeon coop'. Chow wanted to ascertain whether or not Fing was an accomplice in Yuēhàn's kidnapping or merely an innocent neighbour helping out a stranger. Unusually, he let Wong lead the questioning, whilst he looked around Yuck's abode, listening to Wong's cross examination, content on his hunch that Yuck was a witness not a suspect. Chow then thoroughly grilled Fing about the man helping Yuēhàn into his car, plus a description of the car.

Mr Fing Yuck gave a similar description of the man, to that of the obnoxious Maye. "Just above average height, medium build, good head of hair, spoke without a strong Shanghai accent."

Chow, satisfied, probed for more detail about the man's face. "It was dark, the lighting in the area isn't that good," Yuck answered.

"Think, man, think, this is crucial detail, I must have everything you know, your knowledge is extremely important." Chow sharpened Yuck's concentration.

Yuck ran the fingers of both hands through his mop of thick black hair. "He seemed to purposely look away from me, I didn't twig as to why, obviously I do now." He looked at Wong, then Chow. "His eyes seemed to squint, for some strange reason, his face was different, you know." He waved his small hands about, irritating Chow. "His face was more oval shaped than round." Yuck's hands moved around his chin. "That's it, his head was longer than normal." Fing leant back in his chair, as if he'd just finish his maths examination.

Chow wanted more. "How did he behave, what did he say?"

Yuck's face was now distorted with concentration. "He seemed friendly enough, he told me he was taking Yuēhàn to hospital, as he wasn't well, he thanked me before carefully driving off." Fing looked to the ceiling, "He didn't speed off like you'd expect somebody rushing a friend to hospital." He looked at both officers. "Yes, em, I thought at the time he was a careful driver." Yuck leant back in his chair. "Oh, I've just remembered, he wore black clothes, yes I'm sure they were black," he said, looking at Chow for a reward — maybe a square of chocolate?

Satisfied, Chow now turned his attention to the car, nodding at Wong to lead the questioning, while he strode around, mulling over Fing's description, slightly nodding to himself.

"Well, er, let me think." Yuck scratched his head. "Yes that's it, it was a light coloured four-door saloon car." Fing looked at Wong. "I'm not sure the exact colour as you know, the lighting is not good around here."

Wong nodded whilst taking notes. "Can you be more specific on the colour, age and make?"

Fing shrugged his shoulders. "It was either white, grey, silver or light blue." He looked out of the window. "It was getting on a bit, at least eight years old, but I don't know the make or model, I think it could be a Japanese car."

Chow walked back into the conversation, positioned his face inches from Yuck's. "Did you know or meet Yuēhàn's 'friend' before last night?"

Fing Yuck flinched. "No, Mr Chow, no, please believe me."

Chow satisfied with all that he'd heard, said, "We'll be in touch." Proceeding to walkout of the flat, followed by Wong. The pair were just exiting the block, when Chow's phone chirped, the caller was one of Chow's underlings.

"Boss they've found a body, in a car park, in the Baoshan Qu area." There was a pregnant pause. "I think it's the same one as where David and Chynna got killed."

"We're one our way, tell the locals to tape the area off." Chow walked quickly to the car. "No faffing about, I want to be there in five minutes."

Wong bullied his way through the early morning Shanghai traffic. There was little conversation in the car, Chow looked out of the passenger window for the majority of the journey. Wong rightly assumed that his Boss had eliminated Yuck as an accessory to kidnap or murder. He parked the police car in a similar position to the last time they'd been there, however, a body not a pool of blood awaited them.

The officer in charge, until Chow arrived, informed Chow and Wong that the body was found at six o'clock in the morning, by a woman parking her car. She informed the local police, who temporarily took charge of the scene, taping the area off, before deciding to inform Shanghai police murder division. Chow thanked the officer, whilst slowly walking to the body strapped to a stanchion. Both he and Wong knew immediately who it was, but Chow continued walking the scene. A local pathologist, whom Chow had met a couple of years previously, was about to examine Yuēhàn's dead body. "Wait a minute," he snapped. "Whose are those footprints?" he said, pointing to a series of shoe prints created by walking in the blood. "I want photographs of all of them, particularly the bigger ones." He nodded at the pathologist to continue his on-site brief autopsy, he knew the ambulance one of his team had requested, would be arriving forthwith, taking the body to the mortuary for a full post mortem.

"I can't see any other injuries or wounds other than the obvious." The pathologist looked at Chow. "This man's carotid artery was slashed, with at least two cuts." He pointed to Yuēhàn's neck, before pointing to his chest. "I would guess," he coughed, "a single stab wound to the heart, with a small blade." He looked at both Wong and Chow. "No longer than four inches." The pathologist, a middle-aged, bespectacled man could read Chow's mind. "He's been dead for over twelve but less than twenty-four hours." He put his right hand in his trouser pocket. "He was killed here." He pointed to the stanchion with his left hand. "In short, he bled out."

Chow had more or less assumed as much, nodded, thanking the pathologist for his brief summation. Once satisfied all relevant photographs were taken, Chow gave permission for the holding strap to be released, so that the body could be taken to the waiting ambulance, which had just arrived. Wong supervised proceedings, bagging the strap. The ambulance quickly sped off, Chow had instructed he wanted a full post mortem as soon as possible.

Wong stood by the police car waiting for his boss, assuming they would be racing back to HQ to prepare for the next team briefing. Instead, Chow started to slowly walk around the car park, summoning Wong with the wave of his right index finger. "Well, Sergeant your thoughts?"

Wong got over the initial shock at being asked his thoughts. *What's he playing at*, he thought. Whilst fiddling with his half Windsor, he rested his right hand on his chin. "My assumption is that the killer, or killers, are the same ones as Yuēse's." He moved his hands behind his back linking them, as the pair strode seemingly aimlessly around the car park, Chow leading the direction. "In addition, the killings are linked to David and Chynna's." Wong felt quite chuffed with himself, he rightly assumed he'd got the facts correct. Chow slightly nodded.

"Anything else, Sergeant?" Chow inwardly laughed, the stray dog in a neighbouring street could have told him what he'd just heard.

Wong, thinking he was on a roll looked to the concrete ceiling of the car park, maybe for inspiration. "I wouldn't be surprised if the killer drugged Yuēhàn with the same drug, GHB." He put his hands in his pockets, and looked at Chow for acknowledgement.

Chow suddenly stopped, took one final look around the car park. "Okay Zìmò, let's get back to the station, no need to rush, it'll give Wu chance to do the autopsy." Wong didn't realise what Chow was really thinking, his boss was considering the reasoning behind the completely different killing techniques used for both brothers, and whether it was, as he guessed, just one killer.

"This is what I've got for you thus far," said the physician to the two police officers, in a very matter-of-fact manner, almost waving one of his spindly fingers at Chow. Dr Wu leant against a chair. "Pretty straightforward really, firstly a few minor injuries, I'd guess, from an initial struggle, the bruising around his ankles and wrists indicate they were tied before his demise." His thin frame wobbled, Wong thought he was going to fall over, consequently moved half a pace towards the fragile pathologist, but he waved him off. "I'm okay, Sergeant." He steadied himself. "He was cut, twice, quite savagely, with a small knife, slicing the carotid artery, which would have killed him, however, the killer wanted to make sure, piercing his heart with one stabbing, almost certainly with the same knife."

Chow, arms folded, nodded in acceptance. "In your opinion, what is the size of the knife's blade."

Wu looked at Yuēhàn's naked body lying on the slab, and turned to Chow. "No more than four inches, I'd say closer to three," he reflected. "Probably a penknife, the type you could buy in most stores that sell that type of item, typically of the hardware variety."

"So it wasn't a kitchen knife," Wong blurted out.

Chow looked to the heavens, *the stray dog just barked.* "No, Mr Wong, the blade is too thin for one reason, plus the type of cut." Wu's sarcastic tongue admonished Chow's partner.

Chow quickly changed the subject. "Time of death Doctor?" he asked in an apologetic tone.

Wu picked up the olive branch. "Killed before midnight, I'll have a more precise time when I do the full autopsy." Doctor Wu pointed with a spindly right index finger, to his colleague, Dr Huang, who was standing to Chow's left. "Dr Huang has some information for you."

Dr Huang nodded at Chow then Wong. "Gentlemen, I've performed a toxicity test on this man." She looked to the dead body. "He had a large amount of GHB recently injected into him, almost enough to kill him, certainly the quantity would have caused permanent organ damage." She moved her small, plump frame towards Yuēhàn's corpse, pointing at a pinprick and bruising on his body. "This is where the drug was administered." The head of forensics glanced at Wong. "In a somewhat amateurish manner or," switching her eyes to Chow, "rushed, attacking fashion." She stood back, turning to the police officers. "The person who injected this amount of gamma hydroxybutyrate acid into this man, and incidentally, the previous victim, intended to render them helpless in a very quick time; they would have been 'sleeping' in a matter of a few minutes."

She waited for the information to sink in. "He also had smelling salts in his nose and mouth." She faced Chow. "In short, the killer wanted both victims alive, after rendering them helpless, to normally torture, but in both cases," she turned to Wu, "question or interrogate, as we haven't found any evidence of torturing having taken place."

Chow surreptitiously nodded at Wong, who thanked both doctors. Before hurrying off, he asked a question he knew the answer to. "Do you think it's the same killer?"

The doctors looked at each other, nodding in unison. "Yes, almost certainly."

Chow thanked them both, quickly turned, walking out, mentally preparing himself for the delivery of the latest information to his waiting audience. Wong had organised Chow's team, giving them the briefest of overviews on the latest developments, prior to Chow taking centre stage. This was the first occasion the full team were required since the team briefing following Yuēse's killing. Chow had instructed two members to visit chemists enquiring about purchase of the sleeping drug GHB, with special interest in a man fitting the description Maye had given Chow and Wong. He also put a car on observation duties, parked on Beishi Road, when either Lee brother arrived home from work, partly to placate the Lee family, the last thing he wanted was a complaint for negligence. The chemist enquiry reaped dividends on day three of the investigation, the assistant who served Jeff, gave a similar description to that of Maye, although omitting the dialect conclusion. She did, however, inform the officers he used the name Flowers, subsequently Jeff was known as Mr Flowers, the code for the investigation being called Tulip. That was Wong's idea, which tickled Chow's sense of humour.

Chow sat at the front to one side, instructing Wong, much to his surprise, to deliver the latest developments on the Tulip investigation. Wong took his jacket off, rolling his shirt sleeves up in a 'Chowisk' manner, before undoing his shirt top button plus loosening his tie. "Okay everyone, listen up, this morning, Yuēhàn Lee was found in a car park in the Baoshan Qu area, the same car park that David and Chynna were killed." He emphasised same. "Due to the obvious link with Yuēse being placed outside their apartment, in addition, the injection of the immobilising drug GHB, into both brothers," he glanced to his left, Chow gave the slightest of nods, "we think it's the same killer, Mr Flowers." Wong went on to give a full description of the prime suspect, finishing his brief with, "We assume he will go after Zhān mǔ shì Lee next."

"Thank you, Sergeant." Chow got off his chair, joining Wong, slowly walking from left to right, his hands clasped together behind his back. "This is how we're going to play it. I want a car positioned before and after he goes to work, arriving half hour before, in both cases, only leaving when he safely leaves and returns to his flat." He stopped pacing. "That's it, carry on."

In his deepest of thoughts, Chow had a degree of empathy with 'Mr Flowers'. He unknowingly yet rightly assumed that the only people in Shanghai or even China for that matter, in any danger were the Lee family, in particular the only surviving brother. He mused whether or not 'Mr Flowers' might go after the Lee parents, as, after all, to Chow's thinking they were the Frankensteins that created the three monsters. Chow snapped out of his thoughts, he now had the arduous task of revisiting the Lees, to inform them of the latest news about their youngest brother and son. *He'd receive more belly aching about the lack of police protection. Hypocrites*, he thought.

CHAPTER FIFTY-ONE

Fing Yuck arrived back at his flat at six o'clock in the evening, content with his day's work, relieved that the police, in particular, Mr Chow, weren't waiting for him. Fing found Chow quite intimidating, both from a physical and a professional point of view. He held a small bag of shopping in his left hand, unlocking the door with his right one, opening the door with his right knee and foot. Safely inside Yuck was about to close the door, when he heard a rushing sound behind him. *Bloody hell, not Chow again,* he thought.

"Yuck, you treacherous bastard, you've sold our Yuēhàn down the river." Fing Yuck felt a fist hit him on the back of his head, he turned to see the Lee family barging their way into his flat. *Oh shit, I wish it was Chow,* he rethought. The Lees, who'd recently had another visit from Chow, had been hiding in the stairwell shadows, waiting for him to come home. Zhān mǔ shì, who was twice Fing's size, led the way, he was the deliverer of the welcoming punch, followed by the fag smoking Mrs Lee, with the obnoxious Mr Lee behind her. He promptly closed the door, with a slam.

Zhān mǔ shì dragged Yuck by his throat into his small living room, slapping him hard across his face, before chucking him into the same chair he'd sat in during the police questioning, earlier in the day. The Lees surrounded Fing Yuck, taking it in turns to administer slaps and punches. Mrs Lee in particular was the most vicious, scratching his face and neck; it didn't take long before Yuck fell on the floor, whimpering in pain. "We've heard that yesterday, you helped some bloke put Yuēhàn in his car, you fucking moron," Mr Lee spat, before kicking Fing in the stomach. Yuck grimaced in pain.

"Look, I didn't know what was going to happen, I was trying to help Yuēhàn." He looked up at his attackers. "This bloke said his was taking him to hospital, I thought I was doing Yuēhàn a good turn."

The three took it in turns to kick Fing several more times, trying to inflict as much pain as possible. Yuck was crying in agony. Mrs Lee knelt by Yuck, grabbing his throat with her sharp nails. "You helped a stranger kill Yuēhàn, you complete wanker, are you that thick?" She continued to try and strangle Yuck, who tried to get her hands away with his. Yuck looked at his female attacker, he winced at her black rotting teeth and ugly face only inches from his. Her breath reeked. She tried to bite his nose off, being encouraged by the other two and nearly succeeding.

"Please Mrs Lee," he begged. "I was trying to help, please let me go, I won't tell the police, honest."

Mrs Lee, spitting out the tip of Fing's nose, stood up. "He needs some fresh air."

Mr Lee and Zhān mǔ shì grabbed Yuck's crumpled body, putting his arms around their shoulders, ironically in a similar manner to that of Jeff 'helping' Yuēhàn, dragging him out of his flat towards the main staircase. The Lees dragged the moaning Yuck up the staircase, to the top of block B, propping his body against a concrete wall. Zhān mǔ shì kicked the roof access door open, and the Lees dragged the helpless Yuck onto the roof. The fresh early evening air temporarily revived him. "What's happening, what are you doing." He realised where he was.

"You'll find out soon enough, you bag of treacherous shit," Mr Lee replied and continued. "When was the last time you had a leg and a wing?" The three laughed simultaneously, Mrs Lee spitting several times with excitement.

"Zhān mǔ shì you grab his right wrist and ankle, Pop, you do the same with his left wrist and ankle," she instructed, pointing to Fing's wrists and ankles. The pair did as instructed, carrying Yuck to the roof's edge, holding him so he could look down. He tried to struggle but he was too weak and they were far too strong. "After three, throw this traitor off," she barked, spitting at Yuck.

Yuck struggled in vain, his captors' grips were too strong. "One." Mrs Lee held her right hand in the air, the two men laughed hysterically. "Two," she hissed.

"Please, Mrs Lee, please," Fing Yuck sobbed uncontrollably.

"Yucky, you're out of lucky," she lowered her right hand. "Three."

Mr Lee and Zhān mǔ shì swung Fing backwards to gain momentum, before throwing the screaming Yuck off the roof. The three linked arms as they watched him fall. It took Fing Yuck four seconds to hit the ground, the Lees laughing as he splattered all over the concrete pavement below. "Yucked you well and truly fucked," Mrs Lee cackled. "Now let's go and have a celebratory drink."

CHAPTER FIFTY-TWO

Jeff kept a very low profile for the first few days following Yuēhàn's death, deciding to use the facilities in a shopping mall further away from The Golden Flower, as he rightly assumed the police had been checking both chemist and hardware shops to get his identification. What he didn't know was, that Chow and his team had an idea of what he looked like, courtesy of Maye, due to the receipt found on Yuēse. Jeff put the clothes he'd worn on the night of the attack in a plastic bag he found in the bottom of the wardrobe, dumping it in a public bin, because they had too much blood on them. *No point handing myself on a plate,* he thought. When he did venture out, he wore the tinted glasses, plus a face mask and black hat, both bought from the other mall, the object being to conceal as much of his face as he could, without raising suspicion or standing out from the crowd. Conveniently for Jeff, face masks were common place in Shanghai, due to air pollution issues, so he bought a variety that covered as much of his face, in particular his chin, as possible. He could wear one without raising suspicion. At the shopping mall, whilst buying the box of face masks and cheap hat, he picked up the local free paper. The headlines weren't pleasant reading — for anyone.

Two deaths in the spate of twenty-four hours! The article went on to describe scant detail on both deaths. Jeff read the paper on a public bench, he deduced Fing Yuck was the man who helped him manoeuvre Yuēhàn into his car, and rightly concluded the Lees killed him in an act of violent stupidity. Due to Yuck being one of two people that could identify Jeff, it hardened his resolve to finish the job.

After finishing reading the paper, a plan started to hatch in Jeff's brain. He walked back into the shopping mall, buying a baseball bat plus lemon juice in a plastic squeezy container. He put the lemon juice in his jacket pocket, the bat in a large shopping bag, disguising the shape of the bat by crumpling the bag sides. Jeff decided to go for a long walk to try and gather his thoughts. He realised that he was on borrowed time, therefore, sooner or later Chow would track him down, probably by checking passport arrivals and their consequent trail, leading to the hotel plus Joni's car rental.

Jeff enjoyed the walk, the weather was dry, not much breeze. In the sun it was pleasantly warm, although it did get cold at night, not that it bothered Jeff. He walked at a steady pace for three hours, stopping briefly at a cafe for lunch, before heading back to his hotel with a clear head. He'd made his mind up — he had to act immediately.

Early that Friday evening, Jeff, dressed in a pair of new flannels and beige shirt, loaded the car with his toolkit, including the baseball bat and lemon juice, before heading out, driving past the blocks of flats on Beishi Road to check whether the Honda was parked or not. *Good,* he thought, *it's not there, the smug bastard must have gone to work.*

***

Zhān mǔ shì finished his lunch, jumped in the Honda, and sneeringly waved at the two police officers as he headed off to work, content in the knowledge that they'd be there when he got back at ten o'clock in the evening. Not that he was particularly bothered, he wasn't frightened, so he portrayed. He wondered who this mystery killer was that had murdered his brothers. *He certainly wasn't going down without a fight, he'd enjoy exacting revenge.* He knew that Chow knew, he'd been involved in killing that moron, Yuck, the family fobbing the police off with a, 'we were watching television together', bullshit story. They got rid of all the clothing they'd worn, including footwear, by burning it in his parents' flat, long before the police arrived. They knew they'd be the prime suspects — it served Yuck right, in their twisted minds.

It had been several days since both his younger brother's and Yuck's deaths, and he had had the time off work to grieve in addition to celebrating, subsequently he drank heavily with his parents. All they talked about was getting even with the killer or killers, intertwined with braying about Yuck's departure from life. He knew he was over the drink-driving limit as he drove off to work for the first time since the

258

killing, assuming the police wouldn't stop him — idiots had sympathy for him. He wondered who he'd bully at work.

***

Chow had organised his team to take it in turns, making sure there was a police presence both before and after Zhān mǔ shì was at work, after all he didn't want to be sued by the unscrupulous Lees for lack of police protection. He decided to do the last shift of the week. Being Friday evening, he planned to visit one of his girls after seeing Zhān mǔ shì safely tucked up in bed, even though he detested the Lee family. Whilst he couldn't find enough incriminating evidence on them for killing Yuck, he knew they'd done it. He could smell the stench of burnt fabric, presumably their bloody clothes, when he visited Mr and Mrs Lee after the apparent suicide jump had been reported. They fobbed him off with a load of baloney, each saying they were mourning Yuēhàn's death, watching television while getting drunk. The three off them kept repeating the bullshit story, suggesting that Yuck, on realising the gravity of his mistake, couldn't live with himself, belly laughing at each other whilst repeating the story.

***

Jeff drove steadily through the Friday evening traffic, he wasn't in a rush, not like most of the other drivers, eager to get home to their loved ones. He reflected on whether he'd made the right decision because, when he got back to his room after his long walk, Jeff booked a flight out of Shanghai back to the UK on a flexible ticket, which was valid for a week. It was an indirect flight, stopping in five places, taking two days, but was the cheapest option as he was running out of money. He continued his journey, it wouldn't be too long now before he arrived at the SIAC car factory. It would be a waiting game for the rest of the evening. Jeff decided to play it by ear because he, firstly, didn't know if Zhān mǔ shì had gone to work and secondly, how to set up the final attack. He'd have to think of something — and quick.

***

Zhān mǔ shì clocked in a few minutes late, his breath reeked of alcohol, his shift supervisor thought about bollocking him for lateness plus incapacity, but let it go. He, like all the rest of the workforce, was intimidated by this detestable bully. Zhān mǔ shì made his way to the locker room to change into his overalls, which he had left in there. Once changed, he sauntered to his work station. His job was unusual, as it required a high degree of physical strength, consequently he was one of only a few employees that could manage it, giving him macho bragging rights, not that he needed any justification or encouragement. He was feared by everybody, in addition disliked by the majority, however, he did have his hangers on, who name dropped him in exchange for favours.

***

Chow looked out of his office window into the dark Friday night, the lights of car drivers lit up the city landscape. He took his hands out of his pockets, rubbed his chin, and took a quick glance at the clock on his office wall. It was nine p.m., it wouldn't be long now. He looked back out again, pondering on who to visit once he'd done his duty by checking on the safety of the surviving Lee brother. Chow considered what he would do if the attack happened on his watch. Maybe cheering on Mr Flowers. That thought brought a smile, a rare one, to Chow's solemn mug. *Unfortunately, I'd have to help that piece of human garbage,* he corrected his thoughts. Chow walked back to the crime scene board he'd been looking at before his momentary break, joining Wong, who was adding artistic arrows to related boxes. He, too, was filling in the boredom.

***

Jeff pulled up outside the factory, just metres from the front gate exit. He looked at his watch, it was now nine fifteen p.m. He switched the engine off. He contemplated his plans for the evening, subsequently tormenting himself with questions. Was Zhān mǔ shì at work, or did he go out socialising, that was the first question. If he was at work what time did he finish, was the second question, followed by, if he was at work, what would he do other than follow him after he'd finished. Jeff decided, after a heavy deliberating afternoon session with himself, that he would take the first opportunity to fulfil his aim, taking pot luck on chance and just go for it, come what may. *Regardless of planning, I must be fully prepared, tonight could be the night, I must be ready, just in case,* he thought to himself.

***

After working for a couple of hours, Zhān mŭ shì nipped off to the toilet, asking one of his hangers-on to fill in for him. He closed the closet cubicle, sat on the toilet seat and shut his eyes. The factor of drinking nonstop for days without eating a substantial meal, was catching up with him, he needed at least one good night's sleep. *I'll have a good kip when I get home,* he thought, as he dozed off. Zhān mŭ shì was abruptly woken by one of his chums, he'd been absent from his work station for nearly one hour. His chum had stood on the pan of the adjacent toilet, shouting down at him. The pair quickly returned before disciplinary action would be taken. Once again, he'd gotten away with abusing the system.

***

Chow rechecked his watch. "Come on, Sergeant, let's get this charade over with, I want to make sure we get there before he gets home. I don't want a disciplinary on behalf of him, of all people." The pair left the police station at nine forty-five p.m. arriving outside block C Beishi Road, just before ten o'clock, knowing Zhān mŭ shì clocked off at ten that evening. They calculated that it would only take him twenty minutes to drive home, due to the ease of late-night driving conditions. Wong poured them both a cup of coffee from a flask his wife had prepared for her husband and his boss, who she knew he worshipped, regardless of the constant chastisement. In a rare moment of informality Chow joked with Wong, almost apologising to him for choosing the Friday night shift. They talked about what the weekend held in store. Wong, of course would spend the time with his girls, Chow was coy about his affairs. Chow looked at his watch; it was ten fifteen. *the quicker he gets home the better*, he thought.

***

Jeff placed the baseball bat on the passenger seat. He loaded the syringe to the maximum with GHB, putting a small cork on the needle point, the last thing he needed was to clumsily stab himself. He rechecked his jacket side pocket to confirm the lemon squeezy was there, it was more of a nervous gesture, as he'd checked it ten minutes previously. The factory gates opened, and the steady stream of cars started to leave. He started the Nissan up, slotted it into first gear — all was ready. He waited seven minutes, checking every car that went past him. *This could be the Honda, it's that shape,* he thought. It was a Honda, but not The Honda. He waited, more cars drove past, another Honda was coming. Jeff tried to check the number plate, thinking, *this might be it, just maybe.*

***

Zhān mǔ shì managed to get through his first shift since coming back from grievance leave, it wasn't the grief that made him struggle, it was the copious amounts of very strong liquor that he'd been consuming. He clocked out after first changing back into his casual clothing, eventually getting to his car at ten minutes past ten. He chucked his jacket into the back of the car, his forearms revealing the tiger and dragon tattoos he was proud of, before slowly driving out of the car park, following the early charge of other drivers. All he wanted to do was get to his flat and sleep, possibly all weekend. Once through the factory gates, he almost hit a parked car. As he swerved around it, he electronically wound the passenger window down, shouted, "Wanker". Continuing his journey, glancing in his wing mirror, he noticed the parked car had moved off. Zhān mǔ shì smiled to himself, at least he had the pleasure of giving Chow some sarcastic piss take when he arrived back home, which wouldn't be long.

Wong poured his boss another coffee, finishing the contents of the flask. "He'll be here soon Boss. I think I'll have a lie in tomorrow morning." He took another sip of his drink, loosening his tie afterward. Chow looked at his watch, it was now ten twenty p.m. He was starting to get irritable, his impatience, one of his few weaknesses some might say, was coming to the fore.

Chow finished his coffee, checked his watch again. It was now twenty-five minutes past ten. "Phone the factory, check what time he left, he was instructed to drive straight home, that was part of the arrangement, straight home."

Wong rang the car factory. "He clocked out at five minutes past, so, he probably got to his car, say, ten minutes past, driving carefully he should be here anytime now."

***

It could be, it might be, yes I think it is. Jeff studied the car as it approached his, it seemed to swerve slightly, the driver, a big, solid looking character shouted something through his open passenger window at Jeff, it sounded like wanker. Jeff double-checked the car, yes it was a Honda, four-door saloon, yes it was black, yes the registration was what he'd written down once he knew it, from the Yuēse attack. Jeff pulled out into the flow of traffic; he was two cars behind Zhān mǔ shì's Honda. Jeff accelerated, quickly overtaking the car in front of him, slightly cutting the driver up, much to his annoyance. Jeff waved in acceptance of his selfish driving. Zhān mǔ shì turned right at the next set of traffic lights, conveniently for Jeff the driver between them carried straight on. Jeff was now tailgating the black Honda, and both cars were driving slightly over the correct speed limit. Jeff got the impression Zhān mǔ shì wasn't concentrating on his driving, as the car seemed to wander slightly from time to time. The cars were approaching a set of traffic lights, the Honda abruptly braked, the driver suddenly realising the lights were on red. Jeff, driving too close to the Honda, slammed into the back of it — all went quiet for a minute or two.

***

Zhān mǔ shì turned right, he wasn't far from home, he smiled again, thinking, *Chowy baby, here I come, get ready for some shit.* He felt tired, only controlling the steering wheel with one hand. He knew the car swayed a bit. *Fuck'em,* he typically selfishly thought. His eyes closed, only for second, he opened them again. *Shit, the lights are on red.* Subsequently he hit the brakes hard. The car behind his smashed into the back of the Honda. Zhān mǔ shì hit his head on the steering wheel, dazing him slightly. The car stalled. All went quiet — for a moment.

***

Chow got out of the car, leaning against the roof. Wong joined him soon after. He looked at his watch, it was now 10.35 p.m. Chow had a bad feeling. He now contemplated an unwise decision he might have to make, splitting the team. The route to and from the factory had been agreed, the most straightforward direct route, not zigzagging through the back streets. "We'll give him another ten minutes, if he's not here by then, you will drive the route and check to see if he's broken down, or just running late." Chow paced about, looking up and down the road. The minute hand hit the nine, making it quarter to eleven. "Zìmò drive the agreed route back to the factory, he's in for a right bollocking when I get hold of him." Sergeant Wong headed off.

***

Jeff, being more alert, had seen the traffic lights change to red, and subsequently braced himself for the inevitable front-rear collision, hitting his head slightly on the steering wheel before jerking back into his seat. He quickly came to his senses, thinking, *this is an ideal opportunity, quick Jeff, take advantage of it.* Luckily no other vehicle was behind him, so he reversed the Nissan a couple of paces. Jeff exited his car just as Zhān mǔ shì opened his car door. *Good he looks dazed,* he thought.

Tooled up with the bat hidden behind his leg, he approached the swaying, swearing Zhān mǔ shì.

"What are-you fucking doing, you fucking idiot, you've damaged my car." He was now parallel with the rear passenger door, still slightly dazed.

Jeff casually approached him, all apologetic. "Sorry mate, it's my fault, I'll pay for the damage, let's have a look." The occasional car drove past, the drivers gawping at the apparent exchange of driver details as it was a minor accident.

The pair met at the rear of the Honda. "This will cost you dearly, I want the whole car touched up, or else." He pointed threateningly at Jeff, his black eyes piercing at Jeff's face. The men were a pace apart.

Jeff had his left hand in his jacket pocket. "What's that?" Jeff pointed upwards.

Zhān mǔ shì looked up, Jeff pulled the lemon squeezy out of his pocket, squirting several shots into his eyes. "Ah, ah, you bastard." His eyes were stinging like hell.

Jeff swung the baseball bat hitting Zhān mǔ shì's right kneecap. He then quickly hit his left shin, Zhān mǔ shì screamed in pain. Jeff squirted his eyes with more lemon juice. He was screaming with agony as he fell to the floor. Jeff grabbed him, dragging Zhān mǔ shì to the back of the Nissan, opened the boot door, hit him hard a couple of times to the head with the bat, gradually putting him in the boot. Jeff took out the syringe, injecting the GHB into Zhān mǔ shì's right side, in his rush he didn't put the full amount in, before slamming the boot shut. He calmly walked to the driver's door, waved a driver on before driving off, keeping to the speed limit

Zhān mǔ shì tried to struggle, he banged on the side of the car whilst shouting. The initial stinging in his eyes started to wear off, and he now fully realised the damage to his kneecap and shin, consequently the pain started to kick in. He started to feel sleepy, all went black — it was now ten forty p.m.

***

"I'm now turning right, still nothing." Wong looked at the traffic coming in the opposite direction. He was in constant communication with Chow. "Is he at the flats yet?"

"No he bloody well isn't, keep your eyes peeled." Chow was getting anxious.

Wong raised his eyes, he could get away with it on his own. "I'm now approaching the traffic lights, hold on." He stared at a black car appearing to have stalled at the lights in the opposite direction. "There's a black car stationary at the lights, it's…" He slowed down waving passing cars to overtake. "Shit, it's his Honda." Wong pulled over, rushed out of the police car, and crossed over the road, to the empty car. "He's gone." Wong looked around. "He's not here, Boss, there's a slight bump at the rear of the car, one of the tail light cover's cracked."

The line went silent for a few seconds. "He's got him, quick get back here." Wong spun the car round, quickly driving back to Beishi Road, Chow met him towards block A, due to running in his direction. "Move over, Sergeant, I'll drive." Wong slid over the handbrake into the passenger seat, he'd never experienced Chow's driving before. The front wheels spun, smoke exuding from them, Wong buckled up, as the car screeched off.

"Where are we going, Boss?"

Chow, driving like a madman whizzed through the night traffic, the time was ten minutes to eleven o'clock. "North, the Yangtze River." He paused for a second. "That's where I'd go."

CHAPTER FIFTY-THREE

Jeff was careful to keep to the speed limit, he didn't want to attract attention from a speed cop when there wasn't a need for it. He knew his passenger would be soundly asleep for some time. He was ten minutes away from his destination when he decided to ring Shanghai International Airport, confirming his booking from his flexi-ticket for the first available flight to the UK. He felt pleased with himself, he'd be on the morning flight leaving at eight o'clock, giving him plenty of time to get back to The Golden Flower, showered and changed, and leaving the Nissan at the airport. He pondered over whether to leave Joni an apologetic note, thinking, *I'll cross that bridge when I get to it.*

Jeff checked the clock on the car dashboard, it was reading 11.05 p.m. He nodded to himself, it wouldn't be long now. Jeff reflected on the night's event. It was pure fluke how it happened, as he didn't really have a proper plan, similar in a way to Yuēse's attack. *Maybe it was meant to be, possibly poetic justice,* he considered. He could now see the road to Baoshan Port river buildings that both Yuēse and Yuēhàn had described, killing his lights as he approached the entrance, and turning to the right onto a feeder road, stopping where the Lees' van had roughly parked.

Jeff picked up his toolkit plus the baseball bat, as he had a quick look around. *Good, the coast is clear.* He unlocked the boot of the car quickly standing back, with the bat raised for immediate attack. Zhān mǔ shì was still out cold, but unfortunately for Jeff, not as comatose as he would have preferred him to be. Jeff half dragged him out of the boot, leaning the bat against the rear bumper, before tying his hands together behind his back with a cable clip. Jeff didn't notice Zhān mǔ shì's eyes starting to flicker. He finished pulling him out of the boot, propping him up against the bumper, closing the boot thereafter.

Zhān mǔ shì felt the cold evening air flush over him, his legs were in pain, however, quickly realising the danger he was in — he had to think, and fast. He pretended to be unconscious which was quite an effort considering how much agony he felt. He squinted to get his bearings in the semi-dark, his other senses switched on.

Jeff, not realising he hadn't administered Zhān mǔ shì with the full dose, calmly prepared himself on finishing his overall aim, placing his phone in position to record the third Lee brother's confession. Out came the smelling salts from his bag. Sprinkling a dose onto a cotton wool pad, Jeff placed it over Zhān mǔ shì's nose and mouth. This brought him fully round, elevating his concentration to a higher level, his brain was now buzzing. He acted dumb. "Where am I, who are you?" He knew the answers, he was buying thinking time.

Jeff moved his face in front of Zhān mǔ shì's. "You've got blue eyes, fuck me, you look like a freak." Jeff took the knife out of his jacket pocket, opened the blade, and stabbed Zhān mǔ shì in the stomach. "Ahh, you bastard."

"Right, you piece of shit, tell me what you and your scumbag brothers did to my son, yes my son and Chynna." The penny dropped for Zhān mǔ shì. "Any lying and I'll club you." He switched the video record to on, for his phone.

Zhān mǔ shì went through the sorry tale, like the other two previously, blaming Yuēse and Yuēhàn for most of the barbarity, surreptitiously moving his wrists over the hot exhaust pipe. He felt his skin burn, the pain being almost unbearable, however, he achieved his aim, the plastic tie quickly melted, his hands were now free!

***

Wong didn't realise his car could perform 'miracles'. Chow drove like a man possessed. Using supreme skill incorporated with physical power, they 'flew' through the evening traffic. Chow had learnt to drive at an early age, he certainly knew how to handle a car by the time he was sixteen years of age. Chow's right hand was constantly pulling the handbrake, using it for speeding the car around tight bends, by sliding it, using his left hand to control the steering wheel. Wong sat terrified, he held his breath, holding on for dear life, wondering if he'd see his wife and twin girls again. Chow didn't need an excuse to bully his way through what traffic there was. He cut cars up, overtook in dangerous places, in addition he used the car horn, main beam lights plus the siren. They reached the road leading to the river buildings by ten minutes past eleven. The lighting in the area was scant, just one light illuminated the area by the river, where they were heading.

***

Zhān mǔ shì, although in severe pain from several places on his body, realised he was in extreme danger, the man he was with intended to kill him. He flexed his now free wrists, keeping them roughly in the same position. He was biding his time, forming a cunning plan.

Jeff felt relieved that he'd managed to achieve his overall goal. It would now be a matter of a minute or so, to complete the task, smashing Zhān mǔ shì's head to pulp, followed by one stab wound to the heart, before chucking his body into the river. Jeff stood in front of his victim, bat raised. "Have you heard the expression 'he who plays with fire gets burnt'?"

"Please, have mercy." He slowly moved his hands to just behind his back, his left leg, although hairline fractured, could still be used.

"You're about to get burnt." Jeff slammed the baseball bat down towards Zhān mǔ shì's head. Just as it was about to make contact, both men heard a car suddenly brake sharply; the distraction was all Zhān mǔ shì needed. His hands shot from behind his back, in one swift motion he grabbed the bat, snatching it out of Jeff's unsuspecting hands. He hit Jeff on the side of the face with it, at the same time knocking him off balance, tripping him by putting his right foot behind Jeff's left heel in a sweeping action. The combination of the surprise, the impact of the blow, plus the trip made Jeff lose his balance. He fell to the ground. Zhān mǔ shì, using the bat as a prop, got to his feet, the pain he was in seemed to subside, and his renowned evil grin returned. As Jeff tried to scramble to his feet, he felt the excruciating pain of his left ankle fracturing, followed by the cracking of his left ribcage. Zhān mǔ shì had delivered two swift, hard blows to his body. Jeff struggled to his feet, barely being able to stand. In retaliation, Jeff slashed out with the knife, lunging at his intended victim. Adrenaline kept both men fighting, seeming to mask a substantial amount of pain and disability. In addition, they were both now fighting for their lives, this was a winner takes all contest. Although Jeff missed with the knife, his lunge knocked Zhān mǔ shì off his feet, resulting in both men grappling on the riverbank, each gripping the other man's weapon-holding wrist, whilst trying to punch with the other one.

***

Chow and Wong reached the river master's buildings, Chow screeching the car to a halt. He could see the two men, one had his back to him, he held, what looked to Chow, like a baseball bat raised ready to strike the other man propped against the rear of a car. The silhouette of the standing man reminded Chow of somebody, the shape of his head, his height and build. Chow's brain was whirring; he instantly knew who the other man was. Rather than drive down the riverbank, Chow decided it would be quicker to run the thirty paces to where the combatants were. They were halfway to the scene and both men were rolling on the floor grappling. It was clear to Chow by how they moved, that both men were badly injured. Just as they got there, an almighty scream came from one of the men; it was the smaller of the two, he'd been stabbed in the chest.

Zhān mǔ shì's youth, extra weight and physical strength now played to his advantage. This type of fighting suited him, he intended to wear his opponent down, he could feel the strength draining from the blue-eyed freak. "Now we'll see who'll burn," he said in ear shot of both policemen. "I enjoyed killing your son — he cried like a baby." He sneered at Jeff and snarled. "We all relished raping that slut of a girlfriend of his." He started laughing, and continued his abusive barrage. "I'm going to savour killing you, even more than when we murdered that moron Yuck."

This news spurred Jeff. He wriggled his knife-holding wrist free, and was now on top of his opponent. It was now or never, he had a chance. Jeff pulled his arm back, aiming the blade at Zhān mǔ shì's ribcage, hoping to hit his heart. Zhān mǔ shì, anticipating this, grabbed Jeff's forearm, using the leverage of Jeff's movement to roll him. Letting go of the bat, using both hands, he turned the direction of the knife towards Jeff, ramming it into his chest. Jeff screamed.

"That's enough, we'll deal with it now." Chow demanded as he arrived at the scene.

"I'll say when it's over," Zhān mǔ shì sneered, ramming the blade once again into Jeff, who lurched in pain. "Fuck off Chowy and take your sidekick with you, this is unfinished business."

Chow went to grab Zhān mǔ shì's right shoulder, who quickly grabbed the baseball bat hitting, Chow in the ribs, whilst simultaneously getting to his feet. Chow doubled up in pain, Wong moved to support his boss. Chow stopped him with his arm. "If this is how he wants it, so be it." Chow straightened himself, rubbing his ribs. *Two probably fractured,* he thought. Wong looked down at Jeff, who was lying on the floor, gasping for breath.

"Boss he's got blue eyes." He looked again at the skin showing through Jeff's ripped shirt. "And white skin."

Zhān mǔ shì raised the baseball bat for the killer blow to Jeff's head, intending to pulverise it with one extremely hard hit. Chow lunged at him, the two men falling on the muddy embankment, both holding the baseball bat, rolling to and fro. Wong rushed to his boss' aid. "No Zìmò, this is between us, help 'Mr Flowers', or should I say Mr Peters," Chow gasped, whilst tangling with the biggest Lee brother. The penny had dropped as soon as he'd seen Jeff's blue eyes. He remembered Jeff's physical appearance, but dismissed it due to being informed he was dead. The attacks and placing of the bodies all made perfect sense to Chow. He looked forward to interviewing him, if he survived.

Chow managed to get on top of Zhān mǔ shì, kneeing him in the face. Both men held onto the bat with both hands, whilst jostling for the upper hand, seemingly ignoring their disabling injuries. Chow took a chance, temporarily letting go of the bat with his right hand, giving Zhān mǔ shì a couple of quick punches to the face, twisting his knuckles into his flesh in the process, before trying to re-grab it. Zhān mǔ shì moaned in pain, however, having the advantage of both hands on the bat, whilst enduring the punches to his face, he hit Chow on the side of the head, knocking him sideways. Chow winced in pain. He hit Chow again with the tip of the bat, pushing the detective slightly off him.

Wong, cradling 'Mr Flowers' in his arms, looked on in disbelief, as his boss slugged it out with Zhān mǔ shì Lee. This certainly wasn't in any correct procedures police book. He also pondered on what to do if the unthinkable happened — his boss losing. Even worse, the unbearable thought of him being killed. What would his superiors say? Would Wong be culpable of murder? In addition, he could be the next victim. This was all too much for Detective Sergeant Wong, he made his mind up. *I'll get to the car, phone for backup and wait there,* he finally thought. Wong rushed off leaving Jeff on the floor, apologising as he went. Jeff shuffled himself using his arms so as to lean his head against the rear tyre of his car. He'd got a ringside seat to the best fight he'd ever seen, he felt like cheering, but didn't have the strength.

Both men grappled for control of the bat. Blood dripped onto it from both of them, subsequently it became slippery and, as Chow jerked at it, due to the angle plus the force at which he pulled, it resulted in the bat becoming loose, flying into the air and dropping into the river. Both men tried in vain to grab it — the real fight now commenced. The pair rained hard punches at one another, mainly aiming for the face and head, followed by grappling and rolling on the floor, each trying to gain the upper hand. Zhān mǔ shì managed to get up first, kicking Chow in his ribs with his 'good leg'. Chow blocked the fourth kick with both hands forming a V-shape, grabbing his calf, and punching Zhān mǔ shì in the testicles with his right hand. Zhān mǔ shì gasped in pain, staggering back slightly. This gave Chow the chance to get to his feet, and he quickly kicked Zhān mǔ shì in the stomach, roughly in the same place where Jeff had stabbed him. Chow went of the offensive, quick punches, left, right, left, right to Zhān mǔ shì's chin, finally he rotated his hips delivering a very forceful punch with his full weight and power to Zhān mǔ shì's temple, knocking him down. Chow assumed he was concussed and unfortunately relaxed.

Zhān mǔ shì lay dazed on the grass embankment, his head thumping like a bass drum. He grabbed a handful of sandy soil, and waited for Chow to drop his guard. Chow obligingly stepped close to inspect his victim. Zhān mǔ shì threw the grit into Chow's eyes, resulting in him momentarily losing his senses. Zhān mǔ shì picked a rock up, smashing it in Chow's face, the detective fell backwards, almost into the river. Zhān mǔ shì sauntered over to the prostrate Chow, his smug grin returning. He sat on Chow, his evil black eyes glaring down on the helpless Chow, raised his arms in readiness to smash the rock down on Chow's head, as many times as he needed to finish him.

Jeff, on seeing what was about to happen, pulled the knife out of his chest. Blood inevitably spurted out, but he summoned the last of his remaining strength, and crawled the three paces to where the two men now were. With one final act he rammed the penknife into Zhān mǔ shì's carotid artery as hard as he could, pulling out the blade before collapsing, blood spurting out profusely. All was still. The three men lay motionless.

Chow was the first to stir, gradually mustering the strength to push the fatally injured Zhān mǔ shì off him. He realised what had happened, ironically Jeff had saved his life. Chow turned to see Wong standing by the police car, he heard sirens in the distance, he had to make a decision, and quickly. "Help me Jeff, let's finish the job. I guess your aim for being here." He looked at Jeff. "Help me shove this evil monster into the river." Chow grabbed Zhān mǔ shì's right arm, pulling him closer to the river's edge. All Jeff could do was push Zhān mǔ shì's foot. The pair, both very weak, struggled to get the heavy man's body to topple in. Zhān mǔ shì, still conscious, tried to grab blades of grass for resistance, mumbling incoherently. Finally, with one last effort, Chow managed to manoeuvre Zhān mǔ shì's torso so that it was now pointing downward. "Jeff, give him the final push." Jeff pushed Zhān mǔ shì's foot with both hands with all his strength, it was just enough; the dying Zhān mǔ shì plopped into the river. He splashed about for a few seconds before going under, the tattoo panther's glowing amber eyes on his chest, was the last thing Jeff saw, as the fast river current swept him away.

Chow slowly crawled to the dying Jeff, cradling his head on his lap. "Stay with me, Jeff, the ambulance will be here soon."

Jeff could barely open his eyes, he squinted at Chow, whispering, "No, Mr Chow, as you rightly deduced, I've completed my aim."

Chow struggled to say anything positive. "You've certainly gone to a lot of trouble, Jeff, I'll give you that."

Jeff half smiled. "I can see David and Chynna waving at me, it's time to go, tell Anne I'm sorry, I did my best."

Chow, close to tears asked, "What did you whisper in David's ear in the reflection room at the mortuary?"

Jeff's eyes suddenly jerked open. *Fancy Chow remembering that*. "I told him I'd never rest until justice was d…" Jeff died in Chow's arms.

CHAPTER FIFTY-FOUR

Chow was rushed to hospital, Wong taking charge of the small police presence. Both injured men were put in the ambulance, the paramedics confirming what the barely conscious Chow had muttered, that Jeff was indeed dead. Wong instructed the area to be cordoned off, a full search for relevant evidence would be performed at first light, including the removal of Mr Flowers' car. Wong noticed a mobile phone lying on the floor at the back of the Nissan, he bagged and pocketed it.

Chow, whose head was bloodied and swollen, was diagnosed with the following injuries: fractured skull, two broken ribs, broken nose, fractured left arm, loss of blood, plus multiple cuts and bruising. He would have to remain in hospital, much to his protestations, for several days, and he would be resigned to desk duties until the fractures healed, which was a minimum of six weeks.

Wong checked Jeff's phone the day after the incident, which had been left on record, recording the whole scenario. Wong also checked the other recordings, confirming two factors. One, that Mr Flowers was the killer of both Yuēse and Yuēhàn, in addition, the confessions of all three brothers confirmed their guilt, although the confessions couldn't have been used in a court of law because they were taken under-duress. The final recording also revealed Zhān mǔ shì bragging about what he and his parents did to Mr Yuck, prompting a thorough search of their flat, resulting in bloody clothes being found. Dr Huang matched it to Fing Yuck's, subsequently the Lees were arrested, being charged with murder.

Wong, had to write a full report of what happened that night. He completed it in such a way, as to completely exonerate his boss from any possible charges, or accusations of foul play or unprofessional conduct. Wong finalised it by adding that Chow was unconscious, and it was Mr Peters who killed Zhān mǔ shì Lee before pushing him into the river. Chow would have to complete his version of events when he reported back to work; his would match that of Wong's. When Chow did return to office duties, he was given, much to his annoyance, a hero's reception, and his reputation was enhanced tenfold. The investigations for both Chynna and David's plus the Lee brothers' murders were closed.

The Sunday afternoon after the incident Chow, laying on his bed: head swathed in bandages, nose protected by a splint, arm in a sling, face dark blue with bruising, phoned Mr and Mrs Ling. He informed them, off the record, of a very succinct overview of the Lee brothers' killings, with the Lings' first promising Chow it would go no further. The brief phone call finished with Chow promising to visit them, at the first opportunity. The Lings, after getting over the shock of Jeff being the killer, thanked Chow sincerely. They could now, at last, try and get on with their lives.

Chow looked out of his window. It was pitch black, and the wind made it sound cold. *Winter was on its way,* he thought, after waking from taking a nap. Chow had one more important phone call to make before he could finally rest. He looked at the hospital room clock, it read ten p.m. Chow struggled with his phone, wearing a sling irritated him. He eventually scrolled through his contact list, found the number, finally pressing the call button.

CHAPTER FIFTY-FIVE

Anne Peters was busying herself in her house. She'd recently had confirmation from the coroner and the police, that finally she could arrange her husband's funeral. All enquiries resulted in probable suicide, although the police discovered strange banking activity, that Anne wasn't aware of. Apparently, Jeff had set up an account for a Mr Thomas Smith, plus payments had been made from a local mortuary business, which left Anne completely flummoxed.

Anne switched her central heating on. It was a cold, wet, late November Sunday afternoon. She made herself a cup of tea, deliberating on what to have for dinner, if indeed to bother having one. She'd aged considerably, relying on sleeping tablets and antidepressants to get her from one day to the next. *Just get Jeff's funeral over with,* she thought to herself. Suddenly the phone rang. *Who's that,* she thought. *Ringing on a Sunday afternoon, I hope it's not the coroner changing his mind.* She looked at her wrist watch, it was three p.m. She picked up the telephone, "Hello, Anne Peters speaking."

"Hello Mrs Peters, sorry to trouble you, this is Detective Inspector Chow, calling from Shanghai. I have some news for you."